Atlantis: Insights from a Lost Civilization demonstrates supurb research, excellent writing skill, and fascinating details. I predict that it will become a <u>classic</u> in its field."

—Ruth Montgomery
author, *World Before* (Ballentine, 1976)

ATLANTIS IS GONE
BUT NOT FORGOTTEN

There are those who predict that someday, Atlantis will rise from the sea. But others think that the enlightenment and spirituality of the Golden Age will rise again in its place.

If we follow the example of the long-lived civilization of Atlantis and simplify our lives . . . if we emphasize love, compassion, and alignment with nature . . . if we eventually allow ourselves to take advice from helpful celestial visitors, then the human race and the Earth will survive.

And, in spirit, Atlantis will rise a~

ABOUT THE AUTHOR

Shirley Andrews lives on the Concord River in Concord, Massachusetts, with her husband Bill, a professor at Harvard Law School. She is a graduate of Middlebury College and has studied, performed, and taught flute for over twenty years. Her intense interest in Atlantis has always been part of her and she believes it stems from one or more past life experiences there. After raising six children, Shirley was able to devote time and energy to the study of Atlantis and related subjects, which led her to research in the libraries of the British Museum, Harvard, the University of Chicago, and the Association for Research and Enlightenment (A.R.E.) in Virginia Beach, as well as personal travels to the Azores, the Andes, Central America, the Dordogne Valley in France, and the Tito Bustillo cave in Spain. She and her husband have traveled extensively, hiking and mountain climbing throughout the world, often focusing on the customs and beliefs of inhabitants in remote areas as they reflect on the spirituality of the distant past. Her foremost desire is to share what she has learned with others and incite their curiosity to discover more about these fascinating subjects.

TO WRITE TO THE AUTHOR

If you wish to contact the author or would like more information about this book, please write to the author in care of Llewellyn Worldwide and we will forward your request. Both the author and publisher appreciate hearing from you and learning of your enjoyment of this book and how it has helped you. Llewellyn Worldwide cannot guarantee that every letter written to the author can be answered, but all will be forwarded. Please write to:

Shirley Andrews
℅ Llewellyn Worldwide
P.O. Box 64383, Dept. K023-X
St. Paul, MN 55164–0383, U.S.A.

Please enclose a self-addressed stamped envelope for reply, or $1.00 to cover costs. If outside U.S.A., enclose international postal reply coupon.

ATLANTIS

INSIGHTS FROM
A LOST CIVILIZATION

SHIRLEY ANDREWS

1999
Llewellyn Publications
St. Paul, Minnesota 55164-0383

FIRST EDITION
Third printing, 1999

Cover design by Lisa Novak
Editing and book design by Rebecca Zins
Maps on pages 14, 16, 18, and 20 by John S. Moyle

Edgar Cayce Readings Copyrighted © 1971, Edgar Cayce Foundation.
Used by permission.

Library of Congress Cataloging-in-Publication Data
Andrews, Shirley, 1930–
    Atlantis: insights from a lost civilization / Shirley Andrews.—1st ed.
        p.   c.m.
    Includes bibliographical references (p.   ) and index.
    ISBN 1-56718-023-X (trade paper)
    1. Atlantis.   I. Title.
    GN751.A6 1997
    001.94—dc21   97–18360
                                                    CIP

Llewellyn Publications
A Division of Llewellyn Worldwide, Ltd.
P.O. Box 64383, Dept. K023-X
St. Paul, MN 55164-0383

Printed in the United States of America

Read not to contradict and confute,
nor to believe and take for granted,
but to weigh and consider. . . .
Histories make men wise.

—FRANCIS BACON

CONTENTS

ILLUSTRATIONS

ACKNOWLEDGMENTS

Atlantis: Insights from a Lost Civilization would never have materialized without the assistance and encouragement of my supportive family and friends. I wish especially to thank Bill Andrews for his patient assistance with the intricacies of computer technology, his editorial suggestions, and his time and effort in printing repeated new drafts. My sincere appreciation also goes to Katherine Min, Karen Taylor, Marianne Trost, and Rebecca Zins for their careful editing and to Jim Keck, Marian and Dick Thornton, Susan, Carol, and Roy Andrews, Terry Baker, Peggy Davenport, John Reid, and Barbara and Jack Wolf for their helpful comments and suggestions.

The views I have expressed in *Atlantis* are my own and are not all shared by those whose help I have acknowledged.

PREFACE

When I was very young, I constantly thought about a land called Atlantis that I was sure lay in the Atlantic Ocean. Adults finally convinced me it wasn't there but, like an adopted child searching for a birth parent, my insatiable interest in the mysterious country persisted. I now realize that perhaps in a previous life in Atlantis I used my knowledge and skills in evil ways to gain power. As a novice priest I came under the influence of older magi, who encouraged me to take advantage of women and abuse my talents to control others. To atone for these misdeeds, I believe I must publicize what I know about the Atlanteans' accomplishments in hopes of indirectly improving and maintaining life on this planet today.

For years, whenever it was possible, I read about Atlantis. I learned from ancient scholars, scientists, contemporary researchers, Native Americans, and the readings of Edgar Cayce and other reputable psychics. It startled me to discover how well the channeled material from the psychics correlates with more traditional sources, even though they had no access to one another. Before long, I was completely convinced that until about 12,000 years ago, the people of Atlantis *did* thrive on land in the Atlantic Ocean that, like so much else on the surface of our unstable planet, just isn't here now.

An extensive amount of the knowledge I have acquired about Atlantis is relevant to life today. Our Atlantean ancestors managed to live peacefully with nature without destroying it. They developed an admirable life similar to the type we presently strive to attain, a life in which individuals fully understood what lay within themselves, comprehended the magnitude and power of the universe and had a satisfying relationship with it.

Edgar Cayce offers a further advantage to study of the lost country. He maintains that many who lived in Atlantis chose to be reborn into the present time; these people retain latent qualities that influence their behavior today. Some carry an interest in science and technology. Others, because their land was so terribly destroyed, have a desperate desire for harmony, peace, and preservation of the Earth. Buried in humanity's subconscious are vivid memories of the distant past, and for many people today this means experiences in Atlantis. It is my hope that academic and intuitive examination of the lost land and its people will help us create a better world, modeled on that outstanding civilization of prehistory.

Striking parallels between accounts of the advanced accomplishments of Sumerians, who lived in the area between the Tigris and Euphrates Rivers about 4000 B.C., and descriptions of life in Atlantis became apparent during my study of prehistory. Attempting to understand the reason for the unbelievably rapid progress of human beings in Sumeria and its similarity with Atlantean feats, I was drawn to the research of the renowned scholar Zecharia Sitchin and others who suggest that extraterrestrials visited our planet in the past and assisted in the accelerated development of some primitive societies. If beings from outer space frequented the Earth in antiquity, the glacier-free, mineral-rich land of Atlantis would have been a logical destination for them. This explains Plato's reference to the god Poseidon marrying a mortal woman and settling in Atlantis, and accounts for the Atlanteans' amazing achievements.

Most accurate knowledge of long ago is lost in the mists of time but plenty remains in the bright sunlight, apparent to those who search for it. Hopefully what follows will arouse the reader's interest and curiosity, and encourage pursuit of this fascinating subject in new and varied directions.

EARLY ATLANTIS

PART I

INTRODUCTION

MODERN HOMO SAPIENS, our own species, appeared on the Earth more than 100,000 years ago. While devastating floods, earthquakes, volcanoes, Ice Ages, comets, and asteroids completely destroyed many other species of plants and animals, these vulnerable humans managed to survive. Using their highly developed intuition and their minds, which were as competent as ours, they not only persevered but, when natural circumstances permitted, they flourished.

I was taught in school that our ancestors of before 10,000 B.C. were big, strong brutes with hairy bodies who didn't wear clothes, lived in caves, and behaved like wild animals. When I learned of the difficulties modern craftsmen encounter in reproducing

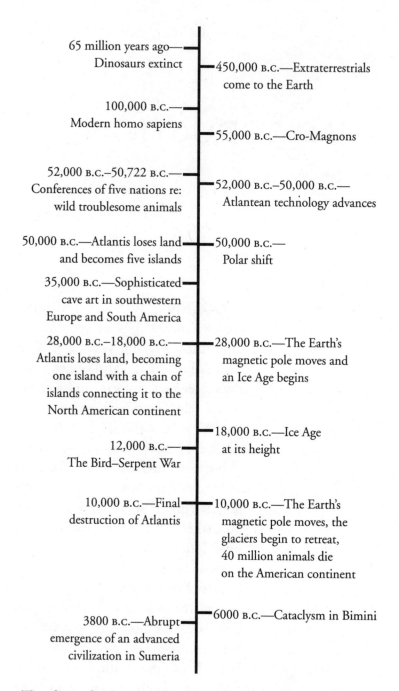

65 million years ago—
Dinosaurs extinct

450,000 B.C.—Extraterrestrials
come to the Earth

100,000 B.C.—
Modern homo sapiens

55,000 B.C.—Cro-Magnons

52,000 B.C.–50,722 B.C.—
Conferences of five nations re:
wild troublesome animals

52,000 B.C.–50,000 B.C.—
Atlantean technology advances

50,000 B.C.—Atlantis loses land
and becomes five islands

50,000 B.C.—
Polar shift

35,000 B.C.—Sophisticated
cave art in southwestern
Europe and South America

28,000 B.C.–18,000 B.C.—
Atlantis loses land, becoming
one island with a chain of
islands connecting it to the
North American continent

28,000 B.C.—The Earth's
magnetic pole moves and
an Ice Age begins

18,000 B.C.—Ice Age
at its height

12,000 B.C.—
The Bird–Serpent War

10,000 B.C.—Final
destruction of Atlantis

10,000 B.C.—The Earth's
magnetic pole moves, the
glaciers begin to retreat,
40 million animals die
on the American continent

6000 B.C.—Cataclysm in Bimini

3800 B.C.—Abrupt
emergence of an advanced
civilization in Sumeria

Timeline of Atlantis in history (all dates are approximate)

their everyday stone implements, I realized that anyone with that amount of skill and patience could easily make a bench to sit on and a house to live in. My picture of prehistoric families squatting on the ground in rock shelters was soon replaced by a more realistic image of their living in dwellings of stone or wood with tables, chairs, and beds.

While their well-built homes turned to dust long ago and no records of them exist, traces of their sophisticated lives remain. Anthropologists are finding necklaces our forebears placed on bodies they buried tens of thousands of years ago in southwestern Europe. Beads that required hundreds of hours to create were carefully strung with delicate needles. Prehistoric peoples could easily have used those needles to sew soft, comfortable garments of animal skins, or of cotton and linen, which were cultivated in antiquity. Once I acquired a more realistic picture of our predecessors and understood they really were similar to us mentally as well as physically, the concept of an advanced Atlantean civilization with superior accomplishments assumed increasing plausibility.

Sources of Atlantean Existence

If we condense the most recent 100,000 years so that it equals only one year of 365 days and imagine that the history of modern humanity took place in that twelve-month period, recorded facts begin in the last week of December. From July until early December the Atlantean civilization flourished. The period from January to the last week of December is referred to as prehistory, a time from which we have almost no written or recorded facts but plenty of information.

A wide variety of sources contribute to a picture of Atlantis from 100,000 to 12,000 years ago. The readings of the gifted psychic Edgar Cayce offer insight into the location and disintegration of its land as well as the society's accomplishments. All of Cayce's data correlate with more conventional reports he could not have been familiar with. Most psychics describe life in Atlantis at only one period in its long history, usually the most recent. Cayce is an exception; although the majority of his readings are concerned with the culture's final 20,000 years, he often furnishes details of early Atlantis as well. Psychics W. Scott-Elliot and Rudolph Steiner also provide information about the beginning of its civilization.

Additional accounts of the people of Atlantis are found in stories from England and Ireland that describe the thousands of individuals who fled to those areas from a country that sank into the Atlantic Ocean. Native Americans recall the lost land in legends they have transmitted carefully from generation to generation since the beginning of their time. Diodorus Siculus, a Sicilian geographer and historian of the first century B.C., was a far-ranging traveler and a trained and experienced compiler of knowledge who recorded many details about Atlantis that he learned from the native people while researching in Africa. Stories and legends of prehistory deserve to be taken seriously, for ancient people were not given to fiction and the information their memorizers handed down in this manner was based on facts; verbal transmission was known to be more long-lasting than recording it on perishable materials. The close correlations in data about the lost country from widely diverse sources are impossible to explain without a belief in the basic concept of Atlantis.

Numerous scholars have added to the overflowing cup of knowledge about Atlantis. Lewis Spence (1874–1955), a Scottish mythologist and ancient historian, compiled reports that related to Atlanteans and their nation from a wide variety of sources including Herodotus—a fifth-century B.C. Greek traveler—Pepi 1st of Egypt (2800 B.C.), and later British treasure-seekers Cuchulain Fionn, Laegaire MacCrimpthian Labraidh, and Mannannan Osin. Greek scholar Plato (429 B.C.–347 B.C.), one of the foremost philosophical writers of the western world, describes in detail the geography, people, and government of the largest island of Atlantis, which he places in the Atlantic Ocean about 9,000 years before his day. He thoroughly outlines his sources, and four times in two dialogues, the *Critias* and the *Timaeus,* confirms the veracity of his statements about the ancient country. His accurate description in 355 B.C. of the geography of mid-Atlantic islands and his references to the continent beyond contribute to the credibility of Plato's information. More recently, the works of Edgarton Sykes, David Zink, Nicholai F. Zhirov, Ignatius Donnelly, and many others are available for enlightenment about the lost country.

A few aspects of life in prehistoric times that are still with us offer more tangible information about life in Atlantis. Shamanism, a form of spiritualism that has prevailed for 40,000 years, is practiced in a comparable manner throughout the world. Sensitive artworks created as long as 30,000 years ago are visible on cave walls and ceilings in France and Spain. These beautiful paintings suggest numerous clues that contribute to an understanding of the lives of the masters who crafted them.

Further details depicting Atlantis were collected in extraordinary libraries in the western world that were available for study and research in the centuries before Christianity. One of the most notable, with over 500,000 books, was located in Carthage, on the north coast of Africa. The Carthaginians were excellent sailors and their archives contained maps and facts concerning the world they and their predecessors explored. In 146 B.C., when the Romans ravaged the library at Carthage, kings of North African tribes managed to rescue some of the valuable books.[1] They guarded them carefully for hundreds of years, and fragments of this knowledge of ancient times eventually reached the European continent with the Moors.[2]

Alexandria, in northern Egypt, was the site of an extensive library that Edgar Cayce says Atlanteans established in 10,300 B.C.[3] The huge university that centered on the library at

Alexandria included faculties of medicine, philosophy, mathematics, astronomy, and literature. In A.D. 391 and again in A.D. 642, ignorant invaders burned the libraries and over one million precious volumes. In the chaos and confusion of these traumatic events, local people joined the marauders and saved various irreplaceable books. Nevertheless, heat from the fires of burning manuscripts warmed water for the baths of Alexandria for several months. When the Moors from North Africa occupied portions of Spain during the eighth to the fifteenth centuries, they carried some of the ancient books their forefathers saved to the European continent.[4] Scotsman Michael Scot (A.D. 1175 –A.D. 1232), who was familiar with Arabic, traveled to Spain in 1217 and translated knowledge recorded in the manuscripts from Africa, including details of Atlantean lives.

A source of information that portrays the skills of Atlanteans is available in sailors' charts from ancient times that were preserved in northern Africa and in the dry Middle East. In the thirteenth and fourteenth centuries A.D., when it became permissible to think that the world extended beyond the Straits of Gibraltar, copies of these detailed, accurate maps appeared in western Europe. They illustrate northern Europe with its lakes and ice as it was before the glaciers melted in 10,000 B.C., as well as unknown islands in the Atlantic Ocean.

Where Was Atlantis?

Plato, psychics, and hundreds of legends describe an ancient country on land in the Atlantic Ocean. Intensive studies of the details of the ocean floor in the vicinity of the Atlantic Ridge—including core samples, the geography of the terrain, glacial residue, lava rock, coral, sand deposits, and plant growth—contribute convincing proof that portions of the Atlantic Ridge were above the surface until 10,000 B.C.

The Atlantic Ridge was a desirable location for people. Fertile volcanic soil was abundant and warm winds from the Gulf

Stream caressed the land. Glaciers plaguing the Neanderthals on the nearby European continent were confined to the northernmost zone of Atlantis. Surrounding ocean waters provided safety from marauders, while chains of small islands offered necessary access to the rest of the world. Just as favorable island conditions supported the evolution of huge wall spiders in the Canary Islands, giant tortoises in the Galapagos, and yard-long lizards in Grand Canary Island, so in Atlantis they afforded the ideal living conditions for developing the first group of modern, fully evolved homo sapiens, known as Cro-Magnons.

Cro-Magnons appeared in various places on the Earth about 55,000 B.C. For thousands of years prior to their emergence the human race was unchanged. Suddenly, without progenitors, these people with larger brains and stronger bodies, whose skeletal modifications from those who lived before them would have required isolation and an infinite amount of time to develop, were present in widely separated areas. Biblical scholar Zecharia Sitchin offers an explanation for the mysterious origin of Cro-Magnons. As he studied the Old Testament, Sitchin was fascinated by references in the Bible to the "Nefilim" who spent time on the Earth, and to the phrase in Genesis 6:4: "When the sons of God came into the daughters of men, and they bore children to them. These were the mighty men that were of old, the men of renown." Sitchin realized that although Nefilim is usually translated as "giants," it literally means "Those Who From Heaven to Earth Come." His search for the origin of the biblical phrases led him to the early civilization in the Tigris and Euphrates Valley and the belief that the ancient accounts of the Nefilim referred to the people the Sumerians called the Anunnaki, "who descended to Earth from the heavens," and that the Anunnaki were extraterrestrials. Sitchin proposes that extraterrestrials became aware of the extensive mineral deposits on the Earth. Hoping to create slaves to extract the abundant gold they needed to protect their planet from the atmosphere, they worked to improve the human race genetically. Cro-Magnons were one of the results of their efforts.

The extraterrestrials conducted their genetic endeavors in the idyllic land of Atlantis, and the Cro-Magnons that resulted thrived in the ideal climate. All dates of 10,000 B.C. and before are approximate, but about 30,000 B.C., due to unstable conditions in Atlantis, many of these superior people left their homes and sailed in small boats to the adjacent lands of southwestern Europe and South America. Their artwork, bones, tools, and jewelry remain in the valleys of rivers leading to the Atlantic Ocean, where they carefully placed them thousands of years ago. While working in Europe and South America, German archaeologist Marcel F. Homet discovered that the burial techniques of Cro-Magnons in the two widely separated areas, as well as remains of their skeletons, tools, and personal belongings, closely resemble each other.[5] In fact, archaeologists have discovered that Cro-Magnons lived in South America before they appeared in Europe. Identical occult practices and other similarities of ancient cultures of Cro-Magnons in the lands contiguous to the Atlantic Ocean offer information about their common source: the civilization on the islands that lay between them.

A jigsaw puzzle composed of only verified, flawless facts about the prehistory of our Earth and its inhabitants at the time of Atlantis, from 100,000 B.C. to 10,000 B.C., will never be assembled using the scientific techniques of conventional archaeology and anthropology. Just as historians are realizing that Vikings visited this continent long before Columbus and that Troy was more than a myth, so Atlantis will eventually be included in our history books. For a thorough description of Atlantis, I combine plausible data from a wide variety of individuals, including channeled information from intuitively gifted psychics. Occasional conjecture is necessary but, as much as possible, I describe my sources and avoid assumptions and exaggerations. I believe what follows depicts that "land of paradise" and its inhabitants as well as is currently feasible, and that much of it will one day be verified, to the benefit of our present civilization. So, with an open mind, return to distant Atlantis and

> Read not to contradict and confute, nor to believe and take for granted, but to weigh and consider. . . . Histories make men wise.
>
> —FRANCIS BACON

1

GEOGRAPHY

TODAY THE ATLANTIC OCEAN covers almost all of ancient Atlantis, whose land once stretched, sometimes in the shape of a serpent, from the present country of Greenland in the north, to Brazil in the south, and from the United States almost to Africa. When the fertile continental shelves bordering the Atlantic Ocean were above the surface, many Atlanteans left their unstable land and settled in those desirable areas. Atlantis' varied topography included vast plains of rich red soil, deep river valleys, and rugged mountain ranges, many of whose tall peaks were covered with perpetual snow. The country gradually returned to the ocean bottom from whence it came. Today's sonar devices, which use reflected sound vibrations to detect the

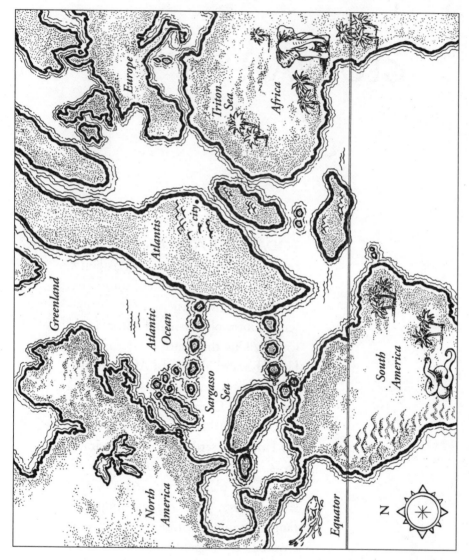

Figure 1:
Atlantis—
48,000 B.C. to
28,000 B.C.

presence and location of submerged objects, portray the physical features of Atlantis just as they were thousands of years ago when the land was above the surface.

Atlantis began to emerge from the hot, liquid bowels of the Earth 200 million years ago when Pangea, the supercontinent that contained all the land of our globe, slowly broke apart. Separations occurred along the lines of the tectonic plates— large rock masses, forty-five to seventy-five miles thick, which cover the surface of this planet. The plates float on a hot, thick liquid, known as the mantle, like pieces of wood floating on a simmering thick soup. After Pangea separated, molten lava and volcanic rocks poured from the cracks at the boundary line between the American plate and the Eurasian plate. These extensive ejections from the inner Earth united to form the Atlantic Ridge, a section of the ocean floor running north–south in the center of the Atlantic Ocean. The Atlantic Ridge plus the Azores Plateau (150,000 square miles of relatively flat land on the northeastern side of the Ridge) comprised the mainland of Atlantis.

Today the sea floor between the American and Eurasian continents continues to separate at an erratic but average rate of about one-half inch per year, or approximately as fast as a fingernail grows. Two hundred thousand years ago, the continents on opposite sides of the ocean were only two miles closer to each other than their current locations. Studies of rock strata reveal that layers of ancient crystalline rock are identical on today's South American and African continents, where they once fit together nicely. The North Atlantic Ridge, when it was above the surface, occupied the space between North America and Europe.

The original southern boundary of Atlantis is defined by the Romanche Trench, a deep underwater valley close to the equator that runs between two chains of mountains from Africa to South America. Deep ocean troughs of this sort are

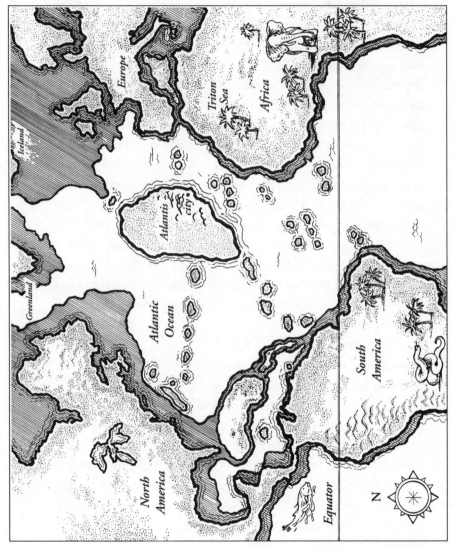

Figure 2:
Atlantis and
continental
shelves
18,000 B.C.

almost always situated close to either continents or islands. The Romanche Trench is the only exception—there is no land near it since Atlantis, once adjacent to the trough, disappeared into the sea.[1]

During the 100,000 or more years when people lived on the Atlantic Ridge, the expanse available for habitation varied. When deep glaciers enveloped large parts of the surface of our planet, their masses of snow and ice contained tremendous quantities of frozen water from the oceans. As a result, the surface of the Atlantic Ocean was sometimes 400 feet below its current level, exposing large zones along the shores of the Atlantic Ridge as well as the continents. Like birds attracted to a recently filled feeder in midwinter, plants, animals, and humans soon flocked to these desirable living spaces.

An Unstable Area

The region of Atlantis was, and still is, unstable for many reasons. Two tectonic plates move at the Atlantic Ridge, disturbing the delicate crust of the Earth and making that area one of the most active earthquake and volcanic sites in the world. Three plates interact in the area of the Azores Plateau. As lava bursts from cracks in the Earth's crust in these troubled regions, the ocean floor sinks to occupy the empty space. The instability of the ocean floor in the vicinity of the Atlantic Ridge was demonstrated dramatically in 1923 as a vessel belonging to the Western Telegraph Company searched for a lost telegraph cable laid in 1898. From soundings of the exact spot where the cable was placed, engineers determined the surface of the ocean bed rose nearly two and a quarter miles during that twenty-five-year period.[2]

Additional factors contribute to the instability of the Atlantic Ridge. It is made of oceanic crust that is composed primarily of basalt, a heavy, dense, volcanic material from the interior of the Earth. Basalt structures above water are relatively short-lived and eventually weaken and break up. Continents,

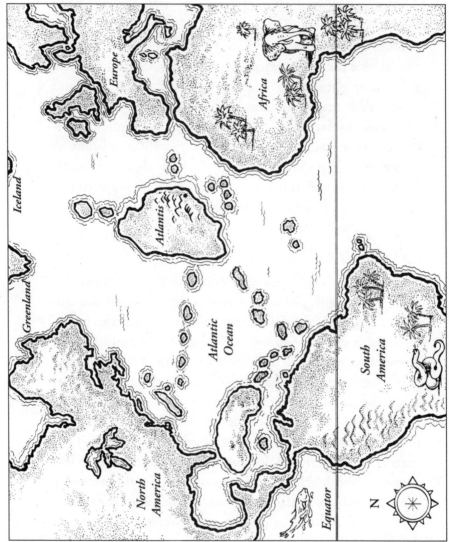

Figure 3:
Atlantis before
its destruction
in 10,000 B.C.

on the other hand, are composed mainly of granite and remain relatively stable for millions of years. Granite is light enough so that continents continue to float on the surface of the mantle even when they move and break apart as they collide. Basalt structures, such as the Atlantic Ridge, are heavy and will sink.

Three Periods of Destruction

The dreadful disintegration of the land of Atlantis took place gradually, but most damage occurred during three distinct periods. Edgar Cayce offers the following approximate dates for major devastations and the consequent disappearance of land into the Atlantic Ocean. They correlate with periods of time when severe upheavals disturbed the Earth's unstable crust. Cayce's dates for the final disappearance of Atlantis correspond with the time when Plato tells us in the *Timaeus* that "the island of Atlantis was swallowed up by the sea and vanished."

Around 50,000 B.C.	Extensive areas of Atlantis sink. Five large and many small islands remain above the surface. Something disturbs the Earth's crust, and the North Pole shifts from the Greenland Sea to Hudson Bay.
Around 28,000 B.C.	Slowly, more pieces of Atlantean lands disappear into the Atlantic Ocean. Eventually only one large island remains, plus a chain of smaller islands connecting it to the North American continent. The Earth's magnetic field moves significantly at this time.
Around 10,000 B.C.	Ocean water blankets the remaining land of Atlantis, except for a few mountain tops. The last major Ice Age ends and a flood covers much of the Earth.

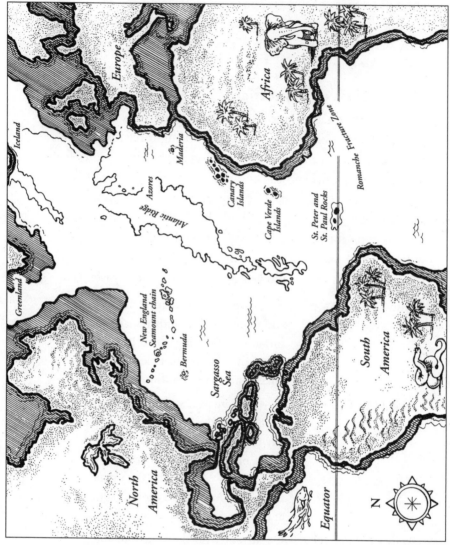

Figure 4:
Atlantic Ridge
and continental
shelves today

These three major catastrophes each continued for hundreds of years and affected the whole Earth. Many species of plants and animals disappeared, and the human beings who survived lost everything, including permanent records of their civilization. The Greeks, the Tibetans, the Hindus, as well as ancient peoples who live on the American continent remember annihilation of the Earth by fire and by water. In the account of the Hopi, who have inhabited the southwestern United States since before recorded history, overpowering episodes destroyed their three previous worlds, or homelands. Like the other traditions, their descriptions of three natural disasters correlate with the three disruptions of the Earth's crust that decimated Atlantis in 50,000 B.C., 28,000 B.C., and 10,000 B.C. The Hopi say volcanic action and fire were responsible for the first calamity. In the second, the Earth ceased to rotate properly, teetered off balance, spun crazily around, and rolled over twice. During the chaos that followed, the twins who guarded the north and south axis of the Earth left their posts and the Earth careened in space, changing the shape of the planet before a new axis and a new world were established. It grew very cold and thick layers of ice covered everything. The Hopis' third world was overwhelmed by water, correlating with the final fate of Atlantis. They believe today's world is the fourth, and that it will be scorched by fire; three more worlds are to come.[3]

Above the Surface?

Currently the Atlantic Ridge is an underwater mountain range with tall peaks rising from the ocean floor. It runs from north to south, although smaller ranges often cross it. A thick layer of mud, lava, and volcanic ash conceals the details of the ocean floor at the Atlantic Ridge. The composition of the lava,[4] analysis of the underwater coral reefs, the location of pteropod ooze that usually gravitates toward islands,[5] plus results of drilling and dredging operations all demonstrate the Atlantic Ridge was above the surface before 10,000 B.C.

In 1948, a Swedish expedition, working at the Atlantic Ridge 500 miles from the coast of Africa, excavated core samples from a depth of almost two miles. The collections contained over sixty species of freshwater algae. Before the sea engulfed them, these tiny, freshwater plants lived in a lake on the land of Atlantis. Tests of the algae indicate the last above-water period of the region was 10,000 to 12,000 years ago. Since 1948, scientists have extracted many similar core samples containing shells of freshwater animals from deep in the Atlantic Ocean at the Atlantic Ridge and the Azores Plateau.

The Mediterranean Hypothesis

Some people believe Atlantis was a land in the Mediterranean Sea, but extensive evidence proves this to be incorrect. One of the initial proponents of the Mediterranean hypothesis was Dr. Spyridon Marinatos. His daughter, Nanno Marinatos, who worked closely with him, has expressed serious doubts concerning the validity of the Atlantis-in-the-Mediterranean proposition. The theory claims that about 1628 B.C., a tremendous volcanic eruption shook the Mediterranean area, throwing fifty cubic miles of rock into the atmosphere with a force equivalent to fifty hydrogen bombs. The site of the volcano on the island of Thera became a huge hole and is now a quiet lagoon. Since 1967, archaeologists have been excavating the nearby cities and towns of the advanced Minoan civilization that was deeply buried by lava and debris from this explosion long ago, and encouraging the misconception that this area is the lost Atlantis.

The followers of Marinatos try to base their assumptions on the Atlantis information in Plato's *Timaeus* and *Critias.* However, when findings about the Minoan civilization do not correlate with Plato's descriptions, as is often the case, they misinterpret Plato, make false assumptions, or ignore or attempt to discredit his work. The Mediterranean Atlantis theory does not correlate with Plato in many ways. The volcano at Thera erupted about 1628 B.C., but Plato establishes the date of the final destruction of Atlantis correctly, at 9,000 years before his time, or approximately 9500 B.C. To justify this discrepancy it is necessary to attribute additional errors to Plato and his credible sources. Plato said the island was larger than North Africa and Asia Minor combined—neither Thera nor Crete begin to approach this size. Minoan land was dry and arid, but Plato refers to "marshes, lakes and rivers." Plato describes a food in Atlantis with a hard shell that was utilized for "drinks, meats and ointments," which is assumed to be the coconut. Coconuts do not thrive in the Mediterranean area. Plato's Atlantis was noted for its abundant use of gold and silver, valuable substances that have not been found in the excavations at Thera. Gold and silver were plentiful in Plato's Atlantis, whose mountains were a direct continuation, via the island of Madeira, of the Sierra Moreno range in Spain where these precious metals abound.[6]

Plato clearly states that Atlantis was in the Atlantic Ocean beyond the Pillars of Heracles (Straits of Gibraltar). He describes a chain of islands that extended westward from Atlantis, making it possible to cross from them "to the whole of the continent over against them which encompasses that veritable ocean." He reports that the people of Atlantis ruled over parts of that distant continent and also in land within the Pillars of Heracles. To combat this discrepancy, Mediterranean advocates imply Plato thought a location less familiar than the Mediterranean would be more impressive to his audience, but it was unnecessary for Plato to be dramatic. He wrote about Atlantis when he was an esteemed philosopher, over seventy years old, who did not need to exaggerate to obtain an audience.

As a source for his Atlantis information, Plato refers to Solon, a highly respected Greek lawyer who traveled to Egypt about 579 B.C. Some Mediterranean advocates suggest that Solon, "the wisest of the Seven Sages," changed the location of Atlantis from the Mediterranean to the Atlantic Ocean. This is, however, highly implausible. While traveling in Egypt, Solon talked with priests steeped in knowledge from the prehistoric world. They told him scientists knew nothing of the ancient times and that natural disasters obliterated all tangible information. The learned men also said there have been and will be many destructions of humankind, the greatest by fire and water. They then taught Solon about the land lost to the Atlantic Ocean 9,000 years before. The Egyptians who told Solon of the lost land were well aware of the relationship of the Pillars of Heracles to the Atlantic Ocean. Their mariners sailed the seas in ships as long as 450 feet, returning to their country with ivory, gold, perfumes, dyes, and other exotic goods from afar. They knew the boundaries of the Mediterranean and the ocean beyond very well.

Peaks of Atlantis

Just as solitary church spires remain above the water when a dam is responsible for flooding a town, so only a few peaks of Atlantis rise above the surface today. The Azores, Madeira, Canary, and Cape Verde Islands, all of whose rocky sides slope straight down to the ocean floor without underwater platforms, were once mountain tops in Atlantis.[7] Mount Atlas was the steepest, most massive mountain of the Atlantis range. Today it is called Pico Alto and is in the Azores Islands. Eruptions from this tall step volcano built Pico Alto higher and higher into a series of terraces before the sea consumed Atlantis.[8] Russian marine geologist Dr. Nicholai F. Zhirov points out that the presence of these terraces offers confirmation that the area was above water for a prolonged period of time and that a change of height took place. At the present time Pico Alto rises 17,600 feet from the ocean floor, although only 7,600 feet of it are above the surface. In the days of Atlantis, Mount Atlas appeared to be a giant column that rose directly from the land into the world above. Steam constantly issued from its volcanic depths so that the clouds that always surrounded its lofty summit seemed to support the heavens. The mighty mountain was named for Atlas, the firstborn son of Poseidon, the god of the sea. Snowcapped Mount Atlas and its companions presented a more magnificent panorama than now exists anywhere, even in the Alps or the Himalayas. What a wonderful sight it must have been to those who approached Atlantis in ships from distant lands!

As time passed, the areas of the Atlantic Ridge and the Azores Plateau that were above the surface became a veritable heaven on Earth, a replica of the biblical Garden of Eden. Captain Boid, who visited the Azores Islands in 1835, describes them in glowing words: "Were they embellished by the arts and refinements of civilized life—they would become a species of terrestrial paradise calculated to render man almost too happy for this sublunary sphere." Nowadays, as was true in the time of Atlantis, the mountains capture moisture from the prevailing westerly winds, and as it condenses to rain it turns into small streams that fall down the steep mountainsides, slowly at first, then faster and faster, creating tumbling waterfalls that splash into crystal-clear pools.

In unexpected places, plentiful, bubbling springs, twenty or thirty feet in diameter, perform like punctured water pipes, spurting boiling water high into the air from deep in the Earth. Plato tells us "the springs they made use of, one kind being of cold, another of warm water, were of abundant volume, and each kind was wonderfully well adapted for use because of the natural taste and excellence of its waters."[9] Mineral springs on the Azores are renowned today for their strong digestive and curative powers. Cattle, sensing the healing capacity of vapors from the springs, place themselves in the path of the strong-smelling, moving air to kill vermin or heal cuts or sores on their skins. Attracted by the moisture and rich soil, colorful, fragrant flowers surround the springs and create lovely, natural gardens, just as they have for thousands of years.

Erosion along the western and southern shores of Atlantis created fine sand beaches, now on the ocean floor. Sand is a product of erosion and is formed only in shallow water along coastlines, therefore it does not normally occur at great depths. When American oceanographer Dr. Maurice Ewing explored the Atlantic Ridge from a submarine in 1949, he reported sighting sand far beneath the surface, sometimes 1,000 miles from land. Testing dated the sand at 10,000 B.C. plus or minus a few hundred years; lower drillings revealed that sand dating to 20,000 B.C. lay beneath it. Debris between the two drillings suggested the land was smothered by volcanic ash.[10] Russian scientists who have carefully explored the Atlantic Ridge from submarines also describe the sand on the ocean floor. Near the Azores, and in other areas, it lies on underwater shelves thousands of feet below the surface in secluded, sheltered places near slopes or in very deep water where it is inconceivable that currents or wind deposited it.[11] Sand in the Romanche Valley is a further indication that it too was once above the surface.[12]

Coral deposits in the Atlantic Ocean offer further evidence of the land of Atlantis. Coral reefs are masses of lime carbonate built up on the sea floor from coral-producing animals who cannot survive in depths over fifty feet. The shallow waters of the western shores of Atlantis attracted a profusion of tiny animals and algae who thrived on the food provided by the steady current. Multitudes of their skeletons accumulated and turned to coral that eventually created reefs, offering protection to the beaches from the powerful ocean's rough waves and storms. Warm water coral formed from lime deposits on the shallow coastline of Atlantis now lies deep in the ocean on the western slopes of the Atlantic Ridge, securely attached to the bedrock.[13] The types of coral found in reefs near West Africa are markedly similar to those found in the West Indies; Zhirov points out that to produce this continuity, a group of islands must have stretched across the ocean from the West Indies to West Africa on a path that included Fernando de Noronha Island, St. Paul's Rocks, and the now-submerged islands of Atlantis.[14]

Iceland, a basalt country on the Atlantic Ridge, provides an opportunity to study land above the surface that is farther to the north but has a topography similar to Atlantis. Lakes, hot springs, and mountains dot the countryside, and plumes of smoke from active volcanoes are often visible. The surface of Iceland is subjected to a series of major earthquakes about every eighty years. The impact of volcanic activity on the people of Atlantis can more easily be understood by considering a volcanic eruption in Iceland in 1783. The discharge of only twelve cubic kilometers of basaltic lava resulted in the deaths of seventy-five percent of all livestock and twenty-four percent of the country's population.[15]

The northernmost area of Atlantis experienced cold weather,[16] but most of the country was blessed with an ideal climate. The temperate waters of the Gulf Stream flowed from the vicinity of the Equator to caress its shores and warm the prevailing westerly winds that flowed over the central and southern parts of the country. Steady air currents furnished a constant breeze, offering relief from the hot sun. The situation was quite different on the European continent when portions of the Atlantic Ridge were above the surface. Since the tall mountains of Atlantis blocked the warm winds from the Gulf Stream, it was considerably colder. Dangerous, moving glaciers of ice often blanketed Europe's northern and central areas. Pollen remains reveal that 20,000 years ago, glaciers extended approximately the same distance to the south in Europe as in

North America, and the climate was similar at the same latitude on both continents.[17] In about 17,500 B.C. snow lines were the same along a north-south transect on both continents, regardless of latitude. This is not the case at the present time. Prevailing westerly winds that blow over the Gulf Stream, no longer blocked by the Atlantic Ridge, carry warm air to the British Isles. Therefore, it is considerably warmer in London, England, than in Labrador, Canada, although both are almost the same distance from the equator. When Atlantis sank in 10,000 B.C., warm winds blowing across the Gulf Stream reached the European continent and initiated the melting of the glaciers, quickly changing the weather in the British Isles to the more moderate present temperatures. Analysis of soil samples from beneath the Arctic seas indicate the first hot flow from the Gulf Stream entered those northern waters 12,000 years ago when Atlantis disappeared into the ocean and glaciers melted in Europe. The location of fossils of cold- and warmth-loving foraminifera in the Atlantic Ocean furnish additional evidence that the waters circulated differently until 12,000 years ago.[18]

Coconut palms lined the beaches of Atlantis, immense ebony trees and verdant masses of laurel filled its forests, and lava-rich soil supported the plant life that enhanced its inland areas. Sweet-smelling flowers perfumed the air, and birds flew everywhere—brightly colored, migrating warblers, mocking birds singing a variety of cheerful songs, busy gulls and high-flying albatross. Except for earthquake and volcanic activity, Atlantis was truly the most idyllic locality in the world when the first people arrived.

2

HISTORY

CONSISTENT PATTERNS ARE obvious as one reviews the 90,000-year history of Atlantis. Mother Nature often tormented them as she violently shook the land beneath their feet, harassed them with boiling lava or volcanic dust, and flooded their lands. In spite of these deterrents, three times major civilizations developed, flourished, and ascended to amazing heights, then decayed and almost vanished. The calamities always correlated with a natural catastrophe that simultaneously affected the rest of the planet.

Just as Atlanteans fled from their unstable country, so too the first settlers of Atlantis arrived, seeking refuge from their own disintegrating lands. Throughout its history, Atlantis was both a refuge and a departure point for many groups of people.

EARLY ATLANTIS UNTIL 48,000 B.C.

Psychic W. Scott-Elliot, a late-nineteenth-century member of the Theosophical Society, tells us that a group of highly evolved people from Lemuria, a land now under the Pacific Ocean, were among the first settlers of Atlantis.[1]

Over 100,000 years ago, astute Lemurians, anticipating their increasingly unstable land would break up and sink, left their homes and made their way to the southern part of Atlantis. Lemuria was an ancient country that, like Atlantis, was subject to constant earthquake activity and volcanic eruptions before most of it disappeared under ocean waters. Numerous psychics, including Madame Blavatsky, who founded the Theosophical Society, believe Lemuria was the birthplace of humanity. Legends in the Pacific region describe island groups as all that remain of the once-large country of Lemuria. At a recent meeting of the Tenth World Pacific Congress, George H. Cronwell reported that discoveries of coal and ancient flora on the island of Rapa, southwest of Mangareva Island, provide evidence that a continent once lay in that part of the Pacific Ocean.[2]

The trip from Lemuria to Atlantis was difficult but possible. In prehistoric times, adventuresome humans walked long distances over the entire globe and innovative people residing near the sea devoted their energy to devising vehicles that would float and transport them more quickly. The Lemurians who settled in Atlantis prospered, and their progeny lived happily for thousands of years.

These earliest residents of Atlantis dwelt intimately with their natural surroundings in small settlements ringed by gardens and trees. Material objects were unnecessary for a sense of personal adequacy; people judged each other by the quality of their characters, not their possessions. Free from desires, individuals looked within for happiness and lived in harmony with the external world. Atlanteans during this period, fully aware of their minds and bodies, were close to what some consider the perfect state of living—approximately fifty percent spiritual and fifty percent practical.[3]

Until recently, some groups of humans untouched by our civilization enjoyed a life similar to that practiced so long ago in the early days of Atlantis. Jacques Cousteau describes the high quality existence of "stone age" aborigines whose distant ancestors settled in Australia in 40,000 B.C. Free from electric appliances and other modern conveniences, the aborigines had security, personal freedom, and fulfillment. Their healthy lifestyle included plenty of time for leisure and a strongly established sense of well-being.[4]

Edgar Cayce indicates that early Atlanteans utilized the power of their minds to control their bodies.[5] This reflected their heritage from their highly endowed Lemurian ancestors. If necessary, they were able to increase their physical strength on demand, just as today when a person in an emergency situation is sometimes able to perform a normally impossible feat, such as lifting an automobile off a trapped person. Muscles of a hypnotized person in a contemporary society may accomplish similar amazing acts, for the capacities of our ancestors are still with us. Today a few highly trained persons succeed in recalling and utilizing these talents to control their bodies, and are capable of altering their heartbeat and blood pressure. Tibetan hermits practice "tuomo," using their minds to produce extraordinary body heat, which enables them to spend a winter in extreme cold without wearing clothing.[6]

Information about the pleasant living conditions in Atlantis spread to the nearby African continent, and powerful, aggressive tribes crossed from there to the desirable land. The invaders slowly forced the Lemurians northward, and for a long period of time gruesome fighting took place between the two groups. They inevitably mingled and the genes of the two diverse groups merged.

Mythology

Plato tells us the god Poseidon and his mortal wife Cleito settled in pleasant and fertile Atlantis near the beginning of its civilization. The couple dwelt on a large island where they raised five sets of male twins, who in turn produced extensive families. Poseidon divided the island into ten parts, one for each of his sons. Atlas, the oldest son, received the most desirable territory, the zone where his parents lived, and the country and the surrounding ocean were named Atlantis for him.[7] The word *Atlantis* means daughter of Atlas in Greek. Atlas, the Greek god who supported the sky, had seven daughters who became the stars of the Pleiades. The word *atl* means water in both the North African Berber language and Nahautl, an ancient Mexican dialect. Poseidon's role in Greek mythology reflects his Atlantean connection. He was regarded as the god of horses, as the god of earthquakes, and as the god of the sea who taught the people of Earth the basics of sailing. When aroused, he was capable of provoking storms, floods, and tremors of the land. With a stroke of his trident he could raise islands from the bottom of the ocean or force them to sink.

In Greek mythology, Poseidon and other gods and goddesses are described as real people complete with emotions and sexual capacities. Possessing powerful weapons and traveling at immense speeds, they are involved in human affairs, yet they are inaccessible. The gods from the great Hall of Zeus bear a striking resemblance to the gods of Sumeria, who are described in Mesopo—tamian tablets as visitors from the heavens. The Sumerians referred to the extraterrestrials as gods because they came from the heavens and seemed all-powerful. Many Greek traditions and religions originated in Sumeria and reached Greece from Asia Minor by way of Crete and other Mediterranean Islands.[8] Plato's reference to Poseidon uniting with a mortal woman is similar to events described in Sumerian texts and pictography, and to the Biblical reference in Genesis 6:4 (see page 9).

The First Conferences

In 52,000 B.C., dangerous large animals and birds outnumbered the human race and terrorized humankind all over the planet. In Atlantis they made life almost impossible.[9] Numerous species of elephants, mammoths fourteen feet high at the shoulders, massive herds of mastodon, hungry cats and wolves, and large wild horses roamed freely where people attempted to live. When these unpleasant creatures trampled orchards and destroyed crops, a whole season's food was often lost. Ruth Montgomery, a psychic who receives information from her spirit guides in the form of automatic writing, describes these carnivorous brutes fighting battles among themselves to determine who would have the privilege of eating the available people.[10] Gigantic birds hovered overhead, eager to devour the leftovers of any available humans, particularly children. When desperate Atlanteans thrust spears and swords against the animals' thick hides, their weapons simply crumpled like paper; flame throwers and explosives were equally ineffective.[11] Something had to be done.

Seeking help from others, the leaders of Atlantis sent messengers on foot and in small boats to every part of the planet. They learned that the savage beasts were a problem to helpless people throughout the world. As they searched for unique ideas to combat the troublesome animals, weary Atlanteans crossed dangerous seas, dry deserts, and icy mountains.

In hopes of finding a satisfactory solution to the problems of the dangerous beasts, several conferences were held in Atlantis. The first meeting convened in 52,000 B.C. Wise persons from five nations attended, representing the five races. They came from what is now Russia and the Near East, the Sudan and upper West Africa, the area that became the Gobi desert, what remained of Lemuria, and Atlantis.[12] Delegates from India and Peru, or Og as it was then named, joined the original group for later conferences.[13] It was agreed that the

Atlanteans would experiment with chemical forces in the earth and air, hoping this extensive research would enable them to expand their arsenal of weapons.[14]

As scientific knowledge and technology advanced in Atlantis in 51,000 B.C., everyday life changed. Agricultural methods improved, education expanded, and material goods assumed increasing importance in the lives of the people. Better mining techniques supplied vast quantities of gold, silver, and precious gems, with which Atlanteans lavishly decorated themselves and their buildings. Minds and thoughts dwelt more and more on material concerns, people became increasingly analytical, and the left side of their brains assumed dominance over the right side. Respect for their fellow human and their close relationship with the natural world diminished, replaced by ambition and intolerance. Most Atlanteans ceased to cultivate clairvoyant thought transmission and other intuitive skills and failed to believe in and trust the inherent abilities they retained.

Two very diverse groups sought power in Atlantis before 50,000 B.C. Edgar Cayce describes one as the Sons of Belial, who worshiped ease and pleasure, sought tangible possessions, and were spiritually immoral.[15] The other, the Children of the Law of One, focused on love and practiced prayer and meditation together, hoping to promote divine knowledge.[16] They were referred to as the Children of the Law of One because they advocated One Religion, One State, One Home, and One God.[17]

Soon after the last conference in 50,722 B.C., the "all-powerful god" rebelled at the decadence of the Atlantean population. A shift in the Earth's poles and the Atlanteans' careless use of explosives initiated earthquakes and ever-waiting volcanoes. Some pole shift researchers propose that when the poles are disturbed, the surface of our planet moves around its liquid center as much as ninety degrees, with disastrous effects on the inhabitants. In 50,000 B.C., most of the dangerous animals died in the resulting chaos and the Atlanteans themselves suf-

fered terribly. As the ground under them shuddered violently, thousands died, overcome by the noxious gases and hot lava that erupted from the interior. Before long, floods covered fields and houses, leaving the survivors without food and shelter. As the land gradually broke up into five large and many small islands, miserable victims piled on makeshift rafts or small boats and abandoned their ravaged country, hoping to start life anew in another place.

The lucky ones who escaped were aware of the advantages and disadvantages of possible havens, for sailors who frequently visited lands around the Atlantic Ocean carried home information from small colonies of fellow countrymen. Nearby Africa was a popular destination of the destitute refugees. The climate was favorable and the numerous animals roaming its savannas provided a readily available source of food. Descendants of the Atlanteans who escaped to Africa lived happily, and as the civilization thrived, the population exploded. Since the supply of wild creatures seemed limitless, swarms of enthusiastic hunters mindlessly slaughtered innocent beasts, often just for sport. Within 1,000 years (around 50,000 B.C.) numerous species of animals who roamed the African plains became extinct.[18]

The fertile Amazon River basin was also easily accessible to Atlanteans in 50,000 B.C., and enterprising families succeeded in making the difficult journey to South America. The possibility of farming the rich soil rather than big game hunting in Africa was attractive, for they feared the changes that resulted in minds and bodies from eating the flesh of animals. These Atlanteans believed that when they were forced to digest meat, the stream of energy running through their bodies was disrupted, resulting in a decrease in psychic powers and physical stamina. The Amazon River basin became home to thousands of intrepid colonists whose descendants established vast plantations with lush fields of grains and vegetables, orchards of bountiful fruit trees, and ornate, colorful gardens of herbs and flowers.[19]

Some Atlanteans who fled to South America discovered strangers already living on the land. Og, or Peru, was a source of minerals for Atlantis, and many craftsmen adept at working with gold and silver moved there in 50,000 B.C. However, before long they encountered the Ohlms, who were already well ensconced in the area. Many years before, the Ohlms had fled to South America from unstable Lemuria.[20] The Ohlms' leader was a weak, unpopular person known for his sexual excesses, and when the Atlanteans' arrival instigated a bloody war, it provided an opportunity for his people to overthrow him. The Ohlms were delighted to get rid of their despised leader and welcomed the newcomers from the Atlantic Ocean, who taught them improved agricultural methods as well as more modern mining techniques. The Atlanteans helped to establish a government that ensured equality, built common storehouses to avoid shortages of food, and improved the educational system.[21]

Atlanteans who left their flooded lands for Africa and South America in 50,000 B.C. fared much better than their friends who stayed behind. The shivering ground and volcanic eruptions in Atlantis seemed endless. As they searched for dry places to live, families trudged up the mountainsides, where they were soon forced to revert to living like animals. The turmoil lasted for approximately 4,000 years, considerably longer than the total time of our current civilization.

48,000 B.C. TO ABOUT 10,000 B.C.

The destruction of unstable Atlantis in 50,000 B.C. was just one of its major natural disasters. The human beings who survived the catastrophes suffered terribly, but civilization always revived and, although somewhat different from ours, advanced in a similar way. Initially, thankful to be alive, people remained close to nature, but as science and technology developed, they became more aggressive, materially oriented, and decadent. In 28,000 B.C. and 10,000 B.C., as had happened in 50,000 B.C., as the emphasis on science and technology increased, moral standards declined, the spiritual quality of life decreased, and a deterioration followed. Just as the thoughts and actions of evil people annoy their compatriots, so the energy emitted from Atlantis at these times disturbed the vibrations of the universe, where all is related and interdependent. Invariably, the Atlanteans' misuse of their powerful sources of energy and/or a natural occurrence disturbed the unstable crust of the Earth along the lines of the tectonic plates. The movement agitated volcanoes and initiated tremendous tidal waves. Fertile, inhabited land and the people who dwelt on it disappeared into the greedy ocean.

In 49,000 B.C., as volcanoes quieted down following the unfortunate events of 50,000 B.C., hardy descendants of the few Atlantean survivors decided to abandon the safety of the sturdy mountain caves that provided them with shelter for countless generations. They longed for a milder climate and a more varied diet. From their high sanctuaries they could see green plants and tiny trees far below, gradually emerging through the volcanic rubble. Carrying their meager possessions, families trekked slowly down to the valleys and plains that were once lush and fertile. Rabbits, squirrels, and other small animals also returned to the lowlands and these, together with shellfish from the beaches, provided food and bare necessities. Only the most industrious and innovative Atlanteans had survived the extremely difficult existence of the past centuries and, once they settled in a more supportive environment, these capable persons made rapid strides. Children watched in amazement as their aging grandparents, recalling stories of their elders, braided and wove grasses to make nets for catching fish and supervised the construction of sturdy homes with windows and doors. Extraterrestrials, always on the watch from above for new sources of minerals from the Earth's surface, undoubtedly observed the improvements in Atlantean life and returned to offer assistance in repopulating and developing the country.

Civilization progressed for hundreds of centuries and gradually a new god, science, assumed increasing importance. Technocrats interested in material goods and disrespectful of religious and ethical customs took control.[22] Deceit and other immoral actions became more and more widespread.[23] Women were mainly instruments of pleasure, crimes like murder and thievery were prevalent, and priests and priestesses even practiced human sacrifice.[24] In 28,000 B.C. the stage was set for the second major blow to their country, and many perceptive families, sensing disaster, hastily departed before it was too late.

Highly skilled artisans, dissatisfied with the increasing emphasis on materialism in Atlantis, daringly sailed small leather boats the relatively short distance to the coasts of Spain and southwestern France and wended their way up the fertile river valleys. At first they inhabited the overhanging limestone rock shelters that abound in the area, but soon they built comfortable homes of logs, animal hides, and stone, oriented toward the sun for solar heat. Free from major problems, leisure time allowed them to return to the artistic endeavors for which they were unusually well trained. Some of their masterful artworks, reflecting the highly developed culture that matured for thousands of years in Atlantis, remain in deep caves in France and Spain. These include sculptures of women, known as Venus statues, that artisans carefully and gracefully fashioned from ivory or stone. Similar statues were carved in the years that followed, but the earlier ones of 28,000 B.C. demonstrate the most expert techniques.[25] The repeated migrations of Cro-Magnons to the European continent came in waves that corresponded with times of destruction of Atlantean lands. The final culture, the Azilian-Tardenoisians, arrived in 10,000 B.C. when the last fragments of Atlantis sank.

Around 28,000 B.C. something severely disturbed the Earth's crust. Australian geologists Michael Barbetti and Michael McElhinney learned from radiocarbon datings that at that time the Earth's magnetic poles were reversed for almost 4,000 years. The changes do not show up in deep-sea magnetism because of the short duration of the reversal.[26] In Atlantis, as if in protest to the depravity of the country, the ground shook violently and the Earth heaved molten lava and rocks from its volcanic mouths. A thick layer of ash and debris covered everything while massive landslides annihilated trees and entombed villages. Atlantis once again became barely habitable.

Leaving Atlantis

Scattered groups assembled a few possessions, gathered with other people on the coasts, and attempted the dangerous journey across open waters. A buildup of glacial ice began at this time, and eventually approximately 14,000,000 cubic miles of water from the oceans was incorporated in the glaciers, making sea levels 400 to 500 feet lower than today.[27] Thirteen percent of the Atlantic Ocean is continental shelf less than 600 feet deep,[28] and most of it became available for settlement. Exposed land off the southwestern coast of Ireland reached almost to Atlantis. This extensive area, plus a shelf 90 to 100 miles wide that abutted the North American coast, and additional space now under the Caribbean Sea were accessible to Atlanteans. Chains of small islands offered convenient paths to the continental shelves of the African, North, Central, and South American continents.

The exposed continental shelves proved a delightful place for home sites. The proximity of the warm waters of the Gulf Stream ensured a pleasant climate, compared to the northern sections of Europe and North America where ice was again piled a mile thick in many places. Atlanteans—ingenious, capable and stronger physically than those they came upon in their new locations—prospered on the rich lands. Food was readily available as abundant quantities of deer, mammoth, and other wild creatures quickly moved to the regions to graze on the lush green grasses. Fishermen today continue to net hunters' harpoon points and mastodons' teeth that recall the activity on the continental shelves so long ago.

Antilia

Another destination of Atlantean refugees in 28,000 B.C. was the island of Antilia in the western Atlantic. Here, not far off the southern coast of the United States, a long ridge rises from the Atlantic floor. Currently only its high points, the Bermuda Islands, are above the surface. Thirty thousand years ago the ridge and an island archipelago north of there, outlined by remains of coral reefs, were available for settlement. Memories of the successful civilization Atlanteans built on this attractive land were transmitted from sailor to sailor for countless generations. Thousands of years later, Antilia was the ultimate destination of numerous adventurers and persons seeking sanctuary. In the sixth century St. Brendan and his followers set off from Ireland in their leather boats, hoping to visit Antilia. They returned after seven years with tales of the wondrous islands they had visited, and "a fine land so vast they could not find the end of it though they tried for forty days."

Antilia was still considered a desirable destination in the eighth century. In A.D. 711, when the Moors invaded the Iberian peninsula, multitudes of Christians fled for their lives. Seven Portuguese bishops and their 5,000 followers, burdened with whatever possessions they could carry, scrambled aboard a fleet of ships and sailed westward in the Atlantic Ocean. They planned to travel to the golden land of Antilia to enjoy religious freedom but they never found it since most of the large island was gone, submerged beneath ocean waters. Some of them landed in Florida and founded the city of Calo, named for the Archbishop of Porto Calo, one of their leaders. Eight hundred years later DeSoto's expedition visited the city of Cale near Florida's west coast. The people of Cale practiced Christianity and were probably descendants of the Portuguese immigrants.

Other possible descendants of the families who searched for Antilia in A.D. 711 are the Melungeons, who have lived in a remote valley in northeastern Tennessee since before the Revolutionary War. These isolated people are Christian and their speech includes bits of Portuguese. *Melungo*, an Afro-Portuguese word meaning "shipmate," and some of their other customs and traditions imply that the Melungeons' ancestors sailed from the western Mediterranean long before Columbus.[29]

Just as memories of Atlantis persist indefinitely, so Antilia was recollected in the time of Columbus. As he searched to the west for India, he carried a letter from Toscanelli recommending Antilia as a convenient halfway point.[30] Unable to find it, when he discovered a chain of islands between North and South America, he named them the Antilles. The lost island of Antilia appeared on maps of the western Atlantic Ocean as recently as the early sixteenth century.

The Yucatan

Other havens for destitute Atlanteans in 28,000 B.C. lay on the shores of the Caribbean Sea. At that time, when ocean levels were hundreds of feet lower, a long mass of land with only two or three breaks for rivers ran from Venezuela across what are now the Lesser Antilles Islands and continued all the way to Jamaica. Eventually the region broke up to form the islands of the West Indies. In the same area, the Yucatan peninsula of Mexico stretched out nearly to Cuba.

Following the second major destruction of Atlantis around 28,000 B.C., a group of religious refugees sailed from their homeland in small crafts toward the setting sun. After weeks on end with little food and water they came to the lovely lands of the Yucatan. People from Lemuria, Egypt, and Og (Peru) were happily living in the most desirable locations but few conflicts developed, since fertile soil and ample living space encouraged peaceful coexistence.[31] The devout Atlanteans focused on their religious services rather than on acquiring unnecessary material possessions. Edgar Cayce describes the energized stone circles they built for worship, similar to those in their homeland. One of the ceremonies that took place at these powerful sites was focused on cleansing the bodies and minds of individuals of undesirable selfish traits.[32]

Members of the diverse groups from such distant parts of the world cautiously explored each other and gradually intermarried. Civilization flourished in the Yucatan peninsula in 28,000 B.C.

Eventually earthquakes and rising water destroyed the buildings of the Atlanteans' descendants on the coast of the Caribbean Sea, but sacrificial altars, red ocher paintings, spiral petroglyphs, and phallic symbols endure beneath the surface. Inscriptions in the twenty-eight chambers of the Loltun caverns near Oxkutzcab in the Yucatan date to over 15,000 years ago.[33] Over the years, water has frequently risen to cover the caves and then receded to expose them. In spite of this, the sanctuaries were utilized for spiritual purposes for such a long time that they radiate an unusual amount of energy. Scuba divers, sensing the intense, concentrated forces in the Loltun caves, consider those catacombs to be more powerful than the Great Pyramid in Egypt.[34]

The Caribs of Central America retain tales of one extensive group that sailed to the west from Atlantis in 28,000 B.C. The entourage consisted of seven large families, each with many cousins, uncles, and aunts, enough to fill ships for seven fleets. When they finally found an island for their settlement, they called it Caraiba.[35] These Carib legends refer to Atlantis as "the old, red land," just as the Toltecs, predecessors of the Aztecs in Mexico, characterize the homeland of their ancestors as "hue, huetlapappan," meaning "the old, old, red land." They say it was located to the east and is now covered by water.[36] Red clay was more abundant in the area above the surface in the Atlantic Ocean during glacial times, which accounts for this widespread nomenclature in old stories of Atlantis.[37] Descendants of Atlanteans dwelt happily in Caraiba for a very long time. Priests who visited from Atlantis taught the people the religion of Tupan and called them the Tupi, meaning the sons of Pan, which was another name for the old, red land.[38]

Many generations later, after a particularly devastating natural catastrophe on Caraiba, the Tupi were compelled to leave their sinking island home. They sailed a little farther to the west in seven even larger fleets and came to a sea they called "Caribbean," after Caraiba, their initial island refuge. Here they separated. Some settled on nearby mountainous islands, where they farmed the land by terracing, a technique their legends pictured their distant forebears employing on the steep mountainsides in Atlantis. Some Tupi moved on to the south and sailed up the Amazon. The Guarahis of Paraguay and other South American natives today continue to worship the god Tupan. While observing and studying a group of linguistically interrelated Indian tribes along the Amazon River, archaeologist Marcel Homet learned that their common language, Tupi-Guarani, contains idioms that are strikingly similar to the Basque language.[39] The Basques were a group of Atlantean refugees who fled to the Pyrenees Mountains of southwestern Europe.

At least one of the seven groups from Caraiba went north to the Mississippi River Valley. For a long time representatives of the seven extended families met every 104 years to coordinate calendars and compare adventures, but communication became an increasing problem, and they gradually lost touch with one another.[40]

South America

South America, although it was a long, difficult voyage from Atlantis, was another favorable destination of emigrants in 28,000 B.C. Clothing, seeds, and an animal or two were all they could squeeze onto the packed boats as they hurriedly took flight from their unstable country. Their lack of equipment forced them to live in a very primitive manner when they arrived. Just as traces of our civilization will disintegrate before A.D. 12,000, so the things Atlanteans produced in the strange, new land of South America inevitably decayed and succumbed to the jungle. Paintings on stone, the longest-lasting of materials, are all that survive.

When the Atlanteans started their lives in a new country, their first implements were of stone. Making effective tools required careful planning and unlimited patience of skilled craftsmen. It was important that the artisan thoroughly understood the composition of each rock in order to select the proper nodule, realize the effects of heat on it, and carve it slowly and carefully for long tedious hours. Few today are capable of duplicating the accomplishments of the stoneworkers of the past. Once they found time, skilled individuals constructed houses of stone or wood and serviceable stools, benches, tables, and beds, all tasks that proved much simpler than forming their finely wrought stone weapons and tools. Remnants of workshops are discernible where skilled workmen spent their days painstakingly chipping stone. One heavily used Cro-Magnon site in the Amazon basin is identical to another in Vilmaure, France, of 15,000 B.C. to 12,000 B.C.[41]

Similar carvings in rocks on both continents also suggest a common background for those who lived there so long ago. Cro-Magnon peoples outlined hands depicting mutilated thumbs or cut off fingers on the walls of caves in the northern Amazon, in southwest France, and in the Pyrenees.

In Atlantis, following the destruction of 28,000 B.C., sturdy survivors slowly clustered together in meager groups and painstakingly rebuilt their lives. Like sawed-off tree branches that sprout anew in several places, many small settlements of meager shelters sprang up, replacing the cities of the past. As a result of their previous experiences, the Atlanteans realized the Earth was a whole, living organism, and everything and everyone existing on its face was closely interrelated and interdependent. For thousands of years they treated their environment and each other with respect, focusing their daily activities on preserving their natural surroundings. Slowly life improved, and by 15,000 B.C., Atlantis resumed its position as a prosperous major power.

During its final period, shortly before 10,000 B.C., invasions from abroad presented problems in Atlantis. A large and dangerous tribe known as the Amazons dwelt in nearby Africa. Their rulers were powerful women who, comprehending their sex's skill as fighters, separated potential warriors from all contact with males so they remained virgins.[42] After intensive training these females became ferocious soldiers who served diligently in the army. Atlanteans living along the eastern coast of their country never knew when hundreds of small crafts carrying Amazon women might travel the short distance from Africa in the darkness of night and fiercely attack their community. Slaughtering and murdering any opposition in a barbarous manner, the Amazons occasionally gained temporary control of defenseless, coastal villages. After helping themselves to the Atlanteans' sophisticated gold and silver possessions, they returned to their homeland to plan and train for another challenging assault. Upon completing their military service, the Amazon women were released and allowed to marry.[43] Many years later, Hannibal—a Carthaginian general who crossed the Alps with 35,000 troops in 218 B.C.—employed Amazon cavalry-women from Africa who carried lances and protected themselves with shields of serpent skins (an Atlantean symbol).[44] While traveling in North Africa in the first century B.C., Diodorus Siculus learned that the Gorgons were also oppressive neighbors to the Atlanteans. In Greek mythology Gorgons are portrayed as females with heads covered by serpents rather than hair, making their appearance so dreadful that those who looked upon them were turned to stone in terror.[45] Gorgons' heads are reminiscent of formidable Atlantean soldiers who carried squirming snakes in battle.

The third and final major destruction of Atlantis occurred around 10,000 B.C., when something once again severely aggravated the Earth's surface. In the natural reactions that followed, earthquake and volcanic activity ravaged the country's last large island and most of it sank into the sea. Within a short time roaring waters from the rapidly melting glaciers covered small islands as well as the heavily populated coastal lands of the continental shelves. Millions of people perished, not only in Atlantis, but everywhere on the Earth. Mammoths died so quickly in Siberia that they were frozen while standing, and recently eaten food remained in their stomachs for explorers to discover over 11,000 years later. Analysis of the animals' cells indicates the temperature may have fallen to minus 26 to 150 degrees Fahrenheit.[46] Simultaneously the woolly mammoth, saber tooth cat, mastodon, horse, dire wolf, large ground sloth, giant cave bear, and antique bison vanished from North and South America, Europe, and Asia. A widespread eradication of plant life added to the devastation.

Various explanations are offered for the possible cause of the agitation of the Earth's crust in 10,000 B.C. Distinguished German physicist and engineer Dr. Otto Muck believes a large, flaming meteorite smashed into the Atlantic Ocean at about that time,[47] instigating earthquakes and arousing volcanoes as well as causing the enormous flood remembered in the Bible. A serious impact of this type could generate a wave hundreds of feet high, so large that it would overwhelm vast sections of the surrounding continents. The tremendous amount of moisture evaporating from the heat of the blazing object would return to the Earth as torrential rains.

It is quite possible that around 10,000 B.C. a comet shattered as it approached the Earth and huge chunks of it hit our planet, just as befell Jupiter in the summer of 1994. If a large, fast-moving body from space smashed into the Earth, it would account for the extreme temperature changes at the time of the final disappearance of Atlantis. When a massive destructive object strikes land, it creates an immense crater from which large quantities of dust and rubble are thrown into the atmosphere. These block out sunlight and prevent the rays of the sun from warming the Earth. Another effect of such a missile crash on our planet's surface, when it hits either land or water, is that liquid of the inner mantle is so violently disturbed by the jolting shock that sensitive volcanoes swiftly eject smoke, cinders, and deadly gases. As these multitudinous particles surge into the skies, they also obscure the sun's warm rays, temperatures drop rapidly, and snow falls over a wide area without stopping. The resulting buildup of snow and ice moves to cover all in its path, including complex civilizations. Ice formed during glacial ages contains approximately thirty times as much dust as more recent layers of ice.[48] Scientists offer a third possible interpretation for the extreme temperature changes from the impact of a hurtling object. If the Earth is jarred with sufficient force to tilt our globe on its axis, it alters the amount of solar energy received at different latitudes. This is similar to the Hopis' description of the destruction of their second world (see chapter 2).

A further explanation for the troubles of 10,000 B.C. suggests that our solar system contains a tenth planet whose long, elliptical orbit takes it from nearby to far away in the cosmos. Numerous ancient Sumerian diagrams depict not only the sun, moon, and the nine planets we know in their relative positions, but they also portray this tenth planet and the extensive route it travels. Noted scholar Zecharia Sitchin suggests that every 3,600 years the tenth planet returns and travels through our section of the solar system.[49] He believes this celestial body is habitable, for radioactive elements in its depths generate heat and the thick atmosphere around it encloses this warmth, making life possible when it is far from the sun. The dense covering also protects the populace from the sun's powerful rays when their globe moves closer to it. Because of its conspicuously thick atmosphere, the Sumerians describe the planet as "clothed with a halo."[50] Sitchin proposes that in about 11,000 B.C., this large mass from outer space passed so close to the Earth that its gravitational pull caused the ice sheet to slide off Antarctica, creating tremendous tidal waves on our planet's surface. This is quite possible, for the pressure and friction of the heavy ice combined with the Earth's heat trapped below would create a slushy, slippery bottom layer that would act as a lubricant between the glacier above and the ground below. A disturbance to the ice sheet could provoke it to come loose and fall into the ocean.[51] Around the time of the gigantic flood, the Bible says "all the fountains of the great deep were broken up and the windows of heaven were opened."[52] Sitchin believes the "great deep" refers to southernmost Antarctica and the shift in an Antarctica ice sheet, plus the rains, were the cause of the biblical flood.[53]

Natural cataclysms in the distant past that eliminated as many as two-thirds of the species of living creatures at one time were often the result of forceful objects smashing into our Earth's sensitive skin. Scientists of the National Aeronautics and Space Administration (NASA) are recognizing that many more large asteroids pass dangerously close to the Earth than previously realized, and that our planet's surface is pitted with hundreds of cavities formed when objects, sometimes two miles in diameter, crashed violently into it. Researchers are developing plans for tracking these potentially hazardous missiles, hoping to divert a flaming body into a new orbit before it strikes and thereby prevent a "nuclear winter," as the human race experienced in the past.[54]

But what about those who lived in Atlantis before 10,000 B.C. and survived the turmoil and chaos that destroyed their civilizations? What do we know of these ancestors of ours?

THE
GOLDEN YEARS

20,000–10,000 B.C.

PART II

3

PEOPLE

EVEN THOUGH THEY LIVED long ago, Atlanteans were basically like us: equally as intelligent, they laughed, smiled, and loved, grew frustrated, angry, and determined. They were capable of calculating, estimating, making plans, and reflecting on the past, present, and future. Their traits changed in 100,000 years, just as the attitudes and goals of most Americans differ from those of their ancestors who lived 200 years ago. The information that follows primarily relates to the last period of their civilization, from about 20,000 B.C. until about 10,000 B.C.

For thousands of years, the strong, spiritual individuals who repopulated Atlantis following the destruction in 28,000 B.C. worked at maintaining a balanced and harmonious life. They were aware of the link between themselves and a greater spiritual being and focused their activities on worshiping and preserving the beautiful natural environment that supported them. When they were able to meet their daily needs in only a few hours a day, rather than fill the additional time working to acquire more personal possessions, they concentrated on loving and enjoying each other and contemplating their role on Earth and their place in the universe. As they stood tall and straight, their beautiful appearance reflected inner strength and beauty.

The lifestyle of these Atlanteans offered additional benefits. Their stories and legends about their past taught that a human being had a better chance of surviving a natural disaster with the help of others. Everyone nurtured and cared for those with problems, producing a race who lived longer. In the harsh conditions of western Europe, Cro-Magnons survived into their sixties, whereas the average Neanderthals who preceded them died before they reached the age of forty-five.[1] Lives focused on love and the appreciation of beauty inevitably led to the development and growth of further interests. The excellent paintings and sculptures Atlanteans and their progeny left on the European continent reveal unusual artistic talents, strong cultural backgrounds, and a high standard of living. Psychic traits also flourished and expanded in the nourishing atmosphere of Atlantis. Adults respected youngsters' insights and dreams and encouraged children's intuition as they matured. Innate talents, such as the capacity to foresee the future and dowsing, which is the ability to locate hidden objects like underground water, were widely supported.

The Atlanteans' highly developed psychic abilities made their lives quite different from ours. Edgar Cayce describes them as very intuitive and capable of communicating by thought transmission.[2] Without speaking, complete rapport could exist at all levels of understanding. They even transmitted messages and images over vast distances, making communication possible when they were separated.[3] Their ability to control their minds also would have enabled them to communicate on a more equal basis with strong-minded visitors from outer space.

Very slowly, toward the end of their last civilization, many Atlanteans changed, although deep within themselves they retained the innate psychic capabilities of their predecessors— hidden talents that human beings still possess. An increased emphasis on scientific attainments was largely responsible for the gradual reshaping of their interests, their skills, and their temperaments. Just as we have disturbed relatively contented aboriginal societies by introducing our modern conveniences, so, perhaps from contacts with extraterrestrials who helped them "raise" their standard of living, the acquisition of material goods assumed increasing importance. Intimate contact and harmony with nature were no longer of major importance. Their attention turned from a relaxed, contemplative life to one of constantly devising strategies to live well under busy, more challenging conditions. They grew indomitable, well organized, and determined. Since their perceptive abilities were more highly developed than ours, they more easily grasped mysteries of the unknown and intricacies of mathematics and philosophy. These characteristics, combined with advice from extraterrestrials, enabled them to improve their scientific abilities to the advanced level Edgar Cayce describes.

Natural catastrophes also contributed to changes in the Atlanteans' temperament. As their interests turned to scientific endeavors, their respect and worship of nature diminished, and unpredictable minor earthquakes and volcanic eruptions increased. Nature became something they tried to fight. In their attempts to hold their own against the destructive natural weapons of the one all-powerful god, they became combative and pugnacious. When it was necessary to procure additional areas for their expanding population and to replace the land the sea was constantly taking from them, they were well prepared to ferociously battle other humans. Plato describes the soldiers of Atlantis as aggressive and militaristic, and Native Americans remember them as cruel.

In addition to innate psychic powers, the descendants of Atlanteans retain characteristics of the survivors of the challenges that resulted from earthquakes, volcanic eruptions and floods that gradually engulfed their land. The admirable traits include ingenuity, fortitude, and perseverance. However, when people today employ violence to achieve their goals, they are partly reverting to the behavior of prehistoric humans whose lives were often a constant battle to remain on the sensitive surface of the Earth.

Two physically diverse groups of people lived in Atlantis. One, the Cro-Magnons described earlier, had long, narrow skulls with a brain capacity of 100 cubic inches, larger than the average modern human. Their teeth were small and even, and relatively long noses, high cheekbones, and prominent chins characterized their faces. The men were tall, often over six feet in height, and the women were somewhat shorter. Their body structure was so similar to ours that a Cro-Magnon walking down the street today dressed in contemporary clothes would not be conspicuous except for his or her handsome appearance. Another race of Atlanteans, quite different from the Cro-Magnons, lived in the eastern mountains of the country. They were dark-skinned, thick-limbed, heavyset and very strong. Mining was their principal occupation. They are remembered for their excellent sense of humor, which helped them to survive in the rugged mountainous terrain. These athletic people were good fighters and a valuable asset to the Atlantean army.[4]

CUSTOMS AND BELIEFS

The following Atlantean customs and beliefs that persisted in areas contiguous to the Atlantic Ocean offer a provocative but incomplete picture of the lives of those who inhabited the now-submerged land during its final civilization.

Marriage

Recognizing the moral values of family life and the importance of sharing one's time on Earth with others, two people of the opposite sex in Atlantis commonly wished to spend their lives together. If women or men preferred to remain single, they joined a temple, devoting their lives to spiritual and mental development and to ministering to others.[5] Homosexuals in Atlantis were generally accepted as well. Atlanteans believed in reincarnation and that, on account of their recent previous life in a body of the opposite sex, homosexuals preferred not to unite with a person of that sex during the subsequent lifetime. Since they wished to remain true to a former part of themselves, homosexuals were actually admired for their faithfulness.[6] In other words, suppose today you are a female, but in a satisfying prior life you were a male. The memories of that past time as a male are strongly fixed in your subconscious. Those recollections are more powerful than your allegiance to your current status as a female. Out of respect to your past self you prefer not to join with another male at the present time.

Marriage was called "union." Two lovers who wished to unite met with a local priest, who used his or her highly developed intuitive powers to assess the evolution of their souls and determine their compatibility. The marriage had a better chance of enduring if the two were at a similar stage of spiritual development, especially if, as happened occasionally, their initial devotion was primarily physical and based on sexual attraction.[7] The Iroquois, Cherokee, and Blackfeet, whose distant ancestors are of Atlantean origin, employed a similar practice in this country. Couples who hoped to marry met with their tribe's medicine man, who studied their auras (bands of colored light surrounding the body) and anticipated the success of the proposed combination.

In Atlantis, after approving a marriage, the priest blessed the two and gave them bracelets of union to wear on their left arms.[8] The partners were equal, although it was considered the duty of the husband to watch over and care for his mate while she was bearing children.[9] In the final days of the last Atlantean civilization two wives were allowed, perhaps because so many men were fighting abroad. These households were usually harmonious, for the children were taught to love and respect their father's other wife, who in turn made every effort to treat them as if they were her own offspring.[10]

Divorce

In the event that an Atlantean couple were miserable, they returned to the priest, who attempted to help them live harmoniously together. If this proved impossible, the religious leader removed the bracelets of union and the incompatible man and woman parted. The Atlanteans believed it was unnecessary to suffer all of one's life for a mistake made when young.[11] When a couple with children separated, if neither adult wished to care for their youngsters, older people, whose own offspring were grown, assumed the responsibility. Neglected orphans also found homes with considerate elderly citizens.[12]

Couvade

The strange, unappealing custom of couvade was sufficiently popular in prehistoric times to survive for thousands of years on both sides of the Atlantic. After the birth of a child, the new father went to bed and for a number of days ate very little while the wife cared for him. In some instances, following the fast, his friends and neighbors, or the group leader, subjected him to lacerating knife wounds and other cruelties. If he bore this treatment well, everyone respected and admired him and believed pain would not bother his latest offspring. If he succumbed to the bizarre conduct, both he and the baby were at risk. During the baby's first year the father refrained from using sharp objects or participating in vigorous activities such as hunting, since he believed any harm to himself might seriously endanger the child. Presumably the practice of couvade started in Atlantis, the central point, and was carried to adjacent lands. It was observed in Mexico, among the Caribs and Arawaks in Central America,[13] and to the east of Atlantis in Ireland, among the Iberians of northern Spain, in France and, until very recently, among the Basques.[14]

Circumcision

Circumcision originated in the hot climate of Atlantis as a sanitary precaution and was carried abroad and practiced by the Egyptians, who told Herodotus in the fifth century B.C. that it originated in "the most remote antiquity." In ancient Egypt, circumcision was not compulsory unless a male wished to study for the priesthood. It was usually performed when the boy was fourteen years old, although the choice was left to the parents.[15] From Egypt it was passed on to the Phoenicians and the Hebrews. Ignatius Donnelly writes that even after metals became readily available, Hebrew rabbi continued to use a stone knife for the ceremony. Donnelly believes this indicates the practice dated to the Stone Age.[16]

Burial Practices

Customs change very gradually, and burial and religious rites are the most long-lasting. New influences may be reflected in a minor way, but in prehistory, stylized burial ceremonies endured almost perpetually, with little modification. Striking similarities dating to before 10,000 B.C. are evident in the burial practices of people who lived in countries accessible from the Atlantic Ocean. These habits, which include the use of red ocher and the preparation of mummies, offer insight into life in Atlantis, their common place of origin.[17]

Immortality was taken for granted in Atlantis, and therefore death was not feared. Since they believed the soul lived on, it was important to preserve some components of the human body to provide a framework for the afterlife; if the soul's home on Earth was totally destroyed, it would lose its immortality.[18] Red ocher, double burial, and mummification were techniques utilized to ready the body for what was to come. The elaborate rituals that accompanied these undertakings assured the concerned family and friends that the deceased was well prepared, and the routines provided stability and strength to everyday lives. Everyone mourned and missed their loved ones when they left this world, but since they knew they would be reunited eventually, they did not suffer the remorse or sense of devastation a permanent loss provoked. The inhabitants of Atlantis spent an immense amount of time and effort preparing bodies of their dead for the next life, partly because it was a religious practice advocated by their highly trained, powerful priesthood. These leaders constantly reinforced the belief that one's soul, created and controlled by the supreme being, did not die when a person's heart stopped beating.

For relatively simple burials, the body was carefully covered with red ocher paint to provide blood for the next life. Loving relatives decorated the corpse and its clothing with necklaces, belts, and bracelets fashioned from shells, beads, or precious stones, and often placed special objects in the grave for use by the deceased in the time to come. Priests moved the body to a sitting, or fetal, position, knees drawn up, ready to reenter this world. Cro-Magnons buried in this manner at the time of Atlantis are found in Africa, western Europe, and across the ocean in South America. Red ocher for painting the bodies was extracted from a hematite mine in Africa as long as 40,000 years ago.[19] Africans who continue to use it in their burial ceremonies demonstrate the long life of burial customs.[20]

To ensure that the cadaver maintained the crouching position, it was necessary to arrange the corpse prior to or immediately following death, before rigor mortis set in. If it was too late to move it into a fetal position, priests wrapped the remains in cloth or fiber and dried them over a fire. After the moisture was removed from the body, they rubbed it with softening fats and oils until it was pliable enough to manipulate. Rhythmic sounds from the mournful chanting that accompanied these elaborate preparation ceremonies, plus the aromatic odor of copal and other burning herbs, helped the participating friends and relatives enter into trance-like states and communicate with the dead.

In some areas of Atlantis the geography was not conducive to underground burial. Sites were limited in mountainous regions and floods were always a possibility along the coastlines. The Atlanteans devised various means of preserving at least part of the body of those who passed on. One was double burials, which were considerably more complicated than the standard procedure. To accomplish them, family members first reverently buried the corpse with the help of a priest. After the flesh decomposed, they removed the skeleton from the grave, polished the bones, and painted them red. Finally, they reinterred the skeleton, often in a jar that could be stored above ground and carried to a new location if nature threatened. Atlanteans and their descendants performed double burials in lands they inhabited around the Atlantic Ocean. In South America, the urns and red-painted bones of Cro-Magnons sometimes date to an earlier period than those of their European counterparts,[21] which indicates that they either settled here first or there has been less robbing of graves in the remote Amazon area than in European caves. People who lived along the Amazon River devised an ingenious method for removing the meat from the bones in preparation for double burials.

Surviving kinfolk placed the dead person in the river, where flesh-eating fish like pacomons and piranhas quickly reduced the body to a skeleton, neatly preparing it for a second burial.[22] Dakota, Choctaw, and Sioux, all descendants of emigrants from Atlantis to North America, put the dead on platforms before polishing and painting the bones red. The bodies were exposed for a year, since they believed the spirit of one who dies is earthbound for twelve months. The time before the remains were buried offered an opportunity for the spirit or soul to learn directions from the birds.[23] The Choctaw say they painted the bones of the deceased red because it was the color of the "old, red land" that is now under the eastern ocean,[24] just as Central American descendants referred to the Atlantean homeland of their ancestors.

Mummification was another technique developed in Atlantis to preserve a body above the ground and assure it would be available for the soul in its next life.[25] The country's many caves provided spaces that were safe from floods and volcanic eruptions for the remains of loved ones preserved in this manner. Mummies displaying the remarkable embalming skills Atlanteans developed are found in Peru, Mexico, Egypt, and the Canary Islands, all lands adjacent to the Atlantic Ocean. The inhabitants of these countries continued to embalm their dead long after Atlantis disappeared.[26]

As civilizations changed in Atlantis and young people discarded old customs, daring individuals experimented with cremation. Trained psychics who altered the rate of vibration, or density, of the components of material objects, thus creating temporary changes in the atomic structures, used their power to disintegrate corpses.[27] Edgar Cayce says that emigrants who settled in the Yucatan practiced cremation and placed the ashes in temples so no burial grounds remain where they lived.[28] When they cremated a corpse, it seemed to the Atlanteans as if the spirits of air, earth, fire, and water were each claiming the aspect of the body that originated from its sphere. Portions of the ritual accompanying this operation have survived in the common burial phrase "ashes to ashes and dust to dust."[29]

CLOTHING AND APPEARANCE

Due to the warm climate that characterized most of the country, Atlanteans usually wore simple, functional clothing. Edgar Cayce reveals that men and women wore similar garments, often of linen.[30] A robe, dress, or a top with short or long trousers were the normal attire. Sandals were prevalent, although bare feet were quite acceptable. Atlanteans preferred to keep their hair long, believing it gave them physical and spiritual power.[31] During the final stage of the civilization, as they placed increasing emphasis on material goods, personal appearance became more important. Men, women, and children elaborately decked themselves with necklaces, bracelets, rings, hairpieces, brooches, and belts embellished with pearls, silver, gold, and colorful precious gems.

Atlantean priests' apparel designated their level of development and their specialty. The basic color of their garments and their sash, earring, pendant, ring, bracelet, or headband indicated whether they were a healer, student, or teacher and what level they had attained.[32] When they started the journey toward priesthood, the novices wore pale green robes. As they advanced, light blue clothing distinguished them, and finally they were permitted to don the white garments reserved for the highest-ranking orders. Special deep blue gowns were passed down from one generation of sages to the next and worn only on rare occasions. A healer who displayed a silver headband specialized in mental healing, while one with an orichalcum headband was proficient in physical medicine or surgery.[33]

Cayce tells us that purple was a popular color for clothing in Atlantis,[34] and Murex sea shells from their beaches offered an excellent source for the hue. Atlantean descendants, including the Egyptians whose traders fervently sought purple dyes, favored purple for thousands of years. The Tuaregs, whose Atlantean ancestors settled in the Atlas Mountains in Africa, continued until the twentieth century to dress only in clothes dyed a very deep blue, almost purple color. Roman scholar Honorius Augustodunensis, writing in A.D. 1300 in regard to the Atlantis of Plato, mentioned that the country was known for a breed of sheep, very white and fleecy, which yielded the best wool for dyeing purple.[35] The warmth of outer clothing woven from sheep's wool was welcome in the mountainous and northern areas of the country.

So, try to picture yourself in Atlantis 20,000 years ago, attired in a cool, white linen dress or trousers with an elegant embroidered purple border. A string of shining pearls and shells hangs from your neck and a simple gold bracelet in the shape of a snake coils up your arm. Soft sandals made from woven palm leaves protect your feet. Perhaps, as a man or a woman, your long hair is held in place with ivory hairpins and you adorn yourself with radiant crystals to amplify your higher consciousness.

When Atlanteans migrated to colder, southwestern Europe, more clothing was necessary. Illustrations painted in caves at that time show people attired in fitted and finely sewn shirts with collars and cuffed sleeves, skirts, jackets, long robes with belts, and trousers with pockets. Socks, shoes, and fur boots cover their feet for warmth.[36] Women are depicted wearing cotton scarves or hats on their heads. Men's hair was neatly combed, and mustaches, goatees, and trimmed beards adorned their faces.[37]

Twenty thousand years ago, Atlanteans and their descendants living in Europe fashioned small needles to enhance their clothing with delicate embroidery. They intricately sewed strings of beads on vests, aprons and other garments.[38]

Some beads were so elaborate that it required 100 hours of an artisan's time to make a necklace containing fifty of the tiny objects.[39] Shells and pearls from the ocean were among the most popular personal possessions in Europe 20,000 years ago. Traders carried them hundreds of miles inland to enthusiastic recipients, who eagerly decorated themselves with these familiar items from the sea.[40]

ENTERTAINMENT

As they grew more materially oriented, Atlanteans moved their worship indoors to tastefully decorated temples. It was important to place these buildings to take advantage of helpful energy from the Earth and the universe. They understood that subtle forces from all realms exert influence on our minds and bodies. To choose the most favorable location, they utilized the science of feng shui, or geomancy. The contours of the land, the location of underground streams, and other natural factors were carefully considered for their influence on the energies resulting from the surrounding gravitational, electromagnetic and electrostatic fields.[41]

These powerful buildings and their grounds, always available for quiet contemplation and refreshing meditation, dotted the landscape of Atlantis. In contrast to their preference for simple homes, Atlanteans lavishly decorated their cherished temples, knowing the buildings would be available for others to enjoy long after they themselves were no longer on this Earth. Artisans carefully covered interior walls and ceilings with exquisite mosaics of gold and silver, or inlaid them with precious stones. Outside, men, women, and children joined together to cultivate lovely gardens enhanced with cooling streams and pools filled with brightly colored fish. They planted tall trees, as well as fruit trees, to ensure that nesting songbirds would supplement the idyllic atmosphere. A nearby temple and its adjacent park were a favorite destination for outings to picnic, swim, relax, and enjoy nature.

Festivals of religious origin, events honoring the gods of nature, and ceremonies connected with birth and death all contributed to the active social life of Atlanteans. The feared gods of the volcanoes often rumbled, and much time was spent attempting to mollify them. On designated days everyone assembled with plates of fresh fruits and vegetables and carried them to mountain peaks or placed them in hollows carved into rocks on the sides of the volcanoes, a custom that some Caucasian people observed in the past as a way of presenting sacrifices to their gods. Hundreds of plates the Atlanteans carried to the mountains survived. In 1949 the Geological Society of America, while conducting a submarine probe in the vicinity of the Atlantic Seamount southwest of the Azores, brought up about a ton of calcified discs from a depth of 1,000 feet. The "sea biscuits," as they were called, were all approximately the same size and shape. They had a depression in the center of one side giving them the shape of plates, and their surface was relatively smooth, except rough in the depression. They were about six inches in diameter and one and one half inches thick. Tests determined the plates were about 12,000 years old and that the material from which they were made was formed in sub-aerial conditions.[42] Limestone discs or "sea biscuits," similar to those taken from the bottom of the ocean near the Azores, were also found in the Bahamas.[43]

One of the most popular events in Atlantis was the Festival of the New Year, which took place for seven days in the City of the Golden Gates at the time of the spring equinox. In 1903, Dr. W. P. Phelon relayed the following description of the holiday, which offered opportunities for spiritual growth and renewal, as well as for visiting with one's friends. The sun was the honored guest at the Festival of the New Year, since each day for the next three months it remained in the sky for a longer period of time. About three days before the occasion, lines of travelers slowly moved toward the metropolis from all directions. When the city was overflowing and inns were full, local inhabitants erected tents of white linen or cotton in parks and gardens to accommodate the visitors. At this point, the level of excitement resembled the emotions of young children before a birthday party.

The initial ceremony of the Festival of the New Year took place at sunrise on the spacious grounds of the Temple of Poseidon. As the first beams of light appeared, the assembled multitude faced the east. A large choir, standing on one of the porches of the sacred building within sight of the crowds, began to sing a low, sweet, rhythmic chant. Gradually, as the voices of the worshippers joined those of the choir, the intensity of the sound increased and the mighty sun rose into view. Thousands of people swayed almost hypnotically to the music, welcoming the light. Suddenly, as the sun's rays shined upon the uplifted faces, a strong blast from a chorus of trumpets accompanied the final note of the chant. The worshippers dropped to their knees, bowing their heads in silent appreciation of the power of this source of all life and strength.

Following the sunrise service, people socialized, played games, and attended discussions and lectures on religion, philosophy, and the sciences. Each day of the Festival everyone paused at noon to face the Temple. When the fiery ball of the sun reached its highest point in the sky, priests swung a crystal from a tall tower, catching its beams and sending brilliant light in all directions. Everyone focused on the magnificent source of energy and gave thanks for its presence. In the evening, as the majestic orb set, the throngs faced west instead of east and, to the accompaniment of quiet sounds from stringed instruments, sang a song of farewell to the beloved heavenly body.

On the final evening, after the sunset service, the Temple choir initiated a quite different, much stronger melody. The masses of worshippers added their voices to those of the choir, and as the haunting, strong vibrations from the music echoed off nearby mountains, a priest spoke to the crowd of the sun's value, his comments reinforced by uneasiness resulting from the lack of light. As he concluded with a discussion of darkness, death, and desolation, and proclaimed, "Let there be light," numerous priests simultaneously lit lamps in the Temple windows and on its towers and roof, brightly illuminating the glorious building.[44]

In addition to the Festival of the New Year, local ceremonies for planting crops in the spring, rituals to Vulcan (the fire god of the volcanoes), services on Midsummer's Day, and events on the nights of a full moon supplemented the Atlanteans' social life. Winter happenings required many bonfires and covered such vast areas that sometimes it seemed as if whole hillsides were ablaze. Everyone in Atlantis eagerly followed the paths of the sun and moon in anticipation of the next event. As soon as the children were able to walk and talk, parents taught appropriate songs and rigorous stylized dances to them, increasing their anticipation and strengthening family unity. The beloved formalities provided stability to the community, elevating participants to the same level and cementing them in a common bond.

Traces of one Atlantean ceremony remain with us today. The early Algonquins, who came to the southern United States around 20,000 B.C., brought with them a dance to the sun. Their descendants, the Dakota Sioux, who believe the dance was theirs "way back to the dawn," continued to carry out the ceremony for thousands of years.[45] In the original performance, as spring approached on the first day of May, a specific number of warriors, accompanied by an attractive young girl who was referred to as the "beautiful enemy," danced off in search of a tree to use as a pole. When they returned, while the women and children attached ropes of colorful flowers to the top of the tree, the men removed its branches. Finally they embedded the tree trunk securely in the ground, and everyone vigorously danced around it, singing and laughing for joy. The event was the predecessor of our May Pole dance.

Atlantis abounded in pleasurable activities. Hiking in the mountains was a favored but dangerous vacation pursuit. A trek to the higher areas sometimes turned into a treacherous adventure as, without warning, the air became heavy and noxious with the acrid smell of ammonia, sulfur, and smoke, and hot, liquid lava forced its way through cracks in the steep, rocky mountainside. As the molten metal quickly twisted down the slope it covered everything it encountered, including the trail. A good sense of direction and agile feet were required to hurriedly find a new route home. Along the southwestern coast, coral reefs protected pink sand beaches from the ocean's powerful waves, and a steady cooling breeze was always available for relief from the hot sun. Atlanteans loved to relax under the palm trees and swim in the quiet waters.

Other diversions became popular during the final years. Throughout the country the masses preferred to attend bloody bull fights and competitive horse races rather than pass time at the beach or quietly relax in the peaceful temples and their grounds. As the possession of material goods grew more important and social classes developed, the rich entertained frequently and extravagantly. Guests carefully ornamented themselves with gold, crystals, and precious gems for the occasions. When they arrived at the door of their host's residence, a servant placed a crown of freshly cut flowers on their heads. Each visitor removed his or her shoes and an aide washed the guest's feet in a copper basin. As the visitors feasted on a wide variety of sumptuous food, attendants served drinks in shiny silver goblets. Entertaining jugglers, singers, and dancers circulated among the guests. The decadent parties often lasted many days, until the participants were bored with rich food and each other.

In the last years of Atlantis many people attached increasing importance to eating, drinking, and socializing. Memories of this widespread atmosphere did not completely fade away. Atlantean descendants living in the West Indies thousands of years later attested that Atlantis was a place where everyone feasted, danced, and sang,[46] and Welsh legends report that if the right sort of music was played, Atlanteans danced in the air like leaves.

PETS

During the last 20,000 years of Atlantean civilization, when wild animals did not outnumber people as they had thousands of years earlier, the people conversed telepathically with animals and birds just as they sometimes shared their thoughts with each other. Deer, lions, goats, pigs, and other animals roamed freely, while an incredible number of uncaged, singing canaries, finches, and thrushes flitted among the homes and perhaps perched on welcoming shoulders. Wild creatures devoted themselves to assisting and protecting their human friends. In a similar way, before the Spaniards came to California, natives and bears picked berries together and communicated with each other to their mutual benefit.[47]

Cats, dogs, and snakes made especially desirable pets, for the animals sensed terrestrial vibrations and the sudden increase in electronic activity that foretold earthquake and volcanic activity. The people also knew that long droughts followed by extremely heavy rains often preceded the movement of earthquakes. These conditions, coupled with a dog or cat's anxious state, furnished a fairly accurate prediction of a forthcoming devastating natural event.

Occultist priests, exceedingly adept at communicating with animals, harbored lions and other large cats. Almost every family kept a smaller cat, believing the pet's psychic abilities were helpful in protecting their owners from the harmful ways of underworld inhabitants.[48] Cats and kittens seemed like part of the family, and whenever it was possible, emigrants found a tiny place in their baggage for these small creatures as they departed for another land. Domestic cats appeared in Egypt long before recorded history; presumably their forebears came with the Atlanteans. Aerial photographs of a formation on Bimini depict a mound in the shape of a cat with a long tail curled over its back as it stretches forward. The animal figure reaches over 700 feet in length and lies next to a rectangular formation that may be ruins of the Temple of Bastet,[49] a temple dedicated to the Egyptian cat goddess that is thought to have been in this area.

The dog we know as the chow is believed to be one of the oldest of all breeds and its origin is unknown. It is possible that, with help from extraterrestrials adept at genetic manipulation, the chow was bred in Atlantis as an aide to the country's vast armed forces. Careful breeding produced these strong animals with heavy bones and very sharp claws, similar to those of a bear. Taylor Hansen offers some interesting insights on the dog's history, which she learned from Robert Beck, a lecturer on Egyptian culture. Beck alleges that the chow was popular in Sumeria thousands of years ago, where it skillfully guarded temples, and it became the war dog of the Hittites. In Cambodia, the chow also guarded prehistoric temples. More recently, in about 150 B.C. during the Han dynasty, the dog was portrayed in China. Hansen suggests the Atlanteans carried the fearless chows on ships to the Far East for use in combat, and when their masters returned home, the animals who were left behind in the Orient were utilized as temple guards.

Sheep, although housed outside, were worthy additions to a household. Children shaped the animals' coats into patterns and enjoyed riding them to visit friends. Sheep's wool served as pillow stuffing or was spun and woven into cloth. The animals' droppings made excellent fertilizer for house plants.[50]

Dolphins were bred as special pets in Atlantis.[51] Atlanteans built pools near their homes for the fun-loving creatures and treated them as equals. They learned to understand their rapid conversation and came to respect the animals' mental ability and intelligence. Dolphins along the coast proved an excellent source of knowledge about the sea. Perhaps we will learn to communicate with dolphins and whales as the Atlanteans did so they may direct us to containers of nuclear waste and other hazardous materials dumped into the oceans.

Horses, a common sight in Atlantis, worked on farms, provided transportation, and were popular participants in races on the huge track in the City of the Golden Gates. They were especially helpful to Atlantean settlers of southwestern Europe, who caught wild horses and trained them to protect their herds of reindeer from wolves and other predators. Discarded bones adjacent to living sights in France and Spain in 20,000 B.C. indicate reindeer constituted over ninety percent of the diet,[52] but reindeer migrate in warmer weather. Riding their horses to collect reindeer, Atlantean immigrants confined the animals in pens so as to assure a year-round source of their favorite food. In nearby caves, careful artists painted and carved horses wearing rope halters and drew pictures of men twirling a stone on the end of a rope, identical to the bolas Argentine cowboys swing today. Skulls of horses of this time frequently show evidence of "cribbing," a nervous chewing habit that wears down their teeth. Cribbing reflects the stress of captivity and is never found in wild horses.[53]

Atlantean descendants preserved their communication expertise with wild creatures on both sides of the ocean, such as the ability to call animals. On the American continent, the Blackfeet established a strong bond with the buffalo, and when they wished to kill them for food or other necessities, they summoned them. A woman holding a buffalo horn over her head symbolized this power. Thirty thousand years ago, a similar picture of a naked woman holding a buffalo's horn high in her right hand was engraved on the wall of a rock shelter in southern France.[54] Ancestors of the Blackfeet, who traveled to the American continent from Atlantis thousands of years ago, used and preserved skills like animal communication they had learned in their homeland. Those who traveled to the European continent did the same.

LANGUAGE

As they sailed, Atlanteans communicated with people everywhere, and their language was gradually accepted for culture and trade. Prior forms of speech grew obsolete as the Atlanteans' vocabulary became the basic vocabulary from which many of the world's languages sprang. The days of one universal tongue are remembered in the Bible at the time of the Tower of Babel, when "the whole earth was of one language."[55] The Popul Vuh, an ancient book of the Mayans, alleges that before their ancestors moved to the western hemisphere they had only one language.[56] A school of linguists called Nostratics are slowly assembling the proto-World language as they attempt to find the predecessor of the proto-Indo-European language family thought to have been spoken 5,000 years ago. The Nostratics believe this group of languages were all offshoots of a common tongue spoken more than 10,000 years ago and are reconstructing the basic vocabulary from which all languages have sprung.[57]

The Basques, a group of 700,000 people living in relative isolation in the Pyrenees Mountains of southwestern Europe, continue to speak fragments of the Atlantean language. This special race maintains that they are descendants of Atlanteans, whose advanced civilization is under the ocean.[58] The Basque language is unique and does not appear to be traceable to any other idiom.[59] Their word for *knife* literally means "the stone that cuts,"[60] supporting their conviction that their speech is the oldest in the world and originated in the Stone Age.

WRITING

Initially Atlanteans considered written symbols unnecessary and undesirable, for they were not dependent on them for stability. Their spiritual lives were thoroughly aligned with the natural world, providing continuity and strength without writing. They believed that if something was written down it encouraged forgetfulness and simultaneously discouraged the cultivation of memory. People feared that in forming the marks for writing they would focus on the appearance of the symbol rather than the true meaning of the thought. In other words, writing an idea limited knowledge but did not expand it. For thousands of years, storytelling was the accepted form of education. Families sat together for hours while respected older people quietly and slowly described the past and relayed ancient knowledge relevant to everyday lives.

Gradually in Atlantis various symbols such as spirals, swastikas, and zigzag lines came to represent abstract feelings or concrete events and other concepts that required several words to express. As they traveled to the lands around the Atlantic Ocean, Atlanteans made these markings in their dealings with others. The signs were universally employed to describe emotions, recent happenings, and plans. In prehistory, sailors and emigrants painted almost identical symbols on cave walls in the Canary Islands, South America, southwestern Europe, and the now-submerged Loltun caves in the Yucatan. It is still customary among persons untouched by our current civilization to tattoo these symbols onto their bodies. They believe the characters help them to gain added strength from the energy of the Earth and the universe.[61]

Using sharp stones, hammers, and bone chisels, the mariners of prehistory painstakingly carved precise petroglyphs throughout the world on rocks and boulders. Their signs endure high above river banks and on cliff faces in places only accessible to people who reached them in boats when the water was far above its current height. Repetitive marks along ancient stream beds, carved before 10,000 B.C., are visible in Africa, the Canary Islands, the Caribbean, around the Gulf of Mexico, and in many other areas adjacent to the Atlantic Ocean where the waters once led to the sea.[62]

The rocks talk in a variety of languages. Since Atlantean sailors used the stars for navigation, their petroglyphs are frequently signs of the zodiac. Calendars are carved in the rocks. Messages or maps sometimes describe the topography upstream. These silent stories in stone assisted travelers in finding food and water or a place to rest and make repairs. Like our international traffic signs, the geometric and animal shapes are similar throughout the world.[63]

One of the most significant occupations of prehistoric people who lived without electric lights was to study and accurately record the movements of the sun, moon, and stars. Thirty thousand years ago in southwestern Europe, viewers of the heavens carefully carved their observations on bones from eagles, mammoth, and deer. The tiny marks precisely chronicle the waxing and waning of the moon through its phases, reminding us of the sophisticated, capable people who lived so long ago.

Written symbols similar to ours slowly developed from picture writing in Atlantis. The earliest marks were based on the sounds of living things, just as the consonants in Hebrew represent the sounds of the Earth. Many references to prehistoric literature have endured. Plato tells us the laws of Atlantis were engraved on a column and the kings of Atlantis wrote their judgments upon a golden tablet when they assembled to make the laws. Ancient Babylonian texts, found in the extensive library of Nineveh in Sumeria, mention the pleasure a king of 2,000 years ago received from reading writings of the age before the Flood.[64] Donnelly offers ten references to information about pre-Flood literature that he assembled from Hebrew,

Greek, Egyptian, Gothic, and Chinese documents. Theologian and educator Clement of Alexandria (first century A.D.) wrote of the gods who lived among men in Egypt. He said they came before the Flood and brought forty-two books, including six medical treatises, which contained the knowledge of the ancient priesthood.[65] As the Phoenicians traveled to the lands around the Atlantic Ocean, they collected fragments of the ancient signs and symbols developed in Atlantis and assembled them into a phonetic alphabet.

The proficient Incas and their predecessors, whom Cayce tells us were descended from Atlantean emigrants to South America,[66] had a system of writing but all traces of it disappeared before the sixteenth century. There is a story that once in the distant past, when a terrible plague was devastating the people of the Andes, the Gods told the leaders that if they abolished all written records and never wrote again the sickness would end. The desperate people destroyed everything containing writing, and thereafter killed anyone who wrote.[67] The Incas developed an elaborate system of colored and knotted strings called the "quipu" to take its place and jog their memories.

EDUCATION

Like young children everywhere, early Atlanteans' education came from their elders and from observing the world around them. Storytelling was a major part of life, and people recited narratives their grandparents told about Poseidon, Cleito, and Atlas, or the past experiences of their people with earthquakes, floods, eclipses, and wild animals. Young people's memories improved as they learned the numerous verses of the songs their community sang at planting ceremonies around the circle of stones or on the nights of a full moon. Encouraged to spend time with their natural surroundings, they talked to flowers, made friends with birds and small animals, sensed that stones and rocks are alive and filled with tiny, rapidly moving particles, and explored additional complex secrets of the world around them.

Girls and boys carefully studied dowsers and, following their example, sought to locate underground water or find a missing article. Children experimented with using the right side of their brains and learned to communicate with animal and human friends, as Saint Francis did many centuries later. Youngsters discovered how to anticipate a forthcoming storm or an approaching herd of dangerous animals before they could hear or see them, a skill that sometimes saved their lives as they quickly raced back to the safety of their stone houses. As a result of their childhood education, Atlanteans were astute, aware adults, at peace with themselves and well prepared for life in the natural world.

All civilizations age, however, and lives gradually changed in Atlantis. Around 14,000 B.C., scientific and scholarly learning increased in importance, and a knowledgeable population became essential to the general well-being. Education for the young expanded to the temples, where children learned reading, writing, astronomy and mathematics. Thought transference, also known as telepathy, was favored as a teaching technique in the temples.[68] To achieve the necessary receptive meditative state, the students relaxed while breathing deeply to low-pitched, rhythmic sounds. When the minds of their students were quiet, the priests communicated to them without speaking. Sometimes the teachers focused a special white light on individual students. The light glowed in noticeable waves, raising the child's energy level and enhancing their ability to learn.[69] In the schools in the temples, written information was recorded on flexible parchment-like material that was rolled into a scroll and secured with a ceramic disc that resembled a napkin ring.[70] Young people received an opportunity to broaden their knowledge during the annual trips to the Festival of the New Year in the City of the Golden Gates, where they might listen with open minds to adults engaged in erudite discussions.

On their twelfth birthday every child was granted a private interview with the chief priest of the local temple. At that time, the highly trained and perceptive leader assessed the young adult to decide what occupation was most appropriate for him or her. One's life work was determined by the level of evolution of the spirit and the characteristics of his or her karmic problems and gifts.[71] Following this interview, the majority of teenagers attended technical schools, where they learned agriculture, fishing, or another practical trade.[72] A few attended academic schools, where the scholarly curriculum was supplemented with the study of the medicinal properties of plants and herbs, plus courses to develop the student's psychic facilities, such as spiritual healing.[73]

The Atlanteans built a splendid university in the City of the Golden Gates with admittance available to all who were prepared, without regard to race, color, or creed.[74] The university was composed of two colleges: the College of Sciences and the Occult College of Incal, which was located in the Temple of Poseidon. Instruction at the College of Sciences was highly specialized, so immediately upon entering students selected a field of study. Popular choices were medicine, mathematics, mineralogy, or any other branch of science that suited the needs of humankind. Courses in government were required and, to increase understanding of their unstable land, everyone received training in geology.[75]

The College of Incal, supervised by priests from the Temple of Poseidon, specialized in occult phenomena with an emphasis on the spiritual growth of the student. Typical areas of study were astrology, prophecy, mind reading, dream interpretation, thought transference, and the use of thought projection to create material objects.[76] Students learned to communicate with the spiritual world for advice and assistance in all affairs.

Healers who studied in the Temple of Poseidon acquired quite different skills from those who studied medicine in the College of Sciences. All Atlanteans benefited from the wide variety of techniques available for diagnosis and treatment of physical and mental problems.

FINE ARTS

A favorable climate offered Atlanteans the opportunity to live without an intense daily struggle for food and shelter, and it assured adequate time for aesthetic occupations like art and music. The talents of the country's artisans were displayed in exquisite temples that are now covered with lava and debris on the ocean floor, but some of their creations survive in lands bordering the Atlantic Ocean. In southwestern Europe a few graceful sculptures, unique paintings, and pieces of lovely jewelry carved from bone, ivory, and semiprecious stones reflect the long period of artistic development in Atlantis. These paintings, sculptures, and jewelry fashioned there were not first attempts, but masterpieces of skilled craftspeople.

We have no way of appreciating the quality of paintings Atlantean refugees created outdoors in the warm sunlight, but their remarkable works of 30,000 B.C. to 10,000 B.C. are visible in caves in France and Spain. Hunting scenes, lists of group activities, and detailed records of the seasons line cave walls near the entrances, but the finest works are in deep, remote, almost unreachable caverns, where painters struggled under the stress of inadequate ventilation and the poor lighting of wavering oil lamps. In spite of the terrible conditions, the animals they depicted display freedom, spirit, and a realistic power of movement in a manner seldom equaled today. Bulls painted in natural colors on the walls of the Altamira cave in Santander, on the Bay of Biscay in northern Spain, stand and recline so realistically one can almost feel their presence. To improve the three-dimensional aspect of their portrayal and enhance the power of the creatures' hefty bodies, the prehistoric artists utilized the natural contours in the cave's stone walls. The head, front legs and one hind leg of a massive bull are shaped from bulges in the rocks. Lighter colors around the eyes and forehead of a bull in the nearby Tito Bustillo cave produce a general impression of inner strength and confidence; this being knows and understands his world and probably more. Nearby a female stag deer runs with her head in the air, displaying an ease of movement that incites joy and happiness. As the well-centered artists created these beautiful animals, they displayed their own positive emotions and self-confidence.

The dedication of these artists of so long ago, and the importance they attached to their work, is evident. They painted beautiful pictures on cave ceilings, where they had to perch precariously on high scaffolding suspended by ropes. Beadwork that adorns skeletons in graves offers another example of their devotion. One style of bead fashioned from the ivory of mammoths' tusks required forty-five minutes just to carve into the correct shape. In preparation for burial, bodies were often covered with more than 3,000 of these lovely beads requiring over 2,000 hours of labor.[77]

The tools of immigrants from Atlantis also reflect their aesthetic inclinations and refined tastes. In 18,000 B.C., new arrivals in southwestern Europe chiseled their spear heads from local stone or bone, but they carved them carefully and delicately, embellishing them with tasteful designs. It was as if they were producing what they needed from what was available, patterning it after prior weapons of much finer materials.

Rather than paint with vegetable dyes, the rigorously trained artists from Atlantis produced permanent mineral pigments that required extensive skills to make. Their various shades of red paint necessitated heating ocher from iron ore to above 250 degrees centigrade. For their white paints they carefully mixed porcelain clay, powdered quartz, and ground calcite. Artists added preservatives to the pigments, binders made from animal fat, and adherents from saliva to ensure the beautiful paintings stayed on the damp cave walls.

Sometimes artists trained by the same master in Atlantis moved to different shores of the southwestern European coast. In a region of the Dordogne River valley of France, and in another area in the Pyrenees in Spain, the details of color markings, shadings, and positioning of animals painted on cave walls is almost identical.[78] Apparently, as they designed and shaded figures in the same manner in separate places hundreds of kilometers apart, talented artists recalled the similar instruction they received in their years of study in Atlantis.

Atlantean craftsmen who left their country retained their longing for the sea and its creatures, both so important in their earlier lives. In Europe, small statues of sea mammals carved thousands of years ago have been discovered far inland.[79] In France twenty thousand years ago, over 100 miles from the Atlantic Ocean, someone treasured a picture of two seals engraved on the bone of a sperm whale. An unknown artist, utilizing his intimate knowledge of the animals, depicted them so realistically that their sex is easily recognized. A similar affection is demonstrated in a cave in southern Spain, where an accurate painting from the time of Atlantis represents three dolphins; two are obviously males and one female.

The subject matter of prehistoric Atlantean painters and sculptors in southwestern Europe reflects the importance of religion in their homeland. When the twelve kings of Atlantis assembled to make the laws, they first sacrificed a bull,[80] the sacred controller of the animal world. Their reverence for bulls is evident in their European art. Illustrations of both bulls and horses, who are regarded as sacred to Poseidon in Greek mythology, predominate in the depths of caves of southwestern Europe, although in that area, when the paintings were created 15,000 years ago, most of the meat eaten was from reindeer.[81] Pictures of reindeer are relatively rare, usually appearing near the front of caves, where ceremonies to ensure a good hunt took place; religious services occurred deeper in the caverns. The largest painting in the Lascaux cave in France is a massive bull, eighteen feet long. The huge animal is painted on the ceiling of a room where people congregated in the time of Atlantis to worship and respect the powerful bull. Sculptors, as well as painters, expressed their reverence for horses and bulls. Miniature statuettes of horses skillfully cut from ivory, the head of a neighing horse at Ariege, and the bison at La Madeleine are considered by experts to be some of the most significant works of world art.[82]

Shamanism and Art

Shamanism provided the strong incentive that induced creative, talented artists of long ago to spend their time in the dark depths of European caves. Here, far from distractions, where the brightly painted birds, animals, and people seemed to come alive in flickering lamplight, priests or shamans more easily gained access to the spirit world and conceived their impressive illustrations. Pictures of wild ducks and other birds they seldom ate predominate, for birds symbolized the flight of the soul.[83] Evidence of taxing initiation ceremonies and paintings of hallucinatory images sensed during the artists' out-of-body experiences in these sacred places reflect the occult practices dominant in Atlantis.

Intuitive skills of shamans enabled these artists to create some paintings that have never been equaled. One of the talents artists cultivated was an ability to communicate with their friends in the animal world. Harsh winters made life difficult in southwestern Europe at the time of Atlantis, and since animals were the main source of food and clothing, it was essential to make every effort to maintain a trusting interrelationship with them. The perceptive shamans not only communicated with animals by means of music, visual language, or body contact as we do, but they learned to mentally enter the animal's mind and have a two-way conversation. The close relationship of shaman-artists with their four-legged subjects 20,000 years ago in France and Spain contributed to the insight and distinction of their accurate, compassionate paintings of freely moving animals.

As long as 18,000 years ago, pictures of bird shamans, who continue to practice in secluded areas of the Americas, were painted in several European caves. One with claws for hands and wearing a bird mask is depicted in the back of the Lascaux cave in France. The bird shaman's penis is erect, something that frequently occurs during trance states, and it points toward a speared bison whose head is turned to look at his own intestines falling from his wound. Next to the man is a staff topped with a bird, similar to those shamans carry today.[84] A similar bird shaman and his staff are depicted in an ancient Arizona rock engraving.[85] The similarities in these unusual carvings suggest the artists had a common heritage: Atlantis, their homeland between the two continents, furnishes an explanation.

South America was also the destination of Atlantean artisans, and although most of their representations are not as noteworthy as the works of those who sailed east from Atlantis, the subjects in Peru, Chile, and Brazil resemble their European counterparts. The principal motifs painted in eight caves near Pizacoma, Peru, represent bison, mammoth, and other animals who lived over 12,000 years ago. Additional cave paintings and relics similar to those in France and Spain survive elsewhere in Peru and in Chile.

Marcel Homet discovered other parallels in prehistoric lives in southwestern Europe and in South America. Deep in the Amazon he explored a place where Cro-Magnons buried their dead between 15,000 B.C. and 12,000 B.C. in the same matter as they did in France at that time. Caring relatives placed with one body a sculpture of a seal that is identical to small seal statues buried with corpses in French graves at the same time.[86] Atlanteans inscribed "the cycle of the seasons" on walls of caves in western Europe and in the Amazon, on the other side of the Atlantic. The circle is divided into four equal parts by diameters at right angles to each other, each segment representing one season of the year. Western Europe and Atlantis have four seasons, but in the northern Amazon, even at that time, there were only two seasons, one wet and one dry. People from Atlantis, as they settled adjoining lands, drew the symbol of the four seasons in their new locations, just as they had at home, even though their new domicile had only two seasons.[87] Early South American artisans' interest in the occult is obvious. At the Abrigo del Sol (Shelter of the Sun), a secret cave deep in the jungles of Brazil, scenes from magical deer dances depict dancing animals, men playing sacred flutes[88] and a leader with antlers on his head wearing a shamanistic animal mask.[89]

Some of the most unusual prehistoric sketches, found not only in the Amazon but also in the caves of southwestern France, are the outlines of hands with mutilated thumbs or cut-off fingers. These are delineations of real hands in this condition, with scar tissue covering the joints of the missing sections of finger.[90] Over 200 similar handprints were pictured on walls in caves in the Pyrenees 26,000 years ago.[91] In 1916, older Crow Indians with similarly maimed hands told anthropologists the disfigurement signifies they are offering a finger joint to the gods and expecting something beneficial in exchange.[92] To achieve this goal, little fingers of babies were often slashed off at the joints soon after they were born or the bloody process was included in an initiation ceremony.

The Crystal Skull

Quartz crystal, a common stone in volcanic Atlantis, was another medium of Atlantean craftsmen. In 1927, a young American girl, assisting her archaeologist father F. A. Mitchell-

Hedges, discovered a delicately carved life-size crystal skull in the Mayan ruin of Lubaantum. Other humanmade quartz skulls, not as fine, are displayed in the British Museum of Man and the Musee de l'Homme in Paris.[93] Since carbon dating does not test quartz, the age of the skulls is undetermined, but scientists at the California laboratories of Hewlett-Packard, after extensively studying the Central American skull, concluded it was made by people from a civilization that possessed a crystallographic ability equivalent to or greater than ours.[94]

Scientists who examined the crystal skull under powerful microscopes found no scratches to indicate it was carved with metal instruments.[95] Diamond-tipped tools are a possibility, or a rock-dissolving paste.[96] Frank Dorland, one of the foremost art restorers in the United States, studied and worked with crystals and the skull for over six years. He concluded that, even with the advanced technology we enjoy today, it would be nearly impossible to re-create the unique head.[97] Dorland estimates it required at least 300 years of constant human labor, or six people working for fifty years, to grind the skull from a solid block of pure quartz.[98] The realistic object, with its movable lower jaw and network of prisms, lenses, and light-pipes, which give life to the face and eyes, is strikingly beautiful.

The crystal skull exhibits strange powers. Sensitive people sometimes see an aura around it; others sense a sweet-sour odor. At times it seems to produce sounds like tinkling bells or a faint choir of human voices.[99] Realistic visions in its presence are a common occurrence,[100] and its power assists sensitive persons in healing and prophecy. Crystal provides additional insight in meditation, for just as it acts as an amplifier as well as a receiver for radio waves, so it affects the energy generated by thought waves.[101] Skulls and other objects like these, carefully carved from crystal, gave assistance in achieving increased perception and vision as Atlanteans and their descendants contemplated their place in the universe.

When mountains trembled in Atlantis and chaos reigned, a foresighted priestess snatched the powerful crystal skull that was later found in Belize from its place of honor in her temple and carefully carried it with her as she traveled westward on a small boat from her troubled land. She eventually settled in Murias and joined the healing temple (in chapter 4 there is a further description of the healing temple at Bimini as described by Dr. Edgarton Sykes). The skull was a prized possession of priestesses in the temple,[102] where its aura, special scent, and amplifying properties were helpful in diagnosis. When waters rose for the last time over the temple, the women carried the sacred object to safer land in Central America. Mayan priests placed it on an altar and, utilizing powers of ventriloquism while opening and closing its mouth, made it "talk" to terrified individuals to attain their selfish goals. When the Mayans hastily abandoned the area, they left the skull under an altar where it remained until Anna Mitchell-Hedges found it.

Only paintings in caves and creations in stone, bone, ivory, and crystal remain from the artistic endeavors of Atlanteans. Today acid rain decays and pits the statues and buildings of our recent past. One wonders if any of our artistic treasures will survive as long as the Atlanteans' to delight our ancestors 20,000 years from now, in A.D. 22,000 . . . .

Music

Music was an important tool in assuring vibrant health and peace of mind in Atlantis. People utilized the human voice and instruments such as harps, lutes, guitars, flutes, pipes, cymbals, tambourines, and drums for the spiritual and physical effects of musical vibrations on their minds and bodies.[103] They also understood the ability of pleasing tones to stimulate the growth of plants and to promote the well-being of domestic animals. At least one flute from the time of Atlantis escaped the scavengers who thoughtlessly pilfered the ancient hiding places. The prehistoric instrument was discovered deep in a cave in France, where its lovely sounds enhanced spiritual experiences 30,000 years ago. Although the bottom half of the bone flute is missing, it still has several holes for fingers and was once capable of producing sophisticated music. The significance of pleasing sounds in the lives of those who settled in Europe at the time of Atlantis is obvious from the number of whistles, pan pipes, drums, and string instruments that accompanied their bones and possessions.

To prepare for sexual intercourse and to facilitate conception, Atlantean women learned engaging songs with particular repetitive tones such as *Ooohh* and *Ommmm* and *Aaaaaah*. The vibrations induced a relaxed state and stimulated the endocrine system, arousing the emotions of both partners.[104] Couples supplemented the sounds with fragrances of jasmine, lotus, sandalwood, and cedar to activate their inner senses.

Sweet flute tones, monotonous, muffled drumming, and tranquil, plucked sounds from instruments similar to harps helped release the mind for meditation in temple services.[105] Music also effectively influenced the body as a supplement to medical and psychological practices. To trigger relaxation, healers employed soft drumbeats with no pounding or metallic tones. They carefully avoided melody and strong harmony and kept the rhythm slower than the normal heartbeat. Patients learned to focus on calming music to lessen their awareness of pain. Drumming and singing were capable of inducing deep trance-like states that could stop bleeding, balance the body, and instantly heal physical and mental problems. Parents sang special songs to sick children and their strong faith in the power of the music was instrumental in a child's improvement.

For depression, Atlanteans combined music with colored rays of light to uplift the spirit and stimulate the appropriate secretions from the body's glands. The ultimate goal, similar to that of a rock concert today, was achieved in a much different way.

In Atlantis the event took place in a sun-filled room with tree branches and blossoms in the corners, ferns, grasses, and colorful leaves on the floor, and crystals dangling from the ceiling. The atmosphere encouraged the participant to relax and sense the power and beauty of nature, the earth, and the universe. Musicians duplicated the calls of birds, a cascading waterfall, or a playful wind with complicated harp-like instruments and flutes. The harp's strings were of different metals so that when the player struck them precisely and delicately with a small hammer they produced a variety of interesting sounds and vibrations.[106] As the tones interacted with colored rays of light from the crystals slowly moving in the sunlight, a marvelous feeling of exhilaration overwhelmed everyone in the room.

GOVERNMENT

Following traditions that originated in its earliest days, Atlantis was governed fairly and efficiently. The country remained divided into ten states,[107] originally one for each of Poseidon's sons. Every territory was ruled by a king with complete autonomy within his area. To ensure the populace did not suffer under these dictatorships, Plato tells us the leaders assembled every five or six years in the Temple of Poseidon to judge the others' deeds.[108] Relying on advice from astronomers, the Atlantean kings held their gatherings just before sun spot activity and planned events focused on the sacrifice of a bull, hoping to appease the potent god who was responsible for this unexplainable, troublesome action of the sun god. They dreaded the sunspots that appeared every five or six years—actually in full cycles of about 11.2 years—because the activity temporarily affected the energy available from the sun, as well as the magnetic currents surrounding the Earth, both sources of power in Atlantis.[109]

The meetings of the Atlantean kings were brutal and bloody as compared to our legislative events today. In the *Critias,* Plato offers a detailed description of the solemn affairs. The leaders' first undertaking was the sacrifice. After praying to the appropriate god that the bull they captured would be satisfactory, they cornered one of the large animals by wielding wooden clubs (not metal weapons since that was not the custom). The kings cut the bull's throat and spilled its blood over the inscriptions on a tall orichalcum pillar in the center of the temple. The old laws of the land were inscribed on the ancient column, which had been used for this purpose since time immemorial. For the next step in this ritualized ceremony, the rulers chanted ancient prayers to the gods and drank from golden cups that contained a mixture of wine and the animal's blood. The remaining blood was splashed on a sacrificial fire. While the bones of the bull burned in the fire, the kings continued to drink from the golden cups and eat slices of the animal's charcoal-broiled flesh. They made solemn agreements, based on the laws inscribed on the ancient pillar, promising to always treat their fellow rulers fairly and unite if their country was threatened in any way. When the sun dropped from sight on the horizon, the rulers dressed in elaborate robes and for the rest of the night sat in the dark near the fire judging each others' actions since their last meeting. When the sun rose, they inscribed their decisions on golden plates and dedicated their plates and luxurious garments as memorials to the Temple.[110]

For thousands of years Atlantis was governed fairly in this manner. When land was lost to the sea, if the affected king desired more territory, he fiercely attacked a nearby continent to replace his missing land, but never a fellow king. The example of the leaders' cooperation with each other, and their sincere concern for the general welfare, filtered down to the general populace. Cooperation prevailed at all levels, and every individual acted toward others as they wished themselves to be treated. As long as the ancient laws were upheld everyone was treated equally, with little sexual discrimination.[111] Since adequate food and energy were available, a high standard of living prevailed, and the civilization developed rapidly. A socialist form of government, in which the state owned all land, all industries, and the systems of public transportation and communication proved the most satisfactory.[112] There was neither poverty nor immense wealth, little dissension, and all were satisfied.[113]

CRIMINALS

Atlanteans developed a wide variety of methods for treating criminals quickly, so prisons were unnecessary. Their techniques also assured the recalcitrants would not repeat their improper behavior. One of the most successful methods employing hypnosis and magnetism is described by Frederick Oliver. In 1884, when he was eighteen, Oliver received his information telepathically from Phylos the Tibetan who lived in Atlantis in about 11,000 B.C.[114]

The goal of the humane rehabilitation Phylos described to Oliver was to change the supply of blood to crucial areas of the brain and raise the level of consciousness of the guilty party's soul. To accomplish this without delay, immediately after his or her conviction, guards strapped the prisoner into a chair in the center of a large, well-lighted room. They placed a magnetic instrument in the shape of a small pole in the prisoner's hands and, as the machine hummed, the man closed his eyes and lost consciousness; he was magnetically anesthetized. After shaving his head, a specialist intuitively examined it and diagnosed the criminal, perhaps as an acquisitive, dangerous character with a destructive temperament, unscrupulous and capable of murder. The expert carefully painted marks on the culprit's head and neck at appropriate points, while attendants rolled a large machine with additional magnetic apparatus into the room. For an hour the healer sent rays of energy from the instrument through a pole to the specified points on the patient's head and neck. When properly performed, this procedure atrophied the blood vessels serving the appropriate parts of the brain. For a thief, the cells concerned with greed and destruction were treated. It also increased the blood supply to the rest of the brain. Meanwhile, a skilled priest communicated telepathically with the criminal's mind, raising the consciousness or soul of the subject to a higher moral plane where unscrupulous behavior was unacceptable.

Recent experiments with moving powerful, fluctuating magnets on a patient's skull—called transcranial magnetic stimulation, or T.M.S.—have enabled scientists to temporarily paralyze small regions of brain tissue. As a result they have relieved depression and instigated mood changes for short periods of time.[115] Perhaps techniques similar to the Atlanteans' for rehabilitating criminals will one day be standard procedure in our society.

ARMED FORCES

Aggressive people in the lands surrounding Atlantis, especially those who lived in the nearby African continent, forced the Atlanteans to maintain a constant state of armed vigilance. Michael Scot provides information about strange techniques developed to defend against possible invaders. After constructing huge magical wooden images resembling ferocious armed soldiers, the Atlanteans stationed these mock defenders on sea coasts. Apparently they believed the sight of them would deter their invaders. Scot also translates that priests imbued similar, larger-than-life-size models with mysterious powers, and Atlantean troops carried the huge fake soldiers into battle to increase their courage and confidence.[116]

The ever-hungry reptilian monsters who lived in the swampy sections on the western approach to Atlantis, although a hazard to the local inhabitants, provided some protection from invaders.[117] Atlantean soldiers even threw captives to the eager beasts, teaching them to search for humans for food.[118] The frightful animals served at least one worthy function—they assured protection from the enemy at night, since they located prey in the dark with their sonar-type devices, similar to those of dolphins. Native Americans tell stories of the difficulties their ancestors from Atlantis experienced crossing to the sunset land (the American continent), since the swamps between were filled with monsters, some large enough to jump on small boats and sink them.[119]

In spite of defenses, hostile soldiers occasionally ventured into Atlantis and were apprehended. Edgar Cayce describes a peculiar punishment the Atlanteans developed for their captives. Temple priests carefully supervised the cremation of dead enemy victims, mixed their ashes with water and forced the surviving prisoners to drink it.[120] This ensured that displeasing vibrations from the bodies of the offensive antagonist did not pollute Atlantis, and if the prisoners were released, they would carry the unfavorable vibrations with them when they returned to their homeland, hopefully causing problems there.[121]

Shrinking land and a growing population forced the Atlanteans to search constantly for additional living space. As they became more desperate, they ruthlessly attacked and destroyed to fill their needs. Atlantean descendants in the United States remember one dreadful global conflict known as the bird-serpent war. Memories of the long-lasting controversy are preserved in chants and dances the Pueblo, the Yaqui, and other Americans have passed down through the ages. The dispute between the Atlanteans, the "serpent people," and the "bird people" took place when the glaciers were still large,[122] about 14,000 years ago. The bird people, who were from a lost Indian empire, adopted the condor, the bird of lightning, as their symbol. Atlanteans motivated the war as they attempted to acquire islands far from their homeland that were inhabited for centuries by the people of the bird. Their reputation as merciless fighters who stole women and sacrificed children assured they met slight resistance when they attacked. Besieged by the Atlanteans, the bird people left their homes and fled as rapidly as possible. As they sailed away from the lovely tropical islands, they carried the infant sons of their leader with them. The serpent people complacently inhabited the distant islands for a while. However, when the sons of the old ruler of the bird people grew to adulthood, the original occupants returned unexpectedly to their island home with strong soldiers and explosive weapons. Caught off guard, the resident Atlanteans were forced to temporarily abandon their pleasant dwellings and flee for their lives. The war continued from generation to generation, and like a hotly contested tennis match, numerous battles took place as power seesawed back and forth between the opponents. Eventually a terrible naval encounter developed. The quantity of blood and flames from the extensive number of explosive weapons that were fired turned the waters red. The people of the bird were ultimately victorious, and the Atlanteans abandoned their efforts to acquire those particular distant islands.[123]

In 11,000 B.C., as the need for additional land grew more urgent, the Atlanteans increased the size and strength of their army and navy. As morality disintegrated at home, so it was reflected in the actions of the soldiers of Atlantis, whose cruelty and inhumanity contributed to their country's acquisition of property. Like the Romans many centuries later, in large numbers they moved to the east and the west with determination, conquering all in their way. Plato describes the total military force they maintained to control their far-flung empire as exceeding one million people.[124] This included sailors for 1,200 ships, charioteers, cavalrymen, foot soldiers, archers, stone-shooters, and javelin-throwers. Once again, their natural environment was Atlantis' helpmate. Two growing seasons a year, lava-rich soil, an extensive irrigation system for over 77,000 square miles of fertile land, and a warm sunny climate made it possible to produce the voluminous quantity of food needed to sustain their extensive army. With the assistance of a sizable navy of oceangoing ships, which proved adequate for transporting supplies and men to the fighting front, Atlantis became an extensive empire with numerous colonies.

Plato tells us that at the height of their power Atlantean kings ruled over all islands in the Atlantic Ocean, parts of the American continent, and as far into the Mediterranean as the present countries of Egypt and northern Italy.[125] Many Atlanteans left their overcrowded land and moved to these areas. One group of mostly women and children who lived on the coast of Morocco before 10,000 B.C. are referred to as the Moullans. Archaeologists, uncovering their graves, found unusual stone tools and bones of animals buried with them. The Moullans' physical features were similar to those of two other groups of Atlantean descendants, the Gaunches of the Azores and the Berbers of northern Africa.[126]

Utilizing their occult talents, Atlanteans devised interesting techniques for gaining power over others. To assist them in conquering a country, they first made an extensive and detailed model of its topography and population centers. Magicians, exercising chants, incantations, and magical operations, attempted to transfer disease upon their prey through the model.[127] An old story says the Atlanteans once tried to do this with the whole world, and Zeus became so angry at their attempt to usurp his power that he directed a thunderbolt against the facsimile.[128]

Magic was not the only tool of the strong, well-trained Atlantean soldiers. Spear throwers were capable of killing from a distance of thirty to fifty feet, and their powerful stone hurlers were the world's best. A fast, dangerous game, played with balls of hardened clay, developed their ability to throw with deadly accuracy. The frightening appearance of the Atlantean soldiers as their mighty troops approached an enemy gave them an additional advantage. Large, fearsome warriors wore tall helmets embellished with feathers or the trident symbol of Atlantis and carried daggers fastened on the upper part of each arm with a metal or jeweled band.[129] Painted faces and flaming torches further terrorized their opponents as the Atlanteans advanced, carrying large, wiggling, venomous snakes, reminiscent of their serpent symbol.[130]

Atlanteans' weapons, although often made of flint, were extremely sharp and dangerous. When Christopher Columbus reached the New World, he was surprised to find natives' knives of stone as sharp as his metal knives. Prehistoric people traveled long distances for special fine-grained and colorful flints. They knew that if they raised the flint to a temperature of almost 1,000 degrees and cooled it slowly, it grew softer and easier to shape.[131] A well-made flint projectile point is sharper and more effective than one made of iron. Flint knives are equal, if not superior to, steel knives, but they do break more easily.[132] The Atlantean military coated their flint spears, javelins, and knives with poison, making them even more deadly.

Atlanteans were adept at using animals and birds in battle, and soldiers who were ruthless but intuitive were in constant demand as trainers. These capable men and women befriended ferocious beasts, communicated directly with them, and developed their love and confidence while constantly encouraging the creatures to obey and defend them at all costs.[133] Leopards, bears, and bulls quickly learned to assist in destroying any opposition to their Atlantean friends, adding to the handiwork of swarms of well-disciplined, extremely quick hawks who flew above the foe, diving down to poke out eyes or bite any exposed portion of skin.[134]

In their effort to avoid nuclear weapons as much as possible, the Atlanteans perfected less deadly explosives to acquire control over others. Some of the oldest tales of Ireland refer to invaders from the Atlantic Ocean who arrived in crystal ships and fought any opposition with rays of fire.[135] The People of the Sea, as the Atlanteans were sometimes called, first carried firecrackers and then gun powder to the Far East. Ancient books of India refer to projectiles, bombs, rockets and guns shooting fire. The Atlanteans' pursuit of superior weapons technology led to the deaths of thousands. These and other deadly arms were utilized on both sides of the bird-serpent war.[136] In *Lost Cities of China, Central Asia & India,* David Hatcher Childress suggests that a destructive battle described in the *Mahabharata* and the *Ramayana* and in esoteric tradition was a segment of a war between the Atlanteans and the Rama Empire of India, a civilization that flourished at the same time. The Indian epics refer to the Atlanteans as "Asvins." They arrived in airplanes, which are described in detail, and threatened to destroy the city. When the Atlanteans ignored the Indian ruler's attempts to avoid a war and proceeded to advance, the ruler raised his arms and using powerful mental techniques caused the leaders of the invading Atlanteans to drop dead, one by one. In retaliation, the Atlanteans returned at a later date with atomic weapons and completely destroyed the seven cities of the Ramas.

RELIGION

During its 100,000 years, Atlantis was home to many cults and beliefs, although basically Atlanteans respected one all-powerful spiritual being who created and controlled the tangible world to which they were extremely close and vulnerable. Trees, flowers, birds, and water, all reflections of this great power, were included in their daily worship. As a result of the severe natural destructions of their land, Atlanteans came to believe this God used physical forces to punish man for improper behavior. They personified, as lesser gods, the forces of rain, lightning, fire, earthquakes, volcanoes, and especially the sun. Religious leaders encouraged the people's daily worship of these secondary deities, offspring of, and supervised by, the one great God.

Religion in Atlantis, although preoccupied with the forces of nature, included a belief in reincarnation. The people were sure each body contained a soul, separate from the mind, which was continuously in existence through the ages either on the Earth in a material creature or in another realm of consciousness. Memories of the soul's experiences in its various lives and forms were retained as it grew in each lifetime toward a perfection personified by the unselfish love of the one supreme deity. Burial practices that were intended to prepare the body for the next life played an important role in the religious lives of Atlanteans.

Throughout the history of Atlantis, people gathered for outdoor services around stones placed in circles, which Cayce said were "of magnetized influence."[137] The powerful circles were symbolic of the all-encompassing spirit of the one omnipotent God and a source of strength to all. Building these extraordinary religious sites effectively was a complicated and difficult process. Only stones with special properties known to the people of long ago were acceptable. The stones, which were often huge boulders, were sometimes transported from a lengthy distance, even though neighboring rocks appeared similar. The site for the sacred circles was carefully selected with the help of dreams, visions, and dowsing to ensure that it took advantage of natural currents of energy from the Earth. The builders placed the center of the circles above underground water, often where a deep spring rose naturally and, instead of breaking the surface, spread out into one or more underground streams. Hills, woods, fields, water, and the location of the sun, moon, and stars were important factors affecting the exact arrangement of the stones. Atlanteans ardently believed in the potency of the circles and that if they worshiped at them, it was possible to improve their health. Their faith undoubtedly contributed to the stones' effectiveness, but the stone circles also generated a natural energy that was a factor in promoting healing of physical and mental problems.

Sacred rituals devoted to the supreme god and the powerful personifications of nature were common events at the stone circles. To honor the arrival of spring, entire communities united in a festival and offered freshly cut tree branches covered with fragrant blossoms. On the nights of the full moon everyone assembled at the stone circles, joined hands, and chanted and hummed harmoniously for hours to give additional energy to the priest while he or she communicated with the gods and spirits. Atlanteans worshiped the sun as a source of light, heat, and life. It was particularly honored as the god of Fire and Life on Midsummer's Day. Communities congregated around the stone circles before dawn and, when the vital entity rose from its bed, joyous women, men, and children joined in singing a special hymn of praise.

Happenings around the stones were oriented toward the welfare of the people as well as the gods of nature. Edgar Cayce refers to ceremonies that were focused on a particular person who wished to purify him or herself by removing lust, greed, selfishness, or other undesirable characteristics.[138] Following the instructions of the priest, everyone monotonously chanted and sang as they rigorously danced around the passive recipient of their energy from the stylized service. Events such as these provided stimulation, focus, and vigor to the lives of Atlanteans.

Priesthood was available to men and women who were considered to be sufficiently evolved. They were often chosen because they carried genes from their extraterrestrial ancestors.[139] The strenuous program of study and initiation required to attain the priesthood assured competence, so that those who successfully achieved the rank were respected and admired by all. Toward the end of the civilization, as science gradually replaced religion in Atlanteans' daily lives and moral conditions slowly deteriorated, many priests took advantage of their power over the people. To gain authority, they conveyed the impression that they constantly communicated with—and had some control of the unseen world of—deities, demons, and ancestral spirits. If individuals in the community resisted their decrees, ambitious religious leaders threatened them with the terrible wrath of these invisible beings.

Strong auras of the priests, visible to the more aware Atlanteans as colored bands of light around the leaders' bodies, increased the profound respect they received from the general population. Priests often wore masks to gain additional esteem. As they played tantalizing, hypnotic music on sacred flutes, the repetitious sounds in the natural setting induced an expanding, tranquilizing effect on the receptive minds of the participants, in much the same way that plants react positively to pleasant tones and supportive thoughts. The energizing spiritual harmony at the sacred circles was in tune with nature and offered positive energy to the leaders, their followers, and to the Earth.

Modern equipment reveals mysterious energy at similar ancient, sacred sites in Great Britain, and that the strength varies with the stones, the seasons, and the time of day.[140] Ultrasonic sound waves from the stones are particularly strong at sunrise. Gaussmeters, which measure static magnetic field strength, reveal unusual amounts of electromagnetic energy circulating in and around undisturbed ancient stone circles.[141] Further tests demonstrate that the stones themselves act as amplifiers and produce spirals of energy.

The knowledge necessary to construct the strong circles of standing stones was transmitted in Atlantis from generation to generation and carried to other lands, where descendants living close to nature retained the ability to locate potent places, select the appropriate boulders, and move them. The belief that the stones absorbed energy from their surroundings and returned it to those who worshiped at them persisted. Similar sacred stone circles constructed in prehistory are found today in France, England, Scotland, Ireland, and the Yucatan peninsula of Mexico. Apparently, the circles were constantly maintained and replaced as civilizations covered them, for archaeologist Geoffrey Bibby estimates that as many as nine different layers of culture are buried under the monuments at Stonehenge, an ancient site of standing stones in England.[142]

Ancient myths that reflect the widespread beliefs in the stone's powers are narrated at locations hundreds of miles apart in England. Usually the legends portray the objects as having a magical life and strength, such as movement to obtain water or to dance. The Witches Stone, near Honiton, travels at midnight to a nearby stream to drink and wash off the blood of sacrificial victims.[143] The rocks at Carnac walk to drink on Christmas Eve. At Rollright stories abound of the stones dancing at midnight, and at Belsen nine boulders once danced at noon. These tales are not literally true, but they preserve the knowledge of the stones' vitality. In Cornwall, the Merry Maidens Stones are said to be young girls who were turned to stone for dancing on Sunday. This is typical of the effects of Christianity on legends, as missionaries attempted to destroy the old beliefs. Recent instrumental tests at Rollright stone circle show the occurrence of ultrasonic sound waves, particularly just before sunrise and at certain times of the year.[144] Obviously our distant predecessors sensed phenomena we are only beginning to comprehend.

As they strove to understand the actions of their most respected God in order to better guide and heal their people, the priests of Atlantis found the energy they received from the stones, plus the rhythmic vibrations from the chanting and drumming of the participants, helped to open their minds. They learned to slow their brain waves from thirty waves per second to one-half wave per second, moving themselves into a trancelike state. In this resulting altered state of consciousness they received messages from the spirit world. Leaders regularly consulted this mysterious realm for guidance in good and evil, for assistance in healing physical maladies, and for advice concerning all other affairs of the individual, the society, and the environment. Communication with the other world was a daily event, not limited to once a week or just when help was needed. Talented priests also utilized their skills to regularly exchange information telepathically at great distances with each other, making every community a component of a spacious network, living and working together.

Emigrants from Atlantis transmitted ancient techniques for exploring the deep unconscious and for accessing universal knowledge to people throughout the world. Everywhere shamans, or medicine men or women as they are sometimes called, employ these skills as they practice a combination of religion and magic in a manner that has remained similar for 40,000 years. Paintings on cave walls in western Europe depict dancing priests wearing bison robes and headdresses closely resembling those worn by the shamans of the Sioux and Plains Indians of North America. A cave painting in Cogul, in northeastern Spain, portrays a number of women wearing skirts and peaked hats, similar to witches of later times. The participants are dancing around a male idol or priest painted black.[145] Prehistoric rock pictures in Stephens County, Texas, practically identical with those found in caves of southwestern Europe, depict dancing women dressed like medieval witches with peaked hats.[146]

To develop their psychic abilities, prospective shamans everywhere undergo an initiation. The rituals follow a similar pattern, although the procedures vary. The initial step is a cleansing that helps to prepare their minds and bodies. This is followed by a near-death experience that tests the individual beyond all imaginable limits. During the intense suffering of this traumatic episode, they first travel deeply within themselves and then open their minds to cosmic wisdom and enlightenment. The extremely difficult incident also eliminates their fear of leaving this world, since they have succeeded in transcending death by undergoing the experience of dying. Finally, there is a "rebirth," or return to life, with newly acquired powers of perception.

Among the Sioux, descendants of Atlanteans who live in North America, it is customary for a prospective shaman or medicine man or woman, under the guidance of a teacher, to first thoroughly cleanse his or her body and purify the mind with a prolonged and very hot visit to a sweat lodge. Following this strenuous experience, the initiate spends up to four days without food and water in an uncomfortable dark place awaiting the dreams that will reveal the future. A cold, windy mountaintop with only a buffalo robe for protection or a tiny, cramped, unlighted vision pit are possible locations for this stage of the initiation.[147] Following the experience, shamans undergo years of intense training. Many are capable of entering deep trance-like states where they leave their bodies and are open to contact with spirits, who offer profound advice for healing and guidance in problematic decisions. When they practice, shamans must exercise extreme caution, for as they grow increasingly adept at controlling their minds, the concentration of forceful energy is capable of destroying themselves and others. Shamanism, utilizing techniques perfected thousands of years ago, is still practiced today. In *Shamanic's Voices*, written in 1979, Joan Halifax describes initiation experiences, journeys, and vision quests of twentieth-century shamans who live in Siberia, Australia, Africa, and North and South America.

Priests or shamans utilized the power of ancient sacred sites but they also devised other successful techniques to induce trances or evoke hallucinatory experiences. Keeping their minds clear and open, they employed meditation, fasting, sleep deprivation, and concentration on symbols. Certain mushrooms and other hallucinogenic drugs also offered access to different perceptions of reality. Shamans frequently use these techniques today but if they follow the ancient rituals carefully, addiction to the drugs seldom occurs.

The fire god of the volcanoes and the dreadful god of earthquakes received special attention in Atlantis. The leaders perfected many ceremonies to appease these frightening deities and hopefully gain temporary protection from their fury. After thousands of years, as the priests began to take advantage of their power and exploit the people, respect for the natural environment diminished. As if in response, the dangerous powers of nature became more active. Hoping to prevent the hostile, volcanic fire god from growing angry, roaring and throwing out hot, molten lava, Atlanteans pushed helpless animals and even humans, dead or alive, into the volcanoes as sacrifices.

Ancient texts, originally from North African libraries, which scholar Michael Scot translated in the fourteenth century, offer details of two Atlantean religious events. The stylized ceremonies were specifically designed to pacify the mighty fire god and the gods of the volcanoes.[148] The Rite of the Earth-fires began at dawn on Midsummer Day and lasted until the sun, a symbol of the mighty god, sank out of sight in the west. The ten majestic kings of Atlantis presided, garbed in voluminous robes dyed deep blue. Hundreds of the strongest people slowly and carefully pushed and pulled stone forms—miniature replicas of the six most formidable volcanoes of the country—that were placed on rollers. As they moved the ponderous models, thousands of observers chanted and beat monotonously on low-pitched drums. When the hardworking people who were moving the cumbersome stone models finally reached the viewing stand and bowed to the kings and priests, the crowds increased their drumming and the chanting turned to shouts. It was as if the all-powerful deity was speaking loudly and sternly to pacify the terrifying but respected fire god. In the shadow of the six replicas of the volcanoes, the priests conducted extensive magical ceremonies, aiming to deprive the greedy gods of the dangerous volcanoes of one of their thousands of lives, thus rendering them ineffectual throughout the coming year. When they finished, the kings carefully spent the night smashing into small pieces two additional massive stone creatures that represented the forces of earthquakes.

The other event translated by Michael Scot was focused on the god of fire and the gods of the volcanoes. In preparation, workmen spent a year constructing an enormous topographical replica of Atlantis on stone pillars. Just before the ceremony, to represent the threatening force beneath the ground of Atlantis, they built a sizable fire under the model between the pillars. As soon as the massive crowd assembled and started chanting and singing, the head priest set fire to the dry wood. When it was roaring furiously, the noisy multitude enthusiastically shouted and screamed as they ignited loud explosives. The officials remained totally silent, focusing their entire psychic energy upon the flames. The goal of this tumultuous procedure was to scare earthquake and volcanic activity from Atlantis for the coming year. At the height of the ceremony, a signal from the high priest launched the release of water from a large tank, and vast clouds of steam enveloped the surrounding area, symbolizing the temporary destruction of the strength of the fire god. Like all rituals, these were undertaken very carefully since the slightest error might evoke the dreaded wrath of the dangerous deities.

Atlanteans who left their unstable country and settled in the Mediterranean continued to respect the natural powers. Sun worship was common among all prehistoric persons around the Atlantic Ocean. Symbols of the sun, considered to be a strong source of personal energy, were carved at the time of

Atlantis on stones in Brazil, especially in the cave of Abrigo del Sol. In Tiahuanaco, Bolivia, they were a common sight to the Spanish monks who first explored the ruins of that ancient city in the sixteenth century. The sun was also sacred in Peru, where the potent festival of the sun was called Ray-mi, a name very similar to the sun god Ra of faraway Egypt whom the Egyptians believed created the Earth.[149] The cult of the sun existed in ancient Ireland and throughout Scandinavia where it acquired increased significance from the long days of darkness and light. In ancient times the Basques, descendants of Atlanteans who live in southwestern Europe, kept fires burning as a symbol of fire from the sun.[150]

THE OCCULT

Unless otherwise indicated, the material in this chapter relating to the initiations and training of the priesthood was derived from Lewis Spence's carefully researched and well-documented *The Occult Sciences In Atlantis*. His descriptions of Atlantean mysteries, including initiations, were primarily derived from the Arcane Tradition, a body of knowledge recorded in English, French, German, Spanish, Greek, and Arabic that dates from the seventh century A.D. The Arcane Tradition, which deals with occult history in its entirety, draws on historical records of mystical societies from the earliest time as they were made available to initiates into occult organizations.

Atlanteans progressed more rapidly than the rest of the world in their pressing search for solutions to unanswered questions, since favorable living conditions in their country extended their daily opportunities for leisure and introspective thought. Atlantean priests, seeking an understanding of themselves and the universe, developed their already potent psychic facilities to a degree few have ever attained. They were far more proficient than the most powerful psychics of our time. Memories of their skills are represented in ancient literature as the secret knowledge of the survivors of a flood. Much of the wisdom Atlanteans contributed to the occult sciences is respected today. However, as their practices gradually combined religion, magic, and science, the results were dreadful.

In the early days of civilization in Atlantis, ritualistic outdoor ceremonies, such as those held on the night of a full moon at the sacred stone circles, granted priests opportunities to experiment with altered states of consciousness. Gradually these leaders realized they did not need to rely on rhythmic chanting and drum beats to raise their minds to a higher level. They discovered that the power was within themselves. They grew adept at slowing their brain waves, entering a trance, and exploring the spirit world, the source of all enlightenment. Activities of this type required few props, but participants believed particular masks offered expanded opportunities while in a trance. For example, a bird mask helped one's spirit fly like a bird.

The Atlantean priests' dramatic experiences as they explored the potentials of their minds, and the unexpected accomplishments that resulted, led them further and further along unexplored paths. Slowly, religion—or a respect and surrender to and belief in one divine being who created and controls the universe—was interwoven with magic. The occult sciences were born.

Eventually, the quantity of magical and scientific information that accumulated in Atlantis was so large that candidates for the most advanced degree of priesthood were required to devote half a lifetime to its study. Fully developing their psychic talents demanded that they master astrology, astronomy, necromancy (communication with the spirits of the dead), alchemy, prophecy, and divination (the use of supernatural powers to foresee the future or discover hidden knowledge). A thorough comprehension of all these subjects was required for candidates as they achieved the three grades or levels of development: Initiate, Adept, and Magus.

Lewis Spence learned that a prospective Initiate was first subjected to the mind-expanding experience of an intense initiation. The event took place in the side of a mountain, not far from the City of the Golden Gates, where the interaction of lava and water for thousands of years created a very large natural cave. Caverns similar to the one utilized by the Atlanteans, such as Algor do Carvão in Terciera, survive in the Azores. They extend 500 or 600 feet in length and often have proportionately high vaulted ceilings. Starting in the days of Poseidon, the Atlanteans improved and expanded the secret space every year, for it was a perfect location for secluded occult functions. Eventually the underground cavity was 1,300 feet long and 900 feet wide and consisted mainly of dark, winding passageways, frequently blocked by locked doors embellished with orichalcum. During an initiation, the doors in the labyrinth did not open unless the correct phrase was spoken, encouraging candidates to rely on their intuition for the appropriate words.

A typical initiation in the Atlantean labyrinth focused on the concept of death and rebirth. Initiation rituals performed in the ancient temples of Egypt and the customs of shamans since the beginning of time have retained a similar focus. Lewis Spence acquired the information that follows about Atlantean initiations from the Arcane Tradition.

When the potential Initiate entered the occult underground labyrinth, a silent, barely perceptible form greeted him or her. After a disconcerting trip down narrow, damp passageways, the individual was instructed to climb into a small space in a wall. Assuming a fetal position in the cramped niche, the person spent many uncomfortable days fasting and meditating. Drugs and hypnosis kept him or her in a semi-hypnotic trance for the following nine weeks. During this time, the potential Initiate endured realistic nightmares of the actual experience of death.

A spiritual rebirth followed, which included interactions with earth, air, fire, and water—all related to the growth of a new spiritual self, just as a fetus develops in the womb. At the end of the gestation period, priests massaged the body with strong-scented ointments and applied magical instruments to restore life to each of the organs. At midday on the seventh day of the ninth week, the supervisors considered the subject ready for its ceremonial rebirth. They passed the body through a shroud and encircled it with a bright light that inferred entry into a new world. Having attained a new level of psychic purity, the potential Initiate was carried from the dark labyrinth to a lovely garden twenty miles from the city. Here, brightly colored exotic birds, flowering shrubs, fruit-laden trees, graceful animals, stately firs, and sparkling pools created the illusion of paradise. A special "fountain of youth" and nourishing food helped the weak individual gradually regain strength.

The following stage of the initiation took place in the same beautiful garden. Barely audible suggestions tested the candidate's ability to ignore the logical thoughts of the Devil and his helpers and rely on his or her own intuition. For instance, she or he might be told of especially delicious fruit on a nearby tree. One set of voices counseled that eating it would be fatal, another said it was an essential source of insight relating to good and evil. The proper approach was to trust their intuition, which should tell them to avoid the fruit from the tree. Those who passed tests similar to this were established as an Initiate in the Temple of Poseidon.

Following the initiation experience in the labyrinth and the enchanting garden, the Initiates underwent a long period of rigorous, intellectual training before rising to the Adept level. They lived and studied in a large section of the Temple of Poseidon. In addition to the occult sciences, they acquired knowledge of ritual symbolism, healing, levitation, clairvoyant communication, and other skills passed down from Atlantean priests and preserved for many centuries. The facilities were excellent. The observatory in the Temple was equipped with powerful telescopes with precisely ground lenses. In the school's libraries, extensive ancient manuscripts contained valuable wisdom from past eras, including sacred writings focused on divine truths.

Meditation was a major component of life at the Temple of Poseidon. Twice a day students assembled in the Hall of Initiates, where sweet choral music and lovely, soft instrumental sounds created an appropriate background.[151] As they surrendered to the music, a sensation of soaring unfettered through the sky enveloped them and they experienced exultation, immeasurable joy, and a profound awareness of their relationship with the whole universe.

As occult students in Atlantis progressed from Initiates to Adepts to Magi, their rigorous training taught them that food, drink, and other material objects served only to nourish or adorn the body and were relatively unnecessary. They expanded their awareness, improved their psychic abilities, and learned to communicate with the divine. It was extremely important to always trust their intuition and not the suggestions of their logical brain. At least twenty or more years of extremely demanding meditation and study were required to bring intuitions and intellects into harmony. The goal was a body, mind, and spirit that worked together successfully, offering the individual maximum strength and power. Ultimately the prospective priests specialized in one of the occult arts of alchemy, healing, prophecy, astrology, clairvoyance, necromancy, or divination. Witchcraft and sorcery were popular pursuits in the later period of Atlantean civilization.

Alchemy

Only the most apt scholars in the Temple of Poseidon were permitted to pursue alchemy, for it was necessary that they thoroughly understand themselves before undertaking the challenging spiritual process. Alchemists' ultimate goals were to know the center of all things, to become one with the universe, to achieve a higher level of perception, and to penetrate the secrets of nature, life, death, infinity, and eternity. Using inorganic matter, and patiently engaged in a prescribed procedure that was extremely difficult to comprehend, they followed a tedious, complex course of study and experimentation. At unexpected moments, without warning, something triggered a glorious enlightenment, similar to experiences of yogis in deep meditation.[152] As alchemists of Atlantis experimented with heat, electricity, light, sound, and their own minds, they contemplated that perhaps an all-powerful god employed techniques of alchemy to create the Earth and life on it. Once they convinced themselves of this, they pursued their work with renewed hope and vigor, searching to attain universal knowledge.

The alchemists of Atlantis personalized metals so they represented certain gods and planets. Gold symbolized the sun, which was the source of life and also the ultimate perfection they sought. From their intense preoccupation with minerals they acquired an excellent comprehension of the structure of matter and its properties, a perception far superior to that of scientists until the present time.

Memories of the varied accomplishments of Atlantean alchemists survived in Greece, Egypt, and northern Africa, where devoted researchers spent their lives patiently attempting to recapture and grasp ancient symbolic mythological references. The African Arabs were the most successful alchemists, since they had access to fragments of texts from the destroyed libraries at Alexandria and Carthage. The body of information these alchemists assembled is known as the *Magnum Opus* (great work). In addition to complicated, ambiguous directions, including difficult instructions relating to timing tasks with astrological periods, the *Magnum Opus* contains beautiful, intricate paintings. These elaborate colored illustrations of strange imaginary people, animals, gardens, designs, and symbols are intended to incite the imagination. Every mark of the brush, every tiny detail is relative and important to the student of alchemy, who endlessly contemplates them, trying to go beyond the surface in the hope that something may suddenly trigger golden enlightenment. Fragments of alchemy and the occult knowledge of Atlantis have endured in the litany of Freemasonry and other secret societies whose origins date to prehistory. The sacred books of these organizations reflect the Atlanteans' worship of sun and fire and their interest in experimentation, numbers, and mathematical codes.

After the Moors invaded Spain, the practice of alchemy spread to the rest of Medieval Europe, where it was widely practiced. Chemistry evolved from it, although the two sciences have little in common. Chemistry is concerned with scientifically verifiable phenomena. Alchemy in Atlantis focused on a hidden reality of the highest order that constitutes the underlying essence of all truth, and it was a worthwhile, productive enterprise. During the Middle Ages, details of the extensive experiments and processes it involved were no longer available, and only indecipherable symbols, a few paintings, and legends of unsurpassed insight remained. Those who tried to work at alchemy were relatively unsuccessful. Once the scientific age arrived, these struggling scientists were regarded with contempt. As we approach the frontiers of knowledge, the techniques of this difficult occupation deserve respect, especially the emphasis on cultivating intuition.

The concluding ceremony to become a Magus, the highest degree of priesthood in Atlantis, took place at the far end of the secret natural labyrinth in the Hall of Illumination. Twelve small chapels, each dedicated to a past king of Atlantis, surrounded the spacious hall with its high, arched ceiling. A brightly lit, lofty altar dominated the center of the immense space. Here the final oaths and pledges were taken, and the remaining secret lore was interpreted to the prospective Magus. On one side of the altar stood a gigantic, hairy, frightful form of Poseidon as a bull. On the other side hung a large metal gong. At the end of a ceremony, when the gong was struck to signify the candidate was entitled to assume the role of priest or Magus, the deafening noise that resulted filled the extensive labyrinth with a tremendous thunderlike sound.

Those who reached the Magus level achieved a high degree of intellectual illumination from their initiation experiences and twenty or more years of study and meditation. They comprehended their own immortality and realized the inevitable transition from this Earth was not the end. Capable of leaving their bodies when they wished, they did not feel trapped by them. Uninhibited by space and time, they envisioned a future beyond their life on this planet. Increased perception of the universe offered the further advantage of more astute observations of the world around them, thus improving their ability to serve their constituents.

Initiation ceremonies were also included in the lives of less sophisticated people in Atlantis, providing them opportunities to expand their minds and better cope with their time on Earth. As a result of their firm attachment to the natural world, Atlanteans believed a particular bird or animal influenced and protected each person. Puberty rituals to introduce boys to their lifelong guardian spirit usually took place in a dark, windowless cavern under a temple. The three presiding priests wore costumes made from the skins and heads of bulls, helping them to identify more easily with the powerful animal. They spent many days painstakingly preparing these costumes to ensure the garments contained the desired powers. For the ceremony, while one leader played a bone flute, the participants solemnly chanted and rhythmically pounded on the floor with their hands. Then, in the dimly lit space, the serious and naked young initiates marched round and round in a circle for hours without food, water, or rest until they collapsed. In the trancelike state that followed, the bird or animal who was to guide them throughout that life appeared in a vision. The unforgettable event strengthened belief in their own intuition and encouraged them to confidently rely on it throughout their lives. Emigrants from Atlantis and their descendants continued to conduct similar ceremonies in dark caves and shelters on the American continent and in southwestern Europe.

The preparation of the bull costume the priests wore in the initiation ceremonies of young boys was an example of the elaborate rituals perfected through hundreds of years of practice and experimentation. After killing the animal, the person in charge stripped the body of all meat, muscles, and organs so that only the skin, two vertebrae in the neck and the connecting skull remained. During a long ceremony of stylized chants and music, they conferred magical powers on the skin and bones as they meticulously sewed them into a costume. Customs such as these were everlasting, for if a given procedure worked, and it did if too much wasn't expected, it was repeated and remembered.

As the Atlanteans' supernatural powers increased, their ceremonies became increasingly elaborate and dogmatic. Belief in the strength of these rites was strong enough so that if they failed, those in charge attributed the problem to a mistake in the ritual. Someone usually suffered. To avoid becoming a sacrificial victim, everyone was willing to expend enormous amounts of care and energy in hopes of achieving a successful result.

Witchcraft

Witchcraft was a popular occupation in Atlantis and Atlantean witches carried their techniques with them as they moved from their country; segments of their know-how survived and were practiced in widely separated areas contiguous to the Atlantic Ocean. Prehistoric traditions of witchcraft in Spain, France, Britain, and the Canary Islands on one side of the ocean, and in the West Indies and Mexico on the other, are remarkably similar. Witchcraft and many other customs that involve magic are so alike wherever they occur that they must have originated in one place. No region in western Europe had an advanced culture sufficiently ancient to serve as the focal point. Atlantis is the only possibility.[153]

In western Europe, the Canary Islands, the West Indies, and Mexico, the women were often virgins who wore long black skirts and tall peaked hats, flew through the air on broomsticks, smeared themselves with smelly ointment to facilitate their trip, and danced vigorously, often twirling around male figures. Witches were partial to crossroads. Owls were their favorite pets. They were skilled with herbs and quite capable of treating ailments and curing diseases. Some could change themselves into the form of another being, and others were able to cast powerful spells.

Societies of female witches were seldom found in Asia, where there was minimal Atlantean influence. Those in eastern Europe were similar to witches in the western part of the continent near the Atlantic Ocean, where their Atlantean techniques originated.[154] After years of intense training from an experienced older crone, Atlantean witches were adept at contacting the ancestors for guidance, and most of them communicated with the spirits of the underworld. As they became proficient at prophecy and necromancy the witches were often consulted for advice. Eventually, traditions of women oracles spread throughout the world.

Sorceresses who levitated and moved from place to place through the air empowered their sticks in complicated magical rites to facilitate mobility. More elaborate vehicles were also popular. A common practice that survived for thousands of years was to make a coffinlike "broom" from a leg bone. To accomplish this, the flesh of a dead man was roasted over a fire, pounded into the proper shape, and wrapped in a cloth. As the witch chanted and danced in a stylized manner, she squeezed the body's carefully prepared skin into the cavity of one of the leg bones. She buried the potential "broom" and left the creation in the ground until it no longer smelled. When it was unearthed, this novel instrument made an excellent seat for a witch's flight.[155]

Sacrifice

The growth of occult sciences in Atlantis seriously altered the culture's sacrificial practices. For numerous centuries, people presented gifts of flowers and fruits to the gods in their attempts to placate them. Gradually, in hopes of more satisfactory results, they gave animals, such as the bull that was sacrificed every fifth or sixth year in the Temple of Poseidon. Many of the temples kept sacred fires burning continuously, available for anticipated victims. Gods of the volcanoes, who threw out smoke, fire, rocks, and boiling liquid, were a constant threat in Atlantis, and the Magi worked hard to subdue their powers. The Rite of the Earth-fires described in chapter 3 was one of the tactics they devised as they sought to keep those demons happy.

The Magi in Atlantis, because of their intensive training and initiation experiences, no longer feared death or possible reprisals from the gods for immoral acts, and the majority of them freely took advantage of the people's belief in an afterlife and the spirit world. Increasingly, these dominant leaders resorted to supernatural powers as they attempted to placate and control the spirits and gods who regulated their environment. As time passed, to improve their status and gain power, the decadent priests implied they communicated directly with the destructive gods. Their magical tricks, plus their terrifying threats of evoking the spirits of the volcanoes, horrified the people. Whenever the ground trembled, their desperate attempts to appease the gods increased.

The Atlanteans fought ceremonial battles for sacrificial victims for the volcanoes. The winners killed the losers, burned their bodies, and threw the ashes into a volcano's mouth. Sometimes leaders supervised the killing of sacrificial victims by means of an electric charge resembling a bolt of lightning. Dust was easier to carry up the steep mountainsides, so the use of crystal rays became a popular means of disintegrating corpses. Slowly the civilization degenerated even further, and people were simply transported up the mountain side and flung directly into the boiling inferno. Negative energy was reaching an intolerable level and the inevitable time for the one all-powerful God to assert authority was approaching.

4

ARCHITECTURE

THE SKILLED BUILDERS OF THE
past had numerous accomplishments
that have yet to be duplicated. Immense
retaining walls now covered by water,
pyramids in Egypt and Central America, Tiahuanaco, the City of the Golden
Gates, and the complex highway system
of South America offer glimpses of
noteworthy talents and expertise of prehistoric people. Immense structures, far
from each other on the face of the
Earth, reveal that advanced persons possessed superior scientific and architectural skills, such as the ability to move
rocks weighing 200 tons for a considerable distance and the facility to shape
these stones to fit together perfectly.
The accomplishments represent the cul-
mination of a long development from
an unknown source. The civilization of

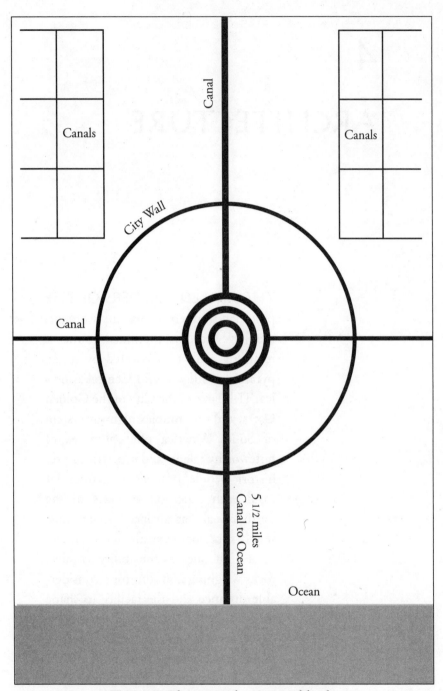

Figure 5: Plain, canals, city, and harbor

Atlantis was partially responsible, and the presence of celestial visitors offers a further possible explanation.

CITY OF THE GOLDEN GATES

The renowned capital city of Atlantis is usually referred to as the City of the Golden Gates. Plato describes the construction and the details of the city carefully, including its huge, elaborately decorated buildings. What he portrays is so unlike anything of his day that it obviously required infinite conviction and courage on his part to ascribe the city to an ancient civilization. However, the City of the Golden Gates was actually very similar to Khorsabad, the walled city of King Sargon II in Sumeria, which was deeply buried in sand when Plato lived. Sumerians' careful writings report the helpful assistance gods and goddesses offered toward their magnificent city's design and construction. The City of the Golden Gates also resembles the Aztecs' opulent capital in Mexico, and Cuzco, the Incas' extraordinary city in Peru.

The Ringed City

Plato reports that the god Poseidon and his mortal wife Cleito raised their family in Atlantis on a hill surrounded by a large plain about five miles from the ocean. Poseidon shaped the city area around their home into three circles of land. The canals that divided the sections of land were filled with water from a river that originated in the mountains and flowed across the plain. Earthquakes and eruptions from nearby volcanic peaks severely damaged the city at least four times, but the Atlanteans always rebuilt it in the same pattern—circles of land surrounded by three rings of water.[1] Other ancient civilizations duplicated this design. Carthage, on the north African coast of the Mediterranean, was almost identical to its layout, and the main city of the Aztecs, with buildings erected

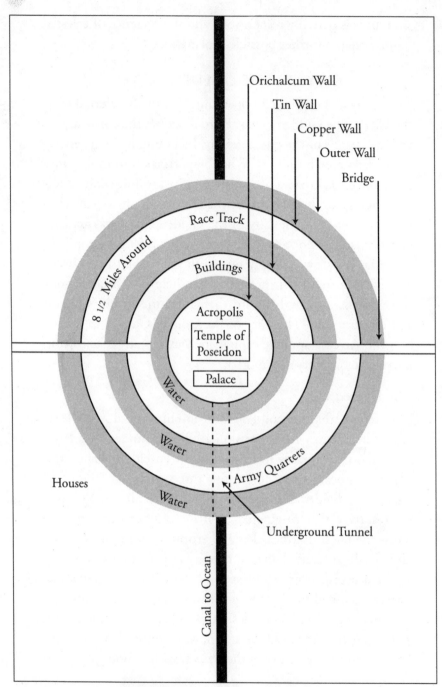

Figure 6: City of the Golden Gates

around an extensive canal network, was also constructed from a similar master plan. Recent radar images taken by the Space Shuttle reveal that many centuries ago a city was constructed on the site of the current extraordinary buildings at Angor Wat in Cambodia. That prehistoric city was surrounded by perfectly round moats, just like the City of the Golden Gates.

Innumerable small boats navigated the circular passageways of the City of the Golden Gates, providing supplies to the inhabitants, in the same manner that small merchants glide in laden shikaris from houseboat to houseboat on Dal Lake in Shrinigar, India, selling food, clothing, and handiwork. Water from the canals in the City of the Golden Gates supplemented the rain, furnishing additional moisture for lush plants, ferns, flowers and trees. Paths along humanmade streams offered cool respite from the city's confusion, and splashing fountains reflected the Atlanteans' love of moving water. Numerous bridges over the canals offered easy access from one ring of the city to another and held aqueducts that transported pure drinking water to the city's residents.[2] The Atlanteans built 200 elaborate towers on the bridges,[3] inlaying them with gleaming metals and precious stones.[4] The towers served as guard houses, storage places, and observation and communication posts. Rising toward the sky from the bridges, the sparkling towers added beauty and vitality to the lives of the city's inhabitants.

Metal Working

The Atlanteans constructed massive stone walls, fifty feet wide and the height of seven-story buildings, to encircle each of the large rings of land. They covered the stones of the imposing outermost wall with copper, the boulders of the middle one with tin, and the wall that encircled the inner circle with brilliant orichalcum;[5] a pink version of gold. The alchemists of Atlantis associated certain metals with specific planets and learned the ions within metals are always in motion and believed these patterns of activity were dictated by the orbit of the particular planet to which the metal chiefly responded.[6] Each metal was associated with one of the heavenly bodies. Walls of copper, tin, and orichalcum were respectively representative of Venus, Jupiter, and the Sun.[7]

Orichalcum, also called "mountain copper," coated the inner wall of the city. It was a popular metal in Atlantis, but its composition is somewhat of a mystery. From Plato's description we know Solon and the priests of Egypt were not familiar with it, although they knew it "sparkled like fire."[8] In ancient Greek, the language of Solon, the word *chalkos*, which is the basis of the word *orichalcum*, applied to all metals, therefore orichalcum literally meant "gold metal." Plato describes orichalcum as something that in his time was only known by name, but was once a metal more precious than any except gold. Memories of the orichalcum of Atlantis appeared 600 years before Plato's time in the works of the Greek poet Homer, who mentions it as a golden metal in the hymn of Aphrodite. Hesiod, another pre-Plato Greek poet (eighth to seventh century B.C.), also refers to it.[9]

It is possible that orichalcum was a combination of gold and meteorite iron, and some of it survived into this century. In 1916 the British War Office in India obtained small elephant statues and incense burners fashioned from a mysterious metal. The ancient objects were preserved for centuries in Hindu monasteries. Translucent stones and crystals inlaid in the incense burners produced a dramatic effect when the wicks were lit in a dark room, for as the odor of incense filled the air, firelight gleamed through the jewels. The British War Office decided the unknown metal was a mixture of a high percentage of nickel and some gold.[10] Nickel is found in meteorite iron, which was prevalent in Atlantis.

The mountains of Atlantis were an excellent source of mineral deposits, including silver, gold, copper, tin, iron, and sulfur. Everyone loved the readily available precious metals for ornamenting themselves and their buildings. To meet their own desires and the demands of their extraterrestrial visitors, Atlanteans also mined gold and silver in Africa and South America and tin and copper in Peru and Great Britain.

Atlanteans observed the frequent eruptions of Mount Atlas, learned the dramatic effects of heat on metals, and devised methods of smelting copper.[11] They also produced and utilized bronze. When they settled in northern Europe and the Mediterranean, where copper was scarce, Atlanteans made bronze as in their homeland by heating copper and fusing it with tin.[12] Due to their influence in northern Europe and the Mediterranean, ancient copper tools, which usually preceded bronze, are rarely found in those areas. The Atlanteans' techniques enabled the indigenous people to move directly from the Stone Age into the Bronze Age.[13]

The passage of time altered all things in Atlantis, but throughout its long history the unequaled capital city reflected the people's creative ability and their adoration and respect for all aspects of nature. This was especially true of the innermost circle of land with its ornate temple and attractive park. As each successive king attempted to surpass the sizable contributions of his predecessors, the temple, sacred to Cleito and to Poseidon, attained unsurpassed splendor.

The Temple of Poseidon

The Temple of Poseidon was so large—600 feet long, 300 feet wide and appropriately high that even Plato admits it was rather "barbaric" in appearance.[14] The Temple of Poseidon as described by Plato certainly was different from the stark Greek temples he was familiar with. He describes the exterior walls of the mammoth building as lined with silver and topped with towers covered with shining gold. A blue-tiled courtyard, complete with graceful fountains, offered an area for people to congregate. Each successive king erected a golden statue of himself and one of his wife to stand around the Temple of Poseidon.[15] The statues were set in gorgeous gardens filled with unusual flowering shrubs and lofty trees from all over the world.

A wall overlaid with gold that enclosed the unique temple and its grounds[16] became one of the sources of the name City of the Golden Gates,[17] which also had an esoteric meaning. Many psychics refer to the city as Chalidocean, its more official name. In the first century B.C., Diodorus Siculus reported it was called Cercenes in Africa.[18]

The interior of the sacred Temple of Poseidon, as described by Plato, was as ornate as the exterior. Ivory enhanced with gold, silver, and orichalcum covered the ceiling, and more orichalcum brightened the walls, pillars, and floors. A gigantic statue of Poseidon standing on a chariot and driving six winged horses, surrounded by statues of graceful sea nymphs riding on the backs of golden dolphins, dominated the center of the main room.[19]

The Incas' immense Temple of the Sun in Cuzco was similar to the Temple of Poseidon. Its interior was lined with sheets of gold, and golden statues stood throughout its lavish gardens. Excavations at the Sumerian city of Khorsabad revealed a magnificent royal palace at its center. The interior walls of this immense building were carved with sculptured bas reliefs, which, if placed end to end, would extend over a mile.[20] Like the City of the Golden Gates, in addition to one gigantic building, the metropolis was filled with temples, walls, gates, towers, columns, and gardens, all completed with the help of their "gods" in just five years.[21]

The Atlanteans erected various wooden buildings in the City of the Golden Gates, but Plato reports that they preferred to construct with the white, black, and red stones they quarried from under the city.[22] It is impressive that Plato knew that white, black and red are the typical colors of rocks in the volcanic islands of the Atlantic Ocean, for many historians believe people did not sail outside the Mediterranean in 400 B.C.

when Plato lived. Stone structures remained standing for a longer period of time than those made of other materials. They were also less apt to topple during the frequent shaking of the Earth. The stone structures in the city displayed the advanced engineering techniques acquired as Atlanteans worked on their earthquake-prone land with tremendous boulders to form their religious circles. These sacred areas required not only the transportation of heavy rocks, but careful placement to exactly the correct depth in the ground, for if one stone in the circle settled too deeply, it was out of alignment and decreased the energy of the site. Atlantean workmen shaped the unwieldy rocks, some weighing many tons, into blocks that fit together perfectly, in an interlocking manner, without the aid of mortar. The same skills are visible in buildings in Cuzco, Tiahuanaco, Malta, Mexico and other sites on the earth, where apparently visitors from space, with knowledge we have yet to acquire, assisted humankind.

The City of the Golden Gates was an agreeable and inviting place to live and to visit. Excellent soil, a favorable climate, and the loving care of its inhabitants assured that luxuriant trees purified the air and flowers bloomed everywhere. Crystal windows enhanced many of the city's buildings, for clear quartz crystal, the result of rapid cooling of the magma from within the Earth, was readily available in Atlantis. Exterior walls decorated with bright patterns of precious stones and mosaics added color and charm. Cayce describes temples with interior onyx and topaz columns inlaid with beryl, amethyst, and other sparkling stones.[23] Atlanteans favored a white marble floor, embellished with a golden altar, for the focus of their religious services.[24]

The citizens of the city created many opportunities for recreation and entertainment, ensuring that it was a place to play and relax. They filled numerous swimming pools with warm mineral water from the natural hot springs. Plato depicts separate pools for men and women and special ones for horses and other beasts of burden.[25] At appealing parks people exercised in grassy fields and attended competitive athletic games. Regular bloody bullfights were popular events. Plato describes the largest, outermost ring of land in the City of the Golden Gates as containing a giant racetrack, the width of a thirty-lane highway and over eight and one half miles long.[26] Here the masses eagerly attended raucous chariot, horse, and elephant races.

As Atlanteans traveled more extensively on the ocean waters surrounding their land, they built larger boats and grew increasingly reliant on supplies from abroad. Administrators decided to make the city accessible to the sea, and like everything else they undertook, they did it in a grand manner. Hundreds of workmen labored for many years to bore a huge tunnel beneath the center of the city to the ocean. Cutting through the circles of land, they hollowed out the spacious underground passageway until, as Plato says, it was one hundred feet deep and fifty feet wide, making it accessible to ships measuring twenty feet across with oars on both sides.[27] Crafts traveled from the outside port through the tunnel to a sixteen-acre cavern excavated under the central island. Here an immense inner harbor was equipped with docks that offered berths for 130 ships.[28] If an invader appeared, watchmen lowered heavy portcullises from the towers above, eliminating access to the secluded shelter.

When the capital city grew overcrowded, the innovative Atlanteans built apartments[29] and additional pleasant, cool housing underground.[30] In rich soil above the subterranean living spaces, residents grew fruits and vegetables for their own use or planted exquisite flowers and shrubs. They placed ledges of rock over the entrances to these homes to provide shade and planted abundant trailing vines to conceal the openings.[31]

In the final days of Atlantis, the wealthy ruling class lived in spacious, elegant open-air haciendas. Their sparsely but expensively furnished homes were designed around a central courtyard to provide cross-ventilation for all rooms. To improve the relaxing atmosphere in this outdoor living area, the occupants fashioned ornate fountains which splashed perfumed spray into marble basins, and surrounded them with exotic plants and flowers.[32] Affluent Atlanteans employed artisans to fashion bronze, silver, gold, and precious stones into artistic decorations for their courtyards in the shapes of trees, plants, insects, and animals. Silver butterflies sat on golden flowers, and carved ivory beetles crawled up bronze stems and branches. Metallic, colorful birds that moved their tongues and wings and toy monkeys that broke nuts with their teeth offered entertainment.

The Temple of Incal

Several miles from the City of the Golden Gates stood the huge Temple of Incal, capable of accommodating thousands of worshippers.[33] The building was in the shape of a pyramid and was constructed without windows. When one entered the temple through an unusually small doorway, it felt like emerging into a natural cave. Enormous crystals, resembling stalactites and stalagmites, hung from the ceiling while subdued, reflected light created a peaceful atmosphere for meditation. A raised platform of red granite that was thirty-six feet across occupied the center of the Temple. The platform supported a large block of quartz crystal from which a constantly glowing light leapt twenty feet into the air like a fiery white flame. The light did not harm the eyes if one looked into it and it did not emit heat, but it had the power to disintegrate whatever came in contact with it. The strange fire was useful for cremations and sacrifices to appease the feared natural gods.[34]

The ocean port of the City of the Golden Gates was a boisterous and exciting place, constantly filled with an interesting variety of hardy sailors and their diverse ships from all over the world.[35] Merchant vessels from South America came with precious gems, copper, gold, and silver, and long thin triremes from the north, with three banks of oars and prows in the shape of serpents, arrived with important dignitaries. Native Americans describe the harbor's entrance as a maze where undesirable visitors lost their way; a local pilot was required to navigate a successful path by ship to the City of the Golden Gates.[36]

BUILDINGS, WALLS, AND ROADS

The City of the Golden Gates was home to many Atlanteans, but others preferred to live more simply and focus their lives on the bounties of nature. Some chose the sea coast, passing their free time enjoying the rhythmic sound of waves on the sand beaches, watching flocks of snowy, white egrets and other sea birds come and go, and appreciating the refreshing ocean breezes. Others preferred the cool mountains, with a splendid view of the vast ocean below, although volcanic activity was a constant threat. Atlanteans enjoyed relaxing on their patios, contemplating the constantly changing shape of a cloud, or passing the time in their gardens where fountains and pools attracted darting birds and fragrant flowers perfumed the air and soothed the mind.

Almost all houses built in Atlantis between 12,000 B.C. and 10,000 B.C. were circular in shape, a custom that was continued for thousands of years as descendants of survivors built stone houses in more primitive lands.[37] A circle was considered to be harmonious to the human spirit and thought to better channel the energy of the universe. People furnished their homes sparsely; comfort and a relaxed life were primary goals, and everyone spent as much time as possible outside. Atlanteans had little interest in acquiring an excess of material objects and were satisfied with old family chests and simple furniture. They built shelves to hold dishes and preferred eating utensils made from orichalcum, for it did not tarnish and therefore seldom needed polishing.[38] A large, open, stone fireplace in the main room was adequate for their simple meal preparations. Colorful murals of flowers or fruit decorated the interior walls of their homes.

Except for the City of the Golden Gates, Atlanteans intentionally refrained from building many large cities due to their negative impact on the environment. Their well-irrigated and beautifully landscaped small communities consisted of one-story round buildings. When families grouped together, they placed their houses in a circle facing away from the center,[39] offering everyone a picturesque panorama of a winding river, lofty mountains, or the daily sunrise or sunset. If no beautiful natural sight was available, the Atlanteans rearranged dirt and rocks, modeling the earth into a more desirable shape to improve their view. They covered the resulting mound with spacious gardens, flowering shrubs, and graceful trees. The central plaza of the community served as a marketplace and hub of social life where everyone congregated for conversation, music, and dance. Fruit and nut trees shaded these central areas, enhanced by colorful flower beds, where strawberry plants might cover the ground.

It was delightful to travel in Atlantis, for the landscape offered a varied and attractive panorama. Exteriors of circular houses and temples were brightly painted, gilded, or tiled, and the countryside was laced with canals for irrigation and transportation. Round towers where towns stored communal food and grain displayed the high standard of living.

Heavenly Structures

Stories were prevalent in early Atlantis of times in the past when flaming bodies from space crashed into the land, instigating earthquakes, volcanic activity, desolation, and death. Countless individuals stoically studied the starry skies for signs of a moving object that might smash into their world and destroy it. The Atlanteans' first attempts at constructing large buildings were designed to assist their viewing of the heavens. If possible they erected observation towers on high places, which not only put them somewhat closer to the world above but also offered protection from floods. As they studied the universe, star watchers positioned their observatories to correspond with astronomical features, points of the compass, or the setting sun at the summer solstice. Atlanteans often held religious services in these buildings and covered them with precious stones, shining metal, and sparkling crystals to reflect their devotion.

Builders, perhaps as a result of advice from celestial beings, learned that structures in a pyramid shape unleashed a mysterious power. To augment the energy channeled from the heavens above and the earth below, Atlanteans constructed pyramids over places of high energy and placed a potent quartz crystal near or at the building's peak. The power available to those who spent time in a pyramid provided a strengthening experience that centered the mind and improved their ability to learn. Pyramids were apparently an architectural form favored by extraterrestrials, for the structures appear in Mexico, Sumeria, and Egypt, all lands favored by celestial visitors. The earliest pyramids in Egypt were constructed with flat tops that served as a site for religious services, but heat forced the worshippers indoors, and the sides of the buildings were gradually continued up to a point.[40] The peaks of pyramid-type buildings in Mexico and Sumeria were usually flat, offering desirable localities for observatories or shrines for religious services. However, near Palenque, in Mexico, there are two perfectly preserved pyramids that are square at the base but pointed at the peak, similar to later constructions in Egypt. And fifty miles south of Florida a pyramid with a pointed top lies in 1,200 feet of water. Sonar images reveal that it is as tall as a twenty-story building.[41]

Retaining Walls

When necessity demanded, Atlantean engineers utilized their technological skills to build mammoth fortifications. Combining rocks and boulders, they constructed enormous walls to create harbors for their seaports and to provide protection from invaders. Eventually glaciers receded, melting water poured into the Atlantic Ocean, and they hurriedly built additional barriers in their futile attempts to restrain the rising seas that drowned their homes and ruined their lives. In 1977 Russians photographed some of the Atlanteans' extensive defenses that continue to stand, even though they are completely engulfed in water, north of the island of Madeira.[42] Similar bulwarks are visible near the Canary Islands and in the Bahamas. In southwestern Spain, harbors and walls of gigantic stone blocks affirm the amazing engineering skill of their Cro-Magnon builders.[43]

The Apaches remember one of the most tremendous retaining walls of their Atlantean ancestors, which Chief Asa Delugio described to Lucille Taylor Hansen.[44] Long ago, when the present Mediterranean was a small enclosed sea, a river ran from it to the west. As the waters of the river encountered high cliffs near the Atlantic Ocean, they divided; part fell down around the barrier and the rest fell with a thundering roar over the cliffs. The two segments of the river united at the bottom, and the combination of wild waters turned toward the left, poured through a gorge, and headed for the ocean. When the rushing torrent passed the "old, red land" (Atlantis), it ate away valuable soil and numerous lovely homes collapsed into the sea. In an effort to prevent this erosion, many lives were lost as engineers spent years erecting a high protecting wall, over a mile wide, along the coast of Atlantis. It was eventually buried under tons of lava and earth.[45]

Atlantis in the Caribbean

Twenty thousand years ago some Atlanteans who were forced to leave their land because of flooding and overpopulation consulted sailors for help in deciding where to go. The mariners' tales of the curative powers of the waters near Murias, in the Bahama Islands, enticed many to the area. The Bahama Islands are approximately 700 small islands and cays extending from the east coast of Florida over 760 miles southeast in the direction of Haiti. The entire region, known as the Bahama Bank, has repeatedly been above and below the surface of the ocean. In 20,000 B.C., due to the huge amounts of moisture assimilated in the glaciers, considerably more land area was exposed than today. Earthquakes often disturb the Earth's sensitive crust in this region, forcing land to rise and fall. When the Atlanteans arrived in the Bahamas, the present ocean floor stood fifteen feet above the surface. Edgar Cayce predicted that in 1968 or 1969 part of Atlantis that was in Bimini, an island in the Bahamas, would rise again, and the remains of an ancient temple would appear. In 1968 airplane pilots sighted cut stone blocks and columns under the water where Cayce predicted. Intensive study of the Cayce readings inspired Dr. David Zink to lead an expedition to Bimini in 1974 to search for remains of Atlantean buildings. His discoveries of submerged ruins of megalithic structures and intriguing artifacts has inspired this expert sailor, underwater photographer and skilled scuba diver to return to the area many times.

Things went well for the Atlanteans in Murias 20,000 years ago. Two psychics, who assisted Dr. Zink in his research in Bimini, transmitted information about the city. The psychics related that highly evolved, loving beings from the Pleiades, discovering the spiritually advanced residents, joined the thriving commercial and religious community.[46] Taking into consideration the alignment of the sun, the moon, the stars, and the biorhythms—the subtle repeating functions that make the life of an organism possible, such as the seasons, rotation of the Earth, the spinning of the galaxy—of our planet, the Pleiadeans supervised the construction of temples and buildings.[47] From the research of Edgarton Sykes we know that the city of Murias in Bimini became the seat of government for the area, and that its extensive facilities included a hospital, a home for travelers in distress and a shipyard with repair facilities.[48] On a hill that rose above Murias, the Atlanteans and the Pleiadeans worked together to build an exquisite healing temple dedicated to the god Min and the Bennu bird, both representative of rejuvenation. The architecture of the building incorporated sacred geometry and it also displayed sophisticated knowledge of the structure of the universe, the solar system, and this planet. The dimensions of the Great Pyramid in Egypt contain similar information. The most unusual feature of the enormous temple at Murias was its crystal windows, which caused it to be referred to in legends as the Temple of the Translucent Walls.

Highly evolved priestesses presided over the unique building. Utilizing plants and advice from the Pleiadeans, they developed an extensive variety of invaluable medicinal potions derived from flowers, herbs, and other vegetation. Sound, in the form of chants, was another tool the skilled women employed to supplement the healing remedies offered to those who came for help and advice.[49] The site at Bimini was an effective place for increasing body energy, since slightly radioactive water in nearby pools produced a rejuvenating effect on the adrenal and pituitary glands, stimulating beneficial hormones. Near South Bimini, Dr. Zink and his companions found underwater hot springs rich in minerals and still emitting radioactive gases. Swimming in the water improved skin tone, diminished facial wrinkles, and was beneficial to one participant's arthritis.[50] In addition to assistance with physical problems, the facilities of the healing temple at Bimini offered opportunities for people to raise their level of consciousness and comprehend that their origins were outside this planet.[51] As the population in the surrounding area increased, spiritually oriented residents erected sturdy pyramids, eventually covered by the waters of the Caribbean Sea but obvious today on sonar scans and aerial surveys. Airplane pilots report seeing these tall, pointed buildings from the air when the surface is very calm.

In 10,000 B.C. ocean water rose rapidly and covered the city of Murias but not the healing temple standing safely on a hill above it. For a considerable period of time the ancient spa was visited by Irish, Egyptian, Greek, Phoenecian, and Carthaginian sailors and travelers.[52] In 6000 B.C. ocean levels climbed again. Simultaneously, earthquakes disrupted the land, broke the retaining walls, and toppled sections of the beautiful building as if it were a glass toy. The once-magnificent structure with the remnants of its translucent windows slowly disappeared from sight. Legends of the Island of the Ruin (of the temple) and the rejuvenating powers of Murias continued to attract adventurers and explorers to the area until the sixteenth century, when Ponce de Leon arrived searching for the Fountain of Youth.

Underwater remains of buildings Atlantean descendants erected in the Bahamas are sometimes encountered by scuba divers. This is most apt to occur after a bad storm that has disturbed the ocean bottom. The findings receive almost no publicity because it is feared treasure hunters will strip them of valuable objects or employ damaging dynamite to explore beneath them. Charles Berlitz describes an account of Dr. Ray Brown who, in 1970 after such a storm, was exploring with four other divers near the Berry Islands about 150 miles from Bimini. Brown recounts that from their boat they saw buildings under the water. They jumped in and near the bottom, at a depth of about 135 feet, he came to a pyramid. He investigated it and swam into an opening near the peak and through a shaft until he came to a crystal ball held in two bronze hands.[53] A ruby, hanging from the top of the pyramid, was suspended over the crystal, a combination of gems ancient spiritual persons employed to magnify and disperse thought.[54] Brown yanked the shining stone free and swam out, eager to leave the dark, mysterious place. He carried the crystal home to Arizona, where he occasionally shows it in lectures. It has a strong energy field and smaller crystals are visible within it. Three of the four divers with Brown the day he found the crystal ball later died while scuba diving in the vicinity of the pyramid.[55] This story was also portrayed on a 1980s national television program, *In Search of Atlantis*. Dr. Douglas Richards, an underwater archaeologist who is currently participating in investigations of the Bimini area, believes Berlitz was possibly deceived by Brown and that the event may be fictitious.

A man exploring off the coast of South Bimini in 1957 discovered a sizable stone column in forty feet of water. Psychics relayed that the column was once incorporated in a building that housed a tremendous crystal. The column aided in regulating and turning the crystal to reflect the energy of the sun.[56] Psychics believe those who lived in the area before the sea covered it utilized the column and crystal for the reception and radiation of cosmic energy for the benefit of one's soul. Photographs of the submerged pillar show peculiar radiation patterns emanating from it that are not visible to the naked eye. Radiation physicists suggest that, through ionization, ultraviolet radiation from the column may increase the energy level of the water, so that radioactivity becomes photographically visible without special film and filters.[57] Satellite mapping in 1984 revealed large geometric patterns with perfectly square corners extending for many miles in the vicinity of Bimini under the surface of the water. Twelve to fifteen feet of sand and water cover them, making them only visible from the air; they cannot be seen from a boat.[58] A group of talented people, including Dr. Douglas Richards, are involved in searching in the Bimini area for traces of the temple and healing waters that Edgar Cayce referred to. They have recently visited the cat mound, a difficult task since it is surrounded by mangrove swamps, but have been unable to ascertain what is beneath it because penetrating ground radar doesn't probe through the sea water that has seeped into the area. Their next step is to try seismic technology. They are also investigating numerous cut stone blocks, including one that is ten feet by thirty feet and protrudes from a bank ninety feet under the water. They are optimistic about their venture and believe this may be the most fruitful archaeological undertaking of the twentieth century.

Tiahuanaco

The ancient city of Tiahuanaco, in Bolivia, offers another example of the extraordinary accomplishments of prehistoric builders who were probably assisted by extraterrestrials. The extensive ruins are now at an incredible height of 13,000 feet, 200 miles from the Pacific coast, but many signs confirm the city was once at sea level, with a passageway to the ocean. Tiahuanaco was built on Lake Titicaca, a vast body of water that covers an area of 3,140 square miles. The lake has diminished in size considerably, so that today the ruins of the city lie several miles from its shores. The water retains some salt content and oceanic plants from the days when it was much larger and at sea level with access to the Pacific Ocean. Cut from solid rocks, docks for ships,[59] with rings on them for cables for fastening oceangoing vessels, are still visible.[60]

Other factors demonstrate that the land in the vicinity of Tiahuanaco was once much lower. Skeletons of mastodon and giant sloths, animals not capable of surviving at the high altitude where the ruins are, suggest the land rose relatively recently when these creatures were prevalent. Stone agricultural terraces, visible on the nearby mountains, outline where the land was farmed at a present elevation of 18,000 feet. Here, where the snow line begins, fragments of an irrigation system are also visible. Even with the moderating influence of the large lake, plants ripen very slowly at the city's current height of 13,000 feet, for the soil at this altitude is extremely poor. The terraces on the nearby mountain were utilized for growing food for the massive population required to build the city at a time when the land was lower.[61] At some point after civilized people settled here, a massive earth change raised the height of this ridge of the Andes and the city of Tiahuanaco over two miles.

German-Bolivian Professor Arthur Posnansky of the University of La Paz researched extensively at Tiahuanaco. His work was translated by J. F. Shearer of the Hispanic Department of Columbia University and assembled into *Tiahanacu, the Cradle of American Man.* Posnansky uncovered five layers of civilization. The oldest is characterized by sandstone buildings and it dates to about the time when Murias was settled. The second civilization, the most advanced, lived in Tiahuanaco about 15,000 B.C. Posnansky believed that about 10,000 years ago a cataclysm destroyed the city.

Atlanteans who followed tributaries of the Amazon and reached Tiahuanaco around 15,000 B.C. found travelers from the Far East living there. In prehistoric times, many sailors navigated the Pacific as well as the Atlantic Ocean, in both directions, as Thor Heyerdahl demonstrated in 1947 when he traveled in a replica of an ancient balsa wood raft from Peru to the Polynesian Islands. In Tiahuanaco the diverse groups of individuals cooperated to create a glorious city, patterned in many ways after the Atlanteans' City of the Golden Gates, with aqueducts, temples, palaces, and observatories. Fray Diego de Alcobaso and other Spanish friars who visited Tiahuanaco in the sixteenth century before it was pillaged by the Spaniards recorded the little we know of its grandeur. Workmen constructed structures as long as thirty-six feet, using perfectly cut stone blocks weighing over 200 tons that were transported from a quarry fifty miles away.[62] The distances the huge boulders were moved, the accuracy of the stonework, and the tremendous size of the buildings are characteristic of the techniques extraterrestrials demonstrated in Sumeria thousands of years later; presumably they advised in Tiahuanaco as well.

On the peak of a truncated pyramid, the citizens of Tiahuanaco built the largest Sun Temple in the world, complete with an astronomical observatory with a stone calendar.[63] Posnansky determined that in 9550 B.C., when the observatory was abandoned, the astronomers were observing the north star.[64] Artisans embellished buildings throughout Tiahuanaco with readily available gold and silver, including silver bolts weighing over three tons that served as rivets in huge monoliths.[65] Workmen paved the streets and sculptors lined them and the popular lake shore with lifelike statues of the cities' citizens holding upraised drinking glasses.[66] Statues of men of the black race and some signs and symbols from the Far East indicate adventurers from all over the world visited and inhabited the magnificent city.

Spanish conquistadores almost totally destroyed the lovely artwork of Tiahuanaco, shipping innumerable boatloads of invaluable artifacts and precious metals to Spain, where it was all melted down. A few objects endure in a museum in La Paz. Stones from the extensive structures were utilized to construct a railroad bed and streets and buildings in the city of La Paz.

An elaborate highway system once connected the northern and southern areas of South America. The main road, constructed of stones that fit together perfectly, ran through Ecuador, Peru, and Bolivia to Argentina and Chile—a distance of over 10,000 miles. Pieces of the elaborate network of secondary roads that linked widely separated communities are still discernible. The sophisticated transportation system included inns where travelers spent the night, bridges over deep gorges and rivers, and 600–foot tunnels blasted through the mountains.[67]

5

INFLUENCES OF LAND, SEA, AND SKY

HUMAN BEINGS SURVIVE ON the Earth in deserts with almost no rainfall where they must spend most of their time struggling for food and water. People exist in isolated areas with little opportunity for travel and few stimulating visitors. Although they are alive and they endure in these unfavorable environments, their civilizations are not apt to thrive or develop. But consider Atlantis—a bountiful land with ideal growing conditions, surrounded by ocean waters that offered protection from invaders and opportunities for travel to faraway places; a country attractive enough to entice sophisticated visitors from space to come, stay, and help them grow. The opportunities were there and the Atlanteans took full advantage of them.

AGRICULTURE

Atlantis was a natural paradise where no one went hungry. Satisfying fruits and nuts hung from the trees, shellfish were readily available on the seashore, and agricultural crops flourished. A typical meal 20,000 years ago might have included oysters on the half shell, charcoal-broiled lamb and, if you were a vegetarian, boiled wild rice, a green salad, fresh fruit, and delicious herbal tea.

Fish was always a popular item on menus in Atlantis, but some descendants developed a tradition of not eating seafood, such as the Iroquois of North America and the Tuaregs who lived in the Atlas Mountains of Africa. The explanation was that during the terrible destruction, when their ancestors drowned under the waves, fish ate them. Therefore, their predecessors became a part of the fish. To their descendants, eating fish seemed like eating their ancestors. Some Native Americans believed that if they ceremonially speared the fish with a trident, the symbol of Atlantis, it became an acceptable meal.[1]

In spite of the abundance of meat and fish, many Atlanteans were vegetarians. They realized that eating animal flesh depleted the flow of energy within their bodies, thus inducing lethargy, imbalance, and susceptibility to illness. In addition, meat consumption was not conducive to psychic practices.[2]

The first Atlanteans were sensitive to the vibrations of growing things, which enabled them to live intimately and respectfully with them. In a similar way, spiritually aware people at the present time use deep meditation and visualization to receive information from nature spirits or intelligences. The intelligent consciousnesses of animate forms of energy in flowers and other plants are often referred to as devas. At Findhorn, an experimental farm in northern Scotland, inhabitants precisely follow the advice they receive from devas. The result is a thriving community focused on a healthy, balanced life in harmony with its surroundings. Findhorn's spectacular gardens produce remarkably large vegetables and flowers with unusually bright colors. A similar undertaking, the Center for Nature Research, thrives in Jeffersonton, Virginia. In *Perelandra Garden Workbook*, Machacille Small Wright describes the principles and dynamics of this unique community, where recommendations from nature spirits are carefully and successfully followed.

As the Atlanteans communicated with plants and flowers, they perceived the guidance the spirits of the plants offered them. This included recommendations as to when to plant their crops, which seeds to place in a north-south direction, and how far apart to sow seeds. They learned that leafy vegetables and other garden plants that bore their fruit above the ground did best if they were sowed before a full moon. Root vegetables thrived when the seeds were planted at the time of a full moon or soon thereafter, before the new moon. Tomatoes prefer to live alone. A quartz crystal in the center of a garden was also beneficial. Atlanteans were in touch with insects as well as with animals. If farmers expected trouble from bugs, they planted an extra field for them. When marauders began to devour their crops, the Atlanteans communicated with their invaders' leader. They persuaded it to leave with its compatriots and to eat only in the space allocated to them.

Atlanteans used many tactics to assure their fields produced vigorous crops. After sowing in the spring, in order to activate life from seeds, they filled the air with reverberations of loud, persistent drum beats and passionately danced in ritual ceremonies to the Earth. While they circled the newly planted area, regularly kissing the ground, men, women, and children sang as enthusiastically as in a Baptist revival meeting. The powerful vibrations, combined with their compassion for the land, were like an injection into the living Earth, invigorating it with positive energy and stimulating plant growth. When rain was needed, priests or shamans supervised specific melodious dances and chants whose sounds and rhythms drew energy from clouds and dissolved them, sending moisture down to the Atlanteans' upturned faces. These stylized ceremonies not only improved the yield of their crops but also increased the people's personal strength. As they worshiped and immersed themselves in their natural surroundings, they became as one with it and partook of the energy of the universe.

Loving attention, plentiful rainfall, and ample sunshine contributed to successful agriculture in Atlantis, but it was the luxuriant soil that made unusually bountiful crops possible. The productive dirt was a mixture of volcanic ash, pumice, lava, and a small amount of sand and minerals from volcanic eruptions. Plentiful moisture ensured these materials decomposed rapidly. In the Azores today, on comparable land, the soil is extremely productive and plants grow unbelievably well. For example, clusters of long, tapering, deep blue lupines rapidly reach three feet in height, becoming so plentiful farmers plow them under for fertilizer. Colorful hydrangeas that grow wild substitute for stone walls to define the roads and picturesque fields.

The flat, fertile plain on the main island of Atlantis covered about 77,000 square miles, approximately twice the size of Indiana. Here an enormous number of industrious farmers worked to provide food for over 20 million people.[3] Today, even though it is under the surface of the Atlantic Ocean, this area, the Azores Plateau, is covered with thick, rich soil.[4] Around the plain the Atlanteans dug a canal 100 feet deep, 600 feet wide, and over 1,000 miles long that carried water from mountain streams to a 14,000 mile network of smaller canals. As these channels crisscrossed the plain, they served several functions. In addition to dividing the land into plots for individual farmers, the running water provided adequate moisture for two crops a year.[5] Farmers traveled on the canals in small boats to visit their friends. Atlanteans supplemented their irrigation system with warm mineral water from hot springs, guaranteeing that their root vegetables would grow to an enormous size.

When it rained an excessive amount, an immense natural lake in the mountains above the Azores Plateau provided storage space, protecting the main agricultural areas from floods and erosion. This very large lake, known today as the Median Valley, is under the ocean, but it is obvious on sonar.[6] When the land was above the surface, excessive rain water filled the lake to overflowing and the unnecessary fluid poured down rivers from the mountains to the canals, which carried it to the sea, thus diminishing the danger of flooded fields.

Sumerian texts describe seeds of wheat, barley, and hemp sent to Earth in the distant past as a gift from the god Anu in his Celestial Abode.[7] Archaeologists found that the earliest of these grains are uniform and highly specialized, a developmental process that requires thousands of generations of genetic selection. Agricultural scientists in Atlantis experimented for many centuries and, probably with the help of extraterrestrials, developed plants for food and medicine. We will never know how widely the visitors from outer space distributed goods and advanced knowledge, and to what extent the seafaring Atlanteans made them available to the rest of the world, but emigrants from Atlantis undoubtedly carried the roots and seeds of many plants to the lands around the Atlantic Ocean. Fifteen thousand years ago, when there was no population pressure in the Nile Valley and a plentiful food supply was readily available, farmers grew wheat and barley, which were not indigenous.[8] Since they did not grow wild there, it would have required hundreds of years and careful manipulation to produce them from wild stock. Immigrants from Atlantis, in the habit of eating these grains at home, brought them to Egypt.

In testimony of the sumptuous soil in Atlantis, gifts from extraterrestrials, and the travels of sailors since the time of Atlantis, visitors to the Azores in the nineteenth century reported that almost every type of vegetation known to humanity was growing wild in those fertile islands. These included bananas, peaches, apricots, olives, oranges, various types of palms, numerous species of cactus, aloe, figs, weeping willows, and vines. Hydrangea, geranium, and oleander were enormous, fuchsia abounded in a variety of fluorescent colors, and camellia japonica resembled large trees.[9]

Gradually, as the Atlantean civilization focused on material objects, lives changed and many ambitious families moved to the cities. The remaining farmers were overworked and pressed for time to provide the large quantities of food required for the growing urban population. They neglected customs from the past, such as planting ceremonies and rituals for communication with the devas, and ceased attempting to return to the land the nutrients they removed. Initially, Atlanteans respected the earth, wind, sun, and water, but in the process of trying to assume control over these elements to produce more food they lost respect for nature and came to regard it as something to be utilized for their own benefit. The fertility of much of the soil in Atlantis declined during its last period, dropping production even further.

And there was a further problem in Atlantis' final years. As their population expanded, to satisfy their increased need for wood for housing and for use as a simple fuel, Atlanteans indiscriminately removed trees and shrubs from mountainsides. Cayce reports that by 10,700 B.C., large quantities of precious topsoil were washing into the valleys and eventually into the sea.[10] This is similar to the erosion and destruction that is occurring on the mountainsides of Nepal and other parts of the world as needy inhabitants ignorantly cut down the trees.

SHIPPING

When restless Atlanteans experienced the urge to leave the confines of their island, they turned to the ever-present sea surrounding them for assistance in finding a new life. With leather or wood they built small crafts and cautiously ventured forth onto the water. At first these enterprising people stayed close to the coastline, carving navigational marks in large boulders on the shores, but gradually their explorations took them east and west, out into the ocean to distant lands. During the period when moisture was incorporated in the glaciers, sea levels were lower and islands consequently were larger. The nearby continental shelves were exposed and distances across the ocean were smaller.

The stars guided Atlantean sailors by night, and for further help with directions they learned about the oceans' streams, currents, and tides. As they rowed their long, narrow boats, they incorporated this knowledge into monotonous songs. A steer person in the bow chanted melodies for hours or even days and nights, simultaneously tapping the rhythm for the rowers. The songs, combined with the speed of the craft and the rate the current was moving, served as excellent maps for traveling to specific places, such as Bimini, or a likely area to find whales. When they wished to return to Atlantis, they sang the songs in reverse.

Shipbuilding and navigational techniques quickly improved in Atlantis. Boats constructed from leather hides stretched over wooden frames proved capable of providing hundreds of miles of ocean travel. Inventive sailors perfected accurate compasses from magnetic iron, such a renowned accomplishment that it is described by Sanchuniathon in *Legends of the Phoenicians*, where he says the first god of the people of Atlantis devised this tool from a type of stone that fell from heaven and had life. The prehistoric compasses he refers to were quite simple but effective. A piece of magnetic iron rested on a small slice of wood that floated in a cup or shell of water. Phoenecian writer Sanchuniathon lived in the fourteenth century B.C., and Philo of Byblos translated his works in the first century A.D. Sanchuniathon derived his information from Phoenician inscriptions on pillars and illustrations in their temples.[11] Excavations in Syria confirm much of Sanchuniathon's information on Phoenician history and religious beliefs.

When the sea no longer imprisoned them, Atlanteans grew to love its vast open expanses, its quiet, peaceful moments and its violent, challenging storms. Their mighty vessels, hundreds of feet long with banks of oars and voluminous sails, displaying the serpent as their symbol, toured the oceans. By 30,000 B.C., Atlanteans had explored the river valleys of Spain, France, the western Mediterranean, and North and South America. Their pictograph messages remain today on the rocks where they carved them. Hardy sailors rounded the tip of South America and explored the west coast of the American continent. They found tar in the pits at Rancho La Brea, on the California coast, and used it to caulk their wooden boats, making them more seaworthy and capable of further travels to Hawaii and across the Pacific Ocean. As long as 50,000 years ago, Cro-Magnons were buried near the Rancho La Brea tar pits.[12] These people had no Asian characteristics, so they must have come by sea. Only the Atlanteans were capable of such extensive travel. Two of the Atlanteans' visits to the Far East made such a strong impression that they are preserved in ancient Tibetan dances. The dances depict their guests from an island in the Atlantic as a very wealthy group on their first visit, but much poorer on the second.[13]

Astronomers of Atlantis sailed extensively, gathering information relative to eclipses for scientists of their homeland. It is necessary to cover three longitudinal bands of the Earth's surface, 120 degrees apart, to accurately predict solar and lunar eclipses.[14] In their travels, astronomers charted the sun, moon, and stars in different locations, making complicated calculations based on their observations. Ancient Greeks acquired and appreciated some of this knowledge. They were aware that our planet was round and floated in space and traveled around the sun. The Greeks also knew the relative sizes of the sun and moon and their distances from the Earth.[15]

Atlantis was the first and most important trading nation of the world. During their journeys, as the Atlanteans enriched their lives with treasures from all parts of the globe, they shared information from their advanced civilization with others. Their instructions concerning sailing and survival at sea were remembered by those who immortalized Poseidon as the god of the sea, who lived in Atlantis and was renowned for his navigational lore. The seafaring Atlanteans were responsible for transmitting knowledge pertaining to mathematics, religion, shipbuilding, metallurgy, astronomy, astrology, alchemy, medicine, architecture, and the occult to early civilizations everywhere.

Cartography

Sailors of Atlantis stored detailed maps for navigation in watertight containers onboard their ships. When land was inundated by immense floods and records and maps were lost, the ships and their containers floated safely, and some of these strongboxes eventually found their way to land.[16] The knowledge portrayed in their sea charts was copied and treasured for hundreds of centuries in the dry countries of the eastern Mediterranean and northern Africa. The voluminous libraries at Alexandria and Carthage undoubtedly contained many ancient maps. During the Dark Ages, when it was heresy to believe the world extended beyond the Pillars of Heracles, information about the lands around the Atlantic Ocean remained carefully hidden. As conditions improved in the thirteenth and fourteenth centuries, hundreds of sophisticated maps, which included details copied from the charts of Atlantean sailors, were printed in Europe and the Near East.[17]

The maps that appeared in the early Renaissance incorporate measurements of longitude although the chronometer, the device for measuring longitude, was not invented until 400 years after their fourteenth century reprinting. The details in the maps indicate that the sailors who made them had an effective chronometer. The prime meridian of these accurate maps was placed in the Atlantic Ocean at the site of Atlantis, which is another indication that Atlantean seafarers prepared them.[18]

Renaissance maps define the geography of northern Europe as it was from 13,000 B.C. to 10,000 B.C.—a glacial moraine with strange lakes on the edge of what appears to be a receding ice cap, and with glaciers in central England and central Ireland.[19] The ancient charts indicate islands directly above high points on the floor of the North Atlantic Ocean, at the locality of lost Atlantis.[20] Continental shelves west of Ireland, now under 500 feet of water, are also pictured above the surface in these early maps, just as they were before the glaciers melted around 10,000 B.C. Rivers in lands adjacent to the Atlantic Ocean are drawn without deltas, where large deltas that took thousands of years to form now meet the sea. Portolan charts (navigational maps) that appeared in Europe before A.D. 1500 depict magnetic north in the vicinity of Hudson's Bay as it was 12,000 years ago.[21]

Charts of the Atlantean sailors contributed to the Piri Re'is map of the world, discovered in the Topkapi Palace in Istanbul in 1929. Dated 1531, the old map was drawn on a gazelle hide by Admiral Piri Re'is. Notes in the margins indicate the Admiral compiled information for it from ancient Greek maps saved when the voluminous library at Alexandria was destroyed and from a map used by Columbus with whom one of the Admiral's slaves sailed.[22] The ancient map shows an island in the Atlantic just north of the equator, 700 miles east of Brazil, over the Atlantic Ridge.[23] The tiny islands of Saint Peter and Saint Paul are all that remain above the waves on the site today. Caribbean islands and the coastline of South America are all accurately located by longitude and latitude on the Piri Re'is map, as are the Azores, Canary, and Cape Verde Islands.

Information for the Piri Re'is map and the Oronteus Finaeus map of 1531 was assembled before the last Ice Age. Both charts portray the geography of Antarctica and Greenland with rivers and mountains, as they were in pre-glacial times before the land was covered with ice and snow. The cartographers who copied the maps in the thirteenth and fourteenth centuries trusted their sources and did not alter them. The extensive information that contributed to these maps was difficult to achieve from the ground and implies that surveying was done from the air.[24] As they traveled to our planet from other stars thousands of years ago, extraterrestrials carefully observed the surface of the Earth from above and were probably indirectly responsible for the unusual details in these maps.

Dangers at Sea

While at sea, the Atlanteans used their highly developed psychic abilities to forecast and predict hurricanes and other dangerous storms, but these extrasensory abilities proved inadequate for dealing with the plesiosaurus and other large man-eating monsters swimming off their shores. The hideous beasts mainly inhabited swampy areas on the west coast of Atlantis, where people traveled in small boats to fish in the relatively shallow water. Plesiosaurus were difficult to kill since they traveled under water for long periods of time at speeds of up to twenty-five miles an hour. If one of these creatures swam close to an Atlantean, the human's ordinary weapons simply annoyed it and would not penetrate its thick hide. Plesiosaurus often came to the surface just to play with and upset the flimsy crafts of the fishermen, sending the occupants into the water, where they made a delicious meal. The monsters posed such an overwhelming threat that Native Americans say Atlanteans resorted to throwing sacrificial victims to the beasts to divert their attention.[25]

Reports of three varieties of similar creatures, such as one encountered in 1969 off the west coast of Florida, suggest plesiosaurus are still with us. Lucille Hansen describes an article in a small magazine by a pre-med student at a Florida university. Five boys jumped from their boat when they heard a high-pitched whine and saw a tall, thin shape moving toward them. Four of the boys disappeared and the lone survivor heard the screams of his companions as they were devoured. Only one of their bodies was recovered, and its condition was not described, perhaps because the coast guard had warned the writer not to repeat the story, as it would provide poor publicity for the nearby resort area. Interestingly, the lone survivor described a terrible smell, which is also a characteristic of Loch Ness in Scotland.[26]

The Red Paint People

When massive floods and tidal waves swept their country, many Atlantean sailors took refuge on their well-built ships until the turmoil subsided. As soon as possible, they settled along the shores of the Atlantic Ocean, where their offspring remained, continuing to love the ocean and depend on it. Some of their descendants, now referred to as the Maritime Archaic, lived in well-organized communities on the coasts of Brittany, Denmark, Labrador, and Maine. Biological traits in the skulls and intracranial skeletons of the Maritime Archaic indicate these people were of the same race as some native North Americans.[27] They were not Eskimos. Artifacts the Maritime Archaic elaborately engraved 7,500 years ago demonstrate that these intelligent people had leisure time and highly developed minds. The Maritime Archaic are also referred to as the Red Paint people due to their sophisticated burial techniques involving red ocher, a custom that originated in Atlantis and is apparent wherever Atlanteans settled.

The Red Paint people often traveled 1,500 nautical miles from Maine to Labrador to collect special flints and slates for their tools. Stone markers, or inukshuks, stand where they placed them thousands of years ago as they sailed along the coastlines of the North Atlantic. Using simple geometric calculations, they followed these signposts from one point to the next. In their strong, seaworthy ships they also sailed far out in the ocean for swordfish and other deepwater fish.[28] The Red Paint people retained many traits and skills of their ancestors who escaped from Atlantis although, as was true of the descendants of survivors elsewhere in the world, their civilization never reached the heights previously attained in their homeland.

AVIATION

Atlanteans, hemmed in by water, were constantly aware of mi
grating birds who freely soared to faraway places. They longe
for similar freedom of flight and eventually learned to ove
come the force of gravity. Solo flight, multi-passenger vehicl
and planes that flew underwater as well as in the air were
included in their varied repertoire of aerial accomplishme
during their extensive civilizations.

Levitation

A few Atlanteans with highly developed states of conscious ss
managed to travel from place to place without vehi s.
Witches mastered gravity with mind energy and learned t se
from the ground and travel in space. Other well-cen d,
trained individuals harnessed the latent energy of the le-
cules within their own bodies and, utilizing this power, c ted
a private force, like a rotating energy field, around em-
selves.[29] With these vibrations and the power of their nds,
they dissolved their bodies, overcame the natural force rav-
ity, transferred themselves to another place, and reso fied.
These remarkable individuals, with minds capable of trol-
ling their physical selves, traveled wherever they wishe nen-
cumbered by time and space.[30]

Atlanteans employed energy from sound waves to t their
bodies and move short distances in the air. Antigravity metal
discs, similar to small trays, were tuned to the vibrations of a
person when they were still a small child. Their voice and
mental concentration provided the vibrations necessary for
movement.[31] When they sang the correct notes and simultaneously struck the disc, they rose from the ground and, with
supreme concentration, moved in the air.[32] Descendants of
Atlanteans passed down knowledge of these levitation plates,
and it has endured in stories of magic carpets in *The Arabian
Nights*. In the Caribbean island of Trinidad they say that in the
old, red land in ancient times, if people wished to climb a hill

they hit a plate, sang the appropriate song for where they wished to go, and immediately moved through the air to that spot. Folklore in Great Britain recalls that a special metal plate helped people fly down the path of a ley line. In prehistoric graves in South America, German archaeologists uncovered objects they called Klang Platten, or sound discs. The discs looked like pendants engraved with pictures of flying bats and eagles. There is no explanation for their name, but they certainly resemble the levitation plates of legends. In 1519, the Aztec king Montezuma gave Cortez two flat discs of pure gold. The plates were ten inches in diameter and round in shape with rough edges.One was one-fourth inch thick, the other thinner. These unusual gifts may have been levitation discs, made for Emperor Carlos V of Spain and his queen, although the royalty were unaware of their extraordinary function. The plates remained among the personal treasures of the Spanish crown until the abdication of King Alfonso in 1931, when they were hidden with other valuable possessions.[33]

Hot Air Balloons

In 52,000 B.C., as dangerous beasts made daily life miserable in Atlantis, it became important to consult with others, often in distant places, who were similarly threatened. Since those they wished to confer with did not have adequate means of transportation to their country, the innovative Atlanteans devised a method of conveying them. Stitching the skins of large animals together to form balloons, they created unique vehicles for transportation in the air, similar to zeppelins. The shape of the craft was determined by the proportions of the animal from whose skin it was made; therefore, some dirigibles resembled elephants or mastodons, and others looked like giant bears. Edgar Cayce carefully describes the techniques Atlanteans utilized to temper metals to make strong light braces for these unusual crafts. He says they filled the shells of these immense, strange balloons with a gas that lifted them just enough to move in the air close to the ground while carrying several passengers.[34] He also mentions Atlantean planes, which were capable of traveling underwater and were useful for transporting destructive weapons for fighting the threatening beasts.[35]

Flying Boats

Long after 52,000 B.C., human beings revived their technology to build flying machines, and the results were not totally forgotten. The Hopi and other American natives describe air travel in the distant past. Memories of ships that required neither sails nor oars and flew through the air also abound in Irish and Celtic legends. Detailed accounts from the Far East of flying vehicles in prehistoric times include aviators' accurate and realistic descriptions of the appearance of the Earth below. The *Bhagavata Purana* and the *Mahabaratha*, written in Sanskrit long ago, describe the gods arriving in flying boats, the building of aerial vehicles for the gods, and large quantities of the gods' flying ships lying at rest.[36]

Innovative Atlanteans, probably with assistance from helpful extraterrestrials, devised varied means of air transportation during their long periods of growth and development. Edgar Cayce refers to Atlantean flying vehicles similar to those Ezekiel describes in the Bible.[37] With energy from the sun, pilots raised, propelled, and directed the crafts. In a later period, strong beams from power stations in Atlantis, also fueled by the sun's energy, moved and controlled airplanes. Cayce describes another flying machine that resembled a low, flat sled. It was capable of carrying heavy loads thirty feet above the ground for long distances in a straight line. The conveyance was steered from the surface and was motivated by the crystal.[38] Rays from the crystal similarly energized small planes that carried one or two passengers and flew two to three feet above the ground.[39]

Frederick Oliver describes airships in Atlantis called *valix* that varied in size from 25 to over 300 feet. They resembled hollow needles with sharp points at each end and were constructed from sheets of a bright lightweight metal that shone in the dark. These passenger vehicles had windows in the floors and along the sides in rows like portholes, and skylights in the ceilings. Books, musical instruments, potted plants, comfortable chairs and beds made traveling a pleasure. A special repulse key enabled the planes to avoid accidental encounters with mountain tops during storms. As the Atlanteans travelled above the Earth in these planes, they frequently dropped seeds as offerings to the sun when it set.[40] Many old Indian books describe these similarly shaped, high-speed planes of the Atlanteans with exactly the same name, *valixi* being the plural.[41] In 1884, when eighteen-year-old Oliver channeled the information from Phylos the Tibetan, he could not have been familiar with the ancient Sanskrit literature.

Technology for transportation in Atlantis so long ago was different from ours but unlimited possibilities are available to us in the fields of fluidics, photonics (involving light and its uses), and magnetics.[42] Perhaps accounts of Atlantis will provide inspiration, enabling us to develop new techniques to conserve our rapidly depleting sources of energy.

EXTRATERRESTRIALS

Einstein, who said, "I worship at the temple of the skies," expressed the deep feelings of awe and wonder we all experience as we gaze at the heavens and try to comprehend the extent of the universe. The concepts that nearly forty million galaxies lie in the bowl of the Big Dipper, or that every minute ten million new stars come into being within the range of our telescopes, inspire reverence and respect. Anxiety may also accompany our thoughtful contemplation of the innumerable objects above us as we realize that, with so many possible sites for life, we probably are not alone in the universe. Recent discoveries of large planets outside our solar system that orbit nearby sun-like stars fuel the concern that other beings live out there. Are they friendly and helpful, or might they ruthlessly attack us and destroy our civilization?

In ancient times visitors from outer space to our planet were openly acknowledged and discussed, just as they are in some places in the world today. Plato describes the god Poseidon settling in Atlantis and marrying a mortal woman who bore many children. The theory that Poseidon was an extraterrestrial correlates with the descriptions in the Bible of "the sons of God who bred with the daughters of men."[43] The Bible says these renowned men of pre-Christian times were "mighty." Poseidon's superhuman feats as he constructed his home, dug huge canals and excavated for the City of the Golden Gates correlate with this description.

Edgar Cayce matter-of-factly mentions extraterrestrials in his readings. In 1938 he described vehicles coming to the Earth during the late Atlantean period, whose occupants warned of the impending destruction of Atlantis.[44] In another reading he referred to visitors from other worlds or planets who were here at the beginning of the Mayan civilization.[45]

The presence of aliens from the heavens is memorialized throughout the world in stories, myths and legends. Usually the visitors are described as gods descending to Earth from the skies. The Zulu, an African tribe that originated in prehistoric times, refer to visits of beings from outer space as the oldest thing in their history.[46] The Dogons of North Africa, whose ancestors migrated from Egypt in the distant past, have an excellent knowledge of astronomy, eclipses and the invisible star near Sirius. They maintain they acquired the information from extraterrestrials who came from the bright star Sirius and spent time with them long ago. This is affirmed by the ancient Order of Egyptian Ammonites who relate that the "Neters," who could fly in the air, move rivers and write on rocks with fingers of fire, came from out of the universe to their people. The Ammonites believe these beings married and lived with them and with the Dogons and Tutsi.[47] The Popul Vuh, from the Quiche tribes of Central America, describes visitors from the skies who used the compass, knew the world was round and understood the secrets of the universe. In the Far East ancient Brahmin books claim friends from the cosmos brought previously unknown fruits and grains to the Earth.[48]

The Bible contains references that may be attributed to extraterrestrials. The term *space vehicle* is not part of the biblical vocabulary, but *chariots*, the primary means of transportation at that time, is used instead.[49] Liftoffs are described as *whirlwinds*—"Elijah went up by a whirlwind into heaven."[50] Pilots were *charioteers*.[51] In the Bible prominent space men were sometimes referred to as the "Lord," and his vehicle was a swift cloud or cloud chariot.[52] The two "angels" who visited Lot and spent the night with him before the destruction of Sodom appear to be extraterrestrials.[53] It is quite possible that a vehicle carrying astronauts was responsible for the smoke and fire accompanying the arrival of the Lord on Mount Sinai at the time of Moses.[54] A similar occurrence is mentioned in Ezekiel 1:4–5: "As I looked, behold, a stormy wind came out of the north, and a great cloud, with brightness round about it, and fire flashing forth continually, and in the midst of the fire, as it were gleaming bronze. And from the midst of it came the likeness of four living creatures."

Extremely sophisticated accomplishments on the Earth long before our current civilization are attributed to the advice and skillful assistance of extraterrestrials. These include the huge ruins at Stonehenge and Tiahuanaco and the fortress at Sacsayhuaman, Peru, whose walls contain perfectly cut stones weighing up to 400 tons. In 4000 B.C. hunter-gatherers lived in Sumeria between the Tigris and Euphrates Rivers. Suddenly these primitive people developed a materially and spiritually advanced civilization. Their accomplishments are elaborately described in documents they wrote as early as the third millennium B.C. These include 25,000 clay tablets discovered in the early twentieth century in the library in Nineveh, the ancient royal capital. Zecharia Sitchin has carefully translated the descriptions in many of these texts relating to their temples, pyramids, astronomy, expert metallurgy, advanced mathematics and other remarkable achievements. Their medical manuals deal with human anatomy, diagnosis, prescriptions, surgical procedures and even fees payable to surgeons for successful operations. Throughout the documents the Sumerians refer to the gods who came in ships from the heavens. They resembled humans, wore helmets, possessed weapons, and were the source of the Sumerians' knowledge.[55] Who were these knowledgeable gods and goddesses? Sitchin believes the visitors to the Sumerians about 4000 B.C. descended from the tenth planet. He offers many examples from the Sumerian tablets supporting his proposition that these intelligent beings from the tenth planet came to the Earth 450,000 years ago, and thereafter visited it at 3,600-year intervals when their world's long orbit brought them closer to us.

Space beings who traveled to the Earth throughout its history also apparently came from the Pleiades, a group of about 300 stars that lie within the constellation Taurus the Bull. Although they are 400 light years from our sun, seven of these stars are visible without a telescope. References to the Pleiades, and to their inhabitants' frequent visits to the Earth, are found in almost every civilization on this planet. The Hopi and Navaho star calendar of fifty-two years is based on a cycle that correlates with the rising and setting of the Pleiades. Initiation of young men into the Hopi spiritual ways takes place only when the Pleiades are directly overhead.[56] In the Bible the Lord asks Job: "Canst thou bind the sweet influence of the

Pleiades?" Legends from Great Britain describe the Pleiades as the dwelling place of giant sky gods who once visited the Earth.[57] Callanish and many other prehistoric stone monuments in Scotland line up with the position in the sky of the Pleiades at the Equinox or other significant astronomical dates. The ancient occasion of Halloween occurs when the Pleiades are directly overhead.

Legends tell us that the idyllic land of Atlantis attracted visitors from the Pleiades, who liked it so much they decided to stay. From Dhyani Ywahoo, a twenty-seventh-generation Cherokee who shares the ancestral wisdom she received from her grandparents and great-grandparents, we learn that long ago people from the stars known as the seven dancers, or the Pleiades, reached the five islands of Atlantis and happily settled there. The Cherokee say that eventually, when many Atlanteans abused their sacred powers and grew corrupt, the islands disintegrated. With their homes in ruins, the Cherokees' Atlantean ancestors sailed westward to the American continent.[58] Atlanteans' close relationship with intelligent beings from the Pleiades is commemorated in Greek mythology where the God Atlas fathered seven daughters, the seven stars of the Pleiades. The Pleiades are characterized in occult literature as the heart for our portion of the galaxy.

Beings from the heavens are still visiting the Earth, instigating approximately 70,000 reports each year.[59] Even if a large percentage of these are mistaken, the number that remain is impressive. The presence of extraterrestrials is not acknowledged as openly today as in the distant past. Each of our recent presidents promised during his campaign to release information about UFOs, but once they were elected and briefed they would not discuss the subject. This attitude is referred to as "The Silent President Syndrome." Perhaps they feared the panic the release of information could create, as people realized that intelligent beings who developed the sophisticated technology necessary to travel to our small planet from a world hundreds of light years away are quite capable of easily destroying the human race. The current United States government policy is to suppress UFO information, but credible accounts surface regularly. When the notification of a $10,000 fine and a ten-year prison sentence to any member of the military who talked about UFOs in public was finally repealed, pilots immediately publicized 24,000 events.[60] The 500 employees of The Center for UFO Research at Northwestern University, now the Heineck Foundation, have recorded over 300,000 sightings of UFOs.

Astronauts have undergone numerous experiences with strange manned vehicles after leaving the Earth. On one trip a doctor in a United States space ship pressed the wrong button, so a comment of his was accidentally broadcast to the public. He said, "NASA, we still have the alien craft in view."[61] The world overheard another similar incident one night when astronauts were sleeping in a capsule. NASA officials in Houston warned them they were on a collision course, because their screen in Texas displayed a bright light moving directly toward the American ship. Luckily, when the unidentified object reached the craft it suddenly stopped. Because of these and a variety of similar inexplicable incidents that suggest UFOs follow and watch our vehicles when they leave the Earth's atmosphere, former shuttle astronauts are working diligently to expand our search for extraterrestrial life.

Photographs of UFOs are extremely difficult to obtain. Sophisticated observations estimate the vehicles attain speeds of 28,000 m.p.h., which allows very little time to focus a camera and shoot.[62] To compound the problem, the crafts can fly erratically, making unexpected and seemingly impossible turns. In addition, if potential photographers think about what they are doing the alien pilots seem to detect them and quickly depart from view. Filming automatically and impassionately is the most successful approach.

In spite of these difficulties, hundreds of pictures exist. At the UFO Conference at the Association for Research and Enlightenment in Virginia Beach in May 1995, astronomer James Mullaney and Ray Stanford, who founded Project Starlight International in 1964 to study UFOs as physical phenomena, projected slides of innumerable space craft. Their photographs clearly depicted vehicles of different shapes and sizes. Occasionally pictures of identical vehicles were taken within a short period of time from different parts of the Earth as the objects flew from one continent to another. Stanford also described the information obtained from computers that assist in the study of UFOs. Some are programmed to register, with a change in colors, the energy of the electromagnetic fields around the space ships as they zoom overhead. Others measure the magnetic and gravity waves the vehicles project. Recorded simultaneous gravity waves and magnetic waves suggest that extraterrestrial "intelligences" may have discovered a relationship between gravity and magnetism, something Einstein never succeeded in doing.[63]

The reverent feelings we experience as we contemplate the universe and the possibilities of other life in the distant heavens are easily overcome by fear and concern for our future safety. Perhaps visitors from the skies have wreaked terrible havoc on our planet in the past, but they also raised the standard of living in Sumeria in the third millennium to a very high level. The striking similarities between the advanced civilization in Sumeria and the Atlantean culture thousands of years earlier suggest that extraterrestrials were active in Atlantis.

6

SCIENCE

JUST AS THE ELABORATE
canal network, temples, palaces,
bridges, tunnels, and docks of the City
of the Golden Gates display the skillful
engineering talents of the Atlanteans
and their celestial advisers, so their
unique methods for procuring energy
testify to superior ability and creativity.
Time was a major factor in their
achievements, for the final Atlantean
civilization flourished for 20,000 years,
much longer than our current civilization. The Arabs, Egyptians, Greeks,
and Romans acquired fragments of scientific knowledge from Atlantis that
were preserved in the prehistoric libraries of the western world and, during the Renaissance, as curious, open-
minded scholars studied this ancient
lore, our Scientific Age was born. We

are rediscovering and mastering some, but not all, of the expertise of our ancestors.

ENERGY

Early Atlanteans acquired energy from an uncommon source that Austrian scientist and occultist Rudolph Steiner learned of from the Akashic records. The Akashic records are pictorial memories of all events, actions, thoughts, and feelings that have occurred since the beginning of time. The information is imprinted on Akasha, the astral light, that exists beyond the range of human senses. It is available to sensitive individuals while in an altered state of consciousness. From the Akashic records, Rudolph Steiner depicts these prehistoric people's ability to tap the "life force," the seed within all living things, for energy. Plants were cultivated not only for food but for the forces latent in them that Atlanteans transferred into power.[1] For instance, when we plant a grain of corn we water it, but basically we just have to "wait for nature to take its course." Atlanteans devised a means of transforming a pile of grain into active energy. Researcher John Michell refers to a similar concept of the aborigines of Australia, whose civilization has changed very little in 40,000 years. They believe that all things will release life energy if the proper rituals are performed.[2]

Sonic Levitation

Early in their civilization, when their bodies and minds were fully aware, aligned, and balanced, the Atlanteans perfected sonic levitation to lift large objects for use in buildings and monuments. Employing intense group concentration to direct the energy from sound waves, they raised and lowered massive blocks of stone without machinery.[3] To accomplish this amazing feat, several people linked arms, and to the noise of drums and cymbals, danced in circles around an immense boulder, chanting loudly in a prescribed manner. As they focused on the large rock, their intense mental strength combined with the energy from the pulsations of sound to raise and lower the heavy object. In time, engineers perfected sonic gongs tuned to the correct pitch of the moving substance to supplement and eventually replace the vibrations from people's shouting voices and stamping feet.[4] When a gong was struck, if the tone was precisely controlled so that it resonated to the material to be moved and the note was prolonged while everyone concentrated, gravity was overcome and the object rose in the air to the desired location. It is possible that the ability to move large objects with sound was retained and used when the pyramids were constructed in Egypt, for Sumerian tablets state that sound can lift stone.

On a smaller scale, it is possible to perceive how the Atlanteans accomplished their feats with sound and focused mental power. The Russians experimented with focused mind energy and succeeded in moving small articles without touching them.[5] Another example comes from the village of Shivapur, in western India, where visitors participate in lifting a granite stone weighing 120 pounds. Following careful instructions, eleven persons place themselves around this boulder, touching it with their right forefingers. As they chant in loud ringing tones the name of Qamar Ali Dervish, the patron saint of the nearby mosque, the rock slowly rises into the air, and then crashes to the ground. Other sounds have no effect on gravity's power over the boulder.[6] Both Central and South American traditions claim that long ago sound was used to move gigantic stone building blocks in the air. An ancient Chinese poem says: "In olden days rocks used to walk. Is this true or false? In olden days the rocks could walk. This is true not false."[7]

Energy from the vibrations of sound is demonstrated in a variety of other ways. In 1891, John Worrell Keeley started an engine in his laboratory in New York with energy from the pulsation of tones from the strings of a violin. When the correct notes were played, it started a motor twenty feet away. Discords on the violin stopped the engine. Keeley also conducted innovative and successful procedures to overcome gravity, but in spite of his unequaled experiments, or perhaps because of them, he suffered much ridicule. One night when he was depressed and discouraged, he burned all his papers, destroyed his models and apparatus, and died.[8] More recently, sonic levitation was employed in a space shuttle. Sound waves securely held glass in suspension while it was experimentally melted and shaped into a delicate lens. This amazing act is possible because in the space vehicle, due to the absence of gravity, less intense sound is required for levitation. Once this process is perfected, optical engineers will successfully create thinner, more complicated lenses with fewer layers of material.[9]

Electromagnetic transducers, piezoelectric quartz crystals, and special whistles are other examples of energy from the reverberations of sound. They all produce strong ultrasonic vibrations above people's hearing range. Sonar, which is helpful in mapping ocean bottoms, is a well-known use of ultrasonic waves. Employed properly, ultrasound is capable of increasing molecular motion in liquids, generating heat, cracking solids, and killing germs. Ultrasound is also a well-known diagnostic technique that provides physicians with images of internal organs. If the vibrations of ultrasonic waves are strong enough, they are capable of killing animals and people, as do equally powerful infrasonic vibrations below people's hearing.[10] As we relearn and employ the power of sound waves, it is possible to comprehend the Atlanteans' astonishing ability to harness it and move large rocks.

Gasses and Lasers

The people of Atlantis constantly experimented with obtaining energy from natural sources. Following the final conference in 50,722 B.C., as they tried to rid their land of the dangerous large animals that were overrunning it, generation after generation of scientists worked intensely to devise weapons for defense against the beasts. Toxic gases were one of their first attempts. When the noxious fumes were ready, desperate Atlanteans optimistically used the wind to blow them into large caves where the dreaded animals lived.[11] Only the young beasts died, and erratic breezes wafted the dreadful poisons toward unsuspecting human onlookers. Simultaneously, the disturbed larger animals left their sheltered homes and, like a swarm of angry bees, furiously attacked anything or anyone within range. For hundreds of years Atlanteans continued to search for means of combating the obnoxious animals. They developed various types of explosives that were advantageous but also difficult to control.[12] Edgar Cayce describes powerful rods, similar to lasers, that skilled Atlantean technicians focused on the beasts from a central location.[13] The intense light killed some, but not enough to alleviate the problem. Lasers are an example of the many things in Cayce's readings that seemed unlikely at the time he described them but later proved accurate. Lasers were reinvented in the 1960s, thirty years after his references to them.

Nuclear Power

Continued experimentation eventually led to the development of nuclear power. Seafaring merchants brought uranium to laboratories in Atlantis from mines adjacent to rivers leading to the ocean, such as the one in nearby Gabon, West Africa, which was mined extensively in antiquity. Probably with considerable advice from their celestial visitors, scientists exposed the dangerous material to vast streams of energy from the heat of the sun and managed to split the atom. Before long, nuclear power was available.[14] It proved valuable for destroying large animals, but Edgar Cayce says its misuse soon stimulated earthquakes and intense volcanic eruptions, initiating the first major devastation of Atlantean civilization around 50,700 B.C.[15] Nuclear energy was also available in the last period of Atlantis, for the dreadful effects of the perilous weapons the Atlanteans used in a battle in India are described in detail in the *Mahabharata* and the *Ramayana*.[16] The manuscripts portray a fierce contest culminating in a blinding explosion from a bomb, and a cloud of rising smoke that gradually expanded into great round circles. Burning elephants crashed to the earth and birds flying in the air above turned white. Human survivors waded into streams, attempting to rid themselves of ash falling from the sky. Their teeth and nails eventually fell out. Skeletons, later determined to be radioactive, were excavated from beneath the ancient Indian cities of Mohenjo-daro and Harappa.[17] The positions of the bodies imply they fell while running from something.[18]

There are other accounts of destruction, apparently resulting from the uncontrolled employment of nuclear power in prehistory. In the Euphrates Valley in 1947, archaeologists excavating through many layers of civilization eventually uncovered a cave culture that lived on a hard surface of fused glass. The composition of the ground under their homes was similar to the desert floor in Alamogordo, New Mexico, after the testing of the first atomic bomb.[19] Zecharia Sitchin believes extraterrestrials instigated nuclear blasts in the Sinai peninsula in 2023 B.C. Sumerian texts describe the dense cloud that rose to the sky followed by "rushing wind gusts" and a furiously scorching tempest.[20] In the aftermath, everything died and only sickly plants grew on the banks of the Tigris and Euphrates.[21] When Dr. Oppenheimer, who was instrumental in the development of the atomic bomb, was asked after the first successful test explosion if that was the first atomic bomb, he is reported to have said that it was the first in *modern* history.[22]

Crystal Energy

During their long civilizations, Atlanteans developed other sources of energy that are relatively new to us. Struggling to rebuild in 48,000 B.C., scientists accepted help from beings from outer space as they researched with crystals to utilize energy from the sun.[23] They placed a large piece of precisely cut quartz crystal in the peak of a tower that served as a solar type converter. In this exposed location, close to the heavens, the facets of the crystal caught energy from the rays of the sun, just as parabolic mirrors do today. The Atlantean building was lined with a nonconducting material similar to asbestos, perhaps serpentine.[24] Edgar Cayce describes the crystal and its housing in detail, including the information that the roof above the stone was movable, to admit sunlight as required.[25] Employing this sun power, Atlantean engineers operated a wide variety of useful machinery, which did not pollute the environment. Sadly, in 28,000 B.C., a fateful accident occurred, and large quantities of potent energy stored underground exploded. The resulting shocks disturbed the delicate seismic balance of the Earth's crust, contributing to earthquakes that once again aroused the ever-eager volcanoes. Knowledge of the crystal was carefully preserved, and during much of the 20,000 years of the final civilization, the sun's rays once again provided energy for Atlanteans.

Crystals that transmit and redirect currents of energy may still be active in the North Atlantic. In 1989, the crew of a Russian submarine reported that several hundred miles east of the Azores, while filming the ocean floor, the sub's engines stopped suddenly and the instrument needles quivered and ran backwards. The crew acted strangely and did not feel well. This state of affairs lasted approximately fifteen minutes before conditions returned to normal. It was as if a mysterious energy field affected the submarine and its occupants. The captain requested permission to dock at Ponta Delgada in the Azores to obtain immediate psychiatric treatment for his terrified crew.

Ship and airplane personnel who travel through or across the Bermuda Triangle, a large area in the Atlantic Ocean east of Florida and the Bahamas, tell similar stories. Many ships and low-flying planes disappear in the Bermuda Triangle, for engines sometimes lose their power and their compasses and other navigational equipment may behave erratically or even cease to function. On November 9, 1956, a P5M patrol bomber with a crew of ten vanished. Its mission was classified, but it was carrying an instrument for studying magnetic flux density or abnormal magnetic phenomena.[26]

There is a possibility we will eventually learn more details of the Atlanteans' successful research with crystals to obtain power from the sun's rays. Edgar Cayce says records of their solar-type converters are accessible in three places in the world. One is in the sunken portion of Atlantis near Bimini; another is in Egypt in the Tomb of Records that "was a part of the Hall of Records, which has not yet been uncovered. It lies between—or along that entrance from the Sphinx to the temple—or the pyramid; in a pyramid, of course, of its own."[27] As to the third, in a reading on December 20, 1933, Cayce said: "In Yucatan there is the emblem of same. Let's clarify this, for it may be the more easily found for they will be brought to this America, these United States. A portion is to be carried, as we find, to the Pennsylvania State Museum. A portion is to be carried to the Washington preservations of such findings, or to Chicago."[28] None of this information has surfaced, although scientists have recently discovered cavities under and around the Sphinx.

Magnetic Fields and Ley Lines

Atlanteans respected their surroundings and, while working in a manner similar to dowsers, became aware of a natural flow of magnetic energy that covers the surface of our planet. The source of this terrestrial magnetism is in the molten iron in the outer core of the Earth's interior. The constant motion of free electrons in the liquid iron generates a current that produces a magnetic field.[29] The intensity of the magnetic field on our planet's surface varies from place to place, from day to day, and over long periods of time. Its strength, as depicted on isomagnetic charts, is measured horizontally and vertically. Fluctuations in the Earth's magnetic field disturb radio communications and are sometimes responsible for aurora borealis, colored rays of light that irregularly appear in the northern skies. At the current time the intensity of our magnetic field is decreasing by six percent every one hundred years. If the trend continues at the present rate, the field will be gone in 1,500 years.[30]

UFOs tend to travel on certain straight lines, which have magnetic characteristics, across the Earth's surface.[31] It is likely that extraterrestrials taught Atlanteans to channel fluctuating magnetic energy surrounding the Earth and move it along tracks for their own use. There is no evidence of another civilization in prehistoric times sufficiently advanced to construct the tracks now referred to as ley lines. The ley lines of England are well known, but these perfectly straight, humanmade paths are visible from the air on every continent. The lines stretch for hundreds of miles over all sorts of terrain, deep into valleys and directly up high hills. In Great Britain, churches, mounds, crossroads, cemeteries, mark-stones, castles, and fords identify ley lines. Although these landmarks are sometimes many miles apart, they are precisely aligned in one direction.[32] Later civilizations converted ley lines to roads, but since they go directly over natural obstacles, like steep hills, and do not follow contours of the land, this was not their sole original purpose. Little is remembered about the strange ley lines except that mysterious currents (perhaps channeled magnetic energy) flowed along the paths.

Considering the immense time and effort expended all over the Earth to construct ley lines, they must have served a worthy function for our predecessors, perhaps assisting in communication or in transportation of people and objects. Legends say that at times when the sun shined directly down one of these courses at sunrise, Druids rose in the air and moved along them.[33] In Australia the aborigines travel on long, straight routes as they have for thousands of years. Using specific old paths, they gain energy as they walk, accomplishing longer, more difficult journeys than on new roads. The minds of people in places of high natural energy provide extra strength to their bodies if they strongly believe an act is feasible.[34] Combining the power from their minds with magnetic energy and sound, it is imaginable that Atlanteans and their descendants moved large objects, as well as themselves, in the air along ley lines.

Ley lines are abundant in China, where the power of terrestrial magnetism continued to be recognized long after the rest of the world forgot. The Chinese call it the dragon force and include it in their science of geomancy or feng shui. To ascertain the strength of the magnetic field at a given location, they fully analyze the features of the land and carefully consider appropriate astrological influences. With the resulting information, the Chinese builders thoughtfully arrange every structure and the nearby trees and boulders so that all is in harmony with the Earth's surface. In the past, care and ingenuity produced an elaborate, sensitive, balanced landscape capable of supporting a very dense population. Following the example of prehistoric peoples, the Chinese built cities, homes, and tombs where they and the dead lived harmoniously with nature, taking advantage of the energy from the subtle forces of the Earth's terrestrial magnetism.

Although the Earth's magnetic field is considerably weaker today than when Atlanteans experimented with it, scientists are rediscovering wisdom of the past as they explore ways to take advantage of this potential source of power. Several years ago Lowell Ponte, a former Pentagon specialist in exotic weapons technology, reported that the Russians built a transmitter complex whose purpose was to alter the Earth's magnetic field on the longitude of the pyramid at Giza, which is on the longitude of Salonika, Greece. Shortly thereafter, in 1978, Salonika was shaken by strong earthquakes.[35]

Unexpected results of contemporary scientists' investigations as they experiment with magnetism and its relation to time suggest we are not quite ready to fully utilize this available source of energy. The Atlantean civilization was in existence a great deal longer than ours before it was able to manipulate space and time or utilize powerful magnetic currents that circle the Earth. In an attempt to bring World War II to an end, under the auspices of the Rainbow Project, the Navy instigated the Philadelphia Experiment, an attempt to make a ship undetectable by radar. Due to problems with experiments on July 22, 1943, and August 12, 1943, the project was culminated. On those dates, while docked at the Philadelphia Naval Yard, the USS *Eldridge* completely disappeared from view and was invisible on radar screens. In each case, when the switches were pulled and the vessel reappeared, the crew members displayed extreme mental instability. The bodies of some were intermingled with the metal of the ship's bulkheads, others were burning or floating in the air.[36] Despite extensive rehabilitation, those who survived suffered permanent mental disorientation and were discharged as "mentally unfit."[37] Similar secret research continued for three decades at the abandoned U.S. Air Force base at Montauk, Long Island. Scientists eventually realized their experiments attempting to utilize magnetism to manipulate space and time were doing irreparable damage to the people involved and the project was abandoned.[38] It has been suggested that beings from Sirius aided the research in these very secret undertakings,[39] and that other extraterrestrials were involved.[40]

Magnetic energy is apparent at ancient stone circles and buildings along ley lines where power is available from both above and below. These early sacred sites frequently coincide with centers of magnetic activity where strips of energy circling just above the earth interact.[41] Stone landmarks oriented toward an astronomical event in the heavens, such as the rising of the sun or moon or a constellation at a solstice, also transmit power. Our distant ancestors placed stone pillars and churches over areas where streams intersected deep underground, so the monuments acted like acupuncture needles, bringing spirals of energy from above and below to the living Earth.[42] Scientists are slowly explaining the phenomena as they learn that these columns seem to attract a kind of electric current. In the past, the heat apparently intensified to the point where it even fused the stones, as in the barrow near Maughold in the Isle of Man.[43]

Descendants of Atlanteans, sensing the power in the areas of strong magnetic energy, used them for religious activities and eventually built temples in these potent places. As time went by, new civilizations, realizing the strength of the age-old locations, built their houses of worship over the original foundations.[44] The French cathedral at Chartres and many other sacred buildings stand over powerful prehistoric religious sites. Most small churches at crossroads in England are located at a spot where religious activities have taken place for over 2,000 years.

Star Power

While some scientists in Atlantis worked with the natural currents circling the Earth, others concentrated on astrology and astronomy. Highly trained individuals intensely studied the skies, believing the sun, moon, and stars, as manifestations of the one all-powerful god, exerted influence over this planet and its inhabitants. In the City of the Golden Gates, in the uppermost area of the Temple of Poseidon, a well-equipped observatory was available to the Atlantean astronomers, who devoted their time to recording the movements of the heavenly bodies as they sought to predict the will of the gods who controlled the star people.

The signs of the zodiac and the names for the constellations date to before 10,000 B.C. when, in the Temple of Poseidon, and maybe with the supervision and help of extraterrestrials, the Atlanteans identified the star formations as personalities and gave them lives of their own. As they studied and named the stars, the Atlanteans took account of the Pleiades' reverence for the bull and named their home Taurus the bull. Thousands of years later the Sumerians, working with their gods from heaven, divided the zodiac into twelve sections and used the same names for the celestial bodies.[45] A Sumerian tablet in the Berlin Museum (VAT.7847) begins the list of zodiacal constellations with the Age of Leo,[46] from 10,970 B.C. to 8810 B.C. Greek scholars, the source of much of our information, copied the Sumerians' science of astronomy, including the signs of the zodiac and how to predict solar eclipses.[47] Fragments of astronomical knowledge from the Atlanteans that were stored in the vast libraries of the prehistoric world were also available to the Greek sages.

Reminders of the astronomical wisdom of the Atlanteans remain with us today. The god Atlas was an astrologer, and his perception that the world was a round globe is demonstrated in the myth that he carried the world on his shoulders. Lunar calendars incised on bone in western Europe in 28,000 B.C. demonstrate the careful and exact measurements observers of the stars made at that time as well as the people's ability to execute and understand abstract mathematical calculations of astronomy.[48] A painting on the ceiling of a chapel in a temple in Dendarah, Egypt, not far from Luxor, depicted the signs of the zodiac as they appeared in the sky between 10,970 B.C. and 8810 B.C., with Leo at the point of the vernal equinox. The aged temple rested on the foundation of earlier buildings dating to before 3000 B.C. In 1821 archaeologists removed the chapel's complete ceiling and its unusual painting and carried it to France, where it is preserved in the Louvre Museum in Paris.

There was an additional reason for the emphasis on astronomy in Atlantis. The amount of energy in the Earth's magnetic field is affected by the relative positions of the sun, moon, and planets.[49] For instance, at the time of a full moon, magnetic activity is stronger near noon and quieter at sunset.[50] When an eclipse takes place, as the magnetic activity normally stimulated by the eclipsed body decreases, the flow of energy diminishes.[51] Advance warning of eclipses was essential to Atlanteans, for if an eclipse occurred, the energy conducted along ley lines suddenly weakened and all movement on the mysterious paths immediately ceased. Objects or people in the air would crash to the ground. The precise placement of pillars in many of the stone circles in Great Britain reveals the accuracy with which prehistoric astrologers predicted lunar eclipses. Terror of the effects of eclipses was so strong in ancient times that a similar anxiety is still prevalent throughout the world.

Symbolic Energy

Single, double, and triple spirals, common symbols in Atlantis, represented the natural forces and physical energy. Wherever Atlanteans traveled, people who interacted with them learned to correlate these signs with unseen power and with Atlantis, the coiled sleeping serpent. Just as the curved serpent symbolized Atlantis, so the dragon stood for China. Irish folklore offers the saying "Knowledge, under the rule of the Golden serpent, was mostly to be found in the West, while Wisdom, an entirely different thing, was to be found under the rule of the Golden Dragon, in the East."[52]

Indigenous people in the lands influenced by the Atlanteans continued to regard the serpent as a symbol of strength long after the powerful country disappeared. Serpent signs embellish many monuments in Great Britain and in this continent. In ancient Egypt, the serpent with a forked tongue and a double penis signified the union of the higher and the lower intellect.[53] The Vikings, descendants of the oceangoing Atlanteans, decorated the front of their mighty ships with carved serpents. The Aztecs of Central America worshiped the sacred serpent, and when a strange man with a white beard appeared from the ocean bringing them civilization, they named him Quetzal-coatl. *Quetzal* stood for the quetzal bird, meaning the sky, and *coatl* meant serpent, for the powerful forces of the Earth.[54]

Other Sources of Energy

With ingenuity, skill, and an ability to seek and accept advice, Atlantean scientists obtained energy in a variety of other ways. They utilized the power of water from rapidly flowing mountain streams and succeeded in harnessing the tides.[55] At one time they developed internal combustion engines operated with carbon fuels. However, when they realized the disastrous consequences of the machines' emissions on the atmosphere, they abandoned them for cleaner, more efficient methods, such as crystals that transmitted energy from the sun.[56]

The ever-burning light, employed for sacrifices in the Temple of Incal near the capital city, offers another example of the superior technology Atlanteans attained. The strange light was capable of changing the atomic structure of an object by altering its rate of vibration until it disintegrated.[57] Solar-charged crystals shined with a blue-white light to relieve the darkness in Atlantis after the sun went down.[58] The ability to produce artificial light survived in Egypt, where it permitted diligent artists to paint on windowless walls of tombs in the depths of dark buildings for innumerable hours. No traces of blackened soot from the smoke of oil lamps or torches is visible on these walls. Our civilization has developed tritium gas-phosphor lamps, which shine for a generation or more without electricity.

From the four elements of nature—earth, air, fire, and water—Atlanteans acquired energy to meet their needs and to enhance their daily lives. The earth offered terrestrial magnetism and materials for toxic gases and nuclear power, the air contained the vibrations of sound waves, fire from the sun was projected through the crystal, and water supplied the force of the rivers and tides. The civilization of the intelligent, resourceful, and intuitive Atlanteans advanced rapidly.

MEDICINE

Thoughtful Medicine

Atlanteans enjoyed excellent physical and mental health as long as they maintained a close relationship with the features of their natural surroundings and incorporated them into their daily activities. They believed all healing ultimately comes from the universal force present in the natural world, and finally from within ourselves. In times of stress Atlanteans put their arms around a healthy, living tree for the strength it offered, or simply paused to appreciate the perfume of a flower, the intense colors of a sunrise, a flirtatious butterfly, or a bird's lilting song.

Regular worship at the sacred sites of standing stones provided opportunities to tune into the unlimited harmony of the universe. The people of Atlantis believed the powers of the stones increased fertility, produced miraculous cures, prolonged life, and resolved mental problems. Potent faith in the healing ability of the stones helped to provide the peace of mind that maintained strong immune systems, increasing their bodies' resistance to infection. Some groups of stones in Great Britain that continue to realign and utilize natural energy are said to cure rheumatism; others are considered effective against fever or paralysis.[59]

Aware of the power of thoughts over the body, Atlantean healers devised unique methods for diagnosing illness. They carefully examined their patients' auras for information in regard to his or her mental state. Auras are fields of colored light, or fluctuating rays of energy, surrounding our bodies, which become more intense with increased concentration or mental activity.[60] From an early age, Edgar Cayce perceived bands of color around people. It was not until he was an adult that he realized auras were not visible to everyone. He enjoyed talking with others who observed auras and comparing notes relating to the meaning of the colors. Cayce learned that when a person is under stress, their aura shifts in color and shape, offering tips to the astute observer of the presence of fear, insecurity, greed, worry, and other deep troubles.[61] This change of color was utilized in Atlantis, where dogs were trained to observe auras and employed to detect liars in difficult situations.

Early religious painters often portrayed auras around people's heads. Today these energy fields are documented by Kirlian photography. In 1961, Valentina Kirlian published a scientific report describing the work of her husband, Semyon Davidovitch Kirlian, a Soviet electrician, who utilized corona discharge photography to photograph the rays of light around leaves, insects, animals, and human beings. Corona discharge photography is chiefly used to detect flaws in metal. Kirlian photography, as it came to be called, is a potentially valuable tool in physical and medical diagnosis and exploring our hidden spiritual dimensions, since in the western world it is usually necessary to see to believe.[62]

In addition to unique techniques for prevention and diagnosis of illness, the Atlanteans developed a variety of methods for alleviating physical problems. Primarily they turned to their bountiful natural surroundings for assistance. Noting the vigor and brilliant colors of foliage around their bubbling springs, they experimented with the waters. They learned that pleasant tasting water from cold springs possessed favorable digestive powers and created an almost instant appetite. Atlanteans who watched animals with cuts in their skin roll in the mud around certain hot springs or stand for hours in the spray and mist discovered this excellent cure for external abrasions, ulcers, infections, and arthritis.

The wide variety of plants growing in Atlantis and its colonies in prehistory offered as many possibilities for curing aches and pains and ways to promote healing as are found in the modern pharmacy. They included antiseptics, narcotics, quinine for malaria, hallucinatory drugs, and herbs to stimulate the heart. Medicinal plants provided treatment for fevers, dysentery, worms, and most medical disorders for many centuries. Cures dating to the time of Atlantis, such as kaolin for the prevention of stomach maladies, are being rediscovered, but the hands of time have torn many pages from the book of history and a substantial amount of invaluable lore will never be available to us. The Spaniards destroyed the medical documents of the Aztecs and Mayans in Central America, and medicine men in North America chose not to share their extensive knowledge with the European invaders, although they kindly helped many early settlers successfully treat their medical problems. In the early twentieth century, valuable opportunities for communication with indigenous healers were dismissed by physicians who believed modern scientific chemotherapy offered adequate replacements for the plant cures of the past.

The priests of long ago knew that the mind and body continuously interact, each affecting the well-being of the other. As they presided at births and deaths and assisted with physical ailments, their rituals convinced the patient that all would go well. Priests were also adept at utilizing energy from higher sources to treat difficulties. If a patient was in pain from a serious injury, the healer smoked a pipe filled with a mixture of the appropriate narcotic herbs and chanted until the person entered a trancelike state, where he or she was more susceptible to the reverberations that the priest-healer directed. If all went well, the focused vibrations corrected imbalances in the patient's metabolism, facilitating its ability to repair the body's problem. Healers worked in pyramids, where energy channeled from the universe was more readily available. The Navaho place healing centers one third of the way up a pyramid-shaped building, where the power is strongest.[63]

Color for Healing

Color helped with diagnosis. The color of the clothing a person wore often reflected their mental condition.[64] Atlanteans also understood that, as well as being helpful in diagnosis, color promoted healing. Light, which makes color, consists of electromagnetic vibrations. As the frequency of the pulsation of the vibrations in light varies, the color changes. Invalids spent time in rooms painted the hue that best served their needs and focused on the color, absorbing its vibrations of energy for the beneficial effect on their neuroendocrine systems. Neuroendocrine systems are color sensitive and variations in light affect the body's production of hormones. This knowledge survived until the sixth century B.C., when Greek scientist and philosopher Pythagoras employed color for healing.[65] Red, the color of life, was considered useful for headaches, diseases of the blood, circulation, weakness, and depression. School rooms were often painted yellow, for it encouraged intellectual and mental creativity, health, and well-being. Orange combined the wilder attributes of red with discipline from yellow and was used for treating chest conditions and troubles of the spleen and kidneys. Healers utilized blue, representing serenity and harmony, for cleansing, for the treatment of nervous irritations, and to reduce fever. Since it influenced the organs of sight, hearing, and smell, blue was considered beneficial for treatment of diseases of the eye, ear, and nose; for example, a blue scarf worn at the neck was helpful for a sore throat with a fever. Green, a mixture of yellow and blue, offered relief from emotional disorders, and individuals learned to focus their eyes and thoughts on verdant trees and grass in times of distress. Walls and ceilings of Atlantean birthing rooms were inlaid with sparkling green crystals, providing a beautiful sight and feeling to a being as it entered the world.[66] Priests preferred to wear clothes of a very deep blue to raise their consciousness to a spiritual level. Purple, the mixture of red (action) and blue (spirituality and calmness), improved nervous problems, rheumatism, and epilepsy.[67]

Sound as Medicine

Pitch, intensity, and timbre of sound influence the blood pressure, circulation, pulse, respiration, metabolism, and muscular energy.[68] Flutists, drummers, and dancers visited indisposed persons and employed sound to cure the body. As the musicians sang and danced around the patient, they encouraged him or her to join them. Positive vibrations from the participants, as they entered into a deep trancelike state resulting from the repetitive sounds, aligned and balanced the body and mind of the sick person. Spontaneous remission of illness was possible. Specific melodies or mantras were assigned for a given problem, and drawings of the human body indicated the appropriate musical scale for the afflicted region. The pentatonic, or five-tone scale, comparable to the black notes on the piano, was the basis of the most simple therapy, but healers also used a wide variety of notes, including half tones, for their influence on the body.

Metal and Stone Healing Aids

Atlanteans employed metals, such as copper, gold, and silver, and precious stones, including sapphires, rubies, emeralds, and topaz, to prevent illness and advance healing. They knew that, like their bodies, each substance has its own intrinsic vibrations created by the minute atomic particles within it. Individuals sensed which element was best suited to their needs and elaborately decorated themselves with it for added strength and insight. Temples, their walls lined with lapis lazuli, provided an effective atmosphere for spiritual healing. The interiors of these useful buildings resembled a large, deep blue cave, where small lights added vitality as they shone on the sparkling pieces of iron compound in the stone.

Crystals were used extensively for medical treatment in At-

lantis. Color changes in large crystals helped experienced healers determine the location of physical ailments. As the keen di-
agnostician slowly moved the clear stone over the patient's
body, slight changes in the stone's hue indicated a change in
vibrations at a troublesome site.[69] Healing ceremonies that employed crystals to focus beneficial energies on an ill person
were a common event, for they were effective in reenergizing
bodies, enhancing the patients' strength, and prolonging lives.
Large crystals that absorbed positive forces from the nearby atmosphere were positioned so as to disperse it to nearby persons. The patient sat on the floor in a yoga position, or lay on
a low couch surrounded with clear crystals. She, or he, held an
additional crystal in each hand while the healer solemnly
arranged more of the bright stones on the top of her head (the
most important site), her navel, on her third eye (the center of
the forehead just above the eyes), and on other receptive areas
of her body.[70] Friends who were present used deep meditation
to send healing energy through the crystals, which expanded it
and transmitted it to the invalid.

Surgery was occasionally necessary in Atlantis, but it was
not an unpleasant experience, for hypnotism provided an excellent anesthetic, ensuring that the patient suffered neither
pain nor unpleasant aftereffects. Atlanteans perfected a surgical knife equivalent to a laser and considerably more powerful.
Edgar Cayce mentions that if the tool was used in conjunction
with certain metals, when the surgeon cut veins and arteries,
the blood coagulated and there was no bleeding.[71] Perhaps it
was similar to the gamma knife we employ in brain surgery.
Healer priests performed surgery without knives, ensuring that
the patient did not experience pain, bleeding, or scarring from
cutting the skin and tiny blood vessels. Utilizing a mysterious
energy, the healer's hands effortlessly entered the body, parted
the skin and tissues, and repaired damage or removed tumors.

To picture the procedure, imagine a mass of ping-pong balls immersed in hardened wax in a bucket. Once the wax is warmed, it is possible to put your hands between the balls, just as the surgeon's hands passed between the cells, separating them without cutting.[72] Reports of healers in the Philippines and South America describe their success removing tumors in this manner.[73]

Extraterrestrial visitors supervised the early Sumerians, who experimented with heart and brain surgery, and presumably they did the same for the Atlanteans. Sumerian medical texts from the library of Ashurbanipal in Nineveh, written about 3000 B.C., contain three sections—therapy, surgery, and commands and incantations. They include instructions about washing hands, using alcohol as a disinfectant, and directions for removing the "shadow covering a man's eye," probably a cataract.[74] Skeletons of graves in Sumeria of that period exhibit brain surgery and other orthopedic operations.[75] In ancient Peru, a common destination of visitors from outer space, surgeons replaced damaged bone in skulls with gold or copper plates.[76] Archaeologists excavating in the ruins of the ancient South American city of Tiahuanaco in Bolivia were surprised to unearth skulls dating to the time of Atlantis with evidence of skillful open-brain surgery and well-healed bone grafts.[77] They also found drills and chisels of high-grade copper for use in these operations in Tiahuanaco.[78]

Dentists in Atlantis cleaned cavities noiselessly, quickly, and efficiently with light from laser beams. No painkiller or anesthetic was necessary. In ancient Peru, dentists capped teeth with gold or silver,[79] and in prehistoric Central America, they filled cavities with gold and jade.[80] Presumably dentists in Atlantis followed similar procedures.

Electrotherapy, combined with hydrotherapy or music, effectively restored movement after paralysis in Atlantis.[81] Similar tools today are the Electro Acuscope, which shoots a tiny electric current into nerve tissue, and the Myopulse, which performs essentially the same function on muscle tissue. The goal is to produce a state of homeostasis, or equilibrium, among cells in the injured area, thus permitting healing to take place at a faster rate.[82]

Longevity Attempts

Like most of us, our ancestors wanted to live longer and they experimented with various ways of increasing their life span. Aware of the power of the energy present in the physical world, they strove to capture and utilize it in unique ways. This natural flow of energy that is present in every particle of matter provides the medium through which magnetic and gravitational forces exert a positive influence on the human body. The late Dr. Wilhelm Reich rediscovered the force and called it orgone energy. He described his experiments with it in *The Discovery of the Orgone.* One widespread attempt that prehistoric peoples used to increase the concentration of orgone energy and expose themselves to it required elaborate preparation. First the builder dug a large pit, similar to a small cellar hole, and lined the chamber with carefully chosen stones. After placing logs across the top, he or she covered the roof with a layer of turf and successive layers of clay and earth. The particular color and type of dirt were carefully selected at each stage, for it was essential to alternate layers of organic and inorganic matter. All was buried under a high mound of sod. After cleansing and balancing themselves, individuals retired to these underground rooms, believing the energizing currents they absorbed there would rejuvenate their bodies and minds.[83] A pit at Stonehenge, lined with bluestones from 100 miles away, is typical of many similar cavities in the British Isles.

Multitudes regularly patronized the temples in Atlantis, where facilities that strengthened and extended the life of both the body and the mind were available. In these impressive buildings, and outside on their well-kept grounds, hundreds of energetic people of all ages danced and exercised. Quiet spaces, where soothing musical tones calmed emotions and reduced stress, offered opportunities for meditation.

Edgar Cayce tells us that the ingenious Atlanteans used crystals to burn destructive forces from the body in a way that encouraged it to rejuvenate itself.[84] In *The Romance of Atlantis,* Taylor Caldwell describes a secret rejuvenation chamber in a temple in the City of the Golden Gates where this procedure was successfully accomplished. Priests carefully guarded the powerful room and allowed only a few respected leaders of the country to enter. While in the chamber, the patient reclined in a comfortable chair, and technicians precisely focused the sun's rays through a crystal onto the elderly body. Simultaneously, the healers produced and magnified varied frequencies of sound, whose energy regenerated the tiny molecules of each cell, reactivating aging tissues.[85] The operation restored the person's hormone balance, wrinkles disappeared, and energy returned. Skill and caution were important, since if the crystal was tuned too high it destroyed the body.[86] One visit was usually adequate, for Atlanteans learned that as they grew older, like one too many days at Disneyland, events they once enjoyed offered less satisfaction when repeated several times. The pervasive sense that it had all happened before made life boring, and the prospect of spending more time in the physical body was not as appealing as the pleasant experience that awaited them after their departure from the Earth.[87]

DESTRUCTION AND NEW BEGINNINGS

PART III

7

DESTRUCTION

AROUND 10,000 B.C., THE self-centered leaders of Atlantis lost interest in material and scientific pro– gress, and their respect for the ancient knowledge vanished. As these powerful Black Priests dedicated their energies to dangerous occult practices, black magic gradually replaced religion in Atlantis. Some mastered the technique of con- juring spirits, not from the higher realm, but from the lower astral or un- derworld. At the bidding of the dread- ful spirits, those who evoked them per- formed terrible deeds to gain material wealth and power over the frightened populace. Devilish human sacrifice was one of the horrible results. To avoid the wrath of the powerful gods and the un- derworld spirits served by the evil men, parents sacrificed their children or cut hearts from fellow humans while they were still living and offered them as gifts to the fearful unknown.[1] People were so terrified of these Black Priests they mindlessly obeyed them, even participating in supervised orgies where human blood was consumed.[2]

To avoid recriminations by the Black Priests, the virtuous magi with higher morals increasingly isolated themselves from the daily lives of the majority of Atlanteans. Just as their warnings of an impending holocaust were ignored by the general populace, so the good priests' frantic prayers for help from above proved fruitless. Discouraged, they withdrew to the inner sanctums of their temples, and like monks today in remote mountain gompas in Zanskar, India, focused on increasing their spiritual development and guarding their religious books and treasures. Without moral guidance, belief in one all-powerful god substantially disappeared among the rank and file. They grew increasingly corrupt, sensual, and self-indulgent. People devoted their lives to eating, drinking, entertaining themselves, and ornamenting their bodies. Marriage became less common. Interest in religion waned. Those who ventured out on the streets alone or after dark were at risk of being robbed, beaten, or tortured.

During this unpleasant final period of Atlantis, the army was engaged abroad protecting the lands they acquired from other countries and constantly fighting for more. In 10,000 B.C., as the merciless Atlantean soldiers were attempting to occupy additional regions in the Mediterranean, they were defeated in Greece. Much later, in Plato's day, an annual festival to Pallas Athene, the patron goddess of Athens, continued to recognize their victory over the Atlanteans. During the ceremony, prominent authorities dedicated a woman's garment that symbolically represented the ancient triumph of the Athenians over the invading Atlanteans. The robe was pledged to Pallas Athene, the sworn enemy of Poseidon.[3]

Victorious Greek soldiers who followed the Atlanteans back to their homeland were captured when they reached Atlantis and taken as prisoners to the City of the Golden Gates. Simultaneously, one of the Adepts described a dream of rumbling earthquakes, mountainous tidal waves, and tremendous volcanic eruptions followed by uncontrollable fires and floods that destroyed Atlantis.[4] In quick response to the combination of the presence of Greek troops on their soil and the formidable vision of the destruction of their land, those in command ordered that all Greek prisoners be sacrificed to the gods immediately. Following this gruesome event, a magnificent banquet was prepared and the leaders, although full of apprehension arising from the Adept's dream, sat down to feast. Just as ominous black shadows grow as the sun recedes, so with the approach of darkness the Earth slowly began to tremble with ever-increasing violence.[5] Lightning flashed, hail fell, and peals of thunder drowned out the screams of the terrified Atlanteans. Before long the volcanoes thrust out lava and deadly, fiery objects that ignited uncontrollable fires. The Earth's shaking disturbed huge underground storage vats of energy, and these inflammable gases exploded one after another with the sounds of a tremendous fanfare. More roaring flames filled the air with vast clouds of toxic fumes and the terrible earthquakes increased. Within a short time, as the last Ice Age quickly ended, the sea consumed all but the mountain tops of the last large island of Atlantis, as well as many other areas of the Earth.

Throughout the world, the flood and devastation that followed are portrayed in stories passed down from generation to generation. Frisians, an ancient Dutch people who were primarily sailors, wrote in *Dera Linda Boek*:

Atland, as the land was called by seafaring people, was swallowed by the waves together with its mountains and valleys, and everything else was covered by the sea. Many people were buried in the ground, and others who escaped died in the water. The mountains breathed fire. . . . the forests were burned to a cinder, and the wind bore the ash which covered the entire Earth.

The Bible and the Sumerian Epic of Gilgamesh, written over a thousand years before the Bible, describe the flood over the Earth in similar ways. In the Caribbean island of Haiti, descendants say rain, floods, and fire from volcanoes preceded the disappearance of the Big Country, the homeland of their ancestors. They believe persons who escaped the Atlantean holocaust came to Haiti from the sinking island and killed numerous people when they arrived.[6]

Comparable accounts of natural catastrophes and excess water are found in almost every culture on the shores of the Atlantic Ocean. Legends told in North, Central, and South America portray the shaking earth, volcanic eruptions, and terrible tidal waves; then darkness, torrential rains, a flood, land sinking, nowhere for people to go, death to all. Usually the sources of the tales believe their ancestors were the only survivors. We will never know what this cataclysm was really like, for people living on the Earth at the time were so completely ravaged that only stories remain, provoking the imagination and perhaps stirring indistinct memories in the deeply buried unconscious we all share.

In the *Critias,* Plato describes in detail the size and composition of the Atlantean armed forces. Based on these figures, at the time of this last destruction of Atlantis, about twenty-five million people lived in the doomed country.[7] Most of the helpless citizens endured terrible pain and hardship as they were crushed by collapsing buildings, asphyxiated by noxious gases, cooked by boiling lava, or drowned when the land sank under their feet. Rapidly flying debris from volcanoes acted like arrows, striking fleeing men, women, and children. Screaming throngs, avoiding cracks in the surface, rushed in panic across the shaking ground to the wharves, but discovered the remaining docks collapsing, boats sinking, and giant tidal waves approaching. At this time of need, generous, compassionate people stayed in Atlantis and assisted the victims. These unselfish souls helped a few lucky persons to escape and eased the pain and suffering of many of the dying. At the last moment, just before they themselves experienced drowning, suffocation, or painful incineration, the Good Samaritans summoned their spiritual powers to avoid the disagreeable experience of a painful death on Earth. Leaving their bodies, they transcended to a higher realm.[8] Others utilized levitation to leave the flaming land and travel by way of small islands to the southeastern coast of North America. Native Americans still describe their remarkable arrival in the air.

One of the many tales about the destruction of Atlantis recalls that at the height of the confusion, the final respected ruler of Atlantis, Votan (or Wotan, Wodin, or Odin as he is referred to in lands adjacent to the Atlantic Ocean)[9] lined up the ships in the harbor of the City of the Golden Gates and supervised stocking them with books, food, and animals.[10] As the Earth shook and fire spouted from the mountains, he climbed to the top of a great unfinished pyramid and shouted to his people to remain proud of their beautiful homeland and never fight against each other. To facilitate this, he commanded the leaders to always wear on their heads two white feathers from the breast of the condor, the bird of lightning. He ordered his son to lead half the people in their boats in the direction of the sunrise and his grandson to take the rest toward the setting sun. Votan stayed on his high perch offering support, even though his voice was lost in the screams of people below him and the roar of the volcanoes. Before long, foaming water covered his helpless body.[11] Without delay, the ships, many of them in flames, like animals racing in terror from a blazing forest, turned and fled to the open sea.

Petrels and other migrating sea birds circle in the Atlantic, just as they have for thousands of years, as if they expect to find land. Their actions resemble birds circling an area where a shopping center is now located on a filled-in salt marsh that was once their home. The catopsilia, a lovely butterfly with orange wings resembling the colors of a sunset, lives in British Guiana. Every year brightly colored clouds of male catopsilia fly out to the Atlantic Ocean toward where Atlantis was located. It is a fatal flight. There is no place to land and they all die at sea.

8

SURVIVORS

FOR YEARS IN ADVANCE OF
the last major destruction of Atlantis,
priests who retained a belief in the omnipotent one god warned of the coming
calamity. Edgar Cayce relates that inhabitants of vehicles who flew to the
Earth also informed the people of the
impending disaster.[1] Wise families who
heeded these predictions gathered in
small groups, built sturdy ships, stocked
them with provisions, and sailed away.
When occasional shuddering of the
ground signaled imminent instability,
whole communities quickly assembled a
few necessities and fled like lemmings
to the sea in makeshift boats. Lemmings are small, vegetable-eating, non-
aquatic animals whose feet are not
webbed. They live in Scandinavia, to
the north of where Atlantis was located,

but periodically a migratory instinct drives countless numbers of them to the southern coast. The tiny, six-inch long creatures pile into the water and swim southward in the Atlantic Ocean toward Atlantis, as if expecting to find dry ground to satisfy their needs. As they swim helplessly in the surf, hundreds sink in the breaking waves, and those who stay above the surface, when they fail to find the sunken land, swim in circles until they die.

When the earth shook and volcanoes threatened, those who hurriedly abandoned their homes took only the supplies most important for their immediate needs. Any delay might mean dreadful death and it was impossible to pack on the crowded ships the equipment necessary to retain their standard of living. When the Atlanteans arrived in their new home, just to survive in the unfamiliar surroundings required all their time and energy. They built shelters, hunted, fished, perhaps grew some food, and retained a few religious customs, but their hands became callused and their clothing turned to rags.

When Atlantis was a thriving country, only a select few were allowed access to the full picture of extensive technical lore, so refugees did not have the knowledge to reproduce the high standard of living of their homeland. The best-informed people were the last to leave their sinking country, and they departed hurriedly and usually separately, traveling to different places, making it extremely difficult to reconstruct any one scientific process. The Magi kept the wisdom of alchemy so secret that most of the emigrants did not have any metalworking proficiency. Forced to adapt to the primitive lifestyle of the natives in their new location, without the proper implements and information to rebuild, their standard of living degenerated. Subsequent floods, earthquakes, and other natural disasters, plus the destruction of the extensive ancient libraries, combined to eliminate detailed knowledge of the skills of the magnificent Atlantean civilization. Eventually only memories of Atlantis remained and the many helpless descendants became the "savages" of the future. What would endure in A.D. 12,000 from our civilization if we were hurriedly forced to leave our homes tomorrow with only what we carried, while earthquakes shook our cities and lava or immense tidal waves covered everything? Perhaps, as with Atlantis, only a few customs would remain, plus myths and fables difficult to confirm as facts.

As panic reigned in Atlantis during the final destruction, desperate Atlanteans climbed to the mountaintops, peering down at the corpses of their friends "floating like seaweed" beneath them.[2] Slowly the land sank, the waters rose, and the mountain peaks became islands. Continuous volcanic activity on what are now the Azores Islands made them uninhabitable, but the Canary Islands were more hospitable. Huge natural caves provided initial shelters until the destitute refugees reconstructed a semblance of their former lives. They built homes and then small cities with buildings of large, closely fitting stones in the style of their past. The canals they dug for irrigation extended their growing season and, as life improved for descendants of these Atlantean survivors in the Canary Islands, they revived other aspects of their past culture. In 1402, during their first recorded visit to the area, the Spaniards discovered ruins of some of the ancient buildings and canals.

A few Atlanteans who eluded the destruction and flooding of their country escaped to temples that stood high on hillsides. The waters rose higher and higher but never quite reached them. When things stabilized, they and their temples were still safe on land but were now at the edge of the ocean. For hundreds of centuries, the fortunate escapees and their descendants held religious services and offered welcome medical and repair facilities to visiting ocean travelers.

Occasionally it is possible to see through the smoky glass that stands between us and the distant past, and fascinating information is partially visible about three complexes maintained by Atlantean survivors. One was in the Madeira Islands and two were in the Canary Islands. Unless otherwise indicated, the following material with respect to the temples of Atlantean survivors is derived from Edgarton Sykes' contributions to *Atlantis,* Volume 27, Numbers 3 and 4, May–June and July–August 1974. He obtained his data primarily from records of the Irish Tuatha-de-danaan, whom he believes were initially employed as scribes in Atlantean temples. The Tuathas fled in ships during the final destruction of their country, and eventually many settled in Ireland, where their knowledge was incorporated in Celtic myths and legends. Stories collected by Sir James Fraiser and records of explorers and treasure seekers mentioned in chapter 1 provided Sykes with additional details.

Before Atlantis sank, the Temple of Gorias rested on the mountain peak that today is the Madeira island of Gran Curral. Agile priests and priestesses, who hurriedly climbed to the temple as the waters rose, continued to live in and near the building. They worked hard at tilling the fertile volcanic soil for food, and Gorias became a thriving community. Its famous orange groves are remembered as the golden apples of the sun sought by Perseus, Hercules, and others.

At the time of the final destruction of Atlantis, a remote temple stood high in what were mountains on the western side of what is now the Canary Islands. Anticipating the destruction to come, wise Atlantean priests and priestesses successfully struggled to transport a large, heavy, sacred throne up the steep mountainside to the temple for safekeeping. They placed the special seat in the main hall of the building. The throne was carved from meteorite iron, a material the Atlanteans referred to as the Stone of Death. Falias, as the mountainous area was called, escaped as Atlantis sank and the ocean waters rose, and its temple served for hundreds of years as a nunnery renowned for the beautiful music it offered its residents and visitors. The daring Tuirenn Brothers of the Tuatha-de-danaan, who worked in the Temple of Falias as scribes, stole the royal seat and carried it to Ireland, where it was known as the Throne of Tara. It is said to have cried out if an impostor sat on it. Perhaps the stone was still radioactive and the impostors shrieked in surprise as they received a slight unexpected shock; the real kings were prepared in advance and said nothing.

The third remaining temple was at Finias in the City of the Sun in the Canary Island of Tenerife. During the final devastation, Atlanteans managed to move another priceless treasure to this safe site: a full-sized, solid gold replica of the Chariot of Poseidon, complete with horses and driver. Once life returned to a more normal state for those who fled to the Temple at Finias, the priests moved the precious chariot to the street for special ceremonies and parades. In 330 B.C., historian Budge wrote in his *Life of Alexander the Great* that Alexander was invited to visit the temple at the City of the Sun with its large golden "Chariot of the Gods." The beautiful carriage has probably disintegrated in the sea between Tenerife and Lanzarotte in the Canary Islands and will never be found. Underwater research has increased in the Atlantic Ocean, but metal or wooden objects from Atlantis are no longer recognizable. This is obvious when one considers that scuba divers exploring residues of World War II in the Pacific Ocean found that a tremendous amount of plant growth covered metal objects on the ocean floor after only twenty-five years. In addition to luxuriant vegetation, solidified lava and a thick coating of volcanic ash hide the lovely artifacts of Atlantis.

Atlantean survivors and their descendants continued to perform simplified versions of the initiation and magical ceremonies that played such an important role in life in their homeland. Caves for those who lived in the Canary Islands provided excellent sanctuaries for these events, as well as long-term storage places for mummies. Descendants of survivors in the Canary Islands arranged their mummies in the crouch position, as did the offspring of their fellow ex-Atlanteans in Mexico, Peru, and very early Egypt.[3] Ceilings of these caves in the Canary Islands where they stored the wrapped bodies are painted red, and the walls are marked with drawings of animals and indecipherable symbols and hieroglyphics in red, gray, and white.

When the Spaniards first arrived in the Canary Islands, 20,000 people of four ethnic groups lived in the thirteen islands. The Spaniards referred to the group whose ancestors built the sophisticated buildings and canal systems as the Gaunches. They were the primary inhabitants of the islands of Gran Canaria and Tenerife. These proud people with light skin, fair hair, and blue eyes had remained independent and not intermarried with Egyptian and Carthaginian sailors and adventurers who visited them in the past. They retained the physical characteristics of their ancestors, survivors from Atlantis. The Gaunches represented the last relatively pure Cro-Magnon stock of Atlantis—large skulls, high cheekbones, relatively long, straight noses and firm chins. Many men were over six feet tall. They believed they had saved themselves by climbing to the tops of mountains that were the former mountain peaks of a submerged land. They were so terrified of the water they did not have boats.

The Gaunches preserved some Atlantean knowledge of astronomy and parts of their ancient legislative system, including ten elective officials.[4] A pillar, similar to the one in the Temple of Poseidon, was important in their religious services.[5] On the summits of their mountains, the Gaunches offered prayers to an omnipotent god who rewarded virtue and avenged sin.[6] A sect of priestesses, the Magades, whose practices resembled those of the witches of Mexico and ancient Europe, worshiped at stone circles. Under the power of a high priest, these virgin sorceresses engaged in symbolic dances. While hypnotized or in a trance, they served as oracles. If dreaded earthquakes shook the land, or volcanoes became active, the virgins sacrificed themselves to the ocean, hoping to prevent the omnipotent sea from covering everything as it had in the past.[7]

The explorers who inspected the Gaunches' region in 1402 found an irrigation system, pottery, mummies, paintings in caves, and ruins of prehistoric cities. The beautiful drawings Gaunche artists left on cave walls were almost identical to those painted by Cro-Magnons in southern France.[8] Their ceramics, some dating to 20,000 B.C., were decorated with patterns similar to the designs on early South American pottery.[9] Another interesting find among the possessions of the Gaunches was a stone statue of a naked man carrying a globe, like Atlas supporting the world.[10] It seemed to symbolize Mount Atlas, the magnificent mountain of Atlantis, which once appeared to be supporting the heavens as it reached into the clouds. Although the Gaunches fought the Spaniards valiantly, the invaders and disease totally exterminated them within 150 years.[11]

9

SAILING AWAY

SYMBOLIZING THE IMPACT of the extensive migrations from Atlantis, Arab geographers drew the country on their maps as a dragon in the Atlantic Ocean. Its head stood for the place where the people originated, and its long tails were their travels as they coiled around the globe. Before the destruction of their country, the Atlanteans traded and shared their knowledge as they journeyed to far-away places. After their land was gone, they simply searched for new home-sites, and eventually found them in central Africa, Egypt, Great Britain, mainland Europe, the Near East, and Central, South, and North America.

Africa

The fertile lands of northern Africa were an easily accessible haven from Atlantis that attracted many enterprising families shortly before the final destruction. Twelve thousand years ago, adequate rainfall assured reliable rivers and streams for irrigation in this area, now covered by vast plains of hot sand. The sources of water formed a network of valleys where humans lived until 4,000 years ago. Today these lowlands are buried several feet below the desert floor, but radar scans of southwestern Egypt taken from the Space Shuttle Columbia reveal this ancient topography.[1] Very old drawings on rocks in the dry Tassili Mountains of Algeria depict an attractive landscape where people and animals lived in harmony.[2] Additional memories of the pleasant life at that time are preserved in paintings in galleries under ruins of the city of Khamissa in the Atlas Mountains in northern Africa.[3]

Atlanteans who traveled up the rivers on the western coast of Africa joined with friends already settled where the Ife nation lives in West Africa today. Ruins of their temples and further aspects of their magnificent civilization are still visible.[4] Other Atlanteans followed rivers to communities on the shores of the Triton Sea, a lovely large lake 100 miles wide. Currently it lies under the Sahara desert, but descriptions of it survive. Diodorus Siculus refers to the lake, and it is remembered in stories of natives in both Algeria and Morocco. Herodotus, in his *Book IV*, tells of this vast body of water in northern Africa, which he called Tritonis. He even refers to one of its islands, Phla. The works of Greek historian Herodotus (484–425 B.C.) portray a mysterious golden treasure guarded by griffins in a distant land, which was not found until recently when archaeologists discovered ancient gold mines in the valley of Pazyrka in Russia.[5] They were richly decorated with griffins.

Thousands of Atlantean descendants lived happily on the shores of the Triton Sea in central Africa until a tremendous earthquake along a fault line broke open the Atlas Mountains. In one terrible night, as the Earth's crust shivered violently and erupting volcanoes thrust deadly rocks and boiling lava into the atmosphere, all the water emptied from the lake. Torrents of foaming liquid, combined with volcanic debris, completely buried 200 cities built around the Triton Sea.[6]

Terrified refugees scattered in all directions, and some of the more fortunate and capable groups survived. One band, now the Berbers, fled to the nearby Atlas Mountains, where they named the highest peak Mount Atlas, for its head was often encircled by clouds in a manner similar to the most memorable mountain peak of their native land. With their aquiline noses, high cheekbones, light skin, blue or gray eyes, and often red hair, the Berbers resemble their Atlantean ancestors, as did the Gaunches of the Canary Islands. Their language is unique except for some similarities with the Gaunche speech and with Euskara, the ancient Basque tongue.

The Tuaregs, whose name means "people of the all-powerful fire god" in the old Algonquin language,[7] were tall, warrior Berbers who continued to occupy the central Sahara, isolated from other civilizations, for thousands of years. Their strongest emperor, Heracles, controlled shipping through the Straits of Gibraltar and named them the Gates of Heracles,[8] a title that persisted past the time of Plato's writing in 350 B.C. The Tuaregs also retained Cro-Magnon features of their Atlantean forefathers. When explorers reached them in the nineteenth century, in spite of centuries of harsh desert life, many Tuareg men were over six feet tall.[9] Their skin was light although, owing to the blue dye of their almost purple clothing which rubbed off on their faces, the Tuaregs were known as the blue people.[10] Their written language, Tamahak, or Tiffinagh, contained over 100 words almost identical to those of the

Gaunches of the Canary Islands.[11] The Sioux of North America also understood many words of Tuareg. One of the more interesting correlations in the two languages was the Tuareg word for "to cast a shadow." The Sioux said the Tuareg word meant to follow and hide behind a tree from something you are tracking, similar to our English interpretation of the verb "to shadow someone." Tuaregs regarded the word as a noun that referred to the partial darkness in a space from which light rays are cut off.[12] After thousands of years the word had acquired a slightly different meaning but it still referred to the same concept. Until the French defeated the Tuaregs in 1905, not even the powerful Arabs succeeded in imposing their language or religion on these noble, dignified Atlantean descendants.

One of the Tuareg ritual dances, similar to the ceremony their ancestors employed to obtain sacrificial victims for the fire god in Atlantis, was the same as a dance of the Mescallero tribe of the Apache nation in Arizona, whose distant ancestors also came from the sunken land. Lucille Taylor Hansen observed the Apaches performing this dance and received a firsthand description of an identical dance as it was recently enacted in Africa. In both formal ceremonies, a single-file line of participants rode on horseback from the direction of the Atlantic Ocean to a fire at the site of the ritual. In Arizona they came from the east, in Africa from the west. On their heads they wore flaming tridents, the ancient symbol of Atlantis, which the sea god Poseidon carries. The fire burning in the headpieces represented a mountain spouting smoke and flames. In each case the dancers approached the blazing fire, worshiped it, and participated in a mock battle at the finale. Ten thousand years ago in Atlantis, where the ceremony originated, the combatants engaged in a brutal, fast fight. Those who survived rode away, leading the riderless horses and taking the hapless victims for quick disposal in a threatening volcano as a token gift to its powerful god.[13]

Egypt

Many well-educated, devout Atlanteans moved to both southern and northern Egypt in the years before the final destruction of their homeland. Although conflicts frequently arose between church and state in Egypt, and migrating tribes from the east constantly threatened, Edgar Cayce recalls that the country became a spiritual, scientific, and cultural center,[14] and that the Atlanteans even found time to conduct archaeological research concerning the past occupants of the land.[15] Cayce also refers to the Atlanteans' establishment of worship of the sun god in Egypt,[16] a practice that survived for many thousands of years.

In their Egyptian Temple Beautiful and in the Temple of Sacrifice, Atlantean descendants continued their ancient practices. They utilized music, dance, and initiations to raise their souls to higher levels. Capable priests and priestesses in the Temple Beautiful assisted uncertain individuals in deciding on their lifetime occupations based on the individual's karmic development. Everyone who sought this advice was given a "life seal," which was a plaque to contemplate when they needed additional encouragement and insight.[17]

When the weather changed and it ceased to rain in southern Egypt, the permanent drought forced Atlantean descendants to abandon their homes and move. They joined the Berbers in the Atlas Mountains or journeyed north and east along the banks of the Nile River to live with other groups from Atlantis where water was not a problem. Archaeologists have recently unearthed numerous settlements of Cro-Magnon farmers who lived in 13,000 B.C. along the Nile, twenty-eight miles down river from the Aswan Dam.[18] From 13,000 B.C. until 11,500 B.C. the successful people enjoyed a golden age of agriculture, utilizing sickle blades and grinding stones to produce a diet based on grains.[19]

Prior to the destruction of their country, wise men and women in Atlantis foresaw the long forthcoming period of devastation and a longer epoch of intellectual darkness. They chose Egypt as a place to preserve some of the vast historical and technological knowledge accumulated in the Temple of Poseidon. Working with scholars, priests, architects, and engineers, their builders constructed pyramids, temples, and a Hall of Records in Egypt in an area of strong Earth energy. Before the final destruction of their country, the Atlanteans placed their most valuable documents in these safer places.

Atlanteans and their descendants in Egypt lived well. Attempting to retain the high standards of their lost country, they transmitted information from generation to generation for hundreds of years. Eventually, natural catastrophes in nearby lands forced aggressive, uncivilized tribes into Egypt from all sides. The ruinous barbarians almost totally destroyed the advanced Atlantean civilization.

In spite of the invaders, priests continuously struggled to guard the valuable lore and to convey it to initiates in secret ceremonies. Learned descendants of Atlanteans, who traveled the seas after their country disappeared and eventually sailed up the Nile River, supplemented the teachings with additional wisdom. As a result, occult practices, levitation, architectural and construction skills, and historical information, such as the communication in regard to Atlantis that Solon received at Sais, were preserved in Egypt.[20]

With wisdom from its past, and perhaps with input from the visitors from the tenth planet, who assisted the Sumerians,[21] the mature Egyptian civilization of our history books appeared very suddenly; it was advanced when it began. In the early years of the First Dynasty (the first period of Egyptian recorded history, about 3110 B.C.–2884 B.C.) the people had a complex written language with signs that represented sounds. Their goldsmiths displayed a high degree of proficiency that indicated a long period of development. Within an unusually short time the Egyptians had expert medical skills and an advanced calendar, complex mathematical concepts, and the ability to construct unsurpassed stone pyramids.

Enlightenment from Atlantis, preserved and passed down by the priesthood in Egypt, contributed to the unusual accomplishments of the people of the First Dynasty. Their early calendar demonstrates this very well. As was often the case in prehistory, it was based on hours, with dissimilar amounts of hours of daylight and darkness, depending on the locality. The longest day of the Egyptian calendar contained 12 hours and 55 minutes, the shortest, 11 hours and 5 minutes. These periods of time do not correspond to the location of Egypt, where the days would be longer in summer and shorter in winter, but they do correspond to Atlantis, eighty miles to the south.[22]

When sacred buildings disintegrated in northern Egypt, new structures were erected over the old. Robert Bauval, a Belgian construction engineer and astronomer, studied the arrangement of the Sphinx, the Great Pyramid of Cheops, and its nearby pyramids and temples. Taking into account the correlation of the buildings to the constellations in the sky, he surmised that the site of the Great Pyramid was first laid out in 10,450 B.C.[23] Edgar Cayce says that these buildings stand on the hallowed ground above the pyramid containing the Hall of Records and its valuable information.

The Great Pyramid

Advanced architectural and engineering skills developed by Atlanteans and saved in Egypt, together with advice from extraterrestrials, were instrumental in the construction of the exceptional Great Pyramid. The building bears a striking resemblance to monumental prehistoric constructions in Tiahuanaco, Cuzco, the Sun Pyramid in Teotihuacan, Mexico, the City of the Golden Gates, and to buildings in Sumeria, where gods from heaven were involved in their construction.

To complete the Great Pyramid, the builders used more than 2,500,000 granite and limestone blocks, some weighing seventy tons, which were excavated from quarries many miles away. The structure occupies thirteen acres, or the equivalent of seven square blocks of Manhattan.[24] Their saws, even with the jeweled teeth of nine-foot blades, required two tons of pressure to cut through the hard granite.[25] Builders placed a limestone capstone, sheathed in gold, at the peak of the lofty pyramid and layered the outer walls with enormous polished limestone casing stones. Each of these stones was almost three feet thick and slightly curved inward. Finished to a precision of $\frac{1}{100}$ inch, they fit tightly together.[26] With its golden peak and white limestone sides that glittered like thousands of diamonds in the sunlight, the colossal pyramid offered an unforgettably glorious sight from a distance. Herodotus and others who studied the casing stones report they were covered with writing. Ancient papyri allege this writing contained the mysteries of science, astronomy, geometry, physics, and more.[27] After a series of earthquakes in the thirteenth century A.D., Arabs removed the invaluable stones and used them to construct mosques and palaces in Cairo.[28]

The wisest of men incorporated sophisticated geographical and mathematical concepts into the design of the Great Pyramid. The building is an exact scale model of the Northern Hemisphere, with the apex as the North Pole and the base as the Equator.[29] Aligned with the cardinal points of the compass, the base line of this tremendous building is precisely the distance any one location at the equator travels around the axis of the Earth in half a second.[30] The length of the pyramid's four bases vary by no more than eight inches, and the base measurement, when divided by twice its height, is equal to 3.1416, the value of pi. The dimensions indicate the designers thoroughly understood the advanced principles of the Golden Section, a useful, constant mathematical proportion rediscovered in the fourteenth century.[31] The knowledge of these ancient scholars is especially striking when one recalls that Euclid, who developed basic systematic geometry, lived during the third century B.C., long after the building was constructed. The Great Pyramid is a lasting memorial to the talented scientists of prehistory and their profound understanding of the interrelations of numbers, geometry, and the human spirit.[32]

In ancient drawings, the Sphinx, which is adjacent to the Great Pyramid at Giza, is pictured crouching atop a stone building.[33] Once the immense stone statue was almost completely covered by sand, so it is possible another building lies buried in the deep sand beneath it. Edgar Cayce says "there is a chamber or passage from the right forepaw [of the Sphinx] to this entrance of the record chamber, or record tomb."[34] Japanese scientists, who recently spent months measuring and scanning the building, discovered underground cavities near the Sphinx and a possible tunnel near the right paw.[35] The Egyptian government is unwilling to permit drilling under the monuments, fearing they might collapse. Cayce advises that when man has evolved to a higher understanding and is ready for it, this concealed knowledge of Atlantis will be revealed.[36]

A form of energy operates within pyramids, but even though this phenomenon is the subject of numerous experiments, no one really understands how it works. The energy was discovered when it became apparent that ancient garbage and dead animals in the Great Pyramid were not rotted, did not smell, and appeared to be mummified. Psychic Paul Solomon reports that the power of pyramid energy has preserved food stored in the Hall of Records beneath the Sphinx and the Great Pyramid and that it is still edible.[37] Researchers propose that, in addition to preserving food, given the proper conditions, the energy of pyramids is capable of sharpening razor blades, improving the taste of tap water, stimulating plant growth and seed germination, recharging batteries, facilitating the healing process, and increasing vitality and virility.[38]

Egyptian Scrolls

The keeper of time has locked the doors to many rooms of the past, but fragments of information relating to Atlantis have slipped out. The *Egyptian Book of the Dead*, written on papyri found in tombs and on mummy wrappings dating to thousands of years before Christ, describes "the abode of the souls" that lay to the west beyond the Pillars of Heracles, where Atlantis lay.[39] Here, canals connected green, fertile islands where wheat and barley grew to great heights.[40] The *Book of the Dead* refers to the god Thoth, the "Guardian of the Two Lands," who brought culture to Egypt from a western land.[41] Egyptian priest historian Manethon mentions an Egyptian calendar that began in 11,542 B.C.[42] Herodotus describes papyrus scrolls in Egypt with the names of 330 kings. The list dates back to 11,000 years before his day.[43]

The Papyrus of Turin is one of two surviving records of ancient Egyptian kings. It documents the names of ten gods who reigned during the First Time, as well as the mortal kings of upper and lower Egypt who ruled after the gods, but before the first pharaoh of the First Dynasty in 3100 B.C.[44] Ancient Egyptians described the First Time as the period when the gods ruled their country and brought it out of the darkness. These gods, whom they called the Neteru, were both males and females. The Neteru were stronger and more intelligent than humans and possessed supernatural powers, but they were susceptible to sickness and death. Their connection to Atlantis is apparent in that the early Egyptians believed the gods could transport people across the water to the "abode of souls." Diodorus Siculus also studied ancient scrolls on one of his trips to Egypt, which referred to a succession of gods, heroes, and mortal kings who reigned for thousands of years. It is very possible that these "gods" and the Neteru were visitors from outer space whose contributions to the early advanced civilization in Egypt were evident long after they departed.

Great Britain

Conditions changed rapidly in Great Britain in 10,000 B.C. when the mountains of Atlantis disappeared. Finally the prevailing westerly winds, warmed as they flowed over the temperate Gulf Stream, were unobstructed by Atlantis and reached Ireland, Wales, and England. The climate improved and glaciers melted quickly. Meadow grasses sprang up, flowers bloomed, and animals moved in. Atlanteans, homeless except for their ships, were delighted when they found the attractive lands.

Tales of the People of the Serpent's talented musicians, poets, physicians, and builders are preserved in ancient legends and Irish books. The eighth century *Book of Armagh*, the twelfth century *Book of the Dun Cow*, the *Book of Lecan*, the *Book of Leinster*, and the *Book of Invasions*, all compiled from even more ancient sources, describe the sequential order of the invaders as Nemedians, Formorians, Fir-Bolgs, and finally the Tuathas. They spoke a similar language, for their cultures all sprang from Atlantis. Their experiences after leaving their native land varied. Before reaching Ireland, some wandered the ocean in ships, others journeyed on foot in Slavic countries, and a few spent time in Egypt.[45]

The first to come were the tall, strong Nemedians, also called Sons of the Sun, who arrived in southwestern Ireland about 10,000 B.C. These Atlanteans sailed silver ships with painted serpents on the front of the vessels. The Formorians followed. Also large in stature, they were known as "People of the Undersea."[46] Irish legends remember that spiritual Formorians controlled natural forces and were from a sinking island.[47]

Hundreds of years later, the Fir-Bolgs arrived. A race of shorter, heavily set Atlanteans, these dark-skinned people from its eastern mountains were adept miners and builders who fought with the sharp, broad blades of their axes. The Fir-Bolgs were known for their trickery and humor and are memorialized in the British Isles as leprechauns and goblins.[48]

Fir-Bolgs channeled energy along ley lines to move great masses of earth for artificial hills where they assembled at prescribed times every year for festivities.[49] Frequently these large hills or mounds were raised in the shape of serpents in memory of Atlantis, such as the one at Glen Flochan by Lock Nell near Oban, which is 300 feet long and 20 feet high. For their metaphysical celebrations of the sacred rites of solar magic, the Fir-Bolgs erected the Hall of Tara, a gigantic building over 700 feet long and 90 feet wide, constructed with huge stones weighing many tons. The sacred Hall of Tara was the site of religious ceremonies and initiations for hundreds of centuries. From plans in old manuscripts and the ruins of the multifaceted Hall, it is possible to reconstruct many aspects of the Fir-Bolgs' complex social organization. The magnificent building provided for musicians, poets, physicians, historians, builders, four classes of nobility, three grades of jesters, chess players, Druids, deerstalkers, soothsayers, teachers, judges, blacksmiths, and more.[50]

Soon after the final destruction of Atlantis, Ireland was invaded by the Tuatha-de-danaan, whose name meant "flood." These fair newcomers from northern areas of Atlantis had long red or blond hair and blue eyes. They used metals, possessed supernatural powers, and are remembered as wise, knowledgeable people. The Tuathas understood the language of the Fir-Bolgs but were unfriendly and overthrew them with strange weapons of fire that created dark clouds of smoke.[51] During one of the battles the leader of the Tuathas lost a hand. A skillful associate who was familiar with the advanced medical techniques of prehistory replaced the hand with a metal one and thereafter he was referred to as Nuada of the Silver Hand.[52] Many more stories of the Tuatha are preserved in Irish legends. The Tuathas, following the traditions of their ancestors in Atlantis, worshiped the sun and constructed massive buildings of cut stone.[53]

After the glaciers melted, people from the Pleiades came to Great Britain and offered assistance to Atlantean emigrants and their descendants. Numerous stone structures erected there in prehistoric times are aligned in the direction of the seven stars of the Pleiades to indicate the exact direction of their rising at the summer or winter solstice.[54] Important dates in ancient British calendars correspond to the movement of the Pleiades, such as the Celtic May Day, celebrated at the time when the constellation rose at dawn.[55]

Songs and stories narrated by older folks in Galway, where Atlanteans landed on the western coast of Ireland, describe the wonderful country of their forbears which lay in islands to the west. They call it Iere, pronounced *Ai-ree*.[56] Pan, the god of Nature, was a god of old Iere, a magical place where the inhabitants were fairies or evil spirits. The buildings had no stairways since everyone had the ability to fly.[57] Stories also describe the land of Ogham or Ogyges, off the coast of Ireland. Today it is on a shallow shelf, about 300 feet beneath the sea, which runs almost to the Atlantic Ridge.[58] Legends say it was once possible to reach Atlantis by way of Ogham, traveling for many months on a well-lit, wide highway.[59] A tremendous granite statue of Og, a king of Ogham, and another of his queen Magog, stood in London until bombs destroyed them during World War II.[60]

The inhabitants of early Ireland continued various Atlantean practices. The country was divided into provinces, each ruled by a king. The kings recruited their armed forces just as in Atlantis, with each province providing the required number of cavalrymen, foot soldiers, and stone shooters.[61] Irish high priests, known as Druids, worshiped around bronze pillars similar to the column in the Temple of Poseidon in the City of the Golden Gates. Periodically assembling to settle controversies, they sacrificed white bulls and practiced human sacrifice as in the last period of Atlantean civilization. The

Druids believed in the transmigration of souls and claimed to be able to levitate, control the weather, and make themselves invisible.[62] Universities of the Druids in Great Britain were among the foremost in the western world, attracting excellent scholars from distant lands. Druid faculty members who visited the continent influenced Pythagoras (582–500 B.C.) and innumerable long-forgotten scholars.[63]

The Romans ruthlessly suppressed the Druids in Great Britain and on the European continent, Julius Caesar ordered the burning of an immense library of the Druids in England and the destruction of all their additional written literature.[64] Druids who survived in Wales were eventually obliterated, and the few who survived in Ireland in the fifth century were converted to Christianity by Saint Patrick.

Numerous Atlanteans settled in Wales, and Welsh folklore abounds with stories of the Old Kingdom, first separated into islands and finally covered by the high seas. *Myvrian Archaeology of Wales*, published in 1870 but drawn from pre-Christian sources, refers to those who escaped from an all-encompassing flood and appeared in an enormous, swift ship without sails.[65] Descriptions and adventures of the Children of Don, immigrants similar to the Tuatha-de-danaan of Ireland, also fill many pages of Welsh literature. When these powerful individuals arrived from a sunken western land, they exercised strong magic to subdue the resident population. One of their leaders had the gift of telepathy. Another was capable of changing into an animal or bird form, a talent retained by shamans, and terrifying to the naive residents of western Wales. The Children of Don possessed other remarkable skills and, like the Tuathas, constructed buildings with extremely large blocks of cut stone.

Lyonesse

Off the southwestern tip of England, just beneath the surface, lie the remains of the island of Lyonesse. Around 18,000 B.C., when much of the ocean water was incorporated into the icy northern glaciers, Lyonesse was an Atlantean colony connected by a chain of islands to Atlantis. Gradually the land of Lyonesse broke up and the surviving pieces were named the Scilly Isles. Fishermen who peer down through the water on a very clear day may see the stately castles of Lyonesse far below, proudly struggling to resist the ever-hungry seas that overwhelm them.

Refugees from Lyonesse fled to southwestern England and established the Sacred Kingdom of Logres, where wandering descendants of Atlanteans were welcome for hundreds of years. The residents of Logres employed the techniques of geomancy to improve their relationship with the universe. Relying on technical knowledge and engineering skills passed down from their ancestors, they molded amazing zodiacs from their surroundings. Zodiacs are also found in prehistoric Assyrian ruins and in Egypt, which probably indicates some extraterrestrial influence. The largest land sculpture in Logres includes a circular area of thirty miles near Glastonbury. Clearly visible from the air, its circumference includes hills, water courses, trees and piles of earth, all shaped to form the twelve signs of the zodiac. Each head of a figure in the zodiac is turned to the west toward the graveyard of Atlantis.[66] The zodiac was so cleverly constructed that, at the time it was built, tidal water partially covered the form of Pisces the fish, a character that required water.[67]

Wotan

When tales of heroes of ancient times are transmitted over the centuries, dominant figures of the past often become mythical characters or gods. Wotan or Votan, the last distinguished king of Atlantis, was revered until Anglo-Saxon times as a god who, because of his ability to control natural forces, was a warlike killer of dragons. When the Christian Church attempted to destroy the pagan religion in Great Britain, Saint Michael was pictured as Wotan's successor. Everywhere, Saint Michael's name was methodically substituted for Wotan's. An ancient, perfectly straight ley line, originally built for energy and later used for dragon processions, was dedicated to the god Wotan in prehistoric England. Ten churches or high points that define the ancient track, and were once dedicated to Wotan, now bear the name of Saint Michael. The line runs for 200 miles from St. Michael's Church in Clifton Hampden through St. Michael's Tor in Glastonbury to St. Michael's Mount near Land's End. To further destroy memories of Wotan, Christians pictured the ancient powerful hero as evil and focused on the Saint, accompanied by a band of angels, waging war against the powers of darkness, personified by Wotan as a dragon. The Book of Revelations describes Saint Michael destroying the powerful beast who represented the Devil and Satan. Statues and pictures of Saint Michael killing a dragon or standing over one he has slain abound in British churches, for it required many hundreds of years' intense pressure to overcome the strong influence of the beliefs of descendants of emigrants from the old, red land.

Mainland Europe

Most Atlantean colonies along the shores of the Atlantic Ocean permanently disappeared around 10,000 B.C., totally destroyed by tidal waves and floods. However, hardy inhabitants of the community of Tarshish on Spain's Atlantic coast returned when the waters retreated. They struggled to rebuild their city and, by 7000 B.C., Tarshish was once again a thriving metropolis, renowned for its poetry, laws, and books.[68] The Bible describes the abundance of gold and silver in Tarshish, and early Greek records refer to the silver anchors of the ships of Tarshish.[69] After 533 B.C., when Carthaginian marauders sacked and burned the beautiful city, it gradually faded away. Remains of structures from other Atlantean colonies, built on the now-submerged continental shelves off the coast of Spain, are visible to divers, but for military reasons the Spanish government prohibits exploration.[70]

Edgar Cayce describes Atlanteans who flew through the air and others who walked inland from the Bay of Biscay to settle in the Pyrenees mountains of southern France and northern Spain.[71] Here, protected by steep rocky passes, they lived in relative isolation for thousands of years. Their descendants, the Basques, still inhabit the region. Isolated from the surrounding world and proud of their Atlantean heritage, the Basques, like their distant Gaunche cousins in the Canary Islands, refrained from intermarrying and retained their striking Cro-Magnon appearance. Their blood type is quite different from their French and Spanish neighbors, for Basques have a much higher percentage of type O. RH negative blood is a characteristic of Atlantean descendants everywhere. Basques have the highest frequency of RH negative in the world.[72] The Berbers of northern Africa, some Amazonian cultures, and the Gaunches have a similarly disproportionate amount of RH negative blood types.

The Basque language, Eushera, reflects the prehistoric language Atlanteans spread around the world. Its common origin with the language of Guatemala enables natives of that Central American country to understand Eushera.[73] It is more similar to some Native American languages than the Indo-Germanic group, but it does not originate from another known language.[74] Similarities between the Basque language and the speech of the Tuaregs and the Gaunches were previously mentioned.

In 1978 Basque poet Jacinth Verdaguer published a beautiful poem, *L'Antantida*, preserving for posterity his people's respect for their ancient homeland of Atlantis. Verdaguer describes the snowy heights of the mountains of Atlantis and its fiery volcanoes. With intense feeling he portrays lovely flower gardens and vast areas of yellow wheat resembling fields of golden hair, totally different from his own mountainous landscape. The high-flying condors of Atlantis and its savage mastodons and corpulent mammoths come alive in his poetry, just as they did in the tales passed down by his Basque ancestors through the generations. He even mentions the famous golden orange groves at Gorias. Verdaguer's sincere affection for Atlantis reflects the love of his distant forebears, like expatriates everywhere, for their native land.

The Near East

The extensive wisdom of Atlantean scholars was also recorded and remembered in the Near East, where the boats of destitute refugees carried them in 10,000 B.C. Noah, with his family and animals as described in the Bible, is the most notorious emigrant from Atlantis, the only land at that time sufficiently advanced to produce the knowledge he carried with him. *The Book of Jubilees,* one of the Dead Sea Scrolls, refers to the written information about medicine and herbs Noah gave to Sherm, and says that in due course these books were passed from Jacob to his son Levi, who gave them to his children.[75] The enlightenment Noah brought to the Near East is symbolized in many legends. Hebrews describe one of these holy books originally given to Adam by the angel Raziel. The Hebrews say the book was made from sapphires and once belonged to Noah, who used it as a "lamp" (light of knowledge) while in the Ark. Ultimately the book came into the hands of King Solomon and was regarded as the source of all wisdom. Information relating to the occult arts that reached the Near East from Atlantis at the time of the flood contributed to the practices of the Essence Order, an ancient learned Jewish sect.[76]

Descendants of Atlantean refugees, such as the relatively advanced Magyars or Finns, roamed throughout Europe, continuing to practice their longstanding customs. Powerful priests dominated the Magyar people, summoning evil spirits and conducting festivities with formalized, bloody rites.[77] The Magyars were renowned for their extensive herbal knowledge and treasured their lovely statues and jewelry of gold and silver.[78]

Central America

The prehistory of Central America is more complicated and turbulent than elsewhere in the world, for in that portion of the American continent earthquakes, volcanic eruptions, and catastrophic floods along the coast constantly destroyed precocious civilizations. Hungry wandering tribes from North America, pushed southward by the glaciers, supplemented the irreparable natural destruction, especially in Mexico. Nevertheless, traces of strong Atlantean influences are discernible as one assesses the customs, skills, and engineering accomplishments of past inhabitants and appraises the legends that refer to the great serpent, or the "big country" to the East where the sun rose, and where, before it disappeared, there were buildings like pointed squares and the inhabitants were very rich.[79]

When refugees from Atlantis reached Central America in 10,000 B.C., hostile people and dangerous animals and reptiles populated the strange new lands. Frequent shuddering of the ground and deadly emissions from volcanoes reminded them of home but also compounded their problems. The fortunate families who survived natural catastrophes often retreated to the shelter of caves, where they were forced to live for several generations. Material relics their ancestors brought from Atlantis were of little assistance, but these survivors spent hour after hour, year after year, memorizing and retelling stories of the superior civilization of the old, red land.

As they waited for conditions to return to normal, Atlanteans and their descendants had ample time for contemplation. They cultivated the talents of the right side of their brains, such as intuition and clairvoyance, and never ceased to carry out initiation ceremonies for the young. When life on the outside improved, the tough, intelligent men, women, and children who remained gradually emerged from their dark, rocky havens and moved to more fertile areas. They utilized occult tactics to gain respect and control of the natives, just as priests had hundreds of years before in Atlantis. Their witchcraft was still evident in Central America in the sixteenth century. Mexicans told the first Spaniards that witches capable of inflicting disease haunted certain crossroads. The creatures were said to fly through the air on broomsticks to their gatherings and utilize charms to change themselves into other shapes.[80]

Descendants of emigrants from Atlantis who arrived in Central America during periods of natural stability fared very well. Combining wisdom from their ancestors with advice from friendly celestial visitors, particularly the Pleiadeans, they built cities with substantial structures that included temples, observatories, and numerous pyramids. Their four-sided buildings with triangular faces, like the Great Pyramid in Egypt, were laid out exactly to the points of the compass and designed to display the high importance the society attached to mathematics and astrology.

A few miles from Mexico City, at Teotihuacan, early residents of Mexico discovered a place where an unusual amount of energy was available from the Earth. The sacred site they created survives today beneath one of the largest pyramids in the world, the Pyramid of the Sun. Under the pyramid a long, natural tunnel leads to a four-chambered cave, created from lava flow over a million years ago. The earliest inhabitants enlarged the cave's four rooms, supported the ceiling with heavy stone slabs, and plastered the walls with mud. The site at Teotihuacan was such a powerful location for religious ceremonies and initiations that dedicated residents of the area built a pyramid above it and a ley line extending straight from the original cave to the north, where Atlantean descendants lived in the southwestern United States. The architecture and placement of buildings in Teotihuacan correlate with the rising or setting of their heavenly home, the stars of the Pleiades, which implies the Pleiadeans were involved. Eventually the huge Pyramid of the Sun was constructed over the sacred cave and the first simple pyramid.[81]

The proportions of the Pyramid of the Sun in Teotihuacan demonstrate the precise distance to the sun and other astute geographical knowledge. The stupendous structure is situated so the shadows make it available as a perennial clock. Mathematical researchers who painstakingly analyzed the building believe its designers understood the relationship in space of the sphere and the tetrahedron. They incorporated into the pyramid's dimensions the message that the physical universe is tetrahedral from the microscopic level of the atom all the way up to the acroscopic level of the galaxies, on a scale of vibrations in which man stands approximately in the center. Peter Tompkins offers a detailed, technical explanation of this concept and its relevance to the pyramid's construction in *Mysteries of the Mexican Pyramids*.[82] Like the pyramid at Giza, no one understands how the stones for this immense structure were transported to the site and then raised to form the huge building. Mexicans say giants who perished in a catastrophe of floods and earthquakes created them. The giants were probably beings from outer space who returned to their homes in the stars when natural disasters struck.

Portions of pyramids built about the time the last Atlantean refugees arrived stand today in Central America. One of the oldest is at Pena Pobre in Tlalpam near San Angel.[83] Another ancient building stands at Cuicuilo near Mexico City. This immense pyramid was in place more than 8,000 years ago when enormous quantities of deadly pumice, ash, dirt, and stones from 12,600-foot Mt. Azusco and from a smaller crater, Xitli, covered the lower third of it.[84] Little is known of the helpless citizens of the surrounding area who fled in all directions after this catastrophic event, but the quality of the sophisticated jewelry, ceramics, and statuettes they placed in the pyramid indicate these prehistoric people were an advanced race who retained and developed the culture of their ancestors.[85]

Descendants of Atlanteans in Central America continued to practice the burial customs of their ancestors' mother country. One of their cemeteries is now beneath an area of Mexico City known as the Pedrigal. It is covered by lava, sometimes fifty feet thick, from a volcano that erupted 8,000 to 12,000 years ago. Many of the bones and artifacts remain untouched, since lovely homes and part of the University of Mexico are located above it. In this cemetery, many years before the volcano's lethal action, devout families buried their dead in the crouching position with red ocher and ceremonial flints. The tools were intended to accompany the deceased in their next life in a similar manner to the artifacts that accompanied their compatriots when they passed away in France, Spain, Africa, and South America.

Seeds and agricultural techniques from Atlantis served the immigrants well in their new homeland. Early settlers in Mexico ate corn very similar to our own, although it did not grow wild in Central America. Nearly 240 feet below the surface of the dried lake bed beneath Mexico City, archaeologists recently discovered pollen grains of corn that radiocarbon testing dates to 25,000 years ago.[86] For irrigation and transportation, knowledgeable engineers designed elaborate networks of canals to serve the vast population. These waterways, constructed thousands of years ago, are visible today, defined from the air by the growth of foliage of dissimilar colors.

In prehistoric times, people traveled and merchants moved goods on roads over land currently covered by the Caribbean Sea. Inhabitants of Cayman Brac in the Cayman Islands remember stories their grandparents told of The Gold Road. When ocean levels were lower, this highway ran north from Peru to Venezuela, and from there the route stretched along firm ground across what are now the Lesser Antilles Islands. The road journeyed on to Puerto Rico and Haiti and terminated in Jamaica. Unlimited amounts of gold, silver, and precious gems, all carried on the backs of animals, were hauled from South America to the Caribbean. Eventually, as the natives say, something tore the land into small islands, the sea poured in from all directions, and the whales swam in.[87]

When the last Ice Age ended and North American glaciers rapidly melted, water flowed in torrents down the Mississippi River, provoking seas in the Gulf of Mexico to rise precipitously. In a vain effort to keep out the floods that endangered their precious homes, descendants of Atlanteans, probably with celestial advice, employed their engineering skills to build cyclopean walls. Today in the Bahama Banks, not far under the surface of the water, bulwarks—which were built from colossal blocks of cut stone that weigh as much as twenty-five tons—extend for hundreds of feet.[88] Extensive fortifications are also visible off the coasts of Mexico, northern Cuba, and Florida. Adjacent to Venezuela, another substantial wall, thirty feet high, reaches for miles into the sea.

Evidence has recently surfaced proving that before 9,000 B.C. people settled in Belize on the southern coast of the Yucatan peninsula at a location that Edgar Cayce described as the site of an Atlantean colony.[89] Their continued interest in mathematical and astronomical concepts is reflected in the Olmecs' culture and the accomplishments of the Olmecs' successors, the Mayans, whose civilization in that area reached its height about A.D. 200. The Mayans' accurate calendar utilizes measurements requiring at least 10,000 years of observation.[90] Edgar Cayce refers to visitors from other planets at the time of the Mayans.[91] Contacts with these extraterrestrials firmly oriented Mayan art and architecture toward calendrical and astronomical calculations and correlations. Inscriptions in the Mayan Temple of the Sun in Palenque, in central Mexico, display detailed knowledge of the movements of the planets. Thousands of years of study of the skies in the observatories of the Temple of Poseidon in Atlantis, combined with information from heavenly visitors, supplied the Mayans with the astronomical wisdom revealed in these unusual carvings.

The Mayan civilization in Central America and early Egyptian culture display striking similarities that are a likely result of their common place of origin in the land of Atlantis that lay between them. These parallels include sun worship, funeral customs, hieroglyphic writing, pyramid-type buildings, and the analogous physical features of the people. After the final destruction of Atlantis there was very little communication between the European and American continents. The reason, as Plato tells us in both the Timaeus and the Critias, is that the Atlantic Ocean was impossible to navigate due to a barrier of thick mud just below the surface. Numerous other writers of ancient times mention the shallow Atlantic Ocean. Herodotus, in the *Melpomene*, quotes Satraps, who told the Persian monarch Xerxes that after a certain point he was unable to go farther navigating the Atlantic Ocean because of thick mud that prevented his ship from moving forward.[92] Plutarch, in *On the Face Which Appears on the Orb of the Moon*, refers to the isle of Ogygian, five days' sail west of Britain, the three islands west of that, and to the sea beyond, which was slow of passage and full of mud, on the way to the "great continent by which the ocean is fringed."[93] *Periplus*, by the Carian geographer Scylax Caryandenis (about 550 B.C.), is another work that testifies to the unnavigability of the Atlantic owing to the "shortness of the sea, and mud and weed."[94] Carthaginian sailors describe the presence of land just below the surface, making the ocean very shallow and unnavigable.[95] Volcanoes mainly eject pumice stone, which floats on the surface for a long time. The enormous amount generated when Atlantis was destroyed remained on the surface of the Atlantic Ocean for a very long time. Eventually it turned to mud and slowly sank.[96]

Native American stories refer to a book written by a descendant of Votan's son who sailed to the west as the waves covered Atlantis. The Mayans carefully preserved the ancient manuscript, titled *Proof That I Am a Serpent*, until the time of the European invaders.[97] It was burned in the Spaniards' bonfires that consumed all their precious records, including scientific knowledge and information regarding the prehistory of the world. Three books that escaped the fires of the Spanish invaders in the sixteenth century have proved difficult to translate and appear to be concerned primarily with astrological matters. Perhaps additional literature Spaniards took to Europe is stored in the Vatican and will be available one day to enrich our understanding of Atlantis.

When Cortez arrived in Central America in 1519, the Aztecs were living in what is now Mexico City and its surroundings. To his surprise, Cortez found the Aztecs' skills with metallurgy and architecture far superior to any in Europe. Spaniards' accounts of a city with zones of land and water, plus the Aztecs' lavish use of gold, silver, and precious stones, resemble Plato's descriptions of the capital city of Atlantis and imply the influence of extraterrestrials. Where did the Aztecs originate? They explained to the Spaniards that their distant ancestors came in boats from Aztlan, a lost country once in the sea to the east.[98] In their language, *atl* means water and *tlan* is a place or land, so Aztlan means "water land" or perhaps "island."[99] The Aztecs remembered Aztlan as a place of many flamingos. Thousands of these birds continue to congregate and breed in Andros, one of the Bahama Islands. The Aztecs told the Spaniards of a sacred mountain in Aztlan with seven caves from whence came their seven tribes. When tremors of the Earth forewarned their ancestors of impending trouble, seven groups left, traveling toward the setting sun to safer land. Eventually some of their wandering descendants settled in central Mexico. This is the same story the Caribs recount of their ancestry.

Despite the passage of time, the Aztecs retained a few customs of their Atlantean forefathers. When they met, the Aztec kings practiced a ritual similar to that of the kings of Atlantis, drinking blood from gold cups.[100] Instead of sacrificing bulls, they employed human victims; there weren't any large animals in Mexico during their time. The Aztecs worshiped the sun and conducted religious and magical ceremonies on their flat-topped pyramids. Psychics believe Aztec priests evoked Kundalini, or the serpent fire, during these rites. Kundalini is a Godlike force within people that is coiled at the base of the spine. When released through yoga or by evolutionary growth, it enables one to engage in astral travel, leaving and returning to the body at will.[101]

In spite of natural cataclysms and troubles resulting from aggressive wandering tribes from the north, descendants of those who sailed west from Atlantis retained and developed skills in mathematics, engineering, and astronomy, as well as strong artistic abilities. Native Central Americans today create lovely, attractive articles without machinery. Collectors everywhere prize their handmade decorated pottery and other exquisite articles produced and utilized by these people who descended, in part, from Atlanteans.

South America

Atlanteans who sailed to South America when their country disappeared in 10,000 B.C. found themselves in a land of high mountains and impenetrable jungles. Some joined descendants of those who preceded them many centuries before, and others mingled with resident Asians. For most of the refugees, life was very different from anything they had experienced in the past and just to remain alive was extremely difficult. Forced to hunt and farm in small groups, they lived in bark huts and dressed in primitive clothing. Those who were defeated by insect bites, infections, poor food, and manual labor soon left this world, but the strongest, most resolute Atlanteans survived.

The immigrants to South America in 10,000 B.C. who settled in the Amazon regions managed very well and multiplied rapidly. They cleared the land extensively to cultivate more and more crops so that eventually the forests were virtually eliminated. As a result, the climate changed. No longer did large masses of trees trap the moisture that wafted overhead. Consequently, less and less rain fell. As the fruitful land turned into an arid plain, vegetation naturally moved to higher surrounding areas and people followed. Further problems, such as aggressive wild animals, continued to pursue them. Survival required an increasing amount of time and their civilization degenerated, demonstrating the maxim that "barbarians" often represent the degeneration of a culture. Enterprising descendants of Atlanteans who left the Amazon basin and followed tributaries northwest to the coast of South America contributed to the magnificent city of Tiahuanaco.

Throughout this early period of hardship, due to lore about the wonders of life in Atlantis reverently passed down from generation to generation, some expertise survived. Visitors from outer space also undoubtedly provided advice, as is evidenced by remains of a prehistoric city high on a mountain in the Cordillera Blanca of Peru. This inspirational site, called Yayno, is a three-day walk over two extremely high passes from the nearest road. Located on the summit of a tall peak, the ruins preside over an expansive circular view of snowcapped mountains and lush valleys. In Yayno, almost inaccessible from our civilization, a highly advanced unknown race lived long before the Incas. In spite of severe earthquakes in the area, walls of their colossal five- or six-story buildings remain standing. The style of the structures is completely different from the Incas, but like other prehistoric constructions, they include huge stone blocks that weigh many tons. The mysteries of this unusual site may never be solved by modern science. How were the gigantic rocks for these large multistoried buildings transported from distant sites to the mountaintop? How did people of such an advanced civilization survive in this dry, inaccessible place? From whence came the knowledge to construct towering buildings that did not collapse in the routine severe shaking of the Earth's surface? Yayno offers testimony to the skills of our predecessors and to the extraterrestrials whose presence is commonly noted in Peru.

From the time of Atlantis, as civilizations came and went in South America, the artistic and engineering skills of the conquered were appropriated by the victors. One thousand years ago, the militaristic Incas overcame all who dwelt in the lands from Bolivia to Chile, including a vast empire, the ancient Kingdom of the Grand Chimu. The warlike, aggressive Incas incorporated the Chimus' sophisticated artistic techniques into their culture and copied their social and political system. In the same way, long before, the Chimus learned from those whom they subjugated, such as the Moche, who constructed gigantic mounds with bases longer than the Great Pyramid of Egypt.[102] The Moches were extremely adept at working with precious metals, and after the Chimus conquered them, Chimu artists carefully studied the Moches' skillful artistic feats and learned to fashion lovely and delicate ornaments, such as feathers of gold almost as soft as the plumes of a bird.[103] The Incas, in turn, acquired these skills from the Chimu or forced these captives to work for them.

The Chimus' capital city of Chan Chan, the largest ever built in prehistoric Peru, covered almost ten square miles near Truijillo on the Pacific coast. Since stones were not readily available, their pyramids, temples, and public buildings were constructed from adobe brick that artisans tastefully decorated with gold, silver, and bronze. The Chimus' impressive engineering capabilities are obvious in the remains of their expansive walls and in their extensive irrigation network, which is similar to the Atlanteans' canals.

The Incas' capital at Cuzco, high in the Andes, reflects the talents of the Chimus and their predecessors, the Moche, and probably those who lived before them. In 1531, when Hernando DeSoto arrived, the elaborate architectural style of Cuzco's buildings and their ornate furnishings and exquisite gardens closely resembled Plato's description of the City of the Golden Gates. One cloister in Cuzco, the Temple of the Sun, which predated the Incas, housed over 1,000 individuals. When the Incas took over the building they layered the cloister walls with sheets of gold and carved the gold-plated fountain in its center from a single block of stone. The main altar, in the shape of the sun, was also covered with thick sheets of gold and surrounded by golden statues of the dead kings, just as the Temple of Poseidon was encompassed by statues of former kings and their wives. In Cuzco, DeSoto found other massive buildings erected from heavy blocks of polished stone carved to fit together so tightly that it was impossible to insert a knife blade between the rocks.[104] Like Atlantis, this mountainous area of Peru is subject to earthquakes, but buildings and walls constructed in this firm manner are able to withstand more of the Earth's shaking than those built with stones that are not fitted so closely together. In many cases, earthquakes actually strengthen them, forcing the perfectly cut stones together even more tightly.

The quipu, a record-keeping device of the Incas and their predecessors, consisted of a thick cord from which dangled as many as fifty or more colored, knotted strings of different lengths. The color and length and position of every string on the master cord and the number of knots and their position on each string were all significant in this complicated tool. Quipus were utilized to jog memories and to record and decipher the detailed, intricate information pertaining to the administration of the sprawling Incan empire. Carefully trained officials operated the mass of strings, resembling the inside of an advanced contemporary machine. The quipu appears to be a simple imitation of an elaborate, technical method of calculating from a scientifically advanced civilization that preceded the Incas,[105] or was devised with the advise of gods from the sky.

Additional reminders of Atlantis persist in Peru. In 1958, in the isolated Mancha Valley, British archaeologist Karola Siebert found evidence of a cult from Atlantis. Next to a seven-foot stone column, Siebert discovered stones piled to form a horseshoe, the symbol of Vulcan, the Fire God. In the center of the horseshoe was an altar holding the bones of a baby. Local residents had planted cacti on a nearby hill in the shapes of the trident of Poseidon and zig zag lines, the symbol of fire and water. Other signs and vestiges in the nearby area convinced Siebert that the seven-foot column was a symbol of Atlantis, worshiped by the natives for thousands of years.[106]

Archaeologists have noted the striking similarities between the Incan and Sumerian civilizations. In *America's Ancient Civilizations*, A. Hyatt Verrill and his wife Ruth Verrill, who is an expert on the Sumerians, list forty-two important matters that were identical, or very nearly so, in those ancient cultures. The account is followed by almost 100 duplicate or very similar words and names that have the same meaning in the Sumerian and Peruvian languages.[107] There has to be a logical explanation for the hundreds of correlations in the Peruvian and Sumerian cultures and their resemblance to Atlantis, despite their disparate geographical locations; one may be extraterrestrial. Celestial visitors were largely responsible for the Sumerian's accomplishments. They aided the Atlanteans and they presumably assisted the Incas and their predecessors.

During the nineteenth century, stories abounded in South America of dead Atlantean cities in the jungles of the Amazon and its tributaries. Explorers and prospectors searched for the vaguely described remote places hoping to find ancient, disintegrating stone buildings covered with twisting vines, once inhabited by descendants of Atlanteans. Colonel Percy W. Fawcett, after twenty years in the British Army as a military surveyor, geographer, and engineer, was one who hunted for the lost communities. From 1906 to 1925, Colonel Fawcett traveled extensively through uncharted country in Brazil and Bolivia, becoming an expert on survival among the hostile people in that difficult environment. Finally he acquired a map indicating an unknown city deep in the jungles of southwest Brazil and set out to find it with his twenty-year-old son and a friend. His last report, from Dead Horse Camp in the Zingu Basin, described them as they were on their way to a ruined city on the edge of a large lake.

No further word came from Colonel Fawcett until ten years later, when Geraldine Cummins, a medium hired by his wife, successfully contacted him. Fawcett communicated that he was not dead but in a semiconscious state in the South American jungle, a prisoner in a small village. He had found a lost city, and as if in a dream, envisioned life there as it was long ago. In the vacant city he saw figures cut in stone and other inscriptions that furnished evidence that Atlantis existed in an area now at the bottom of the Atlantic Ocean.

Fawcett believed structures in the mysterious cities of the lost civilization would offer information relating to one of the Atlanteans' sources of energy. He planned to use this knowledge to benefit humankind. Just before he disappeared, he reported finding white towers that emitted a glowing light at night. In a later communication with a psychic, he relayed that he believed the sun bombards the Earth with electrons and the towers in South America acted as sieves, utilizing the electrons' power. Old stone monuments appear to attract a kind of electric current that produces light which, when uncontrolled, becomes so hot it fuses stones. Photographs of old stone monuments some-times reveal unseen bands, as if they were surrounded by light.[108]

Many other adventurers followed maps from old prospec-tors, seventeenth-century Spaniards' vague descriptions, or whispered local traditions that led them into the wilderness of South America. Stories of ruins of cities containing tremen-dous walls, stone houses on straight paved streets broken by tree roots, archways made from boulders weighing hundreds of tons, and large amounts of gold spurred them onward. Fever, unfriendly natives, and the jungle inevitably overcame them, just as it did the brave individuals who, hundreds of centuries before, sought a safe haven from a land sinking into the ocean to the east.

North America

North America was not available to Atlantean residents thirty thousand years ago when, as snow fell and glaciers formed, the world seemed to be turning into a vast frozen planet. From the Dakotas on south to southern Ohio and east to New York State, mammoth masses of ice, sometimes a mile deep, moved both horizontally and vertically back and forth across the land, decimating everything in their path. Stones and boulders were frozen into the moving masses and, acting like file's teeth, cut into whatever they encountered. Glacial ice cascaded forward at a rate of several hundred feet per hour. The accompanying cold often arrived very suddenly and combined with the rapid movement of stupendous sheets of ice to eliminate not only plants and animals but humans and all their possessions. Men, women, children, and animals fled to the south toward Cen-tral America.

The snow and ice eventually melted, but in 20,000 B.C. glaciers once again took over the land, ocean levels fell, islands grew, and the continental shelves were exposed. Atlanteans sailed the shorter distance from their country to the glacier-free southern coast of the North American continent. The fertile Mississippi River valley and its immediate tributaries became home to many who spoke Algonquin, a distinct language that is totally unrelated to the speech of those who lived in the western United States at a later time. The Atlanteans worshiped the gods of nature and, using the Ohio and Mississippi Rivers, traded by boat with nations to the south in the Caribbean. Access to the north was unavailable, for it was covered with snow and ice.

Between 20,000 B.C. and 10,000 B.C., the Algonquins were not troubled by immigrants from Asia. Glaciers and impassable sheets of ice blocked the Bering Straits between Russia and Alaska, making travel by foot almost impossible. It was so cold on the narrow corridor that even the dwarf tundra birch died out.[109] Animals, essential for migrating travelers' food, chose not to live in such harsh surroundings and roamed far to the south, benefiting the Algonquins.

Finally, in 10,000 B.C., the glaciers receded, and bison and caribou living in southern river valleys traveled northward, eating the tender grass and brightly colored flowers that appeared almost overnight behind the melting snow. The Algonquins also moved, following the animals in all directions across the United States. Edgar Cayce described their descendants, the Iroquois, as direct descendants of Atlanteans.[110] Others—the Dakota, Sioux, Mandans, Delaware, Shawnee, Algonquins, Choctaw, and Cherokee—all retain the aquiline noses, high cheek bones, and long skulls of their Atlantean ancestors. Soon after the glaciers began to melt, people successfully crossed from Asia to Alaska and southward. They constantly clashed with those already living in North America, and individuals from the two groups seldom intermarried. The immigrants from the northwest retained their Asian physical characteristics and blood categories; the Algonquin tribes preserved their Atlantean attributes. East Asians are thirty to sixty percent blood types B and AB, as compared to Algonquin descendants whose blood is zero to two percent types B and AB.[111]

Edgar Cayce discloses that second generation Atlanteans who lived in the central United States were among those known as mound builders.[112] They engaged in geomancy, moving tremendous quantities of earth to build numerous artificial hills, which early Europeans referred to as mounds. Exactly when the mounds were built is difficult to determine and varies, for new hills were often constructed atop old. Remains of comparable structures in Koster, Illinois, are covered by twenty feet of glacial debris, which indicates some were constructed before the last glacier, at least 15,000 years ago.

Mounds often served as burial places or as bases for temples. Sometimes the dirt was moved into significant shapes, like the large mastodon in Wisconsin and the remarkable serpent mound in Adams County, Ohio, which was 1,330 feet long, covered sixteen acres, and reached the height of a ten-story building.[113] Like most mounds formed into figures, its shape is only visible from the air. Native Americans say the enormous mound represented the serpent invading from the south, coming up the Mississippi. In its mouth was an oval, the symbol of the turtle, which stood for the Dakotas who led people to the north.[114] Twenty-two thousand mounds were identified in western Mississippi, one thousand in one county of Ohio, and many more from Georgia to Montana.[115] Among the mounds in Ohio there were numerous pyramids, all of whose sides were oriented to correspond exactly with the cardinal points of the compass. The Great Mound of Cahokia, in east St. Louis, was as large as the Pyramid of Cheops in Egypt. When it was decimated in the nineteenth century, it contained embroidered materials, gold, silver, and copper jewelry, and parchment that appeared to have writing on its surface.[116] In 1890, on behalf of the Smithsonian Institution, Georgia Cyrus Thomas made systematic "explorations" of hundreds of mounds. His work involved gutting and demolishing the structures.[117] Travelers and early settlers ravaged most of the remainder. Other sophisticated constructions of long ago in the southeastern United States, reminiscent of Atlantean engineering feats, included huge towers and walls over 800 feet in length and canals fourteen miles long.[118]

Many mounds in the United States were built over remains of sacred structures erected long before them at places of high energy, just as Christians placed cathedrals in Great Britain and France at the strong spiritual sites of pagan temples. The intersection of two or more ley lines often marks the location of significant mounds. The artificial hill at Portsmouth, Ohio, from which groups of mounds extend in concentric circles into West Virginia and Kentucky, is one such powerful location. Portsmouth is located on a ley line that runs from Marietta, Ohio, over sixty-five miles away, to Lexington, Kentucky. The line is fifty-nine degrees from true north, the exact angle of the sunrise at Marietta on June 21, the day of the summer solstice.[119] This correlates with the legends in Great Britain that say when the sun shined directly down one of these courses at sunrise, the Druids rose in the air and moved along them.

For thousands of years, Native American memorizers retained and transmitted knowledge through memory and word of mouth. The memorizers, who were usually women since they were less apt to be killed in battle, were among the most respected citizens of every nation. Memorizers spent their lives absorbing historical, medicinal, religious, and secular literature from their predecessors, and in turn teaching it to representatives of the next generation. Until recently, Native Americans were reluctant to share this knowledge with the white man, but to avoid its being lost forever, Cherokee Dhyani Ywahoo, Chief Sedillio of the Yanqui Indians, Apache Chief Asa Delugio, and others are generously revealing what is so carefully preserved.

Dhyani Ywahoo tells us that the forebears of the Cherokee came from the Pleiades to Atlantis, where they lived until its final destruction. When their homes sank into the ocean they escaped to this continent. Before the Europeans arrived, Dhyani Ywahoo's people lived a happy life, always harmonious with their natural environment. The Cherokees' advanced mathematical skills, detailed knowledge of astronomy, and legends of their sources of power reflect the wisdom and accomplishments of their ancestors. Cherokee medicine people utilized crystals to capture and manage Earth's energy for their protection. Ywahoo describes this positive energy issuing from forceful dragons the Cherokee called Ukdena. Ancient sacred rituals helped these descendants of Pleiadeans from Atlantis maintain a harmonious balance of power from the sun, the moon, the Earth, and the universe. The Cherokee grew bountiful crops and lived happily for an untold number of years in the southeastern United States. When western civilization encroached, the number of Cherokee medicine people decreased, the shamans lost the dragon power, and their beneficial relationship with the energy currents of the universe disappeared.[120] Only traces of their ley lines remain.

Legends transmitted for generations by descendants of the Algonquin family refer to the great flood and to the big country that sank in the sunrise sea. In their drawings the crescent is its symbol; when the points are up, it signifies the old land is still living, and when the points are down, their homeland is covered by the ocean.[121] The Sioux, like the Aztecs and the Caribs, believe they are the children of seven kings from an old, red land. To this day they still keep seven tribes. Their realistic tales of the flood help to confirm that their memorizers related facts, not fiction. Apaches recall a grand fire island in the eastern ocean and the mazelike entrance to its port. Asa Delugio offers a graphic description of the sacred mountain that "spurted fire like a giant fountain" describing "the fire god crawling through the caverns, roaring and thrashing the land about like a wolf shakes the rabbit."[122] He reports that after his distant forefathers fled from their homeland, they traveled west to South America and eventually reached the mountains. Here they found temporary shelter in immense, ancient tunnels. After leaving the mountains, they wandered with their seeds and fruit plants for many years before coming to the North American continent.[123]

Hopi, who live in the southwestern United States, describe their Third World, the one before this, as being an advanced civilization on a red land where the inhabitants wore shields to fly through the air.[124] Their legends portray an overpowering flood destroying that world and survivors migrating on reed rafts to the present Fourth World. When they finally landed on the shores of a warm country to the south, their ancestors separated into various groups and began their long migrations over the continent. The Hopi expect that the islands of their past home will emerge one day to prove the truth of their memories.

Enterprising prehistoric people, perhaps Atlanteans and probably with the assistance of extraterrestrials who were eager for minerals, mined several thousand tons of copper from deposits on Isle Royale and the Keweenaw Peninsula in Michigan. When the Atlanteans ceased to come, clay, bushes, and massive trees filled in many of the excavations, but indications of the workers' sophisticated techniques for locating veins of ore and removing and transporting the copper are still visible. Tunnels and pits sixty feet deep, drains that remove excess water, stone hammers weighing thirty-six pounds, shafts two miles long in a straight line, and a mass of detached copper that weighs six tons lying where it was left after it was raised five feet by timbers and wedges attest to the unknown miners' advanced engineering skills.[125] There is no evidence that any settlement within a thousand miles of these sites made use of the metal.[126] Local legends say the red serpent came up the Mississippi with an insatiable appetite for copper.[127] The O'Chippewas of Michigan recall ships coming for copper from the distant land of Pahn.[128] Capable miners were active elsewhere in the United States long before recorded history.

A coal mine in Wattis, Utah, that extends over 8,500 feet below the surface is so ancient that the coal residue in the extensive tunnels where workmen toiled long ago has oxidized to the point where it is no longer commercially valuable.[129]

Customs of Algonquin offspring on this continent resemble those of descendants of Atlantean refugees living in other lands bordering the Atlantic Ocean. At one time both the Cherokee and the Iroquois sacrificed the buffalo almost in the same fashion the Atlanteans sacrificed the bull.[130] The Choctaw, descendants of Algonquin-speaking people, practiced double burial. They gently placed bodies of their dead on platforms high in the trees, out of reach of hungry animals but available to birds, who picked off the flesh. After one year, when the bones were clean, another elaborate ceremony took place where relatives and friends polished, painted red, and reburied the skeletons in preparation for the next life.[131]

The destructive effects of excessive materialism in Atlantis were deeply ingrained in the minds of descendants of emigrants to North America from the submerged land. As civilization developed on this continent, everyone placed the highest of priorities on maintaining a life in total harmony with the universe. Remembering their ancestors' homeland, they retained a devout concern for the world around them and lived simply. In A.D. 1600, sixty million people inhabited the United States, but their lives imposed almost no detrimental impact on the environment. Carefully limiting the size of their cities, they never overburdened the ecology of any one area, always respecting and cherishing the gifts of nature.

10

FUTURE

ATLANTIS IS GONE BUT NOT forgotten. Like tiny pearls from a broken necklace that fall to the floor and scatter in all directions, so Atlanteans dispersed from their sinking country. Memories of them and their homeland remain firmly planted in the unconscious minds of their descendants, just as the loose pearls of the necklace lodge unseen in cracks and corners. Universal subconscious memories ensure that belief persists in an advanced civilization that thrived on land in the Atlantic Ocean, destroyed by natural catastrophes.

Persistent recollections of Atlantis are basically correct. Many possibilities exist for confirming the reality of the land of Atlantis, its people, and their descendants. Scientists, with the assistance of the deep-diving submarine

Alvin, are carefully mapping the Atlantic Ridge. As they study its ocean currents and rock samples, it will become apparent that some of the land was above the surface prior to 10,000 B.C. Marine infrared and thermal photography offer the opportunity to search for buried structures.

Dowsers who work with maps, or other psychics adept at describing the history and use of artifacts, are a latent untapped source of information. To improve the reliability of their data, more than one might be employed on a similar project, and the results compared for consistency. Thevet's cave, on the north side of San Miguel in the Azores Islands, should be opened and carefully explored by archaeologists. Thevet, a historian who visited the cavern in 1675, described strange inscriptions on two stellae there, but the cave was closed because investigators died from inhaling fumes emitted from adjoining volcanic craters and thermal springs.[1]

Are Gaunche mummies RH negative, as were so many other Atlantean descendants? Do prehistoric ruins lie at the bottom of the large Lake of the Seven Cities on San Miguel,[2] formed in the fifteenth century when earthquakes shook the island? The excellent sailors of Crete traveled extensively in 7000 B.C. When their written language is completely translated it may reveal further knowledge of Atlantis. Perhaps the Hall of Records in Egypt or one of the three sources of information about the Atlanteans' solar conductors that Edgar Cayce described will be found. Literature of the Aztecs that sixteenth-century Spaniards carried to Europe may surface in the Vatican.

When the actuality of the land and people of Atlantis is confirmed to the satisfaction of the western scientific community, it will stimulate additional curiosity about the lost country and its civilizations—information that will offer lasting benefits to humankind as a prediction of what is potentially in store for us, for the moving picture of the past will always be rerun.

As our insight into the Atlantean civilization develops, we become aware of a country where, for most of its long history, the people lived centered and harmonious lives, an ambience we would like to duplicate. The expertise and knowledge that contributed to their ideal spiritual existence are available to us today. For example, meditation, which leads to mindfulness, ensures a more balanced approach to daily traumas. As we contemplate our inner thoughts, we will further develop our intuition, extrasensory perception, and other psychic powers. Twentieth-century individuals are acquiring faith in their intuition and employing it in personal and professional affairs. The medical community is recognizing the power of the mind to influence the physical and mental health of the body. Physicians are suggesting the age-old techniques of visualization and positive thinking as a means of promoting healing. Other options are available for duplicating the balanced lives of Atlanteans. Spending time outdoors in parks or woods with trees, plants, and birds increases our positive energy. Communing with nature helps to adjust our perspective and reminds us that the mountains, ocean waves, and stars have been here for eons, and they will be here long after we and our problems are gone.

The prehistoric practice of feng shui or geomancy survived in China, and architects throughout the world are utilizing it to design suitable interiors for homes and to place buildings at sites where natural factors will provide additional energy. We could build circular homes, which Atlanteans believed were compatible with the human spirit and effective channels of universal energy.

Let's imitate the Atlanteans by cultivating and trusting our young children's psychic skills. Allowing them plenty of time to acquire a relationship with their natural environment will encourage them to comprehend that a great spiritual power created us, the Earth, everything on it, and all that exists in the skies above. Astronomy should be part of every school's curriculum, and telescopes should be freely available to all people, for study of the heavens enhances appreciation of the universe and assists us in restoring our priorities.

Family and community rituals and respect for the environment were the foundations of Atlantean society. When the Atlantean civilization matured, materialism and lust superceded respect for nature, for each other, and for the one all-powerful spiritual being. Negative energy increased and the country was eventually ravaged. Nature has rebelled in more recent times. When the Pharaoh refused to free the people of Israel, the Bible describes God sending plagues of locusts and flies, thunder, hail and lightning against the Egyptians. As Jesus succumbed on the cross, an earthquake split rocks and destroyed a nearby temple. Port Royal, Jamaica, a Caribbean pirate haven of bars and brothels in the seventeenth century, was renowned throughout the world as a city where horrible crimes were everyday events. In a few short minutes in 1692 that entire community was completely devastated by an earthquake. Once again the all-powerful God used the forces of nature to punish our planet's inhabitants and forced those who survived to start anew. To prevent disaster and promote positive energy on this planet, it is important to have harmonious relationships with each other. We must work at preserving the celebrations of birthdays, holiday traditions, and other age-old customs. Community events at sacred sites to honor the solstices, equinoxes, and the full moon are further suggestions for balancing our lives.

Atlantean civilizations that were aligned with nature developed for over 20,000 years before their interests changed and natural catastrophes destroyed them. Similarly, more recent cultures developed belief systems and strategies focused on nourishing the Earth and meeting the needs of its inhabitants rather than increasing material achievements. Technological development emphasizes the importance of tangible, manufactured objects, and tends to instigate a disintegration in morality as people gradually judge each other by their material possessions rather than the quality of their personal traits. Industrialization also contributes to destruction of the Earth's natural resources, a serious problem today.

In his recent book *How Much Is Enough?* Alan Durning offers concrete suggestions for stemming the tide of consumption in the world's advanced countries. He suggests tactics aimed at decreasing the time and energy expended on creating manufactured goods, as well as conserving our natural resources: consume primarily local produce, eat grains rather than meats, increase travel on trains, buses, and bikes instead of private automobiles, repair old merchandise rather that purchase new, tax television commercials, and impose a tax on manufactured commodities based on how much their production is detrimental to the environment. Fewer hours devoted to work would increase opportunities to develop talents and friendships and allow us to grow spiritually, progressing in the process of contemplating and comprehending our place in the natural world and the universe. If underdeveloped countries taxed the natural resources they export to industrialized nations on the basis of the cost of their ecological destruction, they would have additional funds for basic health, education and family planning programs.

The possibilities for protecting the ecosystem of our planet are unlimited. Edgar Cayce and other psychics offer numerous insights into the Atlanteans' almost unbelievably advanced technological society, which did not pollute their environment. The prospects of energy from magnetism, sonics, the human mind, crystals, and the sun's rays are inspiring.

Study of prehistory points to visitors from the heavens whose advice enabled primitive peoples to improve their way of life relatively quickly. Amazing stone constructions attest to the worldwide influence of unknown engineers and builders with sophisticated techniques and skills. Plato's description of the architecture of the City of the Golden Gates resembles the glorious cities of Nineveh, Tiahuanaco, and the buildings at Angor Wat and Cuzco. As contemporary scientists are groping in the dark, attempting to explain how these anamolies came to be, they might consider the possibility that advice from friendly extraterrestrials was instrumental in their construction. Edgar Cayce's portrayal of the Atlanteans' use of a huge crystal to obtain energy from the sun and their varied means of transportation become more plausible if we surmise that visitors from space assisted them. So many records of the past have vanished that we will probably never know how much extraterrestrials advised the prehistoric peoples of the Earth. Even though the Atlanteans, the Sumerians, and the inhabitants of Tiahuanaco have also disappeared, their celestial visitors are still nearby.

The gods from heaven provided accurate astronomical and calendrical knowledge, unparalleled building techniques, and medicinal and surgical advice to prehistoric civilizations; they could help us too. Scientists today are supervising exploration and travel in space. This may prove valuable if it enables us to discover a possible source of minerals, or if we destroy the world's ecosystem and must evacuate our planet. However, it would be preferable to focus our limited funds on preserving the environment with the goal of ensuring that humankind will continue to live here indefinitely with no need to emigrate. Energy from natural sources is a necessity for the survival of our civilization, and extraterrestrials are capable of helping us utilize it. The work with magnetism in the Philadelphia Experiment attracted many UFOs in the early 1940s, as evidenced by the sudden rash of reported sightings. Apparently, as they journey near its surface, the inhabitants of these space ships are utilizing the terrestrial magnetism circling the Earth.

Observers from outer space are not greeted with enthusiasm at the present time, but they are coming and, as has always been true, they are from a variety of places. The Sumerians' extraterrestrial visitors were primarily from the tenth planet when its orbit approached ours. Syrians instructed the Dogons, and Pleiadeans have always been active here. If our radar locks onto a UFO for ninety seconds, it interferes with computer control and operation of the vehicle. Occasionally the ships are forced to the Earth's surface. In 1948 a craft thirty-six feet in diameter and 380 feet long crashed near Phoenix, Arizona. The Air Force has offered various explanations for the incident, but investigators claim government officials recovered and examined two alien bodies from this wreckage of a vehicle from outer space.[3] Experts believe the saucer-shaped vehicle that crashed near Roswell, New Mexico, in July 1947 was struck by a lightning bolt from a thunder storm and flew about 125 miles before it was forced down. The government's attempt to cover up followed a similar pattern to the one they adopted in 1948, but there were many witnesses to the Roswell event and the incident continues to attract attention.[4] Our leaders maintain very strict secrecy about visiting extraterrestrials, perhaps because Orson Wells enthusiastically broadcast over the radio in 1938 that the Martians had landed. It was intended as a joke, but the panic that ensued would encourage any government to deny all future implications of the presence of beings from outer space on the Earth.

Sumerian texts record a variety of reasons for the travel of their gods from outer space to our world, just as these visitors' incentives currently vary. Some are simply curious. Others are concerned about the sickness of this planet, for the polluted atmosphere surrounding it is obvious from above. The aliens' ability to travel in space demonstrates the extent of their advanced skills, as does their control over those they contact on the Earth. The sons of God bred with the daughters of man to produce stronger humans. Today another group seems to be abducting people for short periods of time and experimenting with them, perhaps with the intention of developing a new race as happened in the past. John Mack, a Harvard psychiatrist who has interviewed over 100 UFO abductees in the last few years, is convinced that his patients' accounts of their experiences are real. Their episodes are external traumas, not dreams, which are internal occurrences. Based on three national surveys by the Roper organization, more than five million Americans may have been abducted, most of whom suffered unpleasant experiences.[5]

Atlanteans and Sumerians benefited from their contacts with celestial visitors, but can we? The helplessness of abductees and the disastrous results of the Philadelphia Experiment and the Montauk Project indicate we are not ready to communicate on an equal basis with these skillful, knowledgeable and strong-minded extraterrestrials. Apparently all aliens do not wish us well, and some are taking advantage of human beings. However we must assume most are not eager to see our planet die. Hopefully we can communicate with those who will assist us in coping with fundamental ecological problems and worldwide dangers such as nuclear war. To maintain our sanity as we interact with highly advanced aliens we must cultivate the skills of the Atlanteans and develop the strength and power of our minds.

As long as we inhabit this planet we have control of our immediate destinies. Nature rebels at appropriate times, but we are not solely its victims. In the past, when people released negative energy with hate, sin, and crime, they contributed to their own destruction. If we, the citizens of the advanced nations, follow the examples of the long-lived civilizations of Atlantis and simplify our lives, place increased emphasis on love, compassion and alignment with nature and eventually utilize advice from helpful celestial visitors, the human race and the Earth will survive. Many predict Atlantis will rise from the sea. What will rise is not necessarily the land but the ambience of immateriality, enlightenment, and spirituality that characterized the Golden Ages. The favorable balance of energy and the harmony of the past will again be reinstated on our planet.

AFTERWORD

A recent trip to the Azores Island brought the beautiful country of Atlantis back to life for me. After thousands of years, the tops of its mountains, which of course are now much nearer to sea level than they once were, have become a natural paradise that closely resembles the lovely land that disappeared. Plato's bubbling hot springs surrounded by ferns and moss-covered trees, a constant concert by omnipresent birds, vast areas of yellow wheat resembling fields of golden hair (as described by the Basque poet Jacinth Verdaguer), magnificent scented flowers growing wild that are larger and more intensely colored than any I have ever seen, and many more gifts of nature reproduce Atlantis as it once was. Irrigation, combining the mineral-rich hot springs with cooler water, makes it possible for the people to produce the two abundant crops a year to which Plato referred. Over all stands the huge volcanic cone of Mt. Pico, a constant reminder of the majestic Mt. Atlas that appeared to support the heavens as it dominated the land.

The instability that constantly disturbed Atlantean lands is still present in the Azores. The clouds of white steam that rise from the sides of old volcanoes like the exhaust from our large electric plants indicate some of this otherwise invisible activity. In June 1997, an earthquake that measured five on the Richter scale shook the island of Terceira. This was followed by almost 1,000 aftershocks measuring four or more. As a result of this type of activity, the sea floor is constantly rising and falling in the vicinity. At the present time, land that is ascending near Terceira is only seven feet under the surface. Perhaps, as Edgar Cayce predicted, some of ancient Atlantis actually will rise again.

APPENDIX

The works of the following authors provided substantial information for *Atlantis*. The short biographical summaries are to help the reader understand the writer's backgrounds and qualifications.

Ancient Scholars

DIODORUS SICULUS, a Sicilian geographer and historian of the first century B.C., was a far-ranging traveler and a trained and experienced compiler of information who recorded many details about Atlantis that he learned from the native people while researching in Egypt, Morocco and other parts of northern Africa.

HERODOTUS (485 B.C.–425 B.C.) was the author of the first extensive narrative history produced in the ancient world. His primary residence was in Greece, but he traveled widely throughout Europe, western Asia, Russia, and northern Africa. Herodotus' eye for detail and his interest in the customs and past events of the areas he visited are reflected in his massive *History* (of the Greco-Persian Wars), which is currently divided into nine volumes.

PLATO was born about 429 B.C. into a distinguished Greek family. His father is said to have claimed descent from the god Poseidon. Plato was initially a politician, but when he became convinced that there was no place for a man of conscience in Athenian politics, he turned to the study of philosophy.

Plato obtained some of his knowledge of Atlantis from his friend Critias. In the *Timaeus,* Plato says that when Critias' grandfather was ninety years old, he told the story to Critias. The grandfather, Critias the Elder, had learned about Atlantis from his father Dropides, who had acquired the data from his relative Solon, a prominent Greek lawyer who traveled to Egypt to study in about 579 B.C. According to Plato's account, while Solon was in Egypt, he visited the thriving capital city of Sais (El Said) where he worked with several priests, including Psonchis, who translated for Solon the wisdom about Atlantis inscribed on pillars. Writings in stone were a respected means of preserving facts in the past, for they were more permanent than manuscripts.

The subject of Atlantis was so fascinating to Plato that he continued to search for information about it to supplement the facts he received from Critias. He was able to consult with learned individuals, including students of Pythagoras (582–500 B.C.) who were acquainted with the historical lore lost when the western world's extensive libraries were destroyed. In his *Commentary on the Timaeus,* the philosopher Proclus (fifth century A.D.) describes a visit Plato made to Egypt. Proclus reports that Plato sold edible oils to the Egyptians to pay for the journey and that while he was there Plato talked with priests at Sais, Heliopolis, and Sebennytus.

Proclus also relates that Crantor, a student of Plato's, went to Egypt and to Sais to search for information to substantiate Plato's account. Proclus says Crantor visited the temple of Neith where priests showed him a pillar covered with writings about the history of Atlantis. The scholars' translation from the column to Crantor agreed completely with Plato's story (Muck, *The Secret of Atlantis,* 16).

Many other academics have researched the veracity of Plato's detailed account of Atlantis and confirmed that Solon, Dropides and the two Critias lived when described, so the transmission of information was possible. There is ample additional evidence that authenticates Plato's sources. Clement of Alexandria, one of the priests who instructed Pythagoras, reported that Solon, while he was in Egypt, spoke with Psonchis at Sais, as well as with Psenophis at Heliopolis (Sykes in Donnelly, *Atlantis: The Antediluvian World,* 17). In the *Timaeus,* Plato wrote that Solon was planning a poem about Atlantis. The Greek historian Plutarch's (A.D. 46–120) *Life of Solon* included a poem by Solon, now lost, titled *Atlantikos* (Ibid).

Plato wrote his two dialogues about Atlantis near the end of his long life, probably as a way of preserving the valuable knowledge. He died about 347 B.C.

Contemporary Scholars

CHARLES BERLITZ (1914–) is the grandson of Maximilian Berlitz, founder of the Berlitz language schools. One of the foremost linguists today, Charles speaks twenty-five languages with varying degrees of fluency. (See Bibliography.)

EDGAR EVANS CAYCE (1918–) is the youngest son of Edgar Cayce. His *On Atlantis,* printed in 1968, is a fine interpretation of his father's readings about the missing land and its civilization. *Mysteries of Atlantis Revisited,* published in 1988, which he wrote with Gail Cayce Schwartzer and Douglas G. Richards, offers a careful discussion of the extent to which mainline scientific discoveries since his father's death correlate with information from Edgar Cayce's readings. (See Bibliography.)

IGNATIUS DONNELLY (1831–1901) was an American politician and reformer as well as a thorough and scholarly researcher. He served as Lieutenant Governor of Minnesota at the young age of 28 and four years later was elected to the U.S. Congress, where he was an extremely intelligent legislator, far ahead of his time. He advocated equal voting rights for blacks, women's suffrage, federal income tax, and protection of the environment. Shortly after he moved to Washington, Donnelly's young wife died. Destitute, he turned to the world of books for consolation and was soon absorbed in the study of myths, prehistory, and Atlantis. Donnelly came to believe an element of truth forms the basis for many legends of events and people before recorded history. He proposes that the gods and goddesses of the ancient Greeks were personifications of the leaders of Atlantis and other advanced cultures of the past. In a similar way, Gandhi, Mandala, Churchill or Abraham Lincoln may be the main characters of legends 15,000 years from now. Donnelly's legal training and remarkable intellect are obvious in *Atlantis, the Antediluvian World,* which contains a vast amount of well-researched information convincingly presented. It was the first publication to rationally suggest that Atlantis could be verified by scientists. In a subsequent book titled *Ragnarok: The Age of Fire and Gravel,* he was the first to propose that the Earth had been visited many times by extraterrestrial catastrophes, such as massive objects from outer space, that destroyed human beings as well as plants and animals. Donnelly also wrote *Caesar's Column: A Story of the Twentieth Century* and *The Great Cryptogram.*

LUCILLE TAYLOR HANSEN. Attorney Hansen conducted extensive field work on the American continent and in Africa as she attempted to trace the heritage of Native Americans back to their origins in Atlantis. Her research included interviews with people like Chief Sedillio of the Yaqui Indians, who held degrees from two European universities. The many other Native Americans who confided in Hansen included a Choctaw, a Pueblo sachem, and Apache leader Asa Delugio.

MARCEL F. HOMET. A German archaeologist, Homet believes Atlanteans were the source of many similarities evident in cultures in lands around the Atlantic Ocean. In pursuit of knowledge, Homet traveled extensively in Europe, northern Africa, the Amazon River basin, and in North and Central America. To his surprise he found that Cro-Magnons whose skeletons and tools resembled their European counterparts lived in South America before they appeared in Europe.

JOHN MICHELL (1933–) is one of the world's premier researchers and writers on the sacred powers and mysteries of natural and manmade structures throughout the world. (See Bibliography.)

OTTO MUCK (1928–1965) was a distinguished German physicist and a renowned engineer with 2,000 patents to his name. His excellent book *Secret of Atlantis* reflects his careful study of the subject and his belief that fertile land in the Atlantic Ocean prior to 10,000 B.C. was occupied by people whose customs and beliefs spread to the surrounding areas.

ZECHARIA SITCHIN (1920–). A Biblical scholar and archaeologist, Sitchin reads many different languages, including most writings of early civilizations. As a result of thirty years of study and travel, he has published numerous scholarly works that provide little-known information about our extraterrestrial forefathers and some of their actions on the planet Earth in the past hundreds of thousands of years. He is one of the few people who have translated ancient Sumerian, Assyrian, Babylonian, and Hittite texts. (See Bibliography.)

JAMES LEWIS THOMAS CHALMERS SPENCE (1874–1955) was a highly respected Scottish mythologist and ancient historian who was vice-president of the Scottish Anthropological and Folklore Society and was awarded a Royal Pension "for his service to culture." Membership in a reputable occult organization offered him access to manuscripts of the Arcane Tradition (records of occult fraternities) written over 1,000 years ago. The age-old books are in English, French, Spanish, German, Greek and Arabic—all languages Spence mastered. Since there are few available copies of these venerable documents, they are read aloud to potential new members of the occult group during their sacred initiation ceremony. Spence's expertise at memorizing folk tales and legends helped him to accurately retain the interesting information he received orally during his initiation. He was intrigued by the numerous references to Atlantis in the ancient Arcane Tradition and began to earnestly pursue the subject.

As is true of many scholars who tackle the enormous job of researching Atlantis, Spence developed a passionate interest in the unique prehistoric country and its people. Spence was convinced that the occult arts, because they are unusually similar wherever they occur in the lands around the Atlantic Ocean, must have originated in one place. He found no region in western Europe with a culture sufficiently ancient to have served as the focal point from which the adjacent countries could have received their similar ideas of religion, myth and magic. He firmly believed our knowledge of the occult sciences originated in Atlantis.

To illustrate his theory that the occult arts came from Atlantis, Spence points out that many of the sorceresses in mythology are related to Atlantis. In Homer's *Odyssey*, Calypso was the daughter of the wise Atlas, and Circe was of the Titan race. Titans are commonly associated with Atlanteans because of their size. The severed head of the witch Medusa transformed Atlas into a mountain of stone, reminiscent of Mount Atlas, the tallest peak in Atlantis. The three Gorgons represent the strong forces of overpowering earthquakes, volcanic action and water that destroyed Atlantis.

To reveal the results of his far-ranging research, Spence wrote prolifically (see Bibliography). Despite his enthusiasm for the topic, Spence decided his position as a trustworthy, accomplished scholar was in danger if he continued to talk openly about the quality of life at the time of Atlantis and the occult arts he believed were practiced there. He stopped all his work on the subject and, according to those who knew him, refused to ever discuss Atlantis again (Michell, *The New View Over Atlantis,* 200).

DR. N. F. ZHIROV, a Russian scientist with a doctorate in Chemical Science, is also a marine geologist and a member of the Soviet Academy of Science. His complex, well-documented book about Atlantis, which was published in 1970, includes a Bibliography of 825 references. Many of his sources are from eastern Europe where the actuality of Atlantis is recognized by respected members of the scientific community.

EGERTON SYKES (1894–1983) was an erudite British student of antiquity who focused on Atlantis. In addition to serving in the British diplomatic service, he was an engineer, a soldier, a journalist and a fellow of the Royal Geographical Society. Shortly after World War II, Sykes founded the Atlantis Research Center in Brighton, England. Here, with the assistance of others devoted to the subject of prehistory, he assembled a large collection of classical references, ancient literature and legends pertaining to Atlantis. In 1949 he edited Donnelly's *Atlantis: The Antediluvian World,* inserting sensible, in-depth comments. During his lifetime he published two periodicals, *New World Antiquity* and *Atlantis.* After his death, the material in Syke's library in England was moved to the library of the Association for Research and Enlightenment in Virginia Beach, Virginia.

HAROLD T. WILKINS was a British anthropologist who traveled throughout Central and South America in the early twentieth century.

DAVID ZINK (1927–) is a physicist who served as a former military communications officer and taught English Literature at the Air Force Academy and at Lamar University in Texas. His study of the Cayce readings inspired Zink to lead an expedition to Bimini in 1974 to search for ruins from Atlantean buildings. (In 1926, Edgar Cayce predicted that in 1968 or 1969 part of Atlantis would rise again, and the remains of an ancient temple would be found at Bimini in the northwest corner of the Bahama Islands. In 1968 airplane pilots sighted cut stone blocks and columns where Cayce predicted.) As a result of Zink's discoveries in the Bahamas, this expert sailor, underwater photographer and skilled scuba diver returned to the area many times. Combining his expertise in the sciences of geology, astrophysics and anthropology with a broad knowledge of mythology and careful on-site readings by contemporary psychics, Zink wrote *The Ancient Stones Speak* and *The Stones of Atlantis.*

Psychics

TAYLOR CALDWELL (1900–1985). At the age of twelve, Taylor Caldwell wrote a detailed novel about a princess of Atlantis during the country's final days. The book culminated in the princess' escape from the sinking land by ship. Caldwell's grandfather, a book editor, was horrified when he read the manuscript, for the philosophical and intellectual maturity it reflected convinced him someone much older composed it. Actually, the contents came unknowingly from Caldwell's remote past, as did an unknown amount of the information in her other writings. Toward the end of her successful literary life, while editing *The Romance of Atlantis* with the help of Jess Stern, she experienced three dreams. The first two repeated and enhanced her unconscious memories of Atlantis, and the third occurred in a strange, hot land of mountains and forests where she lived with a few people who survived the demolition of Atlantis, their original island home.

EDGAR CAYCE (1877–1945) grew up in the southern United States as a poor farm boy with very little education. While he was still a young man, Cayce lost his voice and finally, in a desperate effort to cure his malady, underwent hypnosis. While in the trancelike condition he offered himself advice that proved to be a successful treatment for his problem. Cayce soon discovered that when he was in a state of self-hypnosis he diagnosed and prescribed sophisticated beneficial guidance for physical and mental problems of troubled individuals who were often far away. He decided to devote his life to advancing helpful suggestions for healing those who consulted him.

The thousands of stenographic records of Cayce's telepathic-clairvoyant statements are referred to as "readings." In his trancelike sessions Cayce often alluded to his patients' previous lives, some of which took place in Atlantis, where he portrayed a highly technological society over 12,000 years ago with extensive means of communication and transportation. During a period of twenty-one years, Cayce gave 30,000 readings and referred specifically to over 700 reincarnations in Atlantis. Although hundreds of different persons were involved, he was perfectly consistent in his data. No one has found any contradictory statements of dates or events in Cayce's information on any subject. His sons confirm that he never read Plato's material on Atlantis or other books about that country. Edgar Cayce's readings are available at the headquarters of the Association for Research and Enlightenment in Virginia Beach, Virginia.

Edgar Cayce's wisdom about Atlantis becomes more plausible when one considers facts from his readings that were not known at the time he provided them and were later verified. Archaeologists found the Dead Sea Scrolls eleven years after Cayce gave a life reading on the incarnation of a woman who was a member of a teaching community of Essenes on the northwest shore of the Dead Sea. During the reading Cayce described the exact spot near that lost Essene community where the scrolls were later discovered. In 1937, at the time of this reading, it was assumed the Essenes were communities of only celibate monks, and that Cayce was mistaken when he referred to a female member. However, twelve years later excavations produced skeletons of women as well as men among the Essenes, just as Cayce said. In 1939, Cayce portrayed the presence of Salome at the death and raising of Lazarus, something historians regarded as extremely unlikely until 1960, when a letter believed to have been written by St. Mark that referred to the miracle of Lazarus was found in a monastery near Jerusalem. The letter mentioned that a woman named Salome was present at the event. One of the most striking verifications of geological information from Cayce is his description of the ancient Sahara and the Nile. In 1925 he said that 10.5 million years ago the Sahara was a fertile land, and at that time the Nile flowed to the Atlantic Ocean. With the help of Space Shuttle imaging radar, scientists verified this. They also found evidence of campsites on the upper Nile dating to 250,000 years ago, exactly where Cayce said people lived at that time (Edgar Evans Cayce, *Mysteries of Atlantis Revisited,* 65).

With his talent for accessing information about civilizations as far back in history as Atlantis, Edgar Cayce could easily have used his skills to further his own interests, but he devoted his life to offering healing advice to those who sought his help.

MANLY PALMER HALL (1901–1990) exhibited his immense intellect and grasp of the mysteries at an early age. While in his twenties, he wrote his encyclopedic discussion of Western occult traditions, *The Secret Teachings of All Ages,* and continued to produce a substantial literary output throughout his long life. He founded the Philosophical Research Society in Los Angeles in 1934.

PHYLOS. In 1884, eighteen-year-old Frederick S. Oliver was visited by the presence of Phylos the Tibetan. Phylos dictated to Oliver in the form of mental pictures about his (Phylos') life in Atlantis 13,000 years before, in 11,650 B.C. Oliver reports the information he received from Phylos in *A Dweller On Two Planets,* published in 1952. Like Ruth Montgomery's work *The World Before,* which relies on knowledge acquired in a similar clairvoyant manner, Oliver's information is subject to criticism, but the book is worth serious consideration.

H. C. RANDALL STEVENS grew up as a normal British lad who served as a pilot in the Royal Naval Air Service and then became a well-known singer. He was not particularly interested in occult matters when, in 1925, an Initiate of ancient Egypt relayed to him, through automatic writing, information about Atlantis and ancient Egypt. This series of communications became known as the Osirian Scripts. Randall-Stevens published the first of these Scripts in 1928 and other volumes followed. The fourth, *Atlantis to the Latter Days,* was published in 1957. *The Book of Truth, The Chronicles of Osiris, The Wisdom of the Soul, The Teachings of Osiris,* and *Jewels of Wisdom* are his other works.

NOTES

Introduction

1. Pliny, *Natural History* (Roman, first century A.D.).
2. Spence, *The Occult Sciences in Atlantis*, 38.
3. Cayce, Reading 315–4.
4. Spence, *The Occult Sciences in Atlantis*, 49–50.
5. Homet, *Sons of the Sun*.

Chapter One

1. Zhirov, *Atlantis*, 247.
2. Spence, *The Problem of Atlantis*, 205.
3. Walters, *Book of the Hopi*.
4. Muck, *Atlantis*, 149.
5. Donato, *A Re-Examination of the Atlantis Theory*, 113.
6. Muck, *The Secret of Atlantis*, 46.
7. The thirteen Canary Islands stretch from 50 miles off the coast of northwest Africa for over 300 miles into the Atlantic Ocean. The islands of Madeira are 300 miles to the north of the Canaries, and the ten Cape Verde islands, occupying more than 1,500 square miles, lie 320 miles to the south. The nine Azores Islands are 800 miles west of Portugal, at the center of the Atlantic Ridge.
8. Muck, *The Secret of Atlantis*, 101.
9. Plato, *Critias*, Trans. R. B. Bury, 291.
10. Hansen, *The Ancient Atlantic*, 140.
11. Zhirov, *Atlantis*, chapter 9.
12. Ibid.
13. Ibid, chapter 13.
14. Ibid, 315.
15. Courtillot, "What Caused the Mass Extinction?," *Scientific American*, October 1990, 89.
16. Caldwell, *The Romance of Atlantis*, 35.
17. Muck, *The Secret of Atlantis*, 66–69.
18. Zhirov, *Atlantis*, chapter 10.

Chapter Two

1. Scott-Elliot, *The Story of Atlantis and the Lost Lemuria*.
2. Heinberg, *Memories and Visions of Paradise*, 177.
3. Vigers, *Atlantic Rising*, 31. The information in *Atlantis Rising*, published in 1944, was channeled to Daphne Vigers from Helio-Arkhan, who many years later communicated very similar material to Tony Neate, another British mystic, who had no knowledge of Vigers or her book.
4. Cousteau, *Calypso Log*, February 1989.
5. Cayce, Reading 364–10.
6. White, "Divine Fire: A Little-known Psychic Power," *Venture Inward*, March/April 1990.
7. Plato, *Critias*.
8. Sitchin, *The Twelfth Planet*, 60.
9. Robinson, *Edgar Cayce's Story of the Origin and Destiny of Man*, 53.
10. Montgomery, *The World Before*.
11. Caldwell, *The Romance of Atlantis*, 50.
12. Robinson, *Edgar Cayce's Story of the Origin and Destiny of Man*, 54.
13. Cayce, Reading 262–39.
14. Ibid.
15. Cayce, Reading 1977–1.
16. Cayce, Edgar Evans, *On Atlantis*, 80.
17. Robinson, *Edgar Cayce's Story of the Origin and Destiny of Man*, 55.
18. Cayce, Edgar Evans, *Mysteries of Atlantis Revisited*, 78.
19. Oliver, *A Dweller on Two Planets*, 174.
20. Robinson, *Edgar Cayce's Story of the Origin and Destiny of Man*, 110.
21. Ibid, 111.
22. Montgomery, *The World Before*, 126.
23. Oliver, *A Dweller on Two Planets*, 420.
24. Ibid.
25. Raymo, "Ice Age Venus," *The Boston Globe*, January 15, 1990.
26. Edgar E. Cayce, *Mysteries of Atlantis Revisited*, 77.
27. Donato, *A Re-examination of the Atlantis Theory*, 87. William M. Donato presented his thesis, *A Re-examination of the Atlantis Theory*, to the Faculty of California State University in Fullerton, California in 1979 in partial fulfillment of the requirements for the degree of Master of Arts in Anthropology.

28. Ibid, 75.
29. Mertz, *Atlantis, Dwelling Place of the Gods*, 57.
30. Spence, *Atlantis in America*, 18.
31. Robinson, *Edgar Cayce's Story of the Origin and Destiny of Man*, 123.
32. Cayce, Reading 5750–1.
33. Asher, *Ancient Energy*, 101.
34. Ibid.
35. Hansen, *The Ancient Atlantic*, 384.
36. Donato, *A Re-Examination of the Atlantis Theory*, 185.
37. Ibid, 117.
38. Hansen, *The Ancient Atlantic*, 384.
39. Homet, *Sons of the Sun*, 231.
40. Ibid, 82.
41. Ibid, 109.
42. Spence, *The Occult Sciences in Atlantis*, 90.
43. Ibid.
44. Spence, *Atlantis in America*, 130.
45. Spence, *The Occult Sciences in Atlantis*, 97.
46. Patten, *The Biblical Flood and the Ice Epoch*, 106.
47. Muck, *The Secret of Atlantis*, 184.
48. Bricker and Denton, "What Drives Glacial Cycles?," *Scientific American*, January 1990, 56.
49. Sitchin, *The Twelfth Planet*, 254. The "twelve planets" in the title of this book refer to the Sumerians' descriptions that include the ten planets plus the sun and the moon.
50. Ibid.
51. Ibid, 402.
52. Genesis 7:11.
53. Sitchin, *The Twelfth Planet*, 404.
54. Beardsley, "The Big Bang," *Scientific American*, November 1991, 30.

Chapter Three

1. Begley and Lief, "The Way We Were," *Newsweek*, November 10, 1986.
2. Cayce, Reading 225-12.
3. Robinson, *Edgar Cayce's Story of the Origin and Destiny of Man*, 54.
4. Roberts, *Atlantean Traditions in Ancient Britain*, 32.
5. Montgomery, *The World Before*, 107.
6. Ibid, 89.
7. Vigers, *Atlantis Rising*, 29.
8. Ibid.
9. Ibid.
10. Scott-Elliot, *The Story of Atlantis and Lost Lemuria*, 50.
11. Vigers, *Atlantis Rising*, 29.
12. Ibid.
13. Homet, *Sons of the Sun*, 151–153.
14. Donnelly, *Atlantis: The Antediluvian World*, 152–154.
15. Romant, *Life in Ancient Egypt*, 18.
16. Donnelly, *Atlantis: The Antediluvian World*, 210.
17. Spence, *Atlantis in America*, 99.
18. Ibid.
19. Goodman, *The Genesis Mystery*, 206.
20. Ibid, 250.
21. Homet, *Sons of the Sun*.
22. Ibid.
23. Hansen, *The Ancient Atlantic*, 99.
24. Ibid, 100.
25. Donnelly, *Atlantis, The Antediluvian World*, 180.
26. Spence, *Atlantis in America*, chapter vi.
27. Vigers, *Atlantis Rising*, 26.
28. Cayce, Reading 914–1.
29. Vigers, *Atlantis Rising*, 26.
30. Cayce, Reading 275-38.
31. Vigers, *Atlantis Rising*, 29.
32. Hope, *Practical Atlantean Magic*, 153.
33. Ibid.
34. Cayce, Reading 275-38.
35. Wilkins, *Mysteries of Ancient South America*, 70.
36. Charroux, *The Mysteries of the Andes*, 46, and Begley and Lief, "The Way We Were," *Newsweek*, November 10, 1986, 62–72.
37. Ibid, 83.
38. Begley and Lief.
39. Ibid.
40. Ibid.
41. Hope, *Practical Atlantean Magic*, 115.
42. Zhirov, *Atlantis*, 43.
43. Donato, 188.
44. Phelon, *Our Story of Atlantis*, 90–102.
45. Hansen, *The Ancient Atlantic*, 105.
46. Wilkins, *Secret Cities of Old South America*, 64.
47. Halifax, *The Fruitful Darkness*, 97.
48. Vigers, *Atlantis Rising*, 27.
49. Zink, *The Stones of Atlantis*, 261.
50. Montgomery, *The World Before*, 97.
51. Firman, *Atlantis, A Definitive Study*, 38.
52. Goodman, *The Genesis Mystery*, 7.
53. Ibid.

54. Goodman, *The Genesis Mystery*, 251, and Bahn and Vertut, *Images of the Ice Age*, 96.
55. Genesis XI.
56. Berlitz, *Atlantis, The Eighth Continent*, 56.
57. Wright, "Quest for the Mother Tongue," *The Atlantic Monthly*, April 1991, 39–64.
58. Muck, *Atlantis*, 128.
59. Berlitz, *The Mystery of Atlantis*, 158.
60. Ibid.
61. Asher, *Ancient Energy*, 91.
62. Hansen, *The Ancient Atlantic*, 295–98, from Willian Coxon, "Arizona Highways," *Ancient Manuscripts on American Stones*, September 1964.
63. Ibid.
64. Noorbergen, *Secrets of the Lost Races*, 27.
65. Hope, *Practical Atlantean Magic*, 96.
66. Cayce, Reading 3345–1.
67. Berlitz, *The Mystery of Atlantis*, 173.
68. Phelon, *Our Story of Atlantis*, 103.
69. Herma Waldthausen.
70. David Hall.
71. Vigers, *Atlantis Rising*, 24, and Cerminara, *Many Mansions*, 175.
72. Scott-Elliot, *The Story of Atlantis and Lost Lemuria*, 45.
73. Ibid, 46.
74. Oliver, *A Dweller on Two Planets*, 27.
75. Ibid.
76. Ibid.
77. Bahn and Vertut, *Images of the Ice Age*, 74.
78. Hadingham, *Secrets of the Ice Age*, 163.
79. Bahn and Vertut, *Images of the Ice Age*, 132.
80. Plato, *Critias*.
81. Bain and Vertut, *Images of the Ice Age*, 156.
82. Encyclopedia Britannica, volume 15, 291.
83. Goodman, *The Genesis Mystery*, 238.
84. Halifax, *Shamanic Voices*, 17.
85. Bahn and Vertut, *Images of the Ice Age*, 190.
86. Homet, *Sons of the Sun*, 66.
87. Ibid, 205.
88. Goodman, *The Genesis Mystery*, 251.
89. Homet, *Sons of the Sun*, 207.
90. Ibid, 253.
91. Bower, *Science News*, December 13, 1986, 378, 379.
92. Ibid.
93. Bryant and Galde, *The Message of the Crystal Skull*, 4.
94. Garvin, *The Crystal Skull*, 89.
95. Ibid, 14.
96. Ibid, 87.
97. Bryant and Galde, *The Message of the Crystal Skull*, 48.
98. Garvin, *The Crystal Skull*, 1.
99. Ibid, 10.
100. Ibid, 62.
101. Bryant and Galde, *The Message of the Crystal Skull*, 55.
102. Sykes, *Atlantis*, volume 27, no. 4, July–August 1974, 64.
103. Turnbull, *Sema-Kanda—Threshhold Memories*, 55.
104. Clapp, Anne Lee, Lecture re: Edgar Cayce Readings. A.R.E., September 23, 1988.
105. Turnbull, *Sema-Kanda—Threshhold Memories*.
106. Ibid, 55.
107. Plato, *Critias*.
108. Ibid.
109. Donato, *A Re-examination of the Atlantis Theory*, 135.
110. Plato, *Critias*.
111. Scott-Elliot, *The Story of Atlantis and Lost Lemuria*, 56.
112. Oliver, *A Dweller on Two Planets*, 52.
113. Ibid, 54–58.
114. Ibid, 182.
115. Blakeslee, Sandra, "Pulsing Magnets Offer New Method of Mapping Brain," *The New York Times*, May 21, 1996.
116. Spence, *The Occult Sciences in Atlantis*, 54–55.
117. Hansen, *The Ancient Atlantic*, 312.
118. Ibid.
119. Ibid, 307.
120. Cayce, Reading 364–12.
121. Winston, Shirley Rabb, lecture re: Edgar Cayce Readings. A.R.E., September 22, 1988.
122. Hansen, *The Ancient Atlantic*, 307.
123. Ibid, 395.
124. Plato, *Timaeus*.
125. Ibid.
126. Donato, *A Re-examination of the Atlantis Theory*, 68, 188.
127. Spence, *The Occult Sciences in Atlantis*, from the work of Michael Scot, 55.
128. Ibid.

129. Hansen, *The Ancient Atlantic*, 106.
130. Ibid, 184, 314.
131. Feiffer, "Cro-Magnon Hunters Were Really Us, Working Out Strategies for Survival," *Smithsonian*, October 1986.
132. Prideaux, *Cro-Magnon Man, Time-Life Book*, 62.
133. Fix, *Pyramid Odyssey*.
134. Ibid.
135. Roberts, *Atlantean Traditions in Ancient Britain*, 31.
136. Hansen, *The Ancient Atlantic*, 394.
137. Cayce, Reading 5750–1.
138. Cayce, Reading 5750–1.
139. Hope, *Practical Atlantean Magic*, 106.
140. Michell, *The New View Over Atlantis*, 208.
141. Hitching, *Earth Magic*, 164.
142. Bibby, *Testimony of the Spade*.
143. Hitching, *Earth Magic*, 191.
144. Michell, *The New View Over Atlantis*, 208.
145. Spence, *History of Atlantis*, 223.
146. Ryan, *Notes on the Place of Atlantis in World Evolution*, 19.
147. Halifax, *Shamanic Voices*.
148. Spence, *The Occult Sciences in Atlantis*, 50.
149. Donnelly, *Atlantis, The Antediluvian World*, 283.
150. Homet, *Sons of the Sun*, 208.
151. Turnbull, *Sema-Kanda—Threshold Memories*.
152. Klossowski de Rola, *Alchemy, The Secret Art*.
153. Spence, *The Occult Sciences in Atlantis*, 98.
154. Spence, *Atlantis in America*, 128, and Spence, *The Occult Sciences in Atlantis*, 98.
155. Spence, *The History of Atlantis*, 224.

Chapter Four

1. Plato, *Critias*.
2. Ibid.
3. Ibid.
4. Stahel, *Atlantis Illustrated*, 102. Architect H.R. Stahel attempts to accurately portray the City of the Golden Gates on the basis of Plato's description.
5. Plato, *Critias*.
6. Michell, *New View Over Atlantis*, 91.
7. Spence, *The Occult Sciences in Atlantis*, 82.
8. Plato, *Critias*.
9. Zhirov, *Atlantis*, 46.
10. Wilkins, *Secret Cities of Old South America*, 86.
11. Muck, *The Secret of Atlantis*, 43, and Cayce, Reading, 470-33.
12. Sykes in Donnelly, *Atlantis, The Antediluvian World*, 298.
13. Berlitz, *Mystery of Atlantis*, 107.
14. Plato, *Critias*.
15. Ibid, 291.
16. Plato, *Critias*.
17. Sykes, *Atlantis*, volume 27, no. 3, May–June 1974, 44.
18. Hope, *Practical Atlantean Magic*, 83.
19. Plato, *Critias*.
20. Sitchin, *The Twelfth Planet*, 16.
21. Ibid.
22. Plato, *Critias*.
23. Cayce, Reading 364–12.
24. Turnbull, *Sema-Kanda—Threshold Memories*.
25. Plato, *Critias*.
26. Ibid.
27. Stahel, *Atlantis Illustrated*, 54.
28. Ibid, 52, 57.
29. Cayce, Reading 364–12.
30. Oliver, *A Dweller on Two Planets*, 50.
31. Ibid, 50.
32. Caldwell, *The Romance of Atlantis*, 100.
33. Oliver, *A Dweller on Two Planets*, 135.
34. Ibid, 136–138.
35. Plato, *Critias*.
36. Hansen, *The Ancient Atlantic*, 133.
37. Hope, *Practical Atlantean Magic*, 101.
38. Vigers, *Atlantis Rising*, 25.
39. Hope, *Practical Atlantean Magic*, 82.
40. Donnelly, *Atlantis*, 202.
41. Donato, *A Re-Examination of the Atlantis Theory*, 282.
42. Berlitz, *Atlantis, The Eighth Continent*, 176.
43. Hansen, *The Ancient Atlantic*, 124.
44. Ibid, 282.
45. Ibid.
46. Zink, *The Stones of Atlantis*, 142.
47. Ibid, 143.
48. Sykes, *Atlantis*, Volume 27, no. 4, 64.
49. Ibid.
50. Zink, *The Stones of Atlantis*, 272.

51. Ibid, 142,143.
52. Sykes, *Atlantis*, volume 27, no. 4, 69.
53. Berlitz, *Atlantis: The Eighth Continent*, 108.
54. Lafferty and Holowell, *The Eternal Dance*, 154–155.
55. Berlitz, *Atlantis: The Eighth Continent*, 108.
56. Zink, *The Stones of Atlantis*, 154.
57. Ibid.
58. Edgar Evans Cayce, *Mysteries of Atlantis Revisited*, 168–170.
59. Steiger, *Atlantis Rising*, 17.
60. Tomas, *The Home of the Gods*, 1.
61. Homet, *Sons of the Sun*, 176, 221.
62. Steiger, *Atlantis Rising*, 79.
63. Homet, *Sons of the Sun*, 212.
64. Hansen, *The Ancient Atlantic*, 422.
65. Wilkins, *Mysteries of Ancient South America*, 189.
66. Ibid, 188.
67. Homet, *Sons of the Sun*, 222.

Chapter Five

1. Hansen, *The Ancient Atlantic*, 386.
2. Vigers, *Atlantis Rising*, 26.
3. Muck, *Atlantis*, 41.
4. Firman, *Atlantis, a Definitive Study*, 46.
5. Plato, *Critias*.
6. Zhirov, *Atlantis*, 36–37.
7. Sitchin, *The Twelfth Planet*, 414.
8. Goodman, *The Genesis Mystery*, 6.
9. Boid, *A Description of the Azores*, 24, 33, 34.
10. Cayce, Reading 364–4.
11. Donnelly, *Atlantis: The Antediluvian World*, 445.
12. Goodman, *The Genesis Mystery*, 216.
13. Hansen, *The Ancient Atlantic*, 394.
14. Goodman, *The Genesis Mystery*, 171.
15. Tomas, *The Home of the Gods*, 140.
16. Firman, *Atlantis, A Definive Study*, 8.
17. Ibid.
18. Ibid, 8.
19. Ibid, 13.
20. Ibid, 12.
21. Ibid, 56–57.
22. Cayce, Edgar Evans, *On Atlantis*, 98.
23. Hancock, *Fingerprints of the Gods*, 22.
24. Ibid, 99.
25. Hansen, *The Ancient Atlantic*, 381.
26. Ibid, 312.
27. *Nova*, WGBH Transcripts, December 15, 1987; *Secrets of the Red Paint People*, 6,7.
28. Ibid, 11.
29. Anon, *The Truth About Atlantis*, 12–13.
30. Ibid.
31. Wilkins, *Secret Cities of Ancient South America*, 77.
32. Ibid.
33. Ibid, 78.
34. Cayce, Reading 364–6.
35. Cayce, Reading 1735–2.
36. Hancock, *Fingerprints of the Gods*, 488, 489.
37. Cayce, Reading 1859–1. For references to flying vehicles, see Ezekiel 1:4–5, 15–28.
38. Winston, Shirley Rabb, lecture re: Edgar Cayce Readings. A.R.E., September 22, 1988.
39. Ibid.
40. Oliver, *Dweller on Two Planets*, 148–172.
41. Childress, *Lost Cities of China, Central Asia & India*, 241.
42. Donato, *A Re-examination of the Atlantis Theory*, 153.
43. Genesis 6:4.
44. Cayce, Reading 1681–1.
45. Cayce, Reading 1616–1.
46. John Mack, Conference at Association for Research and Enlightenment, May 14, 1995.
47. Hope, *Practical Atlantean Magic*, 159.
48. Tomas, *The Home of the Gods*, 103.
49. Kings 2:6:17.
50. Kings 2:11–12.
51. Zecharaih 6:1–7.
52. Isaiah 19:1, Acts 1:9.
53. Genesis 19:1.
54. Exodus 24: 15–18.
55. Sitchin, *The Twelfth Planet*, 25–27.
56. Steiger, *The Fellowship*, 40.
57. Roberts, *Atlantean Traditions in Ancient Britain*, 77.
58. Ywahoo, *Voices of our Ancestors*, 11.
59. Kinder, *Light Years*, 67.
60. James Mullaney, astronomer, Conference at Association for Research and Enlightenment, May 12, 1995.
61. Ray Stanford, Conference at Association for Research and Enlightenment, May 12, 1995.
62. Davenport, *Visitors from Time*, 85.

63. Ray Stanford, Conference at Association for Research and Enlightenment, May 12, 1995.

Chapter Six

1. Steiner, *Cosmic Memory*, 45.
2. Michell, *The New View over Atlantis*, 90.
3. Vigers, *Atlantis Rising*, 27.
4. Ibid.
5. Asher, *Ancient Energy*, 18.
6. Tomas, *Home of the Gods*, 92.
7. Tomas, *Atlantis from Legend to Discovery*, 132.
8. Wilkins, *Secret Cities of Ancient South America*, 79.
9. Raloff, *Science News*, November 28, 1987.
10. Donato, *A Re-examination of the Atlantis Theory*, 153.
11. Montgomery, *The World Before*, 61.
12. Cayce, Readings 621–1 and 419–1.
13. Cayce, Reading 262–39.
14. Cayce, Edgar Evans, *Mysteries of Atlantis Revisited*, 38.
15. Cayce, Reading 621–1.
16. Childress, *Lost Cities of Central Asia & India*, 243.
17. Berlitz, *Atlantis, The Eighth Continent*, 215, and Childress, *Lost Cities of Central Asia & India*, 245.
18. Ibid, 216, and Berlitz, *Mysteries from Forgotten Worlds*, 215.
19. Ibid, 215.
20. Sitchin, *The Wars of Gods and Men,* 342.
21. Ibid.
22. Childress, *Lost Cities of Central Asia & India*, 244.
23. Montgomery, *The World Before*, 75.
24. Donato, *A Re-examination of the Atlantis Theory*, 159.
25. Cayce, Reading 440–5.
26. Winer, *The Devil's Triangle*, 212.
27. Cayce, Reading 2329–3.
28. Cayce, Reading 440–5.
29. Hoffman, "Ancient Magnetic Reversals: Clues to the Geo Dynamo," *Scientific American*, May 1988, 76.
30. Ibid.
31. Michell, *The New View Over Atlantis*, 211.
32. Watkins, *Ley Hunter's Manual*, chapter 2.

33. Noorbergen, *Secrets of the Lost Races*, 115.
34. Asher, *Ancient Energy*.
35. Ibid, ix.
36. Davenport, *Visitors from Time*, 248.
37. Moore and Berlitz, *The Philadelphia Experiment*.
38. Nichols, *The Montauk Project*.
39. Ibid, 65.
40. Ibid, 142.
41. Hitching, *Earth Magic*, 256.
42. Ibid, 96.
43. Michell, *The New View Over Atlantis*, 208.
44. Ibid, 47.
45. Hancock, *Fingerprints of the Gods*, 190.
46. Sitchin, *The Twelfth Planet*, 197.
47. Ibid, 189.
48. Marshack, *Reading before Writing*.
49. Michell, *The New View Over Atlantis*, 88.
50. Ibid, 86.
51. Ibid, 87.
52. Wilkins, *Secret Cities of Ancient South America*, 72.
53. West, *Serpent in the Sky*, 71.
54. Carlson, *The Great Migration*, 33, 34.
55. Caldwell, *The Romance of Atlantis*, 42, and Oliver, *A Dweller on Two Planets*, 48.
56. Caldwell, *The Romance of Atlantis*.
57. Oliver, *Dweller on Two Planets*, 136.
58. Hope, *Practical Atlantean Magic*, 110.
59. Noorbergen, *Secrets of the Lost Races*, 117.
60. Dave and Lane, *The Rainbow of Life*, 30.
61. Cayce, *Auras*.
62. Dave and Lane, *The Rainbow of Life*, 13, 61.
63. Asher, *Ancient Energy*, 52.
64. Ibid, 10.
65. Cayce, *Auras*, 15.
66. Herma Waldthausen.
67. Wood, *The Healing Power of Color*.
68. Campbell, "Music: Medicine for the New Millennium," *Venture Inward*, January/February 1996, 11, 12.
69. Alper, *Exploring Atlantis*, 21.
70. Ibid, 16.
71. Cayce, Reading 470–33.
72. Warren Russell.
73. Valentine, *Psychic Surgery*.

74. Sitchin, *The Twelfth Planet*, 33.
75. Ibid, 33–35.
76. Berlitz, *Mysteries from Forgotten Worlds*, 55.
77. Steiger, *Atlantis Rising*, 78.
78. Ibid.
79. Ibid.
80. Goodman, *American Genesis*, 223.
81. Cerminara, *Many Mansions: The Edgar Cayce Story of Reincarnation*, 176.
82. Wood, "The Body Electric," *Backpacker Magazine*, November 1986.
83. Michell, *The New View Over Atlantis*, 88.
84. Cayce, Reading 440–5.
85. Caldwell, *The Romance of Atlantis*, 18.
86. Solomon, *Excerpts from the Paul Solomon Tapes*, 9.
87. Caldwell, *The Romance of Atlantis*, 18.

Chapter Seven

1. Vigers, *Atlantis Rising*, 32.
2. Oliver, *A Dweller on Two Planets*, 420.
3. Spence, *The Occult Science in Atlantis*, 23.
4. Ibid, 92–94.
5. Ibid.
6. Wilkins, *Secret Cities of Old South America*, 68.
7. Firman, *Atlantis, A Definitive Study*, 6.
8. Anon., *The Truth About Atlantis*, 38.
9. Wagner immortalizes Wotan as a God who is a powerful manifestation of the source of life in his vast opera *Der Ring des Nibelungen*.
10. Hansen, *The Ancient Atlantis*, 355, 356.
11. Ibid.

Chapter Eight

1. Cayce, Reading 1681–1.
2. Randall–Stevens, *Atlantis to the Latter Days*, 157.
3. Spence, *The Problem of Atlantis*, 63.
4. Berlitz, *Mysteries from Forgotten Worlds*, 112.
5. Spanuth, *Atlantis of the North*, 124.
6. Donato, *A Re-examination of the Atlantis Theory*, 195.
7. Spence, *Occult Sciences in Atlantis*, 100.
8. Ibid.
9. Roberts, *Atlantean Traditions in Ancient Britain*, 106.
10. Donato, *A Re-examination of the Atlantis Theory*, 183.
11. Zhirov, *Atlantis*, 211.

Chapter Nine

1. Bower, "Rivers in the Sand," *Science News*, August 26, 1989, 136.
2. Berlitz, *Atlantis: The Eighth Continent*, 123.
3. Hansen, *The Ancient Atlantic*, 187.
4. Sykes in Donnelly, *Atlantis: The Antediluvian World*, 223.
5. Tomas, *Atlantis from Legend to Discovery*, 141.
6. Hansen, *The Ancient Atlantic*, 33, 381.
7. Ibid, 130.
8. Ibid, 107.
9. Porch, *The Conquest of the Sahara*, 35.
10. Berlitz, *The Mystery of Atlantis*, 172.
11. Donato, An Examination of the Atlantis Theory, 191.
12. Hansen, *The Ancient Atlantic*, 291.
13. Ibid, 128.
14. Cayce, Edgar Evans, *On Atlantis*, 136–142.
15. Clapp, Anne Lee, lecture re: Edgar Cayce Readings at A.R.E., September 22, 1988.
16. Cayce, Reading 966–1.
17. Cerminara, *Many Mansions: The Edgar Cayce Story on Reincarnation*, 176.
18. Prideaux, *Cro-Magnon Man, Time-Life Book*, 46.
19. Hancock, *Footprints of the Gods*, 412.
20. West, *Serpent in the Sky*. In this extensive, well-documented book, John Anthony West defends the work of the late Egyptologist Schiller de Lubicz, who believed high wisdom was kept alive through the centuries in ancient Egypt.
21. Sitchin, *The Twelfth Planet*, 84.
22. Zhirov, *Atlantis*, 378.
23. Hancock, *Fingerprints of the Gods*, 449.
24. Tompkins, *Secrets of the Great Pyramid*, 1, 220.
25. Ibid, 103.
26. Ibid, 17.

27. Tomas, *Atlantis from Legend to Discovery*, 114.
28. Ibid.
29. Tompkins, *Mysteries of the Mexican Pyramids*, 279.
30. Ibid, 241.
31. Tompkins, *Secrets of the Great Pyramid*, 193.
32. Heinberg, *Memories and Visions of Paradise*, 181.
33. Sitchin, *The Stairway to Heaven*, 302.
34. Cayce, Reading 5748–6.
35. Cayce, Edgar Evans, *Mysteries of Atlantis Revisited*, 151.
36. Cayce, Reading 5748–6.
37. Solomon, *Excerpts from the Paul Solomon Tapes*, 12. Paul Solomon was an ordained minister with a Masters degree in Religion Education. While hypnotized, he offered successful medical diagnoses and treatments as well as information concerning Atlantis.
38. King, *Pyramid Energy Handbook*, 27.
39. Braghine, *The Shadow of Atlantis*, 216.
40. Hancock, *Fingerprints of the Gods*, 438.
41. Tomas, *From Legend to Discovery*, 138.
42. Braghine, *The Shadow of Atlantis*, 111.
43. Mertz, *Atlantis, Dwelling Place of the Gods*, 74.
44. Hancock, *Footprints of the Gods*, 386.
45. Sykes in Donnelly, *Atlantis: The Antediluvian World*, 262.
46. Donato, *Examination of the Atlantis Theory*.
47. Roberts, *Atlantean Traditions in Ancient Britain*, 32.
48. Ibid, 40.
49. Ibid.
50. Ibid.
51. Gregory, *Gods and Fighting Men*, 27.
52. Hope, *Practical Atlantean Magic*, 109.
53. Roberts, *Atlantean Traditions in Ancient Britain*.
54. Ibid, 77.
55. Zink, *The Stones of Atlantis*, 154.
56. Wilkins, *Secret Cities of Old South America*, 71.
57. Ibid.
58. Hansen, *The Ancient Atlantic*, 290.
59. Wilkins, *Secret Cities of Old South America*, 71.
60. Hansen, *The Ancient Atlantic*, 290.
61. Spence, *The History of Atlantis*, 179.
62. Michell, *The New View over Atlantis*, 200.
63. Roberts, *Atlantean Traditions in Ancient Britain*.
64. Ibid.
65. Ibid, 54.
66. Ibid, 9.
67. Ibid, 16.
68. Strabo, Greek geographer and historian 63 B.C.–A.D. 21.
69. Berlitz, *Mysteries from Forgotten Worlds*.
70. Asher, *Ancient Energy*, 123.
71. Cayce, Readings 3541–1, 2545–1, 2677–1.
72. Cavalli-Sforza, "Luigi Luca, Genes, Peoples and Languages," *Scientific American*, November 1991, 108.
73. Siebert, *Atlantis in Peru*, 18, and Braghine, *The Shadow of Atlantis*, 187.
74. Berlitz, *The Mystery of Atlantis*, 157–158.
75. Schonfield, *Secrets of the Dead Sea Scrolls*, from Vigers, *Atlantis Rising*, 6.
76. Vigers, *Atlantis Rising*, 6.
77. Wilkins, *Secret Cities of Old South America*, 369.
78. Ibid.
79. Wilkins, *Secret Cities of Old South America*, 69.
80. Spence, *The Occult Sciences in Atlantis*, 98.
81. Tompkins, *Mysteries of the Mexican Pyramids*, 333–338.
82. Ibid, 280.
83. Braghine, *The Shadow of Atlantis*, 222.
84. Carlson, *The Great Migration*.
85. Braghine, *The Shadow of Atlantis*, 222.
86. Goodman, *American Genesis*, 270, and Eben, *Atlantis, The New Evidence*, 13.
87. Wilkins, *Secret Cities of Ancient South America*, 64.
88. Noorbergen, *Secrets of the Lost Races*, 136.
89. Cayce, Edgar Evans, *Mysteries of Atlantis Revisited*, 105.

90. Zhirov, *Atlantis*, 378.
91. Cayce, Reading 1616–1.
92. Wilkins, *Secret Cities of South America*, 69.
93. Bramwell, *Lost Atlantis*, 269 (translation of O. A. Pritchard, 1911).
94. Ibid.
95. Berlitz, *The Mystery of Atlantis*, 52.
96. Muck, *Atlantis*, 200, 201.
97. Hansen, *The Ancient Atlantic*, 282.
98. Berlitz, *Mysteries from Forgotten Worlds*, 131.
99. Berlitz, *Atlantis, The Eighth Continent*, 56.
100. Spence, *The Myths of Mexico and Peru*.
101. Tompkins, *Mysteries of the Mexican Pyramids*, 340.
102. Hadingham, *Lines to the Mountain God*, 202.
103. Ibid.
104. Beltran, *Cuzco, Window on Peru*, 46–48.
105. Tomas, *The Home of the Gods*, 76.
106. Siebert, *Atlantis in Peru*.
107. Verrill and Verrill, *America's Ancient Civilizations*, 310–315.
108. Michell, *The New View Over Atlantis*, 208.
109. Zhirov, *Atlantis*, 353.
110. Cayce, Reading 1219–1.
111. Zink, *Atlantis*, 112.
112. Cayce, Reading 3528–1.
113. Berlitz, *Mysteries from Forgotten Worlds*, 146.
114. Hansen, *The Ancient Atlantic*, 302.
115. Mertz, Atlantis, *Dwelling Place of the Gods*, 127.
116. Hansen, *The Ancient Atlantic*, 39.
117. Ibid, 99.
118. Ibid, 103.
119. Ted Bauer in *The Marietta Times*.
120. Ywahoo, *Voices of Our Ancestors*, 16.
121. Hansen, *The Ancient Atlantic*, 281.
122. Ibid, 274.
123. Ibid.
124. Waters, *The Book of the Hopi*, 17.
125. Noorbergen, *Secrets of the Lost Races*, 156.
126. Ibid, 156.
127. Hansen, *The Ancient Atlantic*, 292.
128. Ibid.
129. Noorbergen, *Secrets of the Lost Races*, 156.
130. Hansen, *The Ancient Atlantis*, 304.
131. Ibid, 99.

Chapter Ten

1. Sykes, *Atlantis*, Volume 27, no. 3, 48.
2. Braghine, *The Shadow of Atlantis*, 53.
3. Stevens, *UFO . . . Contact from Reticulum*, 139, 386.
4. Davenport, *Visitors from Time*, 33–35.
5. Ibid.

BIBLIOGRAPHY

Atlantis is based on many sources in addition to those listed below. I include only references I believe will be helpful to the reader interested in looking more deeply into some briefly discussed area, or in verifying the information in this book.

Allegre, Claude. *The Behavior of the Earth, Continental and Seafloor Mobility.* Cambridge, Mass.: Harvard University Press, 1988.

Alper, Frank, Dr. *Exploring Atlantis.* Irvine, Calif.: Quantum Productions, 1981.

Alvarez, William and Asaro, Frank. What Caused the Mass Extinction? An Extraterrestrial Impact. *Scientific American,* October, 1990.

Anon. *The Truth about Atlantis.* Albuquerque, N. Mex.: Sun Publishing, 1971.

Asher, Maxine. *Ancient Energy.* New York: Harper & Row, 1979.

Bahm, Paul G. and Jean Vertut. *Images of the Ice Age.* London: Bellow Publication Co., Ltd., 1988.

Begley and Lief. The Way We Were. *Newsweek,* November 10, 1986.

Bellamy, H. S. *The Atlantis Myth.* London: Faber & Faber Ltd., 1947.

Beltran, Marian. *Cuzco, Window on Peru.* New York: Alfred A. Knopf, 1970.

Berlitz, Charles. *Atlantis: The Eighth Continenet.* New York: Fawcett Crest, 1984.

———. *Mysteries from Forgotten Worlds.* New York: Doubleday & Co., Inc., 1972.

———. *The Mystery of Atlantis.* New York: Grosset & Dunlap, 1969.

Bloxham, Jeremy and David Gubbins. The Evolution of the Earth's Magnetic Field. *Scientific American,* December 1989.

Bord, Janet and Colin. *Mysterious Britain.* St. Albans, England: Granada Publishing Ltd., 1975.

Bower, Bruce. Rivers in the Sand. *Science News,* August 26, 1989.

———. Humans in the Late Ice Age. *Science News,* December 13, 1986.

Boid, Captain G. *A Description of the Azores or Western Islands.* London: Edward Churton, 1835.

Braghine, Alexander Pavlovitch. *The Shadow of Atlantis.* Wellingborough, Northamptonshire: The Aquarian Press, 1940.

Bramwell, James. *Lost Atlantis.* New York: Harper & Bros., 1938.

Broecker, Wallace C. and George H. Denton. What Drives Glacial Cycles? *Scientific American,* January 1990.

Bryant, Alice and Phyllis Galde. *The Message of the Crystal Skull.* St. Paul, Minn.: Llewellyn Publications, 1989.

Caldwell, Taylor. *The Romance of Atlantis.* New York: William Morrow & Co., 1975.

Carlson, Vada F. *The Great Migration.* Virginia Beach, Va.: A.R.E. Press, 1970.

Cayce, Edgar Evans. *On Atlantis.* New York: Hawthorne Books, 1968.

———. *Mysteries of Atlantis Revisited.* San Francisco: Harper & Row, 1988.

———. *Auras.* Virginia Beach, Va.: A.R.E. Press, 1987.

Cerminara, Gina. *Many Mansions: The Edgar Cayce Story of Reincarnation.* New York: New American Library Signet Book, 1950.

Charroux, Robert. *The Mysteries of the Andes.* New York: Avon Books, 1977.

Childress, David Hatcher. *Lost Cities of Atlantis, Ancient Europe & the Mediterranean.* Stelle, Ill.: Adventures Unlimited Press, 1996.

———. *Lost Cities of Central Asia & India.* Stelle, Ill.: Adventures Unlimited Press, 1991.

Clark, Thurston. *The Last Caravan.* New York: G. P. Putnam's Sons, 1978.

Coleman, Arthur P. *The Last Million Years.* Toronto: University of Toronto Press, 1941.

Colinvaux, Paul A. The Past and Future Amazon. *Scientific American,* May 1989.

Countryman, J. *Atlantis and the Seven Stars.* New York: St. Martin's Press, 1979.

Courtillot, Vincent E. What Caused the Mass Extinction? A Volcanic Eruption. *Scientific American,* October, 1990.

Cummins, Geraldine. *The Fate of Colonel Fawcett.* London: The Aquarian Press, 1955.

Davenport, Marc. *Visitors from Time.* Tigard, Oregon: Wildfire Press, 1992.

De Camp, L. Sprague. *Lost Continents: The Atlantis Theme in History, Science, and Literature.* New York: Dover, 1970.

Donato, William M. *A Re-examination of the Atlantis Theory.* Self-published, 1979.

Donnelly, Ignatius. *Atlantis: The Antediluvian World.* Edited by Edgarton Sykes. New York: Gramercy Publishing Co., 1949.

———. *The Destruction of Atlantis, Ragnarok: The Age of Fire and Gravel.* New York: Steiner Publications, 1971.

Downing, Barry H. *The Bible & Flying Saucers.* New York: Avon Books, 1968.

Durning, Alan T. *How Much is Enough?* New York: Norton & Co., 1992.

Ebon, Martin. *Atlantis, The New Evidence.* New York: New American Library, 1977.

Ferro, Robert and Michael Grumley. *Atlantis: The Autobiography of a Search.* New York: Doubleday & Co., Inc., 1970.

Firman, George. *Atlantis, A Definitive Study.* Hallmark Litho, Inc., 1985.

Fix, William R. *Pyramid Odyssey.* New York: Mayflower Books, 1978.

Folliot, Katherine, A. *Atlantis Revisited.* Great Britain: Information Printing, 1984.

Garvin, Richard. *The Crystal Skull.* New York: Doubleday & Co., Inc., 1973.

Germinara, Gina. *Many Mansions.* New York: New American Library Signet Book, 1950.

Goodman, Jeffrey. *American Genesis.* New York: Summit Books, 1981.

———. *The Genesis Mystery.* New York: Times Books, 1983.

Gordon, Cyrus, H. *Before Columbus.* New York: Crown Publishing, 1971.

Gregory, Lady Augustus. *Gods and Fighting Men.* New York: Oxford University Press, 1970.

Grigson, Geoffrey. *The Painted Caves.* London: Phoenix House Ltd., 1957.

Guiley, Rosemary Ellen. *Tales of Reincarnation.* New York: Pocket Books, 1989.

Hadingham, Evan. *Secrets of the Ice Age.* New York: Walker, 1979.

———. *Lines to the Gods, Nazca and the Mysteries of Peru.* New York: Random House, 1987.

Halifax, Joan. *Shamanic Voices.* New York: Penguin Books, 1979.

———. *The Fruitful Darkness.* San Francisco: HarperCollins, 1993.

Hall, Manly P. *Atlantis.* Los Angeles: Philosophical Research Society, 1976.

———. *The Secret Teachings of All Ages.* Los Angeles: Philosophical Research Society, 1977.

Hammerschlag, Carl A., M.D. *The Dancing Healers.* San Francisco: Harper & Row, 1988.

Hancock, Graham. *Fingerprints of the Gods.* New York: Crown Publishers, Inc., 1995.

Hansen, Lucille Taylor. *The Ancient Atlantic.* Amherst, Wis.: Amherst Press, 1969.

Hapgood, Charles. *Maps of the Ancient Sea Kings: Evidence of Advanced Civilization in the Ice Age.* Philadelphia: Chilton & Co., 1966.

———. *The Path of the Pole.* Philadelphia: Chilton Book Co., 1970.

Heinberg, Richard. *Memories and Visions of Paradise.* Los Angeles: Jeremy P. Tarcher, Inc., 1989.

Hitchings, Francis. *Earth Magic.* New York: Pocket Books, 1976.

Hoffman, Kenneth A. Ancient Magnetic Reversals, Clues to the Geodynamo. *Scientific American,* May 1988.

Holt, Etelka. *The Sphinx and the Great Pyramid.* Church Universal and Triumphant Inc., 1975.

Homet, Marcel P. *Sons of the Sun.* London: Hapgood, 1963.

Hope, Murry. *Practical Atlantean Magic.* London: The Aquarian Press, 1991.

———. *Atlantis—Myth or Reality?* London: Penguin Books, 1991.

Imbrie, John and Katherine Palmer. *Ice Ages.* Hillside, New Jersey: Enslow Publishers, 1979.

Joseph, Francis. *The Destruction of Atlantis*. Olympia Fields, Illinois: Atlantis Research Publishers, 1987.

Kinder, Gary. *Light Years*. New York: The Atlantic Monthly Press, 1987.

King, Serge V. *Pyramid Energy Handbook*. New York: Warner Books, 1977.

Klossowski de Rola, Stanislas. *Alchemy*. New York: Avon Books, 1973.

Lafferty, Laverdi and Bud Holowell. *The Eternal Dance*. St. Paul, Minn.: Llewellyn Publications, 1983.

Le Plongeon, Augustus. *Maya/Atlantis: Queen Moo and the Egyptian Sphinx*. New York: Steiner Publications, 1973.

———. *Sacred Mysteries*. New York: Macoy Publishing and Masonic Supply Co., 1909.

Levin, Harold L. *The Earth Through Time*. New York: Saunders College Publishing, 1983.

Lovelock, James. *The Ages of Gaia*. New York: Norton & Co., 1988.

Luce, J. V. *Lost Atlantis, New Light on an Old Legend*. New York: McGraw-Hill, 1969.

MacLeish, William H. *The Gulf Stream*. Boston: Houghton Mifflin Co, 1989.

Maver, James W. *Voyage to Atlantis*. New York: G. P. Putnam's Sons, 1969.

Mertz, Henriette. *Atlantis, Dwelling Place of the Gods*. Chicago, Ill.: Mertz, 1976.

Michell, John. *The View over Atlantis*. New York: Balantine, 1969.

———. *The New View over Atlantis*. San Francisco: Harper & Row, 1983.

Montgomery, Ruth. *The World Before*. New York: Ballantine Books, 1976.

Moore, William L. and Charles Berlitz. *The Philadelphia Experiment*. New York: Fawcett Crest, 1979.

Muck, Otto Heinrich. *The Secret of Atlantis*. New York: Times Books, 1978.

Nichols, Preston B. and Peter Moon. *The Montauk Project*. New York: Sky Books, 1992.

Noorbergen, Rene. *Secrets of the Lost Races: New Discoveries of Advanced Technology in Ancient Civilization*. New York: The Bobbs-Merrill Co., Inc., 1977.

Nova, Show #2107, In Search of Human Origins, Part 2. March 1, 1994.

O'Brien, Henry. *Atlantis in Ireland: The Round Towers of Ireland*. New York: Steiner Publications, 1976.

Oliver, F. S. and Phylos. *A Dweller on Two Planets*. Los Angeles: Borden Publishing Co., 1952.

Patten, Donald Wesley. *The Biblical Flood and the Ice Epoch*. Seattle: Pacific Meridian Publishers, 1966.

Pellegrino, Charles. *Unearthing Atlantis: An Archaeological Odyssey*. New York: Random House, 1991.

Pennick, Nigel. *The Ancient Science of Geomancy*. London: Thames & Hudson, 1979.

Pheiffer, John E. Cro-Magnon Hunters Were Really Us, Working Out Strategies for Survival. *Smithsonian*, 1986.

Phelon. *Our Story of Atlantis*. Calif.: Hermetic Brotherhood, 1903.

Plato. *Timaeus and Critias*. Trans. R. G. Bury. Cambridge, Mass.: Harvard University Press, 1929.

Porch, Douglas. *The Conquest of the Sahara*. New York: Alfred A. Knopf, 1984.

Prideaux, Thomas. *Cro-Magnon Man*. New York: Time–Life Books, 1973.

Rae, Stephen. John Mack. *New York Times Magazine*, March 20, 1994.

Ramage, Edwin S. *Atlantis, Fact or Fiction?* Bloomington, Ind.: Indiana University Press, 1978.

Randall-Stevens, H. C. *Atlantis to the Latter Days*. London: Knights Templars of Aquarius, 1957.

Roberts, Anthony. *Atlantean Traditions in Ancient Britain*. London: Rider & Co., 1975.

Robinson, Lytle. *Edgar Cayce's Story of the Origin and Destiny of Man*. New York: Berkeley Publishing Corp., 1972.

Romant, Bernard. *Life in Egypt in Ancient Times*. Geneva: Editions Minerva, 1978.

Ryan, Charles J. *Notes on the Place of Atlantis in World Evolution.* Escondido, Calif.: The Book Tree, 1997.

Schul, Bill and Edward Pettit. *The Secret Power of Pyramids.* New York: CBS Publications, Ballantine Books, 1975.

Scott–Elliot, W. *The Story of Atlantis and the Lost Lemura.* London: Theosophical Publishing House Ltd., 1930.

Schure, Edouard. *From Sphinx to Christ: An Occult History.* New York: Steiner, 1970.

Siebert, Karola. *Atlantis in Peru.* London: Markham House Press, 1968.

Sitchin, Zecharia. *Genesis Revisited.* New York: Avon Books, 1990.

———. *Stairway to Heaven.* New York: Avon Books, 1980.

———. *The Twelfth Planet.* New York: Avon Books, 1976.

———. *Wars of Gods and Men.* New York: Avon Books, 1985.

Solomon, Paul. *Excerpts from the Paul Solomon Tapes.* Fellowship of Inner Light, 1974.

Spanuth, Jergen. *Atlantis of the North.* London: Reinhold Co., 1979.

Spence, Lewis. *Atlantis in America.* Santa Fe, N. Mex.: Sun Publishing Co., 1981.

———. *The Problem of Atlantis.* London: Rider & Son., 1924.

———. *The History of Atlantis.* New York: University Books, Inc., 1968.

———. *The Myths of Mexico and Peru.* London: George C. Harrapt and Co., 1913.

———. *The Occult Sciences in Atlantis.* New York: Samuel Weiser, Inc., 1978.

Stahel, H. R. *Atlantis Illustrated.* New York: Grosset & Dunlop, 1971.

Steiger, Brad. *Atlantis Rising.* New York: Dell Publishing Co., Inc., 1973.

———. *The Fellowship.* New York: Doubleday & Co., Inc., 1988.

Steiner, Rudolph. *The Story of Atlantis and the Lost Lemuria.* London: The Theosophical Publishing House, Ltd., 1930.

———. *Cosmic Memory.* West Nyack, New York: Steiner Publications, 1959.

Stemman, Roy. *Atlantis and the Lost Lands.* New York: Doubleday & Co., Inc., 1977.

Stevens, Wendell C. *UFO . . . Contact from Reticulum.* Tucson, Ariz.: Wendell Stevens (self-published), 1981.

Sugrue, Thomas. *There is a River—The Story of Edgar Cayce.* New York: Dell Publishing Co., Inc., 1970.

Sykes, Egerton. *Atlantis.* Volume 27, No. 3, May–June 1974. Brighton, England: Markham House Press.

———. *Atlantis.* Volume 27, No. 4, July–August 1974. Brighton, England: Markham House Press.

Temple, Robert K. G. *The Sirius Mystery.* New York: St. Martin's Press, 1976.

Tomas, Andrew. *Atlantis from Legend to Discovery.* London: Robert Hale & Co., 1972.

———. *The Home of the Gods.* New York: Berkeley Publications, 1972.

———. *We Are Not First.* New York: Bantam Books, 1971.

Tompkins, Peter. *Mysteries of the Mexican Pyramids.* New York: Harper & Row, 1976.

———. *Secrets of the Great Pyramid.* New York: Harper & Row, 1971.

Trefil, James. Stop to Consider the Stones that Fall from the Sky. *Smithsonian,* September 1989.

Turnbull, Coulson. *Sema-Kanda—Threshold Memories.* New York: Mayflower, 1978.

Valentine, Thomas. *Psychic Surgery.* Chicago: Henry Regnery Co., 1973.

Van Sertima, Ivan. *They Came Before Columbus.* New York: Random House, 1976.

Velikovsky, Immanuel. *Earth in Upheaval.* New York: Dell Publishing Co., Inc., 1973.

———. *Worlds in Collision.* New York: Macmillan, 1950.

Verrill, Alpheus Hyatt and Ruth. *America's Ancient Civilization.* New York: G. P. Putnam's Sons, 1953.

Vigers, Daphine. *Atlantis Rising.* London: Aquarian Press, 1952.

von Daniken, Erich. *Pathways to the Gods.* New York: G. P. Putnam's Sons, 1982.

Warshofsky, Fred. Noah, the Flood, the Facts. *Reader's Digest,* Vol. III, No. 665, September 1977.

Waters, Frank. *Book of the Hopi.* New York: Penguin Books, 1963.

Watkins, Frank. *Ley Hunter's Manual.* Wellingborough, Northamptonshire: Turnstone Press Limited, 1983.

Wauchope, Robert. *Lost Tribes and Sunken Continents: Myth and Method in the Study of American Indians.* Chicago: Universtiy of Chicago, 1962.

West, John Anthony. *Serpent in the Sky.* New York: Harper & Row, 1979.

WGBH Transcripts. *Secrets of the Lost Red Paint People.* Boston, Mass.: WGBH Educational Foundation, 1987.

White, John. *Pole Shift.* Virginia Beach, Va.: A.R.E. Press, 1986.

White, Peter. *The Past Is Human.* New York: Taplinger Publishing Co., 1974.

White, Robert S. and Daniel P. McKenzie. Volcanism at Rifts. *Scientific American,* July 1989.

Wilkins, Harold T. *Mysteries of Ancient South America.* New York: The Citadel Press, 1956.

———. *Secret Cities of Old South America.* London: Rider & Co., 1950.

Winer, Richard. *The Devil's Triangle.* New York: Bantom Books, Inc., 1974.

Wood, Betty. *The Healing Power of Colour.* Wellingborough, Northamptonshire: Aquarian Press, 1984.

Wright, Machaella Small. *Perelandra Garden Workbook.* Jeffersonton, Va.: Perelandra, Ltd., 1987.

Wright, Robert. Quest for the Mother Tongue. *The Atlantic Monthly,* April 1991.

Wycoff, James. *The Continent of Atlantis.* New York: G. P. Putnam Sons, 1968.

Ywahoo, Dhyani. *Voices of Our Ancestors.* Boston: Shambhala, 1987.

Zhirov, Nicolai F. *Atlantis.* Moscow: Progress Publishers, 1970.

Zink, David D. *The Stones of Atlantis.* New York: Prentice-Hall, Inc., 1978.

———. *The Ancient Stones Speak.* New York: Prentice-Hall, Inc., 1990.

INDEX

☽ REACH FOR THE MOON

Llewellyn publishes hundreds of books on your favorite subjects! To get these exciting books, including the ones on the following pages, check your local bookstore or order them directly from Llewellyn.

ORDER BY PHONE
- Call toll-free within the U.S. and Canada, 1-800-THE MOON
- In Minnesota, call (651) 291-1970
- We accept VISA, MasterCard, and American Express

ORDER BY MAIL
- Send the full price of your order (MN residents add 7% sales tax) in U.S. funds, plus postage & handling to:

  Llewellyn Worldwide
  P.O. Box 64383, Dept. K023-x
  St. Paul, MN 55164–0383, U.S.A.

POSTAGE & HANDLING
(For the U.S., Canada, and Mexico)
- $4.00 for orders $15.00 and under
- $5.00 for orders over $15.00
- No charge for orders over $100.00

We ship UPS in the continental United States. We ship standard mail to P.O. boxes. Orders shipped to Alaska, Hawaii, The Virgin Islands, and Puerto Rico are sent first-class mail. Orders shipped to Canada and Mexico are sent surface mail.

International orders: Airmail—add freight equal to price of each book to the total price of order, plus $5.00 for each non-book item (audio tapes, etc.).

Surface mail—Add $1.00 per item.

Allow 2 weeks for delivery on all orders.
Postage and handling rates subject to change.

DISCOUNTS
We offer a 20% discount to group leaders or agents. You must order a minimum of 5 copies of the same book to get our special quantity price.

FREE CATALOG
Get a free copy of our color catalog, *New Worlds of Mind and Spirit*. Subscribe for just $10.00 in the United States and Canada ($30.00 overseas, airmail). Many bookstores carry *New Worlds*— ask for it!

Visit our web site at www.llewellyn.com for more information.

TIME TRAVEL

A New Perspective

J. H. Brennan

Scattered throughout the world are the skeletal remains of men and women from long before humanity appeared on the planet, and a human footprint contemporary with the dinosaurs. Where did they come from? Are these anomalies the litter left by time travelers from our own distant future? Time Travel is an extraordinary trip through some of the most fascinating discoveries of archaeology and physics, indicating that not only is time travel theoretically possible, but that future generations may actually be engaged in it. In fact, the latest findings of physicists show that time travel, at a subatomic level, is already taking place. Unique to this book is the program—based on esoteric techniques and the findings of parapsychology and quantum physics—which enables you to structure your own group investigation into a form of vivid mental time travel.

1-56718-085-x $12.95
6 x 9, 224 pp., photos, softcover